The
Puppet Master

J. Lewis-Thompson

Beacons Hill Publishing

This is a work of fiction. Names, characters, places, and incidents are either the product of the author's imagination or are used fictitiously. Any resemblance to actual persons, living or dead, or to events, or specific locales is entirely coincidental.

Copyright © 2019 by J. Lewis-Thompson

J. Lewis-Thompson has asserted her right to be identified as the author of this work

All rights reserved. No part of this book may be reproduced or used in any manner without written permission of the copyright owner except for the use of quotations in a book review.

For more information please contact:
info@jlewis-thompson.com

First paperback edition April 2019

V6 09/2019

Book cover design by Michael T. Skirving

ISBN 978-1-9160752-0-7 (paperback)
ISBN 978-1-9160752-1-4 (e-book)

www.JLewis-Thompson.com

This book is dedicated to the most important people in my life...

...you know who you are xxx

1

Anglesey - Mid October

Charles sat in the corner of the room, his knees drawn up to his chin, hugging his legs as he swayed from side to side. Occasionally he banged his head on the wall trying to focus. The visitor had been busy all afternoon. Charles couldn't recall what time he'd arrived, and he didn't want to remember what he'd had to say. He'd lost count of the number of pills he'd taken, washing them down with cheap vodka from the corner store. Apart from dulling his reactions, they didn't seem to be having much effect. The pulsing beat of an overloud stereo, a permanent feature of the neighbourhood, echoed in his head, adding to his confusion. It seemed to grow louder with each passing moment.

Charles had been holed up in this God forsaken place for three days. He was desperate for news, but terrified to leave the basement of the squat he called home. The events at the cottage were a blur. He'd only taken the gun to show them how serious he was. He'd never intended to use it, but as he'd approached the house his head had started to throb. They weren't going to stop him, and if that meant using the Glock, well then, so be it.

He remembered banging on the door, the look of terror on the woman's face as he waved the gun at her. He hadn't meant to hurt anyone. He only wanted to talk to Maria, to his son. But those people were trying to keep them apart. His friend had told him on the phone that morning, along with their location.

He could remember pulling the trigger, the woman falling to the floor, movement on the landing. Another shot, then someone running at him in the hallway… more shots. He banged his head against the wall again, willing the images to change, they didn't.

He detected a movement across the room and tried to focus, rubbing his eyes, desperate to regain control. His visitor loathed any show of weakness. He clawed his way out of his drug-induced reverie, concentrating hard on the figure now sitting watching him. In the dim light, he could just make out the blurred silhouette. The man had been busy since arriving, Charles wanted to ask what he was doing, but every time the question formed in his brain, it melted away before he could ask it. Eventually he settled for watching, hoping that an explanation would be offered. He didn't have to wait for long.

'Shall I tell you what we're going to do Charles?' the man asked the room in general; Charles could tell he wasn't interested in his reply, in any case, it was difficult to speak. His mouth had gone dry, his tongue felt swollen and was stuck to the roof of his mouth.

'You see,' his companion continued, 'in simple terms, the police are going to look for a motive for what you've done, for killing an innocent woman and her son, and that's what I'm creating, a motive.'

Motive, what motive, thought Charles? He struggled to process the words. He didn't have a motive; he didn't need one. All he wanted was, was…what was it he wanted, he wasn't sure anymore? Words floated over his head. *Justified…too close…ruined the plan.* It was all too much.

'Stop, please stop,' he managed, using what little strength he had left. The visitor stood up to carry on with his task. Charles watched him pinning pieces of paper to the wall, sorting through what looked like photographs. He chose a few and added them to the arrangement. Charles couldn't see any of them clearly. He felt that this was the only person that would understand what he'd done, he had to explain his actions.

'I didn't know!' he pleaded, 'How could I have known? It had all happened so quickly. I just wanted to see Maria and Sam, just talk to them, to beg them to come back. They wouldn't…they wouldn't let me see her,' he yelled, 'they wouldn't listen! I had to make them listen.' The man ignored him and carried on sorting through the mass of papers. He discarded some, others he pinned carefully to the wall.

'Charles, you killed them, Maria and Sam. You shot them, in cold blood, why did you do it? I told you that you had to keep a cool head, didn't I?' The calm emotionless voice resonated around the room. Charles shook his head in denial.

'No…no, it wasn't them, it was the others, the ones who locked her up. You weren't there, you…' He was fighting to remember what had happened, to see the faces in the hallway. A woman, not Maria, someone else, taller, slimmer, well dressed, same colour hair, but not her. It couldn't have been her, could it? He was sure, he was sure. Charles wept silently, banging his head against the wall. His legs were beginning to cramp. He drew his knees tighter towards his chest. He could see her now, the woman, the look of shock on her face, pleading. It *was* her, oh God, it was Maria… and Sam, he had shot his own son…

'Help me,' he begged, 'please, tell me what to do.' His companion didn't answer for what seemed like an eternity.

'I can't,' the words sliced into Charles' brain as painful as any bullet. 'Only you can decide where you go from here. The police have been asking questions. It's only a matter of time before they arrest you, and then…'

'No, no, I'm not going back inside' Charles sobbed, 'not again, I'd rather die!' He drew his hands over his head, trying to protect himself from the awful images that played over and over in his throbbing brain.

'As far as I can see, you have three choices,' his companion continued. His voice was calm. 'You can run, in which case you will forever be looking over your shoulder, or you can wait for them to come and get you.' He paused; Charles looked up.

'That's two,' he said, struggling to stay calm, his speech slurred, 'you said I had three, three choices, what's the third?' He heard a thud as a small plastic bag landed on the floor beside him.

'There's your third option, virtually painless. You're halfway there already.' Charles reached for the bag, more pills. They reminded him of a kid's pick and mix. Of course, he could do it, why not? After all he had nothing to live for now, not now that...

'Will you stay with me?' he begged, 'until the end, I don't want to die alone. Will you help me?'

'Of course, you don't think I would leave you to go through this on your own do you?' came the reply. The fact was that he had no intention of allowing Charles Whittaker to die alone. Watching the life flow out of the pathetic piece of human filth, the predator turned prey, was part of the reward. *It was justice*, he thought, *natural justice*.

Charles opened the bag and took out a handful of tablets, throwing them into his mouth. He was past caring. He swigged some vodka which made him gag, but he forced himself to repeat the process. His visitor watched intently, after a while he stood and crossed to the cupboard that housed Charles' regular medication. He removed several boxes and placed them in his holdall.

'What are you doing?' Charles asked, 'you said...don't take them away, please.' He reached out mustering all his strength.

'Don't worry, you've got more than enough to get the job done.' The room had grown eerily quiet. Charles wept quietly, the bag of pills cradled on his lap. *So many pretty colours* he thought. The noise of the stereo flared up suddenly, a steady dull thud in the late afternoon gloom. He knew his companion was still there, watching him, even as his vision became blurred. His head felt thick, his stomach ached to reject the fetid mixture, but his determination was stronger, fueled by his grief. Eventually the bag fell to the floor, the contents scattered amongst an unidentifiable mix of rubbish. Charles couldn't quite recall how the pills and the booze had materialised, had he managed to get them himself? He hoped they wouldn't let him down as they had so many times in the last few months. He was barely conscious as the Glock was placed in his hand. Words floated towards him, only a few registered.

'You shot your wife Charles. Sam died from a massive head wound in agony, he called for you. How could you?' On and on, a litany of accusations, on and on...

'No, I didn't mean it. They were shouting at me...I just, I just wanted to talk to them, please, please, help me,' he whispered, his voice growing weaker with each breath, consciousness slipping away.

'She hated you, you know, Maria, she didn't want you. Your son was afraid of you, and now they're dead and you killed them.' Charles tried to focus on the cold metal object in his hand, and then back at his onetime friend, now turned tormentor.

'You're dying Charles, soon you'll be with them, why prolong the agony, why not get it over with?' The voice was smooth, seductive. 'What if the pills don't work, what if you wake up. Best this way don't you think?'

'Why are you doing this?' Charles pleaded. 'Why are you torturing me?'

He watched as his visitor picked up the polythene sheet that had covered the seat, taking time to fold it neatly. He placed it inside the holdall, smiling as he surveyed the room.

'Because,' came the reply, 'you are no longer useful. Now go on, there's a good lad, put yourself out of your misery.'

Charles placed the barrel in his mouth and used his remaining strength to pull the trigger, the noise conveniently lost as an ambulance passed by. The man peeled off his surgical gloves and placed them in his bag. He pulled up the hood of his jacket and picked his way through the building and back to the main road.

...oo0oo...

2

10 weeks before

There was something odd about waiting in a hospital room on a sunny day in August. Not that Ellie wanted to be there at all, but she'd promised Graham that they would try once more, and she'd kept her word. The door opened and a young nurse entered. She was wheeling a trolley, bearing implements that Ellie was all too familiar with. Ellie knew what to expect, she'd been through the ritual twice before, the injections, the waiting, the harvesting of viable eggs, if there were any. How could something as simple as conceiving a child involve such a painful and complicated process?

Yet it wasn't simple, was it? Ellie had tried to tell Graham so many times that she knew she would never have a child. But how could she explain it? There was no medical problem, no physical reason.

It had nothing to do with not liking children. She adored her nephew, Max, but she just wasn't maternal, never had been. While other girls were playing with their dolls, she was outside collecting plant specimens, collecting stones and climbing trees, the total opposite of her sister Ruth. She didn't fully understand what happened that day, so many years ago. She'd been watching Ruth pushing the doll's pram around the yard, totally absorbed in her game, but from that moment she knew she would never be a mother. She'd had what her mother would come to describe as a 'glimpse'. It happened now and then, until the 'glimpses' got too weird, until she started fighting against them, she tried to ignore them, finally denying them altogether. Her 'glimpses' got stronger after that, more frequent. They became clearer, and they had scared her ever since.

Ellie winced as the needle pierced her thigh. She'd promised herself that this would be the last time she would endure this procedure, no matter how much Graham tried to talk her around. This time she was serious. The decision left her with a sense of guilt. She knew how much having a child meant to Graham, but she also knew what the result would be, the same as their two previous attempts. The thought of his disappointment settled like a dark mass somewhere in her soul.

...*I should tell him,* she decided, *try to explain.* But how could she explain to him, when she couldn't explain it to herself? She resigned herself to one last try, if it happened, it happened. If it didn't, she would console her husband as best she could, and then get on with what she wanted to do more than anything else...her job.

3

It was 8.45 as David Morgan paced up and down in the untidy back garden of his semi-detached house smoking his fifth cigarette of the day. He was unwashed, hung over, and his greasy hair hung limp, almost touching his shoulders. His jeans were filthy, ripped at the knees, his tee shirt stunk of a mixture of beer, vomit and stale cigarettes. His wife's parting threat as she bundled the kids out of the house rang in his ears. He scratched his head as he turned and walked back towards the kitchen, stepping in dog shit on the way. He swore, convinced that the whole world was conspiring against him. As he reached the back door, he tore off the worn trainers and hurled them down the garden path. His remaining strength deserted him, and he held onto the door frame, sagging forward as the situation overwhelmed him.

What the hell had he got himself mixed up with? More to the point, how was he going to get out of this mess? It had all seemed so exciting in the beginning, helping him come to terms with what had happened all those years ago. When did it all go wrong? Why couldn't he be satisfied with what he'd achieved? The excitement of devising a plan for getting back at his nemesis had felt good at the time, especially when he had been praised so highly by those he had secretly come to admire. Who knew there were so many fellow victims out there? Their stories of recovery had become his life-line.

David shook his head trying to clear his thoughts. *Coffee*, he decided, he needed coffee, or maybe something stronger? No, he had to stay sober, keep a clear head; he had to think this through. Cheap instant was all they had; all they could afford. He hated the taste, yet another situation he could blame on...he stopped. He wouldn't think about Tony Berwick right now, he had to figure out how to get out of the mess he'd landed himself in. The front room was a mess. Discarded toys, books and clothes covered every surface. David swept piles of stuff onto the floor to find a space to sit, but he couldn't settle. He crossed to the window, swearing as he stepped on a piece of Lego.

'Fuck this,' he shouted as he dragged on a battered pair of shoes and his old parka. He left the house, heading for the park just across the road. He sat on a wooden bench by the lake, the only one that hadn't been completely wrecked by the local Neanderthals and tried to put his thoughts into order.

David didn't consider himself to be a stupid man, far from it. A few years ago he'd gained a promotion in his career as an insurance broker. He made pretty good money, enough to buy a house, keep his wife happy and himself in good clothes. The kids never wanted for anything, they had a nice holiday every year, life was going well. That was until he'd come across a file on Tony Berwick in his in-tray. It was a business insurance renewal, one in a long list.

It was then that the nightmares had started again…and the shame, which of course he realised had been slumbering all these years under a thin veneer of coping. He couldn't count the number of times he'd woken up in the middle of the night screaming, his body bathed in sweat. His wife was concerned in the beginning, but when he refused to go for a stroll down a well-worn therapy path, she lost patience with him. Work suffered, and he was told that the company would have to let him go if he didn't improve his sales record. He didn't, and it lost him his job. That had been almost a year ago, and he hadn't worked since.

Finding the website seemed like a blessing in disguise… *eyeforaneye.co.uk*. it was called. In the past David had tried a variety of techniques in order to cope with his memories. This one seemed to work a lot better than most. Every morning, as soon as Maggie left to take the kids to school, he'd log on. It gave him a sense of belonging. He read how members had suffered in the past, some had never got over their feelings of guilt. He was tentative at first, just dipping into the chat room occasionally. Even a few minutes here and there made him feel better.

Eventually he was spending hours reading feedback from 'satisfied members' of the group, telling himself that it couldn't hurt to give it a go. He would never have imagined that opening up to an anonymous audience would provide such an overwhelming sense of relief. Over the years he had developed various distraction techniques which helped him to avoid thinking about Berwick, although his nightmares continued to haunt him periodically. Giving free rein to his imagination somehow felt like he was taking control. He managed to delude himself into believing that he had the upper hand against his Nemesis, if only in his imagination, and it felt good.

It was about a month later that he had a message from one of the group. *Would he like to discuss their respective experiences privately, provided he didn't think it too much of an imposition?* David felt flattered. The member, who called himself *Puppenspieler74*, was one of the most prolific contributors to the site. His story which was remarkably like David's, featured heavily and his success in dealing with the aftermath of his experiences had generated a hero-like status around him.

At first David was nervous about leaving any comments on the site, but after a while he started to post the odd phrase agreeing with his newly elevated mentor, even using the odd 'emoji' on occasions. When he received an invitation to 'talk' privately, David was overawed at the prospect.

At his new friend's suggestion, he created an email address in order to carry out their conversations. In the days that followed, David gained a sense of peace which he hadn't experienced for many years. The tight, guilty shame that he felt had restricted his life, loosened a little. Here was someone who understood him, someone he could really talk to, someone who didn't judge him.

Sitting staring out at the dull water of the stagnant lake, he switched on his phone and logged into his email account, scrolling down to a message that had heralded the change, innocent sounding at the time. He hadn't realised what it would lead to, if he had... he read the message for what seemed like the hundredth time.

Puppenspieler74: I'm glad that our talks have brought you some peace. It feels good when I can help a fellow sufferer

David: thanks for your help, I've never felt so free of the guilt I've lived with all this time, I can't thank you enough

Puppenspieler74: you're welcome, we have so much in common. I feel like I've known you for years, like a brother almost!! I have a suggestion to make, something that I feel might be of benefit to you, although I'm not sure if you are ready yet so maybe I should wait before telling you, I don't know...

David: you must tell me, if it helped you, maybe it could do the same for me, after all you said how similar we are.

And so, it started, the remote 'friend', about whom David knew nothing, revealed his method of exorcising the demons that had plagued him. Quite simple really, harmless enough thought David, once he'd tried it himself. Write down what had happened, include all the details, as many as he could remember or bear to think about. Then formulate a fictional 'plan' to exact revenge on the perpetrator.

Simple yes...easy, no. It was far harder than anything he'd been asked to do in therapy sessions. David hesitated when writing down the details of the event itself. Eventually he managed to record it second by second. For a while the nightmares became worse, so much so that eventually Maggie made him sleep on the couch. They seemed to subside as he worked on the second part, which he found was a lot easier. His imagination was fueled by late night crime series, watched when Maggie had thrown up her hands in despair and stormed off to bed.

Did he feel better, asked his mentor? *Yes, he did*, writing down what he would do to Berwick was cathartic, as predicted. *Was he entirely satisfied with his description of what he would do to his attacker? Yes, well sort of*, he wasn't sure that it would work. He'd seen something on the TV and fantasised having his prey in a similar situation, but...*would David like a second opinion?* David wasn't sure.

Of course, he reasoned as he gave free rein to his imagination, *this was still academic, so it really didn't matter*. David shook his head, bringing himself back to the present. The latest email seemed more like a challenge, one that he was tempted to accept, but one that he knew would take him into uncharted waters.

Could he summon up the courage to carry out his plan? Not the whole of it of course, that wouldn't be right, just up to a point where he would be able to frighten Berwick so that he would think twice about committing such an act in the future. Would he have the balls, because if he did, *Puppenspieler74* could help him? If he didn't, well he had nothing to lose, did he?

4

The Crown and Anchor held just a few stragglers as Tony Berwick sounded the bell for last orders. It had been a busy night, and he was keen to get upstairs for a well-earned rest, a catch up on some TV, and a drop of the good stuff, a bottle of Glenmorangie Signet no less. Not for him the blended rubbish he watered down for the peasants. No, he felt entitled to some reward for enduring the dross he suffered from his clients.

Even when he had a night off there were still demands on his time from his barely competent staff. Bags of change, connecting a new barrel, the list was endless. Tony rarely made it through the evening without the internal phone ringing. Even when he switched it off, some member of staff would come bounding up the stairs to disturb his relaxation, and he was fed up with it. Still, he consoled himself, owning the pub afforded him a reasonable living, and he enjoyed being the repository of so much gossip.

'Going up now,' he called out to anyone within earshot. 'Don't forget the towels Myra! We've got none left so put them on full cycle!'

Myra tutted, her hands full of empty glasses, she didn't need to be told what to do, she'd worked for Tony for long enough. At the end of every shift she would run through her checklist and action it efficiently before locking up, turning on the alarm and retrieving her ancient 2CV from the pubs' car park. A quick stop off at the late-night corner shop for any last-minute bits and pieces and she would be on her way home.

Tonight, was no different. She watched Tony with a certain amount of resentment as he flicked a bar towel at an imaginary mess, and unlocked the door leading to his flat. He disappeared through it, leaving Myra with the clearing up. Truth was she could run this place with one hand tied behind her back. Tony was little more than a figurehead.

Must be nice to relax having done very little work for the last few hours, she thought. Oh yes, he would start the evening off with gusto. The cheerful 'mine host', chatting to the locals, students and tourists, who would sometimes buy him a drink. He never failed to make a show of pottering about in the cellar making, '*Look at me, I'm breaking my back to make your evening enjoyable*' kind of sounds. After an hour or so he would stand at the end of the main bar chatting to whoever was his companion for the evening, leaving the work to Myra and an ever-changing coterie of air-headed young girls. In Myra's experience they barely made the grade as barmaids having been chosen mainly for their looks.

They had nothing to worry about with Tony. He didn't go for girls; a fact Myra became aware of during an incident some years before. A student called David Morgan had been with them for a few weeks. He was shy, this was his first job, and it was obvious that he was distraught about something. He wouldn't have dreamed of taking it further, but he had confided in his mother, who was a friend of Myra's. They both arrived one day at her flat to see what could be done about it. The mother was beside herself. As she ranted on, Myra suspected that by the look of him, her son hadn't told her the whole story.

A few weeks before, when Myra and the rest of the staff had left for the night, David stayed behind to play one of the pub's video machines. It was gone twelve when Tony called down and asked if he had finished, and could he bring the evening's takings up before he left? David didn't suspect a thing as he entered the flat, expecting to hand over the money and leave.

What happened next had changed his life, but it was only when his mother sat him down and dragged the 'truth' from him, that they approached Myra as the senior member of staff. David sat as the two women discussed what they could do, occasionally shaking his head. He was in denial about his experience, and terrified that people would find out.

The two women decided not to take the matter any further. The shame of it would probably scar the boy for life, upset the lad's father and cause no end of gossip. David managed to look relieved and shocked at the same time. Myra didn't blame him. She had a feeling that the incident was more serious than David had admitted. Tony should have been made to answer for what he'd done. But she promised, for all concerned, that she would keep it to herself. She also assured both David and his mother that she would find a way to have a word with her boss.

She then approached Tony about the incident, it was a move so audacious for her that even now it astonished her. Not her sort of thing that, telling someone that they should be careful. It was a small town, people, might not mind him being a newcomer who preferred his own gender, but they would turn nasty if they knew that he'd made certain suggestions to a young and vulnerable member of their close-knit community. She had no problem with Tony's sexuality, she considered herself broad-minded about 'that sort of thing', but she felt responsible for recommending the lad for the job in the first place. Her instincts told her that he had downplayed the severity of the incident, and she was relieved when she found out that he had gone to work at a local café in another part of town. Whenever she ran into him in the street, though, he would cross the road and scurry away.

Tony had treated her differently after that. He'd raised her pay, not by much, just enough for her to enjoy a few little extras, and put her in charge of some of the admin. There was a regular turnover of staff, all female. Some lasted a few weeks; some were there throughout their three years at the University. Only one other was local, and when one day she asked Myra what it was she 'had' on Tony, it finally dispelled any illusions that her boss kept her on because of her hard work and loyalty. She knew about his lifestyle, and what had happened with David Morgan. She could never shake off the niggling feeling that Tony was trying to keep her sweet to ensure that she never gossiped about either, a belief that upset her. Was he afraid that she would spread rumours? Her suspicions were confirmed one day as they were spring-cleaning.

'Always count on you Myra,' Tony had said, perched precariously on a ladder to reach a particularly large cobweb, 'always got my back, haven't you?'

'Don't kid yourself,' said Annie Jeavons, 'you know too much about him, eh Myra?'

Tony harrumphed and climbed down, dusting imaginary specks from his sweater. Myra stood, mouth open, she had her confirmation. Still, that was some years ago, and now Myra felt like part of the furniture. She never asked personal questions, and Tony never volunteered information. He was especially circumspect about his holidays in Thailand. Most importantly, there had been no repetition of the incident with David Morgan, at least not to Myra's knowledge. Now, as the last customer peeled himself off the barstool and stood unsteadily, she sighed, grateful for the job, but despising herself for staying on.

'Off now Myra,' he slurred, *thank God, she thought.*

'See you tomorrow darlin',' he shuffled across the room in search of his coat, waving in her direction before putting it on. He bumped into the long pine table on his way out. Myra crossed the room following him into the small hallway, locking the door behind him. She gave a sigh of relief; he wasn't always that quick in leaving. It took less than an hour to wipe down the tables, picking up empties as she went. When the glasses were all clean, towels on wash, alarm set, she left, making sure the door was locked on her way out.

Myra saw shadows playing on the curtains in the lounge of Tony's flat as she backed out her car. *He's still watching TV,* thought Myra, as she drove off towards home and bed, oblivious to the fact that her boss was lying unconscious, gagged and bound on the floor of his bedroom.

…ooOoo…

So far, so good, David smiled as he prodded the mound of flesh that was Tony Berwick. Even though the prospect of carrying out his plan had given him many sleepless nights, he was pleased with his progress. *Puppenspieler,* as he had started to call his anonymous mentor, had been so supportive. He talked David through his fears, assuring him that once the plan he had so beautifully crafted had been executed, he would feel much better. After all, where was the harm? Berwick was hardly likely to make a fuss, was he? Especially as details of his activities on his little trips had now come into David's possession, a bargaining chip if ever there was one. Yes, he had a lot to thank *Puppenspieler* for. Exactly where the information had been obtained from, he didn't know, nor did he care. The prospect of hitting back at Tony, establishing justice and, he hoped, regaining his former life was overwhelming.

David had contacted Tony earlier that month after hearing on the grapevine that the pub had been broken into. He had arranged an inspection of the premises, suspecting that Tony would still be figuring out how to approach the Insurance Company to get the most money out of them. He had no doubt that Tony would try to inflate the value of some items and claim for others fraudulently.

Posing as an insurance agent was a stroke of genius, even though he did say so himself. It was a part of his plan that he had been complemented on by his mentor, whose approval he sought constantly, and received unwaveringly. It gave David a high to be praised for his initiative, but being back in Tony's flat had caused him so much stress that he came within seconds of aborting the whole plan. Seeing the eager look on Berwick's face at the prospect of triumphing over the Insurance Company helped strengthen his resolve.

The false paperwork had been all too easy to generate, after all he had dealt with claims and renewals for years. He hoped that Tony would give them scant attention and relied on his anxiety about his new premiums to distract him from the finer details of the documentation. David's biggest concern had been that Berwick would recognise him. He'd arranged that the two of them 'bumped' into each other on several occasions in the run up to their meeting. Tony was so self-absorbed that even when David had 'collided' with him at the Post Office earlier that week, and made a huge fuss about apologising, Tony hadn't recognised him. Nevertheless, the possibility of discovery remained David's abiding fear. It had been years since the night in question. He would have recognised Tony anywhere. Berwick, it seemed had no memory of him.

There were a few formalities to carry out. Tony conducted a tour of the flat, recounting the break-in. David spotted a broken window catch that Berwick hadn't mentioned. The window itself wasn't the original point of entry, and it was obvious that other corners had been cut. The alarm system had only covered the downstairs area when David had worked there, nothing had changed. Tony confided that on the night of the robbery one of the staff could have failed to set it.

'Or had it been an inside job all along?' Tony joked.

The code could have been a stumbling block, but Tony hadn't bothered to change it. He keyed in the numbers as David watched, smiling to himself, *nothing changes,* he thought, *the lazy bastard.*

'So, Mr. err...Davies, what do you think?' Tony asked nervously, not wanting the expense of a hike in his monthly premiums. David enjoyed introducing himself as 'Davies', curious to see if it would stir up any recognition for Tony. It hadn't, and that had left him both satisfied at not being found out, and angry that Berwick should have no recall of the events that had changed his life.

'I'm sure we can match your previous premiums,' David announced in a measured voice to a delighted and relieved Tony, who was secretly gloating about the overlooked catch.

David loathed people like Tony, not least because of what he had done to him. The fact that he had downplayed the incident had more to do with the shame David had felt than not wanting Tony to get into serious trouble. He knew what the result would have been if he had reported the incident to the police. No one knew what really happened, and he wanted it to stay that way. That was why he had to be careful that Myra wasn't on the premises when he made his initial visit.

David also knew that what he was offering Tony in respect of the insurance renewal was irresistible. They signed the bogus paperwork there and then.

The first premium was collected, in cash, and David took his leave, gloating over the success of the first part of his plan. He could imagine the congratulations he would receive, and the thought gave him a warm feeling, as though anticipating a delicious meal at the end of a fast. Within days he received another email, a set of instructions.

> *Park your car at the train station – there is no CCTV, gate is never locked.*
> *A black van will be left just inside the yard at Pearson's Garage. Keys in plastic bag taped under the driver's wheel arch Further instructions will be waiting at your destination.*

The journey from the Crown and Anchor was nerve-racking. Not many people on the roads, but those that were everyone seemed hell-bent on hindering his progress. He couldn't allow that to happen. He'd already managed to avoid being flagged down at an accident involving livestock. He laughed nervously as he drove on. To be stopped at this stage would have been disastrous, to say the least. He glanced round nervously. The great mound in the back of the van was still, the tarpaulin stretched over the body of his captive.

He smiled nervously; it was actually happening. Here he was, driving steadily to a facility provided by his new friend. Somewhere isolated, private, where he could scare the living daylights out of Berwick and exorcise the demons that had plagued him for long enough.

5

Tony's mind was buzzing, like the morning after a heavy drinking session. His head hurt. It was cold, very cold, too cold for his flat, not just cold, freezing... and wet, he was wet. He couldn't see anything. It was a while before he realised that his eyes were bound. As his senses cleared, he felt the restraints, his hands were tied together, as were his feet. There was something around his neck that prevented him from raising his head. The trickle of fear that had started in his lower gut spread up through his stomach and into his chest. He had felt like this only once before, when a risky sex game he and his first boyfriend had been playing had gone badly wrong. Tony had almost died, now he felt the same panic. He was cold and wet...how had he got so wet?

It was only when Tony tried to call out that he felt the gag. The fabric was tied tightly, and something inside his mouth was causing him to retch. The bonds around his hands tightened as he pulled against them, causing him to gasp, he retched again. The more he struggled, the more his movements became restricted. His senses now on overload, he caught a faint sound, a footstep. Someone was there. He tried to twist around, which caused him to gasp again. This was going nowhere, and he knew it.

Footsteps to the left...Tony tried to turn his head towards them, they stopped. A door opened. More steps...door closed...silence. He knew he wasn't going to be given a chance to talk his way out. He was fighting to keep calm trying to bring his breathing under control.

What the hell had happened after he left the bar? He never locked the door at the bottom of the stairs in case he was needed. But the door to his flat, he was sure he'd locked that. Doubt crept in, his blood pressure was increasing, the surge of his pulse thundering through his brain. *No, no, keep calm, you must think*, he tried to take another deep breath, to calm down. Next...next...he'd gone straight to the kitchen, got a snack, cheese and biscuits, a little chutney. Was that it, had the cheese given him nightmares? He tugged on the bindings. This was no nightmare; it was only too real. A great sob attempted to escape, only to be silenced by the gag.

Think...think...breathe, slowly...calm down.

He remembered fixing his drink, not too much, he wanted to be able to concentrate. He'd set up the next episode of 'Breaking Bad', sat down, then nothing.

6

David made his way back to the room next door. His plan was going well. He just needed to leave the son of a bitch where he was for long enough to spook him. Then he would hose Tony down again, loosen the ties just enough for him to free himself, and leave before he could escape. David had spent hours writing a cryptic note that would give just enough clues to his identity. Tony would then know that justice had been served and live with the humiliation of it for the rest of his life. It was important, however, that there was nothing to incriminate himself should the bastard decide to go to the police. David hoped that the satisfaction of having put the fear of God into the man who had raped him all those years before would heal the past... at least that was the theory.

David watched as his prey struggled in the next room. Waves of doubt washed over him, as it had so many times in the last few days. His great plan had seemed so daring when he had first devised it and submitted it for comments. He'd taken comfort in the fact that it was all theoretical, never expecting what had arrived out of the blue, a manila envelope, his address typed in bold black letters. Inside was a detailed critique of his plan, complete with a set of suggestions, modifications and subtle improvements. He asked how *Puppenspieler* had obtained his address but was satisfied when told that the information was freely available from the internet. This way he didn't have to print out the lengthy email, did he? The suggested changes had been general, obvious in a way, and David had no qualms in accepting them.

Rendering the subject unconscious and transporting him to an appropriate location, is inspired, however, once you arrive at the venue, may we suggest the following minor alterations?

Item – remove subject from van and transfer to destination via a trolley

Item – place subject in Perspex tank, check all fastenings, block and tackle would be required, a tank with self-sealing sides would be preferable

Item – secure subject's hand and feet, either rope or cable ties would suffice

Item – tie rope around neck and then to metal ring to secure to floor of tank

Item – to ensure subject's discomfort and disorientation, suggest you douse him in water, a hosepipe would be provided

Item – retire to adjoining room and observe subject's reaction once he regains consciousness

Additional suggestions – recording the event would be a way in which you could enjoy your experience repeatedly in the future, recording equipment would be needed, set up in the adjoining room.

Clear, precise, well thought out, David could imagine himself doing this. His mentor had obviously given his plan a great deal of thought.

I have shared your plan with a select number of other members, we are proud of the progress you have made with this exercise. We appreciate how events such as those that you have experienced have, in some cases, resulted in individuals being unable to live happy and productive lives. We hope that by using this website, you will be able to exorcise your fears and/or neuroses. There are, of course, other steps that you might chose to consider in order to put an end to those sleepless nights when you wake in the middle of your worst nightmares...

On and on it went describing moments that David had experienced many times; seeing someone who reminded him of Tony, watching a programme on TV that echoed his experiences. Now that he had brought that dreadful time back into his consciousness, it was only too easy to be reminded of it. The letter hinted that there were other ways of making the memories go away. David wanted to know more.

Somehow, they didn't feel like suggestions, more like instructions, as if he was really going to carry out his fantasy. He dismissed that thought as ludicrous. How would he find the money, let alone the locations, equipment, and more especially the nerve, to carry out his plan? The offer came in the next email, *Puppenspieler* knew someone who could arrange the whole thing, translate his plan into reality. The point was, did David have the guts to carry it out?

No! Was his first reaction, no, that wasn't what he wanted at all, he just wanted. What did he want? Was it possible, that he could carry out his plan, wreak revenge on Berwick, get rid of his nightmares? He dismissed the possibility as ridiculous.

Over the next few weeks he received many more emails, had he made his mind up? Didn't he want to achieve justice? He was the one with all the power. No permanent damage would be done after all, just a lesson that his nemesis would remember for the rest of his life. Didn't David owe it to himself, to others that Berwick might have targeted?

No, he kept saying, to *Puppenspieler* as well as to himself, *no, he couldn't do it...* back and forth went the emails. There were so many on one day, that David was constantly checking his computer for the next one.

Then they stopped. Nothing, no contact at all. Minutes went by, minutes that turned into hours, then days. David paced the room, watching the screen out of the corner of his eye, scratching his head, slumping in the corner onto the floor. He screamed at the kids if they approached him. Maggie packed clothes for her and the kids and left...David seemed oblivious. Alone in the house, David refreshed the screen constantly, waiting for further contact. In the end, panicked at the thought that he had lost the only person he felt understood him, he emailed *Puppenspieler*.

What's happening, why haven't you emailed me?

Silence...

Please reply, you know how much your friendship means to me

Nothing, hours went by, days. David never left the room except for a trip to the bathroom and to fetch water. It was as though he could feel himself melting away. The last vestige of hope that he could recover his previous life seemed to be disappearing. He sent message after message, each one more desperate than the last, begging for a reply.

A week passed before *Puppenspieler* replied, short, concise.

> *How do I know that you are serious? I offered you the chance to turn your fantasies into reality, at no cost to you by the way, and you turn down my offer? The least you could do is consider it, take a look...I thought you were serious about getting even...maybe I was wrong?*

David assured him he was deadly serious. It was just, well, he had never considered the possibility of carrying out his plan. Please, he would do anything just if he could still contact *Puppenspieler*, talk to him when he needed to. It was made clear that either David 'progressed' by stepping up the process to the next level or there would be no more contact.

The result of his decision now lay before him in the next room, tethered, and soaked, undoubtedly fearing for his life, and it made David's stomach turn. As Tony Berwick squirmed in the tank, a mixture of satisfaction and dread began to manifest in David's gut. He had to put an end to this. Rather than the soaring triumph he had expected, he felt only the fear that he had taken things too far. But it was worth it wasn't it? Wouldn't Berwick remember this and be looking over his shoulder for the rest of his life?

As David moved towards the door, he saw a folder on the table. It was labelled *'Further Instructions'*, along with Tony's name. He hadn't seen it when he first arrived and switched on the camera, yet it was within full view. He flipped it open and stood transfixed, reading and re-reading the neatly typed sheets. Disbelief surged through him as he struggled to comprehend. At first, he thought he'd misunderstood, surely this wasn't serious. Yet here it was in black and white, instructions that carried his plan to a whole new level.

Icy fingers wound their way around his neck, curling up into his hair and down his back. The back pages were aimed at him. Warnings, details of what failure would mean. He read them with increasing panic. Graphic threats, underlined to add emphasis, '...*we will send others to seek out your family, your wife, and your children if you fail to carry out the instructions to the letter.*' Included were photos of his family, taken recently, the implications obvious. Shit, what had he done? All very well to get carried away in his imagination. The reality was different, it was staring him in the face.

The words danced before him, burning into his consciousness.

Item – re-enter room containing the subject
Item - operate red wheel in right hand corner of room, allow tank to fill to the marked line. Turn off water
Item – wait until subject ceases to struggle
Item – stand between the table and the window to enable a good view of both you and the tank for the camera
Item - remove anything that may obscure your identity, glasses, scarf etc.
Item – state your name, address, date and time
Item – operate lever on the side of the tank, this will empty the water from the tank
Item – once death has been established, you may leave the premises, all traces of your activities will be taken care of.
N.B. – ensure that all instructions, along with the film of the night's activities are placed in the envelope and deposited at the pre-arranged drop off point.

David swallowed hard, shaking his head. He looked back into the other room. The marked line was way above Tony's head. What the hell had he got himself into? He had imagined taking revenge so often that, given the chance to do something for real, he had been eager to become involved.

His experience so long ago at Tony's hands had left him with such a sense of shame, that talking about it to a stranger had been a huge relief, but this? David's hands shook as he stared through the window at his victim. Berwick was barely moving.

Unsuspecting, maybe...or maybe he had long since realised what danger he was in. David shook his head, he couldn't do it, he couldn't just kill someone in cold blood.

No...MURDER someone in cold blood because that's what it was wasn't it...Murder? What could he do, not a goddam thing? It was this virtual stranger or his family, and he knew it. No choice really. David grabbed his phone, he had to contact *Puppenspieler*. He had to make sure this wasn't a sick joke. His fingers shook as he fumbled with it. It rang, and he stared at it in disbelief. The screen displayed his daughter's name and he swiped to accept the call.

'Daddy...Daddy...please help us,' the call ended before he could reply. David screamed, howling in the empty room, whoever this bastard *Puppenspieler* was, he was threatening his family. David had no doubt that they were in danger. He couldn't take the chance, he had to do what *Puppenspieler* wanted, or...

A strange feeling overwhelmed him, a feeling of not being inside his body. It separated him from the reality of what was happening, and he was glad of it. It gave him the strength to do what he knew he must do or suffer the consequences. His mind was clear at last. *After all*, he thought, what was Tony Berwick to him? The source of all his problems and the answer to so many more. He felt calm as he got up and re-entered the first room, watching the man in the tank who by now had stopped wriggling. He reached up and turned the red wheel until it would go no further. Tony thrashed about as the water hit him, ignoring the pain, panic instantly setting in.

David turned away, sickened by the thought of what was about to happen. He was unable to imagine the panic sweeping through his victim. As soon as the water reached the designated line, he turned the wheel the opposite way and bolted out of the room. He'd been forced to commit this unimaginable act; he didn't have to watch as it reached its inevitable conclusion. Stumbling down the darkened corridor, he burst out of the security doors into the cold night air. His stomach lurched with each step. Holding onto a pipe at the corner of the building he heaved, emptying what little food there was in his stomach onto the dusty track. Almost immediately his phone started to ring. David wiped his mouth and fumbled for it, his hands shaking. The number was unfamiliar. Terror forced him to answer.

'I hope you are going to clean that up!' The voice was impassive, cool, commanding, strong. It took several seconds for David to realise that he was being watched. 'We don't want any clues left behind do we? That wouldn't do at all. Your DNA is in that disgusting mess, don't leave a trace!' The caller hung up and an eerie silence hung in the air.

David looked around, panic flooding his mind. He wondered how his tormentor knew what had just happened. It was then he heard it, an almost imperceptible sound in the still night air, a faint whirring noise. A drone hovered in front of him, suspended at eye level. It seemed that no matter where he went, someone was watching him. He'd carried out each instruction to the letter, what more did they want? Someone was playing with him, and the thought was terrifing.

Maybe whoever had planted the new file was also operating the drone. Perhaps they were close by, not only relaying his progress to *Puppenspieler*, but able to see him in person...perhaps *Puppenspieler* himself was there?

'What do you want from me?' he yelled, 'what do you....' he slid down the wall, staring around, afraid to move. The hum of the drone filled the night, reverberating in his mind. He grew cold and began to shiver, more with a backlash to the adrenaline rush than because of the temperature. David wiped his tear-streaked face with his sleeve, staring at the alien-like technology. He saw it dip once, as if nodding; it turned and flew towards the gate, rising higher and disappeared into the night.

David stood and retraced his steps back to the killing room...silence. He knew that Tony was long past dead. He carried out *Puppenspieler's* extended instructions, placed the recording and paperwork in the envelope and sealed it carefully.

The drop off was three miles away, an old telephone box, used now as a book swapping venue. He placed the envelope on top of a pile of books, then drove back to Pearson's garage.

Within an hour he was sitting back in his own car, his mind a whirl. Despite the lack of CCTV, he'd taken the precaution of parking it well away from the entrance, at the far end, in the dark. By the time he retrieved it and had driven back past the garage, the van had gone. He wondered who was clearing up the mess, but then that wasn't his problem, was it? He'd done what he'd been told to do. He'd pushed through the barriers. David knew that things would never be the same again. He had to find his family now, make sure that they were safe. How was that going to work out? He could hardly go to the police, could he? He slammed on the brakes...the mess...the vomit, he hadn't cleared it up.

Panic overwhelmed him, what if whoever was watching him had noticed? Of course, he'd notice, he noticed everything didn't he? He had to go back, he had to check, to clear up anything that would incriminate him. Within seconds he'd turned the car around and headed back. He looked around checking the area as he approached the gates. He got out and ran towards them, grasping hold of the bars and shaking them...they were locked. His phone rang. This time he answered it in seconds, gasping when the now familiar voice spoke.

'Careless, aren't we? Very careless, I even warned you about your faux pas. Don't worry it's been dealt with.' David breathed out sharply, not having realised that he was holding his breath. The caller interrupted before he could speak.

'That's two you owe me,' he warned. 'You know don't you, that it's three strikes and you're out?'

'I'm sorry, my family' David whispered, 'I'm so sorr...' a shot rang out. David fell forward clutching his chest. A figure approached, prodding the dying man with his foot.

'That's your third mistake, never apologise,' announced the one-man audience sitting at a computer several miles away. He watched dispassionately as David's life ended. The shooter turned and walked back to his car, stashing the Glock safely in his jacket pocket.

Within the building a two-man team moved stealthily, efficiently. For them the evening had just begun. They bagged the body, dismantled the equipment, and sanitised the murder scene, erasing signs that anyone had been there. Now, of course they had two bodies to dispose of instead of one.

7

S usie Walker was fed up with her placement. This was her third year in Catering College and all she could find was a poxy washing up job in a lousy seaside cafe. Her attitude over the last few weeks had resulted in a stern warning from the owner. It went along the lines of, if she couldn't up her game she would have to go, irrespective of the arrangement with her tutor. So far, she had managed to toe the line, and as a result she'd been 'promoted' to waiting on tables.

She enjoyed her new role only slightly more than scraping food off holiday-maker's plates. The place was only half full as the last of this year's visitors stretched out the dwindling hours of their holidays with a final visit to the harbour. Floorboards creaked overhead as the curious visited the museum which featured the history of the local copper mines and some maritime artefacts. Susie had seen the display. She couldn't for the life of her understand why it could be of so much interest, but then she was only here under sufferance.

The afternoon was warm, the outside tables occupied with hungry customers. Susie's table craned their heads as she approached with the tray loaded with tea, scones, jam and butter pats, eagerly anticipating their afternoon treat. So it came as a huge shock when, just a few steps short of its arrival, Susie dropped it with a scream of shock. She pointed, hand shaking, at the harbour wall, clearly visible from where she stood. Eyes followed, heads turned, people stood. Curiosity replaced frustration at the wasted food now being trampled underfoot as they pushed forward to get a better look. A woman screamed, several reached for their phones to call for help, some to take photographs which Susie suspected would later appear on Facebook or Instagram.

'Police,' barked a man dressed like a seasoned walker. 'There's a body...' he swallowed hard, 'hanging from a rope...in Amlwch Harbour.'

Within 24 hours Graham Shaw was performing his first PM of the day...on Tony Berwick.

...oo0oo...

A few miles away Richard and Andrew Lincoln climbed over a gate. They strolled hand in hand along a well-trodden path on their way to the shore. They'd visited the island before and were here to get pictures for an annual competition back in the Midlands. Their dog strained on her lead, eager to run off pent-up energy.

'First this time,' said Richard, determined not to be beaten again this year. Andrew smiled, not his thing, but indulging his partner's hobby meant they could get away from the judgmental eyes of the woman that lived next door. Andrew fiddled with the dog's collar, watching as she sped away from him.

Lady had never been what you could call an obedient dog. She had a mind of her own and never let her owners forget it. They knew there was no point in trying to train her to come to heel as they explored their various holiday destinations. They'd also given up trying to calm down her boisterous nature. The upside was that she hardly ever strayed out of their eye line, and always returned when they called her. This time was different. She headed like an arrow straight for the thickly wooded area, at right angles to the way they had intended to go.

'Bloody dog,' Andrew grumbled, as he headed off in pursuit, 'what the hell is she chasing now?' he looked back at Richard, strolling along as casually as you please, and shouted to him to help.

'Not my turn!' Richard replied in a sing-song voice, smiling to himself. 'I got caught out the last time,' he chuckled as he watched Andrew enter the thicket. He would give it a few minutes, he decided, before making a move to help. The dog barked incessantly, followed by shouting. Richard stopped walking when he heard Andrew scream, he watched open-mouthed as his partner careered back towards him, his arms flailing about, his face screwed up in horror.

'Richard, Richard, oh my God, phone the police, quick, phone....' Andrew's breath ran out as he collapsed on the ground.

'What the...?' Richard was torn; terrified that Lady might be in danger. He knelt by Andrew's side, placed his hands either side of the terrified man's face, then fumbled for a water bottle in the knapsack he carried.

'No, no,' Andrew gasped, 'a...a body, phone the...' he said, clutching his chest. Richard found his phone...no reception. He hesitated, looking round. In the distance he saw what looked like a quad bike.

'Help,' he screamed, 'help...over here, over here.' He snatched a hand towel from his bag and waved it frantically in the air. Within seconds the quad bike changed direction and was heading towards the two men.

'My God, Richard, what if...what if that's the killer?' sobbed Andrew. It was too late, killer or not, the bike was almost upon them. Richard knelt again, his arms around Andrew, staring at the approaching figure. The bike stopped; the rider dismounted and walked towards them. He wore wellingtons, jeans and a workman's shirt.

'Can I help?' he asked. He looked at the two men, now huddled on the ground, he could sense their fear. 'Sorry...are you all right?'

Andrew realised he'd been holding his breath. He managed to tell the stranger what he'd seen, pointing back towards where Lady had disappeared. Within seconds he'd returned to his bike, picked up a handset and pressed some buttons. A radio crackled into life. He strolled some way from the stricken walkers.

'Phil, Sean here...problem up at Treetops, phone the police, someone's found a body...' there was a garbled response. Sean checked on Andrew, then made his way into the woods. Within minutes he was walking back leading an exuberant Lady on a length of rope. She obliged by not pulling as she trotted obediently at his side. She gazed at him with adoring eyes, her owners watching nonplussed.

'Finest Golden Retriever I've seen in years,' he gushed as they waited.

8

Autumn was busy gathering up the greenery of the island, colouring the landscape with a different palette. Within weeks trees would stand bare, divested of their foliage, all but the evergreens, immune to the arrival of colder days. The change always seemed to surprise people, yet every year was only a slight variation on the preceding ones. Snow some years and not others. Sometimes whole communities would be cut off for weeks.

The threat of flooding, storms, school closures; a brutal time of year but one for which the long-term residents of the island were well prepared. The first perpendicular swirls of smoke rose throughout the countryside, highlighting the positions of long hidden farmhouses and secluded cottages. Stores of seasoned logs raided to stoke wood burners; stalwart Agas pressed back into service as temperatures dropped. The smell of wood smoke permeated the air, adding a unique layer to the scents of the season. The harvest, long collected, was transformed into preserves, jams, pickles. Dehydrated fruits stored in well-stocked larders would provide variety throughout the winter months.

The narrow lanes were always a trial this time of year, twisting down into the valley. Sharp turns shrouded in pockets of cotton wool mist so that only full beam and wipers gave Ellie a fighting chance of getting through unscathed. Even after all these years, she dreaded the onset of autumn, once her favourite season.

'Give me New England in the fall any time…God damn,' she cursed under her breath narrowly missing the gnarled oak at the end of the drive. The mist was even thicker the closer she got to the main road. Ellie drove forward cautiously, swerving several times until she reached the T-junction. She slammed on the brakes as a motorbike sped past, well over the speed limit. She sat for a few moments, breathing deeply, her pale hands gripping the wheel. The tension she had felt building up over the last few days almost spilled over. She had to calm down. This morning was too important, she couldn't afford to screw it up. She pulled out onto the main road and headed towards the village. She was in the habit of stopping at the newsagents most mornings to pick up her supply of sugared almonds. They'd become her only vice since giving up smoking the previous year.

'Maybe I shouldn't bother anymore,' she thought, as she entered the shop, eyeing the shuttered cigarette cupboard, 'after all, it's not as though it matters now.' She sighed; she couldn't afford to go down that road either. How was she going to tell Graham that their third, and as they had mutually agreed, their last attempt at IVF had failed? Mr. Rossi took Ellie's money, counting out the change onto the counter.

'You ok love?' he asked. The tone of his voice threatened to tip Ellie's emotions over the top. Most days he never said a word, nobody did. She often felt as though she'd just arrived in a spaceship, the way most people stopped talking and waited until she made a move to leave. Then the interrupted conversations would resume. She'd often heard the low buzz as she stood outside.

In the eleven years since Ellie had lived on Anglesey, she'd tried hard to fit in. She'd learned names and family backgrounds, tried to treat people like old friends, bought cards for birthdays, christening and weddings. She'd even sent flowers when someone died, but nothing changed. People would stop talking as soon as she approached, either that or start speaking in Welsh. In their eyes she would always be 'that American that works for the police'. It gave them a double reason to distrust her.

Once she had left the close community where she lived, she felt she could pull on the cloak of anonymity that most people in large towns and cities seemed to wear. Things became slightly better, but only just. People seemed to accept her in her professional role, after all she was her own boss most of the time. But even at the station she felt as though her colleagues regarded her as a crank whenever she suggested a deviation from procedure. She seemed to do this frequently, she couldn't help it. Her 'Sixth Sense' that's what Graham called it; it was uncanny how many times she was right.

'At least I don't see dead people,' she told her husband after his reference to one of her favourite films, 'not yet anyway!' *Can't argue with the results though,* she told herself as she climbed back into her car. Ellie was excited at the prospect of her new role. Profiling was an absorbing career move, and she was justifiably proud of the results she'd had in what she regarded as her second job. *Second job? More like second chance....no, don't go down that path either...* she resolved, *not now, this morning's too important...* so much that she needed to sort out. Was there any part of her life that she could think about without getting dragged into emotional turmoil? Sadly, she had to admit that the answer was a resounding 'no!'

She flipped down the sun visor to check her appearance. Her face was pale, framed with short flaming red hair. A sprinkling of freckles over her nose and along her cheekbones made her look younger than her age. She wore little make up due to her propensity to emotional outbursts at the most inappropriate times which often resulted in what Graham affectionately called 'Panda eyes'.

To Ellie it was no joke. She'd resorted to having her sandy eyelashes dyed to avoid any embarrassing moments.

She tried to focus on the imminent meeting as she drove steadily towards the Menai Bridge. The mist had delayed her more than she'd realised. The traffic lining up to cross to the mainland was heavier than usual.

Ellie checked the clock...8.45; she still had at least thirty minutes' drive. She sighed, resigned to arriving late. At least she could give some thought to her section of this morning's workshop. She was terrified at the prospect of talking to a room of experienced police officers, trying to persuade them to buy into the benefits of profiling. She also knew she'd be quizzed for a progress report on the current investigation. She had nothing new to tell them. If she could only email her findings in, even Face-timing DCI Horton would be preferable, anything other than having to 'perform' in front of people who she was convinced sneered at her behind her back. A car horn interrupted her thoughts, the traffic in front of her had moved. Eventually she reached the station and scanned the car park, it was already full.

'Hell, more delay, I'm going to be so late!' She checked the time, ten past nine. She needn't have worried. Just five minutes in the meeting had been turned upside down.

9

Hardly anyone noticed Ellie's entrance. Officers stood in small groups, some talking loudly others whispering. DS Connett steered her to one side. Another body had been found, Ellie shuddered, not again. Questions came, who, where, when, how ones. Not the why ones, no one knew why, not yet. Details began to filter through. Male, late forties, early fifties, so far unidentified, had been found dumped on overgrown wasteland in Amlwch. Workmen had begun clearing the land that morning. A JCB driver clearing bricks and rubble from the corner of the site had spotted a shoe, not realising that it was still attached to a leg. By the time one of his fellow workers had screamed at him to stop, he'd moved several tons of rubble.

'Graham won't be pleased,' thought Ellie irreverently, 'it'll ruin the crime scene.' She was immediately ashamed; the victim deserved more respect. The conversations were dying down, she was aware that she was being watched. Expectant eyes scrutinising her, she squared her shoulders, taking a deep breath.

'May I have a word please DCI Horton, in private?' She asked. Horton, the Senior Investigating Officer nodded and walked towards the door, motioning her to follow.

'Porter,' he shouted, 'you as well.' DI Porter grabbed his phone and hurried after them. The rest of the assembled crowd resumed their low-level grumbling. Horton headed to an empty office, held the door open and followed them in. He by-passed the desk and chairs, and headed straight for the window, keeping his back to them.

'God-damn sh..!' he breathed, shaking his head in denial, 'this is the third one in five weeks!' a fact that both

Ellie and Porter were aware of. 'And what have we come up with? Fuck all!'

Ellie hesitated, standing just inside the office door. She was trying to still the panic that was rising from somewhere south of her stomach. How was it he always made her feel that these events were her fault? She had to focus hard, in order not to take her failure to come up with anything concrete as personal. Horton spun round suddenly, grabbing onto the edge of the desk for support.

'You have no idea the pressure I'm under,' he moaned, 'Chetwynd's on the warpath again, overtime's through the roof,' Horton seemed to be talking to himself. 'Tell me you've got something, please,' he begged suddenly aware that they were watching him. He looked at Ellie, then at Porter in desperation, his flaccid face a mask of misery.

Porter sighed, pacing around the perimeter of the room, hands clasped and raised to the back of his head. He had a habit of waiting for others to start speaking first, getting them to play their cards before he committed himself. It wasn't popular, but it was effective. He had to admit that the team's lack of results was becoming ridiculous. No one they'd interviewed seemed to have seen or heard anything, and there had been no new leads for the last two weeks. The lack of discernible physical evidence was baffling. Apart from the appalling injuries that the victims had suffered, he could almost believe that they had expired independently.

Ellie also played for time, knowing that what she had to say wouldn't go down well. She sat down, opened her brief case and extracted several beige files. Her hands were shaking as she placed them on the desk. What she wouldn't give for a drink right now.

'Well?' demanded Horton, 'I haven't got all day *Ms.* Shaw!' he hissed emphasising the *Ms.* Ellie took a deep breath.

'I, err,' she faltered, there was no easy way to tell him. 'I've studied the reports on Ellis Franklin, and that of Noel Parker. As I explained to you at the time, I didn't have many points of comparison to go on. I went back several years to try and find similar cases, nothing showed up. If you're expecting me to make any comment about this new incident, I know as much about it as you do...'

'Obviously!' snapped Horton, patience now expended.

'We need more to go on before it can be established whether these murders are connected in any way. Apart from the victims living on the island, and both being men of course,' she went on. It sounded weak, but for now it was the best she could offer. What was she supposed to say? She knew as much about this new incident as the rest of the station, less in fact.

For a moment she thought that Horton was about to implode. He seemed to fold back on himself as he negotiated his way around a chair and lowered his considerable weight onto it. Porter meanwhile had stopped pacing and was looking at her, his steel-blue eyes narrowing, listening intently.

'You mean that you have nothing to contribute, again?' breathed Horton, his voice barely a whisper. He had little time for the woman sitting opposite. In his opinion she was nothing more than an egotistical foreigner, foisted on him by his boss. He gave her no credit at all for her past record.

'Sir...' Porter cleared his throat. Horton was being unfair, telling him that was going to be risky, 'Sir, it's only been a few...' Horton rounded on his most senior detective.

'...and what kind of results have your team come up on the Franklin case, or, or the Parker lad, I'd like to know...nothing so far, eh, eh?' Horton snapped. He jumped to his feet with a movement at odds with his bulky frame, his red face deepening with every word. He began pacing the room. No one spoke for several minutes.

'I need...' Ellie said slowly, measuring the effect of each word on the seething officer. 'I need to see the reports on this latest killing. I need to find a link before I can say for certain that there is anything to connect them.' There it was said, out there. Horton should have known this, but she knew that his anger with her was personal as well as professional.

'Explain!' Horton snapped.

'How the hell can she,' Porter said, 'when we've only just got the call on this one? It's not her job for God's..."' Horton stared at him. Was that a flash of fear on his face? That and panic too? Horton didn't have a clue what to do, blame and bluster was all he had to offer right now, and Porter knew it.

Horton spoke slowly and quietly. 'Watch yourself, Porter, remember who you're talking to.' He grabbed the phone and dialled the switchboard. *More grandstanding* thought Porter, he could just as well have called direct.

'Put me through to Dr Prothero's office!' he barked. Ellie sighed, that was all she needed, her brother-in law called in. It was a threat she lived with every day, that she would be judged by her mentor, and that he would conclude she wasn't good enough.

10

Ellie's treatment room could only be accessed by passing through a neat reception and waiting area, a domain ruled over by Rosa Pritchard with efficient authority. It housed a large oak desk, a run of ancient filing cabinets, and a worn, though impressive leather sofa to accommodate waiting clients. The offices also included a restroom with dated facilities, and a small kitchen area. Two moderately sized rooms served both as consulting and treatment areas for Ellie and her business partner, John Prothero.

Ellie's room boasted modern furnishings. A cream sofa for her clients, with a faux fur throw and several cushions flanked one wall. A corner desk coupled with an off-white swivel chair, and a pair of canvas and wooden Scandinavian chairs took up the rest of the space. The paneled walls gave testament to the age of the place, the building having been a bank in a former life. They, along with the dark oak floor were protected by conditions in the lease.

Ellie had tried to relieve their gloomy effect with light rugs which were a devil to keep clean. Qualifications hung in gold edged frames, a modern print the only other decoration. Two windows allowed for adequate light, but the view from them was such that Ellie had had them frosted. She'd tried to lighten the area further with cream curtains. These were drawn back and held with ropes intertwined with beads that ended in intricate shell-woven tassels. John hated the look, and had made his feelings quite clear. He said it reminded him of one of the cheap gift shops that taken root in the High Street during the last few years.

But Ellie felt comfortable there, and no matter how many hints he dropped about changing it he had failed to influence her. John had the larger of the two offices, as befit his seniority. It was as dark and sombre as hers was airy, with a large oak desk, a traditional swivel chair, two medium sized Oxblood Chesterfield sofas, and heavy lined linen curtains. He was hardly there these days. His recent promotion meant that he was away for lengthy periods.

Coffee was served almost as soon as Ellie had hung up her coat. After the morning she'd been through, it was more than welcome. Miss Pritchard had bought Rich Tea biscuits again, even though Ellie never ate them. The coffee was good though, and as Ellie sipped the scalding brew, she reviewed the day's appointments. Two clients today, one later this morning, one…oh damn, she'd forgotten, lunch with her sister Ruth. *I could cancel*, she thought. With everything going on she needed to focus. Ellie had been alcohol free for two years, four months and five days, but social occasions were still difficult. With what had just happened at the station, she didn't feel up to socialising.

'It's just a habit,' she sighed, causing Miss Pritchard to pause, tray in hand.

Oh, nothing,' Ellie sighed, seeing her puzzled look, 'just thinking out loud.'

Miss Pritchard was used to Ellie's 'little ways', as she called them. She admired her young employer, though she would never be so bold as to tell her. She knew of Ellie's personal battles and of her successes in her new role with the local police. She was proud to have played a small part in those successes.

'She's a 'Profiler'!' Miss Pritchard had told her best friend Mrs. Pargetter at their weekly outing to the tearooms. She made quotation marks in the air, a habit which she usually despised.

'What's that when it's at home?' Gwen Pargetter asked all agog, suspending the teapot mid-air for a second or two. Miss Pritchard preened herself, explaining in a slightly patronising tone that Ellie Shaw helped the police to put a picture of a villain together. She studied cases and worked out what the perpetrator was like, and then submitted findings to the police investigators.

Truth was that Rosa Pritchard had only recently heard of the term 'profiling'. She considered it to be some 'new-fangled' name for what her other boss, Mr. Prothero, had been involved in since before she'd come to work for him. It seemed to her that some bright spark had come up with a new label, and now she seemed to see it everywhere. Ellie's efforts had been acknowledged in a few national newspapers, and Miss Pritchard's standing within her social group had risen as a result. They seemed to be fascinated at the element of mystery it conjured. Rosa basked in the reflected glory of her young employer, whilst at the same time maintaining strict confidentiality.

Ellie checked her diary again. She made up her mind to cancel the lunch date when the phone rang.

'Hi Ellie...' it was Ruth sounding buoyant. Ellie thought she could detect a slightly manic edge to her voice, '...just got into town,' she enthused, 'so looking forward to seeing you!'

'You're early Ruth, its only 10.30!' Ellie spluttered. She began to wish she'd rung and cancelled last night.

'I know, but I thought I'd get some shopping done, need some new clothes for my trip home!' Ruth sounded bright and Ellie was reluctant to spoil the moment.

'Well don't spend too much!' laughed Ellie, resigning herself to the lunch date after all.

'You know me honey, see you at one!' With a slightly forced giggle, Ruth hung up. Ellie sighed, she was glad Ruth sounded happy, but experience and a lurch in her gut made her suspect that her sister hadn't been taking her medication again, and at this rate it wouldn't be long before she entered another manic phase. She felt guilty for contemplating cancelling their lunch date. It was a scenario that reminded Ellie of a similar case from her past. The dangers of her sister's behaviour filled her with a mixture of sadness, dread and anger.

Ellie liked John, she got on well with him, even if his professional persona still intimidated her. He had after all bought some stability into Ruth's life, and a family which she had always craved. He had also been instrumental in Ellie's career, recommending that she replace him when he'd been promoted. She'd learned so much from him in her early days.

She was soon assisting him in investigations, attending his lectures to augment her understanding of the role for which she hadn't realised he was grooming her. He teased her about her uncanny abilities to sidestep the obvious and flush out the obscure. It was a good-natured teasing, not like her fellow students when she'd first demonstrated her skills at Uni. Her daydreaming took her back to the lecture rooms; to the silence with which some of her more outlandish suggestions had been greeted. Most of her peers had mocked her theories, resulting in some serious arguments, they were incredulous when she was almost always proved right.

Over the last few years Ellie had assumed the role of Ruth's informal guardian. She would watch Ruth from a distance to ensure that she was taking care of herself. Ellie wanted nothing but the best for her younger sister, but she

sometimes resented having to 'babysit' her when John was
absent. In many ways she reminded her of...the phone
rang again, scything through her reverie and making her
jump. Miss Pritchard announced the arrival of her first
client.

Ellie finished her coffee and stood to greet her.

11

I t was past one as Ellie dashed towards the Red Man
Bar and Grill. It was regarded as the 'trendy new
place', even though it had been open for the last five
years and had just been through its second refurbishment.
All morning she hoped that Ruth would call and cancel.
She had to admit she had been too busy to spend much
time with her sister these past few weeks. She felt annoyed
when John had reminded her of his own commitments
elsewhere. Perhaps Ruth would understand, maybe she
would allow for the fact that Ellie was involved in a case
that was threatening to overwhelm her. Ellie had to admit
that that would be giving Ruth too much credit.

She and her sister were as different as day and night.
Ellie tried to appreciate what Ruth was going through, but
she was in despair that her sister wasn't prepared to co-
operate in trying to manage her condition. Ellie had lost
count of the number of times she had fallen into the
'feeling sorry for Ruth' trap. She braced herself for the
telltale signs.

Ruth would announce her latest interest, some quite
reasonable, some downright weird. She would immerse
herself to the point of excluding even her husband and
son, let alone the other people in her life. Then, just as

suddenly, she would run out of steam, emerging some time later, either bored or disillusioned. She would complain that she was 'down', which would be followed by long periods of depression during which she would try to draw others into her negative state. This was the point at which Ellie made excuses to avoid her.

There seemed to be only a few constants in Ruth's life, John, who seemed oblivious to her short-comings, and their son Max, who Ruth loved to distraction. There was also her habit of spending money on disparate items. 'Investments' she called them. They ranged from jewellery to property, paintings by unknown artists, to speculative investments over the Internet, much to John's despair. His wife's spending had caused so many arguments, he'd lost count. They usually ended with him storming off to sleep in the guest room. Ruth would sit fuming in silence in the lounge until fatigue overcame her and she would crawl into his bed in the early hours.

'I'm only concerned for you,' he would tell her as she wound herself around him. 'I know you have your trust fund, but it's not going to last long if you go on like this.' Ruth would laugh and kiss his neck until all thoughts of her spending had been overcome by other emotions. The next morning would be as if they'd never had a cross word. Ellie knew that Ruth saved up most of her complaints for when they met up, which they tried to do as often as they could.

'Tell me what's wrong with me?' Ruth would beg, throwing herself on the sofa, dramatically sweeping her arms, and sighing deeply. 'You're trained to deal with people with depression, aren't you?'

'Ruth,' Ellie said, trying for the umpteenth time to get through to her, 'you don't have depression, you're bi-polar, remember?'

'Oh, yes, well, that then?' Ruth would brush off Ellie's words, as though the two conditions were interchangeable.

What Ruth didn't understand was that Ellie and John were the last people who could help her on a professional level. They were too close, and both knew that Ruth would take absolutely no notice of what either of them said anyway. But, so far, Ruth refused to see anyone else.

It went on and on, and it was exhausting. Ruth was like a kitten distracted by a bouncing ball or a shiny light, followed by a period of self-imposed disappointed seclusion. A pattern had emerged over the years and Ellie knew that soon Ruth would emerge, re-energised, and a lot calmer. That was, of course until something else caught her attention and she would be off chasing the next obsession, then disappointment would hit again. It was at that point that she would want everyone to drop what they were doing and join her in contemplation of her latest failed venture.

'Misery loves company,' their Mother told Ellie back in the day. Ruth certainly enjoyed reliving her failures if only for the sympathy she could gain. Ellie and her sister had always been close. Ruth, the proverbial 'Wild Child' to Ellie's almost convent like obedience to her parents and teachers alike. This left her trying to work out how her sister got away with it. There was no 'middle of the road' with Ruth. It seemed to be all or nothing, which made it exhausting to be in her company for any length of time.

Probably what made her so endearing as well, Ellie thought, catching a glimpse of her sister through the great glass door.

The aroma of smoked meat wafted towards her as she entered the main dining area, reminding her that breakfast had been hours ago, she was starving. As she approached the table, she saw someone sitting with Ruth, a young woman with silvery white hair. She wore it braided and it reached down her back. The stranger rose and turned as she approached. Ellie hesitated for a split second when she saw that the right side of the stranger's face was badly scarred. She realised that she was staring and stammered as the young woman thrust out her hand in greeting.

'S... Sorry, I didn't mean...' she faltered.

'Odelia, Odelia Mathers,' she announced totally unfazed. 'I'm so pleased to meet you Ellie, I may call you Ellie?' she asked with such warmth that Ellie immediately felt at ease.

'Of course,' Ellie murmured. They sat down as Ruth signalled the waiter and ordered another round of drinks.

'Mineral water please' Ellie managed to cut in, slightly annoyed that Ruth had ordered three more glasses of wine.

Same for me,' said Odelia. She smiled as she turned back to Ellie. 'Ruth tells me you work for the police. You're a profiler, aren't you? She says you have your own practice as well, that must be interesting.'

'Did she?' Ellie said staring at the top of her sister's head. Ruth was studying the menu, oblivious to anyone's needs but her own. 'What else did she tell you?' Ellie asked.

'That you get hunches, that you're usually right. That must help with your work.' Odelia went on. Ellie felt uncomfortable, they had been talking about her, not only that but Ruth had shared something that Ellie never felt at ease with, her instincts, 'glimpses', whatever they were called. It wasn't that she was ashamed of them, or that she didn't believe that they were real. But Ruth had no right.

"Glimpses," she said, without taking her eyes off Ruth, she could sense Odelia's confusion. 'That's what my Mother used to call them. If you two are going to talk about me behind my back, at least get the terminology right.'

Ellie stared at Ruth, willing her to take her head out of the menu. Odelia looked from one sister to the other, sensing Ellie's anger. Ellie cleared her throat loudly. At last Ruth looked up. She saw the look on her older sister's face and sighed.

'What?' she snapped defensively, 'what have I done now?' She looked sheepish, like she had when she was a child and was caught misbehaving. Ellie sighed. She really despaired of Ruth's behaviour sometimes, couldn't be discreet if her life depended on it. At least she had the good grace to blush this time.

'All I said was that sometimes you get these feelings. Odelia understands don't you honey, she reckons you might be psychic, just like her.' Ruth shook her head and tutted, really this was too much. Since when had it been a crime to discuss your own sister with a friend? Ellie stood up, preparing to leave.

'Odelia, it was nice to meet you. Ruth, I'll call you later.' Ellie stood and picked up her bag and jacket. Odelia stood suddenly, reaching for Ellie's arm, she grasped it firmly, pulling Ellie towards her so that she could whisper to her.

'You're right...they're linked...' she hissed, 'the murders, they're linked.' Ellie jerked her arm away. It felt like a surge of electricity was snaking towards her shoulder. She stared at Odelia, shock, anger and confusion flooding her body. How dare Ruth put her in this position? If she'd been discussing confidential matters with this woman...how did she know, had John told...how dare she? Without a backwards glance, she hurried to the door and left them alone.

…oo0oo…

Odelia sighed as she sat down. From the moment Ellie entered the restaurant, she had sensed something, something different. It was disturbing, something she had only felt a few times in her life. She was amazed that no-one had picked up on the signs, and that Ellie seemed to have no clue as to what was going on. It was Ruth who'd mentioned Ellie's 'situation' as she had called it. She'd told Odelia that her sister was 'a bit weird, too serious by far, and had never had much time for having fun.' She obviously had no idea what was going on.

'She gets these, I don't know, intuitions, kinda cool sometimes. She sort of...' Ruth hesitated, searching for the right words, '...knows things, don't ask me how though,' she laughed, shaking her head. At first Odelia wasn't sure why Ruth had sought her out, except that it was obvious that the woman felt that she had no one else to talk to. Eventually Ruth began to talk about Ellie. It had become clear to Odelia that it was fate that had brought them together. Their weekly sessions left Ruth with a degree of peace she hadn't experienced in a long time.

At first Ruth said she just needed to talk. Odelia tried to explain that counselling wasn't usually something that she offered in her practice, but there was no putting Ruth off. Their initial consultation was a doleful litany that included a long list of those people in her life who couldn't make time for her. Her husband, her best friend, God, even her own sister...no one to talk to, no one. She didn't know if Odelia could help her...she just needed to talk.

Odelia reluctantly obliged, and they spent the next two hours together.

Ruth talked and talked, repeating herself again and again. For the entire time she was in the treatment room, Odelia felt negativity breaking like waves over her. She closed her eyes at one point and imagined herself surrounded by silver light. Visualising Ruth's words bouncing off it, mollified the effect. It was when Ruth started to talk about her family that Odelia felt the strongest pull at her core. This had always been a sign that here was something she should pay attention to.

'My husband, John, well he's busy all the time,' complained Ruth with a self-pitying whine. 'He's a Psychiatrist, how about that, a shrink who doesn't understand his wife, huh! He's away most of the time, comes back every three weeks or so, expects me to adapt all the time, oh don't get me wrong...'

On and on she talked. Eventually Odelia realised that Ruth's family consisted of 'The Holy Trinity' a nickname that some hack had recently coined. Her husband was John Prothero, the leading local Psychiatrist and Profiler recently elevated to a position within a government department. Her brother-in-law Graham Shaw was a Forensic Pathologist and Professor lecturing at a local University.

Then there was Ellie, her sister, Odelia found her the most interesting of all. Ellie Shaw, the Criminal Profiler, helping the police to investigate the current murders. Together the three of them had solved some difficult cases in the past few years and were gaining quite a reputation.

Odelia had had some strong instincts about the cases in the past few weeks. Maybe she had been offered a potential entrée into the investigation, something that she had been hoping for. Odelia's attempts to arrange a meeting with DCI Horton had met with a blank wall. She'd looked for opportunities to break through, believing that she could help in some way, but to no avail. Even one of her clients, DS Mason, who came to her once a week for Indian Head Massage couldn't help. Despite her strict code of not talking about her clients' work, Odelia felt compelled to ask Doris Mason if she would pass a letter to her boss. She agreed to try, returning it when she arrived for her next visit, unopened.

'Sorry Odelia,' stammered Mason, 'he asked me who it was from and refused to look at it when I told him. I'm so sorry,'…and Odelia knew that she was.

Anyway, now she had met Ellie, she felt that she had a foothold. Whether she could convince her to meet up, to talk, to take what she had to say seriously, well that was another matter. What was even more important, she believed, was getting Ellie to recognise and embrace her own abilities.

...oo0oo...

Ellie didn't go back to the office that afternoon. She was furious that she had been tricked into meeting with Ruth's latest acolyte. She drove back across the island and made for a small cove that she sometimes escaped to. She parked the car and sat breathing deeply until she calmed down. She left the car and walked up a winding path to the top of the cliff, heading towards a large rock that she had come to regard as her 'thinking stone'. She sat down and stared out over the calm blue sea. The temperature had dropped during the last few days, but it was still warm enough for her to loosen her scarf and unbutton her coat.

The scenery that surrounded her, however, left her untouched.

...how dare she, how dare she engineer such a meeting. It was never about what you thought it was about was it?

Ruth had developed a charming way of capturing her attention.

'Let's have lunch, catch up on things,' she would say. What she really meant was, 'I want the opportunity to tell you what's going on in my life. I'm going to do it in such a way that you can't help but feel sorry for me. I want to unburden myself on someone, and, despite the fact that you have really important things, life or death things, you need to get on with, indeed, have to get on with, I intend to monopolise you for the time it takes to siphon all my negative shit into you. Once I have done that, I'll feel much better, and you'll feel like a wrung-out rag!'

Almost immediately Ellie felt contrite. She reminded herself that Ruth couldn't help her condition. But then again, she wasn't even trying to help herself. After years of self-diagnosing, she had finally agreed to see a colleague of John's, but as for following the required regime, that was another matter.

She breathed in deeply and tried to relax, willing herself to review the situation objectively. Ruth had hardly said anything in the brief time they had been together at the restaurant. To accuse her of using the encounter for her own needs was unfair. On the other hand, she had placed Ellie in the position of having to meet someone who she didn't know, and who, quite frankly had spooked her more than she cared to admit.

The wind was picking up. Ellie's eyes started to water. At what stage did Ruth's condition become this acute? Ellie sighed, bi-polar or not, Ruth shouldn't have discussed the case with that woman, she shouldn't have set her up.

A thought suddenly struck her...if she had...if she had discussed it at all? What if this Odelia Mathers had some sort of agenda and wormed her way into Ruth's life. What if she'd played Ruth to gain access to those involved? It wouldn't be difficult; Ruth was susceptible to flattery. As much as it pained Ellie to admit it, her sister was a bit slow when it came to judging other people's characters.

That was it...she decided, feeling calmer now that she believed that she had figured it out. Ruth had been seduced into this meeting by a manipulative individual who wanted, for whatever reason, to have access to Ellie or any others involved in the case. A sudden need to find out about Odelia Mathers consumed her. Something wasn't right. The woman might even be involved in the recent murders. She'd have to be investigated, and Ellie believed she knew exactly the right person to consult.

12

John Prothero sat in DCI Horton's office. He took a deep breath.

'I agree with Ms. Shaw,' he announced, 'you just need to give her more time to work on the case and distill her findings that is of course when you can provide her with something to go on. I notice that there are few if any statements from witnesses. Profiles don't appear out of thin air, you know. I think Ellie Shaw has achieved more within the constraints she has encountered than some of your officers themselves. If you want me to assist, then of course I will. However, my time is limited, I have commitments elsewhere, as you know.'

John's outward calm masked his growing frustration, not only with the lack of progress being made by Horton's team, but also because they were not allowing Ellie enough time to do what he knew her to be capable of. He had to admit that he was also annoyed with Ellie herself for her on-going lack of confidence in her own abilities.

He'd been packing to leave the island again, having spent a few days with his family when Horton had phoned. John's gut instinct had been to ignore the ringing telephone, but he'd made the mistake of answering it on his way out of the door. Now he'd been delayed, and not for the first time. He'd got caught up again, in a case he felt Horton could have handled if only he would delegate and have faith in his officers, and in Ellie.

It was mid-afternoon, Horton, Porter, Graham Shaw and John Prothero had convened at Horton's request, at extremely short notice, to 'compare notes and findings' as he put it. Graham was uncomfortable about not including his wife. In his opinion it was her case, but Horton had been adamant.

'Not needed,' Horton snapped when Graham had asked why she was absent, 'she's got enough to be getting on with!'

Horton sighed, he had been counting on Prothero's backing that Ellie wasn't up to the task in hand and had been wasting everyone's time. He wasn't pleased with what he'd just heard. He watched the others over tented fingertips. *This is all too cozy* he thought, too incestuous for his liking. Graham Shaw, he knew, had an excellent reputation. Horton couldn't fault his work on any level. How the hell he found the time to conduct most of the postmortems for the area, fit in his lecturing at the University and write several well-respected tomes on Forensic Pathology was beyond Horton's understanding.

Prothero had assisted Horton's department for many years, and was in his opinion an exemplary man, fellow Mason and a member of the golf club. Horton felt that they had developed a good working relationship. That was until Ellie Shaw had come to town, with her degree in Psychology from God know which Yankee University, her 'new-age' ways and uncanny abilities. Prothero had sung her praises to anyone who would listen. John was all that his department needed, why did he have to suggest that Ellie come on board? Nepotism, pure and simple, that and an overwhelming desire to curry favour with Ellie's sister, Ruth. It had worked though, hadn't it?

Within six months of their meeting Prothero, upstanding member of the community had gone completely gaga for a girl twelve years younger. They were married and she was pregnant within the year. Now here he was, beguiled with his sister-in-law, an incompetent hanger on, agreeing with her crazy theories. Why the hell hadn't Prothero been content with his lot? Why had he got involved in promoting this new-fangled profiling lark? If he had only been content with the way things were, everyone would have been happy.

What was it with people? Horton wondered, having never been head-hunted in his life. *What was so attractive in working for a Government Department anyway?*

Horton railed against the fact that Prothero had been offered the opportunity to step up the ladder and become involved in a specialised area. Horton himself had been happy to exploit him in the past, but he had never acknowledged the contributions that profiling had made to solving cases. He realised that the others had stopped talking and were waiting for him to speak.

'John, I want you on the case,' he announced. Graham started to protest, but Horton waived his hand. 'Professor Shaw, I respect the work that your wife has done, I really do, but that's my final word, I'm sorry!'

John sighed; Graham knew that any objections would be futile. Horton stood up, gathered his papers in silence, and left the others to return to his office.

'I'll spend some time with him, listen to what he has to moan about this time. I can only reinforce Ellie's findings. Hopefully he'll take more notice of her in the future,' John said, trying to reassure Graham.

'That's all very well, John,' said Graham, 'but when's this going to stop? When's he going to take her seriously and realise that she can do this job just as well as you can? This isn't the first time he's pulled you back into one of her cases, and you know it.' Graham thought he saw John's left eye twitch, his manner seemed to change. It was, Graham concluded later, as though he was stunned at the thought that Ellie's abilities were being placed on an equal footing with his own.

John took another deep breath. 'Ellie is very capable,' he said, his voice steady, measured, 'but it's not her competence that's being questioned here, at least not by me. Horton is desperate, he's getting nowhere with the current cases, and now there's another body. He feels that he's being shown up as the buffoon he is. If I'm not mistaken, he may even have been threatened with being taken off the case if he doesn't start making progress. If I can reassure him that Ellie has my full support, well, hopefully she can take back the reins. God knows I need more involvement with this case like I need a hole in the head.' John's smile was forced, Graham thought, but then he did have a lot on his plate just now. John was watching him intently.

'Graham, there has to come a time when you step back from your role as Sir Galahad. You can't protect Ellie from everything in life you know. Besides, she's a lot stronger than you think,' he patted Graham's shoulder, as he turned to go. Graham couldn't help feeling patronised.

He and Porter gathered their things and left Graham alone as they headed out of the office. Graham remained alone, trying to decide how to break the news to Ellie. How the hell was he going to tell her without damaging her self-confidence even further? The temptation to pass the buck and feign surprise when she found out was almost overwhelming. He knew that Horton had assumed that he would tell her about the meeting as soon as he got home.

What a coward that man was, Graham thought, *leaving others to do his dirty work. All up in your face and 'I'm in charge' attitude 'don't do anything until you hear from me.' Unless it was something that meant he had to get his hands dirty, then it was, 'Oh I thought you knew, I thought someone would have told you.'* God, he hated that man. There had been more arguments between him and Ellie since Horton had started stirring things than he could remember in the whole of their time together. *Unless you counted...best not go there,* he sighed. Thinking this way wouldn't change things, would probably make them worse if anything.

Graham glanced at his watch, four thirty. Traffic would be building up on the approach to the Menai Bridge around now. He'd wait for an hour or so for the worst of it to disperse. His stomach growled, and he realised that he'd eaten nothing since breakfast. That was it, he would go to the canteen, have coffee, maybe a sandwich if there were any left, and then make his way home. *All delaying tactics*, he acknowledged, returning once more to look out of the window.

He noticed John backing his black Jaguar out of the crowded car park. Graham knew he had an up-coming lecture to a slew of high-ranking police officials and members of a Government department on the advantages of *Psychological Profiling in the Detection of Murder Suspects*, or whatever his programme was called. It was a project that John had been working on for some time and had been greeted with enthusiasm by the powers that be. Graham was conflicted about his success. On the one hand he conceded, there was evidence for the need of such a programme, he only had to recall the number of cases both John and Ellie had been able to help with in the last few years. On the other hand, though, he lamented the lack of vital funding being withheld from projects that he believed were equally worthy in his own field of Forensic Science.

'Sour grapes,' he said out loud, bringing his thoughts back to the afternoon's meeting. The fact that Ellie knew nothing about it didn't sit right. Horton had gathered them together using subterfuge that would have been worthy of MI5. None of them had been prewarned, it was obvious that this was so Ellie wouldn't find out.

How could he break the news that John had been drawn back into the case? Damn Horton, why couldn't he give her a chance? Graham considered spending the night at his office at the University, or phoning with the excuse that he had an emergency postmortem. In the end, he decided not to. He'd promised her no more lies, she didn't deserve that, she deserved his support. She'd been dumped on again, but this time not by him, thank God.

Over the last few weeks Ellie had outlined her theories, coming up with some inspirational insights. He in turn had clarified some of the finer points of any injuries that she asked about. That was where their strength lay. They would take turns to play devil's advocate, each enjoying their own and the other's success. Graham sighed, there was no choice really. He would have to go home and tell her what had happened. He gathered his things and walked through the station. The everyday business of the place carried on as though his problems didn't exist.

The canteen was virtually deserted. The sandwich was dry and stuck in his throat as he swigged his cooling tea to wash it down. Graham tried several ways to arrange the facts to shield Ellie from the full impact of the days' events. None of them sounded any better than the others. He cleared the remnants of his snack onto the tray and returned it to the counter. He couldn't avoid it for much longer; he'd take a toilet break and head home.

Graham gave a double take as he caught his haggard reflection.

God, I look old, he thought, his brown eyes were tired, his face made paler by his dark shaggy hair. *Since when did I start looking older than my father? Stress,* he concluded, no wonder IVF wasn't working, hadn't he read that being stressed could affect the results? They had to get off this merry-go-round. They had to reduce the effects of their respective careers, even if it meant them stepping down, taking on fewer responsibilities. He wondered if Ellie would agree with him. She seemed to be enjoying her new role, despite all the aggravation.

As he left the city centre behind and headed towards the bridge, Graham gave way to the temptation that had plagued him for the last few hours. He recalled the only time he had ever let Ellie down, not a memory in which he allowed himself to indulge in very often.

The first three years of their married life was spent in the Midlands. He worked at a local Pathology Lab; she upgraded her qualifications to enable her to work in the UK. One of Ellie's case studies was a young girl...Josie Blewitt. Josie was a seventeen-year-old recently diagnosed insulin dependent diabetic who suffered with depression caused by outright denial of her condition. Up to the age of twelve she had been an energetic sporty ball of energy, once diagnosed she came to regard the restrictions of her condition almost as an enemy. She refused to work with her parents to manage them, sliding straight into deep depression.

Josie's parents were at their wits end. Her doctor recommended therapy, and Ellie was assigned as her health care professional. They got on well, hitting it off from the start. Ellie empathised with her issues, and gradually enabled Josie to come to terms with her condition, and she started to co-operate with her doctor and parents to master the regime that they worked out together. After a few months Ellie restricted the sessions to follow ups only, in accordance with her department's policy, and in response to her workload which seemed to grow daily. Ellie was still in the qualification period of her training, but there had already been a huge demand on her time.

Two months later, Josie was dead. She had fooled everyone into believing that she had mastered the routine, taking bloods, administering insulin and watching what she ate. She managed to persuade her parents to allow her to go on a school trip to France. Ellie was asked for her opinion which was that she believed that Josie would be more than able to cope. Two days in and Josie had been found in a coma, having taken no meds for forty-eight hours. She died the next day. There were two draft texts on her phone, one saying sorry to her parents...that she couldn't cope with her limitations. The second text was to Ellie, asking her why she couldn't have 'fixed' her. During the ensuing enquiry Ellie was cleared of any professional negligence, but the papers had had a field day. Ellie had taken leave, blaming herself, unable to contemplate going back into a therapy room. It was then that she started drinking.

Graham shuddered, dragging himself back from the brink. What happened next had been, and would always be in his view, the ultimate betrayal of the love of his life. He wouldn't think about that now, he decided, he couldn't. He had to be strong, Ellie would need him once she found out about this morning's meeting. He remembered John's parting words from that afternoon. Something about being Sir Galahad, not being able to protect Ellie forever...*strange comment*, he thought.

It was almost dark as he drove up the narrow lanes he had known and loved his entire life. Gravel crunched as he parked close to Ellie's car. Hell, she was already home. He'd hoped for some respite, so he could plan what he was going to say to her. He let himself in, dreading what he knew would be a devastating blow for his wife. Delicious aromas wafted from the kitchen, should he tell her now, or after supper? He acknowledged his shallow desire to delay the inevitable.

Ellie was standing gazing out of the window. The garden was lit by scattered solar lights.

'You don't have to worry,' she sighed. 'John rang me, I already know.'

13

Ellie chewed on the end of a pencil. She sat alone in the tiny cubicle allotted to her by a begrudging Horton. The only furniture was a table, which served as her desk, and what she considered to be the most uncomfortable chair she had ever sat in. Files lay open in front of her, some of which she had generated, some provided by Horton's sidekick Dai Connett, who, she believed, despised her almost as much as his boss did. She and Horton had met with Detective Chief Superintendent Chetwynd, during which Horton had been warned that he had one last chance to get his act together. Chetwynd stressed that Ellie had to be kept in the loop at all times. This gave her the confidence that at last she had been acknowledged as a bona fide member of the team. She wasn't sure whether that was a good thing.

It was after six, not so long ago the station would be winding down for the day, now it seemed to be open 24/7. Ellie could understand Horton's concerns, he was up against increasing pressure for a breakthrough, but they could only work with the evidence available. That was precious little considering the number of officers drafted into the team.

She hoped that closing the door, drawing the thin blind, and focusing on nothing, would inspire her, generate something, anything. Reports on the murders lay side by side. She read the names for the umpteenth time, Ellis Franklin, Noel Parker, Robert Tranter, Tony Berwick and David Morgan, although very little was known about the last two. *Five murders*, she thought, *five*. Ellie needed to find a link if there was one, the end of the thread. She'd scoured the files countless times, trying to establish a connection. Horton seemed hell bent on identifying the murders as carried out by one perpetrator, but the methods were so different that Ellie couldn't say for certain. Graham was sure that he held onto this theory so that if, when, the murders were solved, Horton could take the credit for bringing down a serial killer. Ellie was inclined to agree. Something was telling her that there was a link between them, but at this stage she couldn't identify what. She remembered her meeting with Odelia Mathers, and what she had whispered to her. The thought made her shudder.

Although it pained her to admit it, she agreed with Horton, but had her reluctance to commit herself to announcing that this was a serial killer cost them precious time? So far, she had consoled herself with the belief that it was too early for that conclusion, but the possibility of having five murders in the area carried out by unconnected individuals was almost unthinkable. What she lacked was that all-important link, it had to be established, there had to be one. She shook her head, stuffing the paperwork back into their respective folders when she heard an almost imperceptible knock on the door. As it opened Ellie's heart sank.

DS Mason stood on the threshold, file in hand wearing her habitually surprised, startled look. Mason glanced around, as if expecting to see someone else in the room, and Ellie realised that she must have been talking to herself again, another quirky habit that others apparently found unsettling.

'Come in DS... Mason isn't it?' she fumbled for the woman's name, not having spoken to her since her arrival at the station.

'I'm, I'm sorry to bother you, Ms. Shaw,' Mason stuttered, 'I...well...I was just going over a few files...'

Ellie sighed, *who wasn't* she thought, nodding to Mason to continue.

'I was doing some digging yesterday, and I came across something. I don't know if it's anything important, only you said that anything...' she thrust a file at Ellie, who took it reluctantly. Ellie skimmed through the first paragraph. The typed report was comprehensive and was backed up by newspaper reports and several clips printed off the Internet. Ellie went back to the first page, re-reading it from the beginning.

'Tell me about this,' she said. She remembered that her 'office' only contained one chair. She fetched a second and offered it to the now thoroughly embarrassed and flustered Mason. A few hours later, Ellie had her link.

14

The briefing had been called for 10a.m. Horton felt slighted, furious that he hadn't been consulted. Ellie had gone straight to Chetwynd, despite knowing that her actions wouldn't earn her any Brownie points with him. She could tell by the curt way in which Horton greeted her, and his insistence that he should introduce the meeting, that he was peeved. She hadn't briefed him on what she'd prepared. As he handed over to her, she surveyed the assembled team, overwhelmed at the enormity of what she was about to say, considering how little proof she had. She had also taken the unprecedented step of asking DI Porter to go and interview someone who she suspected could establish a further link. She knew that this could alienate Horton even further; he liked to issue all the orders. She consoled herself that this was the kind of step that John might have taken. In any case it was too late now.

Following her discussion with Mason the previous night, they had worked until the early hours. Eventually Ellie was satisfied that she could present a reasoned argument. She still had no idea if the theories could be proved, or that Horton would take any notice at all. With Porter yet to arrive, and the assembled group chomping on the bit, she felt more under pressure than ever before. It was no use; she couldn't put it off much longer. As she got to her feet, the conversation died down.

'Thank you for coming,' she murmured, clearing her throat. She scanned the front row where Horton sat with his arms folded, classically defensive, a smirk on his flabby features.

'Can't hear you!' shouted someone at the back. A few people giggled. Ellie couldn't tell whether the remark was serious or if it was deliberately made to put her off. She realised she was shaking and tried a few deep breaths. Her vision narrowed as she spotted Mason in the centre of the crowded room and was unexpectedly overwhelmed with a feeling of empathy for her. Ellie knew the avoidance tactics used by Mason's colleagues; she had seen the way in which they almost blanked her. They would whisper behind her back, snigger whenever she spoke. It was as though her hard work; her abilities, didn't mean anything to them. She didn't fit in, a situation that Ellie was only too familiar with. Mason seemed to be willing her on, her face contorted. She bit her lower lip in an effort to convey her camaraderie...and something inside Ellie snapped. How dare they treat people as though they were worthless? How dare they belittle someone's work? Doris Mason had, through her own efforts, and mostly in her own time, provided a clue, a link. Maybe it was worthless, maybe it wouldn't break the case, but it was worth pursuing, and it was more than anyone else had come up with. The babble of conversation had resumed, people were looking at their watches...Ellie's temper snapped.

'QUIET!!!' she shouted, startling the whole room into silence, and herself into a state of shock. She shuffled her papers as she spotted Horton about to speak, she pre-empted him.

'I've called this meeting to advise you of what I consider to be an important discovery.' *Oh God, please let Porter get here in time*. Ellie cleared her throat again, sure now of their attention.

'This breakthrough has come about as a result of the efforts of one of your team, DS Mason.' All eyes turned to Mason, who cringed as a result. Ellie didn't want to spotlight Mason like this, to subject her to unwanted attention. But she hoped to make her feel as though she was being acknowledged, and besides it gave her a few more seconds. Ellie picked up a small pile of index cards on which she had written details of the murders. She knew that what she was about to say could explode in her face but was convinced of their findings.

'In mid-August, a body was found in a derelict house in Bangor. The victim was a Property Developer...Ellis Franklin. He was killed elsewhere, and his body dumped in the house.' Ellie attached a photograph of Franklin onto the whiteboard, which stood at her side.

'Less than a week later the body of a man was found at the base of a cliff close to the decommissioned Wylfa power plant. He was identified as Noel Parker. The local paper reported the tragedy, suggesting that he had killed himself after his parents died in what was believed to be a joint suicide pact. As you will no doubt remember, it was believed that they had ended their lives by gassing themselves in their garage. The usual MO, pipe on the exhaust, etc.,' a picture of Noel Parker joined that of Franklin.

Someone raised their hand. Ellie pre-empted the question... yes, she was aware that Noel's death was the second murder on their books. The papers hadn't been told that he had died before landing on the rocks below, and the police hadn't corrected them. As far as they were concerned the case was still open, but like Franklin's, the trail had grown cold.

'So... the link Ms. Shaw?' Horton demanded.

'*If* you will allow me to finish,' Ellie hissed, her eyes narrowed, determined not to concede any advantage she had gained. Horton's mouth gaped, shocked at her riposte, unused to being talked to in that manner, especially by her. He wasn't going to stand for it and was about to launch into protest when the door opened, and Porter made his way to the front of the room. He handed a piece of paper to Ellie who took a moment to skim read it. She saw Horton fidget out of the corner of her eye. She fore stalled his interruption.

'Thanks to DS Mason's enquiries, we have found out from Noel Parker's sister that their parents had been approached about selling their family home to Median Homes, a Development Company owned by Mr. Franklin. The Parker's home was the last property remaining in a group of houses which occupied a piece of land that Mr. Franklin was desperate to develop. It was a project that would have made him a small fortune. Mr. and Mrs. Parker initially refused to sell, and according to their daughter, they had been subjected to a sustained campaign of intimidation. This apparently led to Mr. Parker's ill health, and ultimately their capitulation to Franklin's demands.' Ellie paused, looking around the room; she had their attention.

'Two days before they were due to complete the sale of their house, they committed suicide, or so it was believed. Connie Parker swears that her parents were reconciled to the deal and would never have taken such a step. However, her brother made a statement to the effect that his mother had had second thoughts and was about to call off the deal altogether.'

The room was silent, no one moved, Ellie swallowed and continued.

'A few months after they died, Ellis Franklin's body was found. Noel Parker was discovered less than a week later. I suggest that it's possible that Noel Parker killed Franklin in revenge for what happened to his parents.' The noise level in the room grew louder '...the point is, if Noel didn't commit suicide, who killed him?'

The room erupted; Horton jumped to his feet, waving his fist, his anger palpable.

'We're here trying to solve murders, not to create imaginary ones,' he shouted, walking towards the front of the room.

'SILENCE!!!' a roar from the doorway, Horton stopped, rooted to the spot, he knew rather than saw who it was. All heads turned; Celia Chetwynd viewed the assembled throng. By her side stood John Prothero who headed straight for Ellie. She swallowed, her throat dry, head pounding. Oh God, had she gone too far? John stood in front of her, his back to the room. Always able to command a crowd, every eye was on him.

'You're doing well!' he whispered, 'keep going, this is interesting.'

She smiled at him, grateful for his support as he sat down. She cleared her throat once more, longing for a drink.

'My findings, er, suggestions, are further backed up by this,' Ellie continued, flourishing the piece of paper that Porter had handed to her. 'The 'fourth' murder that we have been investigating, that of Tony Berwick, whose body was discovered entangled in mooring rope in Amlwch harbour, and the 'fifth', that of David Morgan, found last week in a woodland site known as Tree Tops. According to a statement made to DI Porter this morning, these two victims had history, in that....' a low rumble of something was building again. It was quashed by John standing and staring pointedly around the room.

'...in that,' Ellie continued, 'according to a reliable source, Tony Berwick assaulted David Morgan some years ago, when Morgan worked for him as a student. We will of course have to investigate further to establish these facts, but it would be naive of us to assume that these two groups of murders were coincidences, which in my opinion, don't exist,' Ellie took a deep breath, 'as before, if we can establish that David Morgan killed Berwick, then my question is, who, in turn, killed Morgan? I submit that there are links in the motives behind the killing of Ellis Franklin and Tony Berwick, which I believe, is revenge taken by their victims. At this time I've been...' she looked at Porter, who seemed enraptured by her delivery, '...we have been unable to establish where Robert Tranter fits into the picture, ' she turned once again to the whiteboard, and lined up pictures of Berwick and Morgan, then one of Tranter to the far right of the others.

Ellie sat down, there was a momentary silence followed by a tsunami of voices, which subsided almost as suddenly

as it had exploded as those present realised that Celia
Chetwynd, John Prothero and DI Porter were clapping.
They were soon joined by Doris Mason, others joined in,
some hesitantly, until the whole room was applauding. The
only exception was Horton, who stood, red faced
surveying the room which he regarded as a perfect
example of a world gone mad. He turned abruptly, facing
the assembled officers before barging his way back to his
office, leaving the din behind him.

Ellie shivered as she realised what she had done. Not
only had she gone ahead and taken control, but delivered
the longest, and what she hoped was the most effective
speech of her life. She believed in it, she believed that there
were links, and she was determined to prove those links.
Now she had something to work on, there was someone
out there that was orchestrating these murders, for what
reason... well that would come, she had no doubt. What
she couldn't figure out was why Horton had taken the
hump. After all, she had presented him with the possibility
of his serial killer, hadn't she?

Then she realised, there was just no pleasing some
people.

15

The team picked up the pace with renewed energy. It was as though Horton didn't exist. Most enquiries by-passed his office and went straight to Porter. Statements were re-examined, witnesses re-interviewed, connections established, white boards filled up and spilled over. Officers liaised on what was now regarded as a cluster of connected crimes. Horton blustered, trying to steer attention away from the work carried out by Ellie and Mason, in a clear attempt to gain back control of the investigation. Ellie avoided confronting him, she had had the nod from on high that her efforts were approved of. With Chetwynd's backing, she gained a measure of belonging that she had never experienced before.

A few days later, bag in hand, she made her way through the station, glad to be going home, looking forward to spending a quiet night in. She knew that sooner or later Graham would bring up the subject of their latest IVF attempt, a conversation that she wasn't looking forward to. She hoped he'd finally get the message; this was the last time she was prepared to go through the process. Graham had assured her that he understood, and that he would let the subject rest. For her part, having a child was never a deal-breaker, for him it was obviously paramount.

She had to tell him the real reason for her decision, even though he would find it hard to believe. During one heated argument, he'd even expressed an opinion that somehow it wasn't natural for a woman not to want to have a baby.

She shook her head to clear it as her phone rang, it was Porter. 'I'm just about to interview one of Rob Tranter's associates,' he told her. *Nothing unusual about that,* she thought.

'It's just, well, he seems a bit jumpy. Wondered if you'd like to listen in?' *To turn down this opportunity would be a mistake,* her instinct told her, as she doubled back and headed towards the interview rooms. Porter stood in the corridor, file in hand.

'Just to bring you up to speed…' he said, handing Ellie a single sheet of paper, '…name's Whittaker, Charles Whittaker, long record, been in trouble for most of his life. Apparently, he worked for Tranter for some years before they had a falling out, his name came up when we were looking into Tranter's past. For the last few years he's been on his own on the island. No fixed abode, separated from his wife and son, not sure where they are now. Thought we'd bring him in and see if he can shed some light on what happened to Tranter.'

Typical Porter, thought Ellie as he ran quickly through the pertinent facts, *how much better it would be if he was in sole charge of the case?* At the same time though, his inclusion of her in this latest interview was reassuring, making her feel more like a team member than ever. She watched as he disappeared into the interview room and made her way next door to observe.

Porter settled into his chair and started recording the pre-interview information. He was right, Whittaker did seem nervous. He looked around the room, folding his arms, unfolding them, scratching his head and clearing his throat. With the preliminaries completed, Porter started slowly, gradually asking more in-depth questions. Whittaker seemed to relax as time went on, answering with increasing confidence. *No,* he hadn't seen Tranter for many years... *yes,* he was familiar with his track record...*yes,* he had worked for Mr. Tranter, but that had been a long time ago. He'd lost contact with him after a misunderstanding. That and the fact that he had spent five years in prison for aggravated burglary and grievous bodily harm... with time off for good behaviour. By the time he was released, Whittaker maintained, he was a changed man. He'd learned a trade, carpentry, and had put those times behind him. Tranter never contacted him, and Whittaker never sought his former boss out. Since then he had picked up occasional casual work, backed up with benefits. He'd recently applied for a council flat but wasn't holding out much hope of getting one.

'Didn't you ever think of contacting Mr. Tranter to secure employment, Mr. Whittaker?' asked Porter, having listened intently to the slick flow of information, 'I mean, he did have a diverse range of business interests, including a building firm, which as a carpenter would've suited you extremely well.'

'No, I told you, we had a falling out before I went to prison,' Whittaker repeated. 'I didn't think Mr. Tranter would be inclined to give me a job after that.' Porter stared at Whittaker for a few seconds, was that sweat on his forehead? After the initial nervousness had dissipated, he had delivered an almost faultless breakdown of his activities during the last few years. Now he seemed very nervous again.

'What did you fall out about?' Porter asked without thinking, he detected a sharp, almost imperceptible intake of breath before Whittaker answered.

'He, er, he wanted me to do something that I felt wasn't right.' Whittaker shifted in his seat; his discomfort obvious. Porter wasn't going to get anything else without digging further.

'What was that?' he asked as casually as he could. Whittaker shifted again, clearing his throat.

'He wanted me to kill someone,' he had Porter's full attention now. Although Tranter had accrued a record a mile long, and that record was well known throughout the area, no one had been able to pin anything onto him during his lifetime. If it took Porter the rest of his career it would be worth teasing information out of Whittaker that might mop up cases that had had to be put on ice for lack of information.

'...and who would that have been?' he asked.

Whittaker paused, chewing the inside of his cheek, wondering if he had gone too far. He sighed, placed his hands on the table in front of him, eyes darting from side to side, and it seemed an age before he answered.

Eventually he cleared his throat 'My wife,' he whispered.

16

Porter stood in Horton's office. *How many more times,* he thought as he waited for him to speak. Horton had demanded to be informed of any developments, no matter how small.

'...and you didn't arrest him?' Horton yelled, 'even though he had a motive as obvious as...'

Porter sighed; Horton's reaction was nothing less than he'd expected. 'Whittaker has an alibi for the time of Tranter's murder,' he explained, 'we've already taken a statement from a witness.'

'A reliable witness?' Horton snapped. He snatched the file from Porter's hand and scanned it. Horton sat down heavily; all bluster gone as he read the witness statement. Whitaker had been at an outpatient's appointment with his Psychiatrist... John Prothero. He'd been seen by one of Prothero's team and not by John himself, but confirmation of his appointment had been easily obtained. For now it had placed Whittaker in the clear.

Porter was itching to speak to Ellie, something didn't feel right. He wanted to know if she felt the same. It was early evening, and he found her back in her cubicle making notes. She agreed with his uneasiness at how Whittaker had presented at the beginning of the interview, how he seemed to relax during Porter's questions. The slick way in which he delivered his later answers had surprised them both. She speculated that he might have taken something to calm himself in preparation for the session, and that whatever it was had taken a while to kick in. Either way, his answers sounded rehearsed, to sounded like someone had coached him.

Porter nodded, 'We need to watch out for Mr. Whittaker,' he said.

Ellie shivered; she had a similar feeling herself

.

17

Celia Chetwynd's rise to rank of Detective Chief Superintendent was nothing short of meteoric. Some who had been passed over for promotion in her favour claimed it was baffling. She was astute, tough, with a penchant for detail and an apparent unending source of energy. She was never one for taking a back seat, and although many of her male colleagues sniggered behind her back, some even suggesting that she had 'slept' her way to her current position, she had received many commendations for her performance.

Her record was unblemished, her leadership inspirational. Three national newspaper articles based on her style of policing had been at pains to point that out. A mixture of tough love and uncompromising standards had been laid down for her 'troops' as she had christened the officers within her command.

She had unwavering concern for the welfare of her officers, holding regular 'team building weekends', and introducing a programme of Holistic Therapies for their on-going health. It might have been for this reason alone than Horton loathed her. But he had bigger reasons. They had been together at the start of their respective careers. It had been obvious from the first days at training college who would progress in the force, and who wouldn't. Horton had convinced himself that she'd had a leg up, and he meant that in every sense. He had no idea of the effort she put in, or the sacrifices she had made in order to reach her present position. Either way, Chetwynd was a daily reminder of how little success he had managed to achieve.

What Horton failed to appreciate was that Celia's work was her life, and, apart from a brief interlude during which she almost gave it all up for marriage and kids, she allowed no hint of personal interests to interfere with her dedication to the job. Hardly a day went by when Celia arrived at her desk later than 7.30am, or left before the cleaners, monitoring everything at a discreet distance. Her policy was to give officers their heads to follow their instincts, to oversee discreetly. She would only intervene if she was asked for her input, or when it was obvious that matters were getting out of hand, as in this recent debacle. With her no-nonsense style of leadership and her severe, though immaculate sense of dress, she never failed to cut an imposing figure as she progressed through her domain.

Horton had been in her office three times in as many weeks, and he still didn't get it. She'd tried to encourage him to open up about the lack of progress.

'I understand your frustration,' she told him patiently, listening to a litany of complaints. He moaned about how he wasn't being supported, that his team were letting him down, what with John Prothero going off to mess around with this new-fangled government profiling lark...well...how was he supposed to make any kind of headway? As for that Ellie Shaw, huh, don't get him started on her.

By doing some work yourself, she thought as she watched him squirm at their last meeting. His whole appearance caused her to sigh inwardly. She had long since got his measure, but somehow, he always managed to redeem himself by getting good results. She knew, from a variety of sources, that the bulk of the work was shouldered by his team. Horton was an ineffectual leader, who inspired little loyalty, but he had a warped gift of being able to present reports that cast him in the role of 'hero of the moment'. He would grab the spotlight and take most of the credit for himself. His actions did little to generate the team spirit that Chetwynd so enthusiastically encouraged.

What nobody knew was that Celia had a collaborator within the team. She'd approached this officer several months ago, and asked, without pressure, to be kept up to date with the general mood of the troops. She'd agonised over the move, but recent events had proved her instincts correct. Direct intervention would have meant she'd never have formed a clear picture of how well the troops were performing. She'd nicknamed the officer her 'secondary self' but had to admit that a better name would be her spy. The file she was preparing on the progress of the investigation was growing daily. Celia knew it would only be a matter of time before her own bosses held her to account for Horton's shortcomings. What more could she do? She'd offered to sit down with him on a regular basis to monitor progress an offer which he hadn't accepted.

Since Ellie's seismic speech, Celia had focused almost entirely on the current investigation, and she didn't like what she saw. A lack of leadership by Horton, yes, she had already identified that. She knew that most officers in the squad thought little of him, but that wasn't all. She had examined every statement, sifted through the records of procedures followed, and analysed the information provided by her informer. In the end she was appalled at Horton's incompetence. A series of 'chats' with various members of the investigation team followed, including Porter, Mason, Ellie Shaw and DS Connett, as well as several other officers. She'd tried to make these 'chats' general in nature. How where they doing, what progress were they making? But it was only when Porter sat in her office that she finally had the confirmation that she needed to act.

'So, how do you think DCI Horton is coping with the investigation?' she asked, the genial smile never faltering. 'Do I need to intervene?'

Porter had taken a moment before answering. He wasn't comfortable talking about Horton's shortcomings. How to answer, should he be diplomatic, or honest? Celia could sense the conflict she'd stirred up. No one wanted to be labelled as a snitch. Once word got around that you had dobbed a fellow officer in, no matter how inept everyone thought they were, no one would trust you again. Porter hated what he said almost as soon as he'd said it, but he knew that something had to be done. At the very least it might mean that the team could make progress, maybe even save lives.

'We...we need to be given some latitude in our approach to the investigations,' he was choosing his words carefully, being diplomatic. Chetwynd's method of questioning was clever, one of the cleverest he'd dealt with in his career. He'd often found himself incorporating some of her tactics into his own way of working. Starting off with general enquiries, and then flooring him with a direct question. She sensed his discomfort.

'Excuse me,' she said, barely above a whisper. 'I should never have put you on the spot like that, but you can understand my frustration.'

Was that a question, he thought, or a statement, and how clever of her to ask his opinions of a fellow officer, and follow up with an apology, excusing herself, claiming that she had overstepped the mark? He realised that her question needed no answer, she'd didn't expect one. Rather, a message had been sent, the Super had no faith in Horton's abilities either, and the knowledge that they were singing from the same hymn sheet gave him a degree of hope.

'Now, tell me about Ellie Shaw,' she asked smiling.

18

There was no doubt that Ellie's intervention had fired up a renewed sense of urgency. The lethargy that had settled over the investigation had been dispelled. However, the idea that she might have created a reputation for 'hauling them over the coals,' as Porter had put it, filled her with horror. Wasn't it enough that all those people had died? Hadn't that been enough for people to do the job that they were paid for? She was aware of Horton's failings, wasn't everyone, but abhorred the fact that no one seemed to be doing anything about it. When she'd put all the facts together, she'd done what she had through frustration, rather than wanting to take charge. Yet here she was being treated like a superhero. Almost the entire department was asking her for advice. They sought out her opinion on almost every detail... it was getting too much.

Ellie was now so busy with her police work that her practice was suffering. Appointments had to be rearranged or cancelled, and she was seeing only urgent or on-going clients. Even that was becoming a strain. John was busy with his governmental commitments, some days she didn't know which way was up. Graham was worried, even though Ellie assured him that she could cope. Despite this, he was continually asking her if she was ok. Did she think she had bitten off more than she could chew; after all, assisting John was one thing, but this? They hardly saw each other anymore did they? She seemed to be at the station most of the time, while he was busy supervising a second postmortem on the Parkers. When would they get a chance to have a private life? His attitude left her feeling both touched, and angry that she felt he was employing double standards regarding their respective careers. This in turn had led to several heated discussions.

'I had a chat with Celia Chetwynd this morning.' Graham said almost as soon as Ellie walked in that evening. She stopped in the middle of taking off her jacket.

'Superintendent Chetwynd?' she asked, 'why on earth were you talking to her?' She threw her jacket on the sofa, then sat down to remove her shoes, her eyes never leaving his face. He took a deep breath, shaking his head.

'Ellie, I am part of this investigation you know, a fact that some people forget, unless of course you get another body, or want me to provide you with information within ridiculous time frames,' he snapped.

Ellie sighed hoping this wasn't going to be another row. She wasn't used to Graham in this mood. She was tired and could feel the threat of another headache, but had to admit that perhaps Graham was right. His part in the investigation did sometimes get pushed into the background, and that had to be galling for him.

'I'm sorry,' she murmured, getting up and crossing the kitchen to where he sat at the table. 'It must be difficult to be part of the back-stage crew,' she placed her hands on his shoulders. He jumped up brushing off the gesture and stormed out of the room. She heard him stomping up the stairs to his tiny office, the door banged, then silence. She sighed as she sat down on his recently vacated chair.

It was meant as a joke, she had been trying to lighten the mood. This wasn't like Graham, what on earth was the matter with him? *Then again, he's not used to me being in this position,* she thought, considering the changes that had taken place in the last few weeks. She was a lot more confident now, more sure of herself. From the moment she had conducted the briefing, Ellie had felt a surge of self-belief, and it made her feel good. Perhaps that was it, perhaps Graham didn't like the fact that she was changing. Maybe the shift in their dynamic made him feel uncomfortable and, dare she say it, that she might not need him anymore. If that was the case, little did he know that she needed him now more than ever? Or was it to do with their conversation a few days ago, the one she'd been avoiding?

She'd at last found the courage to tell him about the failure of their last attempt to conceive. His obvious pain had been almost too much to bear, and she realised how much he had been counting on a positive result. Now, for whatever reason, he had taken umbrage at what was meant as a flippant joke. His uncharacteristic reaction made Ellie uncomfortable. Her hold on her newly found confidence was tenuous to say the least. She had to set him straight, try to get back on an even keel.

Standing up was painful; her body ached from too much sitting at her desk and too little sleep. As she climbed the stairs, she could hear voices from inside. Although he'd slammed the door, it had rebounded and was slightly ajar. She could see an image on the screen, a woman, talking directly into the camera, not quite loud enough for Ellie to hear.

'I think that's a good idea...' said Graham, he hesitated. It took Ellie a few seconds before she realised that the two of them were having a conversation. The woman started to talk again, something about 'not trying to fix...' something, Ellie wasn't sure.

'I don't think I could, you don't know the pressure.'
Graham stopped as the woman interrupted. What she said
was indistinct, but Ellie had heard enough. Memories from
years ago flooded back, the times she had caught Graham
on his phone, only for him to stop talking when he
registered her presence. She would call him at his office,
only to be told that he hadn't been in that day or catch an
exchange between him and a 'colleague', although their
conversation had been anything but work like.

Ellie headed back down the stairs as quietly as she
could, her head swirling. She needed to think, the last thing
she felt like now was another huge row, she was too tired.
She swayed, momentarily overcome by a mixture of
fatigue, low blood sugar and a swirl of emotions. She
needed something to eat, something to drink, preferably
alcoholic. When it came to it, she realised she couldn't face
food, just like she couldn't stand the thought of another
row. She sat looking out of the window for what seemed
like hours, considering what to do; the idea came to her
suddenly. She pulled on her shoes, closed the kitchen door
loudly, and walked back up the stairs. She made enough
noise to alert him, and by the time she reached the landing
Graham was coming out of the office door. He smiled
nervously.

'Sorry love,' he said raking his fingers through his hair,
'shouldn't have blown up like that, been under a lot of
pressure, haven't we?' Ellie cringed. He'd used a similar
phrase to the woman on his computer screen. Now here
he was all guilty looking and eager to make amends for his
previous outburst. Ellie swallowed, trying to stop herself
from crying. Was this how it was going to be every time
they reached a crisis point in their lives? Would she ever
be able to trust him again? If this was the same

woman...she couldn't bear to think about her. Ellie tried to smile as he put his arms out, and stepped towards her, but her body language betrayed her as she turned slightly to avoid him.

'We're both tired Graham, it's been a difficult time lately, hasn't it?' she said. She tried her hardest to relax as his arms went around her. Let's try to get a good night's sleep,' she murmured, 'I'm sure things will look better in the morning.' Ellie cringed; the well-worn clichés tasted bitter in her mouth, they sounded so false, but Graham seemed placated. He took hold of her hand leading her to the bedroom. Ellie knew where this was heading.

'Look, don't take this personally,' she forced a smile, nodding her head slightly in emphasis. She was praying that he wouldn't take offence and start another row. 'I'm going to take a shower and sleep in the guest room; after all you nearly woke the neighbours with your snoring last night.' She smiled weakly and was relieved when Graham smiled back.

'OK, go do what you have to do. To be honest I don't think I'm up to it either, you sleep in our room. I've got a bit of work to do, then I'll turn in,' he said, kissing her on the forehead and squeezing her hands before turning and going back into his study.

Ellie sighed in relief, not realising that she had been so tense. She watched him close the door, then turned and went into their room. The events of the last hour replayed over and over in her troubled mind. How could she find out who Graham had been talking to? It wasn't a case of having someone look at his computer, that's what they did to suspects and victims. She stopped dead in her tracks, how could she have been so stupid? In all the information that she had studied in the last few weeks, where were the reports of either the victim's or the suspect's Internet activity? She couldn't remember seeing any mention of either, yet she'd assumed that this was part of routine procedure. This had to be her first task in the morning... she stopped, shocked once more...wasn't dealing with what had just happened between her and Graham her number one priority?

…ooOoo…

Graham sat in his study his face creased in concentration. He was uncomfortable about earlier, saddened to see the gulf between him and Ellie growing wider. It seemed to be spinning off uncontrollably, and he was more than a little shaken that he had resorted to...no, he couldn't think about that just now. He had to have someone to unload to, but shouldn't that have been Ellie and not some stranger online that demanded his credit card details before she would talk to him?

Everyone was suffering, yet it was no one's fault. They were all just trying to do their jobs. It was when doing their jobs impinged on their family life that he found it all too much. He had watched Ellie beating herself up in the early weeks of the case. Now she seemed to have turned into a messiah for the entire station. It left her with little time for anything else.

The galling thing about it was that she seemed to be enjoying every minute of it. It looked as though she was coping well in her new role, but the demands on her time were swallowing up everything else. He shook himself, *get over it*, he thought, *this is what Ellie is good at, that and being a wonderful wife and, hopefully soon a fantastic mother.* He had been thinking about their latest failure a lot. He couldn't believe she'd meant it when she told him that she wasn't prepared to go through IVF again. He was convinced that he could talk her round. But that was just the point, in the last few weeks they hadn't had chance to do much talking at all.

For years he had tried to encourage Ellie to give full rein to her talents. Now, here he was, resenting the fact that she was totally immersed in the current case. He almost wanted her to forgo the opportunity she had to establish herself. But to go back to what? If he was honest, the answer was like an elephant occupying every room they were in the same time. He wanted kids, and she didn't, there he had said it, and now this last attempt.

He stood up suddenly and walked to the window remembering how it had been when they first arrived at the farm. Ellie had been so down after the Josie Blewitt affair, but she'd made a huge effort to adapt to a new way of life. It had been difficult for her, yet she'd persisted, and now... he sighed, making up his mind to show her more support in future, after all he owed her that much, didn't he?

Maybe after a few months, maybe he could talk to her about trying again? Perhaps he could persuade her to give it one more try. She'd looked so tired earlier, was his snoring that much of a problem? If it was, he knew a good doctor... what was it that had set him off earlier? He'd been looking forward to a relaxing evening as he'd watched her take off her jacket, sit down on the sofa, kick off... hold on, that wasn't right. She took off her shoes, in the kitchen, right before she made that remark, the one that flipped him out, the one that started that stupid row. So why would she put them back on to come upstairs? She always said that once she had her shoes off for the night they would stay off. That her feet would swell, and she couldn't get them on again even if she tried. It was a joke, but she never... unless... unless she wanted to let him know that she was coming up the stairs, but why?

Then he knew. Because she had already been up the stairs, and if she had then she might have seen him...Oh no, please don't say she had heard his conversation with...Oh shit! That was it; she'd come up, overheard him, gone back downstairs, put on her shoes and come back up, making sure he'd heard her. No wonder she'd suggested that they sleep separately, that excuse about his snoring was just avoidance tactics.

He realised that he was pacing, he sat down and opened his computer, he needed to talk to someone. All thoughts of his conversation with Celia Chetwynd were forgotten as he logged back into the website.

19

The note read... *'Call-out in the night, sorry I was such a grouch, talk tonight. Love you honey....Graham xx'* Ellie re-read it as she sipped her coffee and picked at a slice of toast. Last night she had found her husband talking to a woman on the Internet, a woman she didn't recognise. 'Grouch' didn't even cover the description she held in her mind. Her night had been fragmented, snatches of sleep lasting no longer than a few minutes. Those brief periods had been peopled with images of Graham with a variety of unrecognisable bodies. In the end she had taken another shower and studied her notes.

Around 4.30 she heard Graham's phone ring. Within half an hour he'd left. Once again sleep eluded her, she gave up trying and got up. At that time of day, the house was eerily silent. Ellie found the note in the kitchen, she tossed it to one side, unsure of her next move. She was determined that she wouldn't be the one to bring the subject up, she would wait and see if Graham did. What was it he said during their last row?

'The trouble with you Ellie is you're passive-aggressive, how am I supposed to put right a mistake when you won't even tell me what I've done?' At the time she was hurt, now she had to admit he might have a point. No time for self-analysis, there was so much she needed to do. By 7.30 she was on her way to the station. The morning traffic flowed without a hitch, and soon Ellie was approaching the car park, determined to find out about the computers. She went, not to Horton, but to DI Porter, being careful how she phrased the question. She was building a good working relationship with him and didn't want to alienate him in any way; his reaction was priceless. The realisation that they hadn't followed up on something as important as obtaining the devices shocked him, it wasn't possible...

'I'm... I'm not sure,' he blustered. 'I think DCI Horton assigned Connett to handle...' he jumped up, grabbing the file she'd been reading, looking for the relevant chain of evidence form. 'Stay there...' he said and headed out to find Connett. Soon he was back, and Ellie was startled at the change in him...he was rattled. He sat heavily on one of the new chairs that had come with her larger office. He leaned forward and buried his head in his hands. He sighed deeply, and sat back shaking his head, she could sense his frustration.

'I don't believe it,' he said quietly. Ellie waited, holding her breath. 'I've sent Connett to chase...' he stopped, 'excuse me, I have to check something out,' with that he jumped up again and headed back to the incident room. Ellie went back to studying the case files, and it seemed like an age before Porter was back, sticking his head round the door and asking if she was free for a briefing that afternoon. He left her again, and she wondered what had happened to necessitate it.

Ellie found it almost impossible to do any work, she headed to the canteen, and sat nursing a mug of coffee, staring out of the window. She jumped as the swing doors opened admitting Celia Chetwynd and... Odelia Mathers. Her heart sank, was there nowhere in this building where she could just sit and think? In any case, what the hell were these two doing together?

Chetwynd spotted her and turned to head in her direction. Odelia put her hand on her companion's arm and halted her progress, murmuring something, she nodded to Ellie as the two women turned around and left. Ellie felt a rush of gratitude. It was as though Odelia had summed up her mood in a split second, decided on the best course of action, and headed off Chetwynd before she could disturb Ellie's reverie. Maybe there was more to this woman than Ellie had given her credit for?

She considered something to eat but she wasn't hungry... *must be nerves*, she decided. Still, she could just have one more coffee before she collected her things for the briefing. For the next half hour, she thought about Odelia Mathers... her connection to Chetwynd, and whether she had judged her too harshly.

20

Porter's briefing was a textbook delivery. How had he managed to get the information together within such a short space of time? It was a mystery to Ellie, as it was to the rest of the team… *then again, he does have Mason,* she thought later as she studied her copy of his findings. Bullet-points made for ease of reference; short and to the point. Within twenty minutes Porter was back in her office, asking for her first impressions.

'Not quite finished yet,' she admitted, he came in anyway and sat down. She read through the rest of the document as quickly as she could, sighing as she placed them carefully on the desk. *He looks tired,* she thought as he passed a hand across his forehead, stress was taking its toll on everyone.

'I know its early days,' he started, 'but does anything strike you yet, any link you may have spotted?' Ellie shook her head, re-reading the report.

<u>Brenda & Edward Parker</u> – Devices retrieved from home address - 2 laptops – 1 tablet – 2 mobile phones
Information obtained – Series of emails from Ellis Franklin on both accounts, more frequent and intimidating, up until their deaths.
Series of phone calls made from the time they were approached about selling their property until their death, becoming more frequent during the last week and made around the clock. The duration of some of these calls was a few seconds, some lasted several minutes.

<u>Ellis Franklin</u> – requests for devices made, search of home and office revealed that devices were missing - believed stolen.

Suspicion that laptops were hidden by either spouse or members of staff - unsubstantiated.

Requests for records from provider initiated.

<u>Noel Parker</u> – requests for devices made, search of home address revealed that his laptop was missing. No mobile phone located, although sister confirms existence. Requests for records from provider initiated.

The rest of the information ran along similar lines. Requests for access to devices had been made in each instance, much to Porter's relief.

Tony Berwick's laptop had revealed little relevant data, other than an obsession with the kind of pornography that would have landed him in court had he lived. The searches at both Rob Tranter's office and home addresses had revealed nothing. That, Porter was at pains to stress, meant little as his 'employees' or his wife could have stashed them away as soon as they were told of his death. It was the sort of thing they would consider a safeguard against having his past activities, criminal or otherwise, uncovered. Porter drummed his fingers on the desk. It was beginning to annoy Ellie as she tried to concentrate on the facts laid out before her. After a while she put down the sheaf of papers and stood up.

'I'm going for a walk,' she announced. She saw the look of surprise on Porter's face. 'There is such a thing as not being able to see the wood for the trees. I need to clear my head,' she explained.

She picked up her bag and headed for the door, she looked back. 'Coming?' she asked.

Porter shrugged, he got up and followed her. They walked down to the reception area and out into the main street. Within minutes they were seated under a beech tree in a nearby park. Children, just released from the confines of the classroom, ran screaming and shouting to each other on their way to the slides.

Porter watched them for several minutes. 'Do you have kids?' he asked, regretting his question almost as soon as he'd asked it. He watched as she hesitated, a faint blush creeping up her neck.

'No,' she said, taking a bag of sugared almonds out of her bag and offering him one. They sat in silence for a few minutes. Porter cleared his throat, he wanted to bring the subject back to the morning's meeting.

'I want to thank you Ellie, you don't mind if I call you...?' he hesitated. Ellie shook her head. 'Anyway, I wanted to thank you for bringing my attention to the matter of the devices. I didn't know... I think it goes to show how off track we've become, as a team I mean.' He sat forward on the bench, elbows on his knees, hands clasped. 'I'm sorry if you feel that I'm hustling you, it's just that...'

'You're not hustling me, but I think I'm going to need a little more time to try and spot any patterns, if that's what you're asking me to do,' she admitted, watching a squirrel scamper up into the branches.

'That's exactly what I need you to do,' he smiled; something Ellie had rarely seen him do. She'd never paid much attention to him, other than in a professional role. He really was quite good-looking in an 'older man' kind of way. She stood up suddenly, ready to head back.

'Are you hungry?' he asked, 'I could murder some fish and chips.' He stopped realising what he'd said, 'sorry, slip of the tongue.'

It was Ellie's turn to smile. 'In that case,' she replied, 'I'm in, but you're paying.'

21

DS Connett had never worked so hard. Horton was in the shit again, and he was determined he wasn't going down with the ship. It was all very well being the SIO's sidekick, but if his career was being threatened, he didn't intend to be tarred with the same incompetent brush. Still, it meant that his other 'job' was shielded, and he could report to Chetwynd on a regular basis under the guise of being given a watered-down version of the bollocking she gave Horton.

It wasn't that he minded being viewed with derision by his fellow officers. He was sure that Chetwynd would look after him. If there was one thing that Connett was good at, it was backing the right horse. She didn't ask much, after all, just a heads-up as to whether everything was being handled as it should be. It was just that in the last few months everything seemed to have gone tits up. People were running around like headless chickens. Then there was the debacle about the missing devices. Connett had been responsible for getting the information on them. He'd handed that information straight to Horton, and now...

Some people knew exactly the right time to leave a party, and Connett was one of those people. He knew when to throw his lot in with a better side, which was why he had been working so damn hard for the last few days to curry favour with Porter, who seemed to have become Chetwynd's new favourite. It seemed to be paying off. For a while he thought that Porter and Mason had become welded at the hip, but with Mason busy with mountains of paperwork, something that Connett would die rather than be assigned to, he'd seen his chance. The report on the devices that she had typed up had come largely from his original notes. Earlier that day he'd found himself with Porter and Ellie Shaw in the incident room reviewing it. Connett hoped he'd done enough to ensure that he was well on the way to becoming integrated back into the team at large, rather than Horton's stooge.

He'd been called into Ellie Shaw's office where, along with DI Porter, they were going over her observations. It had taken Ellie only a few minutes to summarise her findings, her adept delivery impressed Connett more than he wanted to admit.

Ellie stood by the side of a whiteboard on which she had written:

Parker Brenda & Edward - 2 laptops 2 mobile phones 1 tablet

Franklin Ellis	- no devices recovered
Parker Noel	- no devices recovered
Tranter Robert	- no devices recovered
Berwick Tony	- 1 laptop 1 mobile
Morgan David	- no devices recovered

'We suspect that Franklin was killed by Noel Parker in revenge for the death of both of his parents. Initially these looked like a joint suicide pact, but could have been murder,' she looked at Porter for confirmation, he nodded. 'If that is the case, then Ellis Franklin could qualify as both a suspect for their deaths, and a victim of murder by their son. The Parker's devices were found at their home address, no attempt had been made to remove them. The same situation exists with Tony Berwick's laptop and mobile, no attempt to remove them from his flat. However, neither David Morgan's computer nor his mobile phone have been traced.' She could detect Connett's confusion and chose her next words carefully.

'Data on the devices that were stolen could lead us to the person orchestrating the whole shooting match, what do you think DS Connett?' She stood, board marker in hand waiting for him to speak.

'The information would still be on the hard drives, no matter how hard someone had tried to get rid of it, wouldn't it?' he offered. Ellie nodded, 'and if someone didn't want us to find that information...'

'...they'd ensure we wouldn't find them.' finished Porter. 'So, if we did manage to find a device belonging to a suspect, we might find data that would lead us to...'

'...Mr. Big. The absence of devices belonging to Franklin, Parker and Morgan is a common denominator. It suggests contact over the Internet, which we could have established if we had had the missing devices to hand,' said Ellie, relieved that they were all singing from the same hymn sheet. 'Have you been able to get anything else off the ones we do have?'

'We've got a team going over the stuff recovered again,' Porter said, 'Seems they hadn't had time to look into all the files. We've sent for that chap that helps with deleted data recovery. Cooper, I think his name is, Alan Cooper. Runs a computer repair shop just off the High Street, apparently, he's the best there is. If there's anything there, he'll find it, he's helped us out before.'

Yet more expense for Chetwynd to moan about, he thought.

22

The incident with the missing IT devices was a turning point for Horton. Mishandling a vital step on one occasion was careless, repeating that mistake several times was incompetence. Ellie didn't want to think about Celia Chetwynd's reaction. It would, without question, have far reaching repercussions for the beleaguered SIO. However, dwelling on the team's shortcomings was a waste of time. She herself had been certain that the correct procedures had been followed, but it was becoming obvious that this wasn't the case. Seasoned detectives should have appreciated the importance of obtaining the devices in the first place. If they had neglected to action this step, then the fault was much more widespread than she had realised, and implied that several of the team were culpable.

Ellie shuddered, realising that if that was the case the blunder could result in the deaths of more people. One thing was for sure, she felt a lot more confident now that Porter was over-seeing the case, along with his unlikely new partner, Connett. They seemed to work well together in the brief interactions she'd observed. Almost as well as...she swallowed hard, thinking back to the previous night. If she was honest with herself it was a situation she would rather put on hold, but she needed to know more about the woman that Graham had been talking to. She would bring it up tonight she decided, ask him outright. Ellie picked up a file and started to re-read the report she had read several times already, but nothing was going in, she soon gave up and went in search of coffee.

23

Horton stood in front of the mirror in the men's toilets, trying hard to bite back his anger. One more embarrassing session in Celia Chetwynd's office. His mind tried to grasp the implications of her tirade. *Incompetence and ineffectual leadership,* she had said in that superior voice of hers, her anger brought on no doubt by increasing pressure in this case. Then, just as suddenly she backtracked, she was worried she told him. Worried that because of the magnitude of the case he was being asked to do too much, which had led to mistakes being made. Not just by him, she stressed, but by others as well. It was then that he admitted that perhaps he had made errors. Before he knew what had hit him, she pounced once again.

'In that case DCI Horton, you won't object to a little extra help, will you? I suggest we split up the cases, assign more personnel to each one, and have a reliable officer in charge of each. We'll arrange for a communal meeting every couple of days so that any new information can be shared and considered,' she went on barely drawing breath. 'Oh, and one other thing, DS Connett will be working alongside DI Porter for the time being,' she announced scrutinising his face for his reaction. He only realised after leaving her office that she had worked out the plan well in advance.

So here he was...supposedly still in 'overall charge' but having to hand over each case to a DI with whom he would 'liaise' at regular intervals. *It doesn't matter which way you look at it,* he thought, *I've just had my arse kicked.* Horton wondered how many others had been told of Chetwynd's plan. He suspected there were a few, or had she paid him the dubious courtesy of having to inform the rest of the team of what was happening? He doubted it, he could imagine the welcome he would get when he returned to his office, running the gauntlet of grinning subordinates, all gloating at the news. All the same, he was relieved that she didn't know the truth, and if he had to grovel to Connett, it would never come to light, at least not from him.

Connett's reports, handed over directly to him in the aftermath of each murder, had languished in the top drawer of his desk until a few hours ago. When the shit hit the fan, he'd panicked. He'd shredded them, only to realise that he could have left them in various locations and claimed that he had asked someone else to carry out the task, someone like Mason.

He couldn't delay the inevitable. He splashed his face with cold water causing rivulets of liquid to run down his neck and onto his shirt. Cursing, he grabbed a fistful of paper towels and dabbed around his collar. There was no avoiding it, he would have to run the gauntlet of the Incident Room. Celia Chetwynd's voice grew louder as he approached, he pushed the door open and stepped inside. She was already announcing the plans that they had discussed barely half an hour ago. *Bloody hell,* he thought, *she really had had it all worked out, hadn't she?* He moved sideways as quietly as he could, hoping that no one would see him, only to catch DS Mason staring at him. He felt oddly exposed, but at the same time relieved that someone at least wasn't paying full attention. Mason blushed slightly and turned her head back to Chetwynd. *Yes,* he thought, *she would have made the perfect patsy, and deserved it.* It was then that Horton saw another woman standing by Chetwynd's side. He recognised her but couldn't come up with a name.

'...and in order to ensure that each of you is comfortable with the level of stress that these investigations may be causing, I have asked our guest here to provide those of you who may feel the need to talk about any issues, to be available on an appointments basis.' With that Chetwynd turned and beckoned the visitor to step forward. 'For those of you unfamiliar with our guest, this is Odelia Mathers.'

24

Alan Cooper had been interacting with the online group for several weeks. At first his activities reminded him of being back at University. There were Module guides complete with notes, advising participants to allow their imaginations to run free.

'Include as much detail as you can, write them down, let it all come out. Recount as much of your experience as possible, just as long as it doesn't distress you too much.'

That was considerate, he thought, *concerned for his welfare... nice.* It didn't take long for him to start writing with a fervency that had surprised him. Once he'd started, he couldn't stop, he described the overwhelming emotions he'd felt, going into details that it made him physically sick. For the first time in many years he'd allowed himself to remember. The next stage was creating scenarios in which he exacted his revenge for the things that had been done to him. That was when he began to enjoy the process. Pressing 'send' once he had perfected his submissions was almost orgasmic.

Anticipating the replies became an exquisitely agonising wait. It put Alan in mind of an 'X' rated distance learning course. You invented all kinds of horrific things that you wanted to inflict and wrote them down in essay form. Members were encouraged to describe the methods they had chosen and reference their sources. When complete they were required to type up their submissions before emailing them off. Then the wait. Alan started checking his inbox every few minutes, hoping that his online mentor would approve of his efforts. Days went by; he almost gave up hope of a reply. Then, when he least expected it, an email – *Puppenspieler74*.

Now he couldn't quite remember when the theoretical and reality merged into one.

...oo0oo...

It had taken a while for Alan to absorb the fact that he had carried out his plan. He was shocked to realise that the emotions that he experienced weren't all negative. Everything had gone smoothly, and in a perverse twist, after the initial euphoria started to wear off, he felt as though he had done society a favour. After all a drug dealer wasn't exactly the kind of person that decent folk would mourn for very long, especially one with a past as sordid as Colin Evans. But he'd done it. He'd taken revenge on the bastard for the years of misery suffered at his hands. He hadn't counted on the nightmares though.

They'd been at school together. Colin, or 'Col' as he liked to be called, was a year ahead of Alan. He was one of the worst bullies that Alan had encountered, and he'd met quite a few in his time. He shuddered as he recalled an episode when Col and his gang had bounced his head off the toilet wall. They'd forced him down to his knees, urinating on his back, the foul liquid mingling with the blood coursing from the deep gash on the back of his head.

'What's up speccy four eyes?' the acne-inflicted Col crowed, 'can't take a joke? Go crying to anyone and we'll really getcha! Fancy a bit of arse action do ya?'

Alan had kept quiet after that, arriving at school before 8am and hanging around until he was as sure as he could be that he was the only one left on the grounds. His salvation was that he excelled at IT, and joined the after-school club, remaining late each night under the tutelage of Mr. Roberts.

'I don't know Alan,' chuckled the rotund man who Alan regarded as his saviour, 'you go on like this and you'll be competition for the big Silicone Valley guys when you grow up!' Alan was good, writing programmes became his refuge; learning code seemed a simple process. But it seemed that his achievements gave the bullies even more of an excuse to pick on him. Alan was relieved when Col was expelled during his final year. Their paths had never crossed again, until a few weeks ago. The years rolled back as a horrified Alan watched Evans walk into his shop, his sidekick, a gorilla lookalike following close behind. As with most school bullies, Col's recollection of the torture he had inflicted on the young Alan was rose tinted in his favour. He spent the next few minutes chatting as though they had been the best of mates.

'Remember that time me and the boys teased you about your computer stuff? Eh? That was so funny, eh?' Col sighed, grinning as though they had shared happy times together. Alan nodded, swallowing hard, praying that Col would leave, but his ordeal wasn't over.

'Nice shop,' Col observed, 'got any space out the back?' He moved towards the door behind the counter, just as

Alan's assistant Lloyd Matthews opened it. Lloyd was built like a heavy weight boxer, with skin the colour of an Americano coffee. He glowered at him as Col backed away, realising that the possibility of acquiring storage for his merchandise here was unlikely. He didn't care; he had plenty of other options. It would've been nice though to have Alan doing his bidding again. Maybe he could try again, get something on this lad standing resolutely before him?

'Never mind,' he breathed, just as the front door opened and Lloyd's two equally large cousins walked in. 'See ya'round Al!' he breezed in his best fake American accent and left the shop.

'Y'all right Alan?' Lloyd's voice belied his size, it was soft, almost a whisper. He'd worked for Alan for two years now, first a Saturday job, now three days a week when he wasn't at college. He and his cousins were good lads, went to church every Sunday and loved their mothers. Alan thought the world of them all. Lloyd, in turn, worshipped Alan.

'Yeah, thanks Lloyd... y-you go through. I'll be there in a minute mate.'

Lloyd held the internal door open for his cousins, muttering something as they entered the back room. It was a class that Alan had run for some time and was proving very popular. Lloyd doubled back to his boss, standing quite close, he leaned down to whisper in Alan's ear. Alan, who was holding onto the counter as though he would never let it go, barely heard him.

'I'll start the class, you'd better go get changed mate,' Lloyd said. Alan turned to him, confusion clouding his face.

'Wha...' he stammered still shaking.

'Your trousers are wet man,' Lloyd said quietly, he turned and retreated into the back room to join the others. Alan realised that he had pissed himself.

He'd been more careful after that. He installed an intercom on the shop door to screen callers before allowing them entrance. He stopped going out at night, the usual behaviour of the terrified underdog, which he realised he'd become... again. He spent sleepless nights trawling the internet, looking at gaming sites, checking up on the latest trends. He would try out as many as he could find, satisfied that he could create equally engaging challenges for a games-obsessed public. It was during one of these sessions that he realised that some of his anger would dissipate when he imagined his enemy as Col Evans. He fantasised about being more confident and planning how to carry out revenge on people who had exercised power over him. There had been quite a few over the years, but no one more than Col.

One site that came up when he Googled 'Therapeutic Role-play' caught his attention...called *'eyeforaneye.co.uk'*. It fed his imagination of what it would be like to settle long festering emotions about his nemesis. He visited the site more frequently during the next few days, his interest drawn to one specific member. Soon they began to email each other regularly. Within a very short space of time he had told *Puppenspieler74* his entire story. The replies were sympathetic, understanding, Alan felt listened to for the first time in years.

The next big step came about by chance, when he was out collecting a computer from one of his housebound customers. Alan ended up just a few miles from his old school, an area he'd studiously avoided for many years. Now he found himself drawn towards it. He knew, of course that it had been derelict for years, but something was urging him to go there. Maybe to take one last look, could this be part of the healing process that *Puppenspieler* had told him about. He left the client's house and drove a few miles further on. There it was; the place where he'd spent some of the worse days of his life. It was on the outskirts of the town, and it had taken a young Alan an hour to get there on his bike. That meant that if he wanted to avoid any confrontation, he had to leave home before 7am each morning and cycle hell for leather to arrive before Col and his gang. Mr. Roberts was almost always there, but some mornings when he was held up, Alan would spend what seemed like an age hidden behind the outbuilding that masqueraded as a bike shed. He knew that if he left his bike there, Col would know he was somewhere around, so it was always locked in a small room to which Alan had managed to acquire a key.

The room had been a coalbunker, complete with a shoot that lead to a cellar, which had been rendered redundant when the school switched to electric storage heaters. Now it was the domain of Mr. Woodall the caretaker, who used it for various 'important' projects, such as making mid-morning cups of tea on an old camping stove. Alan had had to wheedle his way into Mr. Woodall's good books by volunteering to pick up litter during break and at home time. This meant that he left even later most nights, but he felt it was worth it.

Alf Woodall had seen it all before. The thin boy reminded him of his own days of being bullied at this same establishment. Why he had come back full circle and adopted the care of this hellhole was beyond him. He suspected it had something to do with wanting to help others who were experiencing what he had gone through himself. Alan was the current whipping boy, and Alf

Woodall was determined to do all he could to make the boy's life easier. They'd decided on a hiding place for a key to his bolt hole during the summer term of his second year, Alan's gratitude knew no bounds.

Now Alan saw the buildings for what they were, ugly concrete monstrosities. They would be no loss to the area. Over the years since the school had closed there had been a great deal of vandalising, but the 'bunker', as he had named his grimy sanctuary, was still there. Remarkably it still had the metal door. He tried pushing it open, it was locked. His heart pounded forcibly in his chest as he felt for the key. It fell from the moulding as he ran his hand along the frame.

A long forgotten feeling of relief swept over him. He gazed at the key as though it was a talisman, still overwhelmed by the sense of safety it had meant to him as a child. Unlocking the door, he prayed that there was clear access to his former refuge. It opened freely and for a moment he stood, moved beyond any emotion he had experienced. The years slipped away as the pungent aroma of coal dust and oil overwhelmed him. The memories of sipping tea with Mr. Woodall when the old man offered him safety during the worst of the bullying flashed across his mind.

After that day Alan submitted his fantasies to paper, allowing his imagination to run wild. He drew detailed diagrams and typed meticulous notes to accompany them, finally launching them into the Internet ether. He was shocked to receive a reply a few days later that had turned even his comprehensive work into a precise military-style operation. There was a short note praising him for his innovative ideas and attention to detail. In addition, his mentor asked him if this was a theoretical exercise or was he serious about carrying out a modified version of his plan, just to teach Evans a lesson of course. To confirm that he was interested, all he needed to do was to type a few words on a certain social media website to which he belonged, and they could work out the details from there.

Later he couldn't believe that he had even considered the suggestion. Did he have the balls to go ahead, he asked himself repeatedly? More than that, would he get away with it? He laughed, this must be a joke, but no, a few hours after the first email came another, then another, bombarding him with questions about how the past had impinged his life. Did he recognise the reasons for his alienation from his ex-wife? Didn't he realise that Col Evans had set up a series of events that had guaranteed him a miserable future? He was afraid of his own shadow, wasn't he? He had little to look forward to except years of horrific memories and a pathetic back-street business. He was afraid to venture out into the big bad world... wasn't that the truth?

After the first half dozen emails, Alan panicked. There was no more conciliatory language, no more 'understanding of the events of his past', just a barrage of cruel jibes, bordering on abuse. He made up his mind and set to work erasing every trace of his interactions with the website. He knew that there was a record in the computer's hard drive, but it didn't seem important to get rid of it. After all, he hadn't done anything wrong, had he?

Communication stopped almost as suddenly as it had begun, and over the next few days Alan relaxed a little. He'd started working on a new game calling it 'Best Eaten Cold' and smiled to think it had been inspired by his recent experiences with *Puppenspieler74*. He hadn't figured out all the nuances yet, but it was loosely based on revenge.

A week later Alan was opening his post as usual, throwing away junk mail and offers for cheaper broadband. He wondered later how the sender of the newspaper clip knew his address, but that question seemed irrelevant when he read it.

A report on Evans and his gang, detailing how they had been arrested for aggravated burglary, and conspiracy to commit burglary. His blood ran cold as he scanned the piece over and over. Evans was out on bail, the house he and his gang had 'allegedly' robbed, just around the corner. The emails started up soon after that, several in the space of a few hours. Had he seen the report, what was he waiting for? Didn't he want to see this piece of scum taught a lesson? Didn't he owe it to society? He didn't have to go the whole hog after all, just far enough to scare Evans into mending his ways.

'If we could show you a way in which you could lay all those ghosts to rest...' *Puppenspieler* had asked in one of many emails, 'wouldn't you at least consider taking a look?'

Alan ignored them for as long as he could, but they became incessant. They reminded him of his plan, of his experiences. They quoted chunks of his story, his memories back at him. In the end, what could he do? He replied early the next morning.

'What do you have in mind?'

25

Lloyd was the first to comment on his change of mood.

'Al, you ok man?' he asked, as he watched his boss dusting around the small back room, "onny you seem, well sorta happy like.' Alan stopped, smiled at his protégé and nodded.

'You know something Lloyd, I'm ok,' he said nodding, 'I'm more ok than I've been in a long time.' Lloyd shook his head, something was up, and he knew it. Alan hadn't been the same since that bloke had called. What was his name? Lloyd couldn't remember, but he sensed trouble.

'Pass me that new mouse, would you?' Alan asked. Lloyd knew he was trying to change the subject but did as he was asked. Alan watched him as he ambled through to the tiny kitchen to make some tea. He didn't want any of his activities to affect other people, least of all Lloyd. He'd decided to teach Evans a lesson and had modified his original plan so that his objective could be achieved without any permanent harm. *Puppenspieler* had promised him help with his project and had assured him that even putting the frighteners on Evans would have a massive effect on his self-confidence. Hadn't he read the experiences of others on the website? There had been a few second thoughts, but each time he expressed them the reassurances were there. Now everything was set for his plan to go ahead.

Puppenspieler74 suggested that his old school would be a suitable venue to carry out his plan, and Alan visited it again, walking round in a state of other worldliness. He asked himself for the umpteenth time what the hell he'd got involved in, but the visit seemed to strengthen his resolve. He went down to the basement of the old boiler room. It was there that he found the parcel. It was addressed to him, and contained a disposable phone, with a pre-programmed number to call. Talking to the man gave him back his resolve. Why not do it, why not exact revenge? Evans had made his life a misery, wasn't he attempting to re-enter Alan's life, to mess it up again? Wasn't this just one more piece of filth, ruining other people's lives?

…oo0oo…

He arrived earlier than arranged and waited in the dark. The plan was that someone would dump Evans in the coal chute, which would deliver him directly to Alan's feet. This was an irony that wasn't lost on him. Then it would be down to him to carry out his plan…Alan couldn't think any further ahead. The boiler room, he had discovered when he arrived earlier that day, had been transformed into a cross between a film set and a torture chamber. The latest message, contained in a fresh set of instructions, told him that there had been a few minor adjustments that he needed to familiarise himself with.

The notes were headed:

SUGGESTIONS TO ENHANCE YOUR EXPERIENCE.

Filming the entire process, is highly recommended, for two main reasons.

1 - you will be able to savour your experience again later, in the comfort of your own space. If this sounds vaguely macabre, we completely understand, but now you may be too psyched up to immerse yourself fully in the subtle nuances of the process. You will appreciate the suggestion later.

2 - the resultant tape, if the quality is up to a high enough standard of course, will be considered for inclusion in any training sessions offered by the Company.'

In order to avoid being recognised by your intended victim or online, you may wish…

The notes went on, an effective disguise had been provided.

Alan considered this a reasonable argument, but it did little to quell the vague feeling of discomfort he was starting to regard as a permanent fixture. He knew, of course, that anything recorded was easy to post on the Internet. Once it was there…he swallowed hard, he'd always considered tonight to be the end of the whole experience. He was sure that he would never want to relive it repeatedly. A black balaclava lay on the table, it took him several minutes to pick it up and put it on.

He spent what seemed like forever familiarising himself with the camera. He checked his watch…6.30; another half hour and Col Evans would be here. The thought shocked him, was the hell was he doing? 6.45, his heart was racing, what if he couldn't do it, what if Evans found out who he was? His life wouldn't be worth living. 6.52, that was it, he'd call it off, he'd leave now. Maybe he could waylay whoever it was that was supposed to deliver his prey, tell him it was over, he'd changed his mind. Alan pulled out his phone, but his fingers refused to work…the phone rang, unknown caller. Probably a sales pitch, he thought, but it might be… he answered it on the fourth ring.

'Not thinking of changing your mind, are you? Only by the look on your face, I think that's exactly what you're contemplating.'

The line went dead. Alan stared blankly at the screen; his mouth had gone dry. His eyes darted around the room.

He spotted the tiny LED light in the corner of the room. He approached it, a camera high up on a bracket, just out of reach. Why hadn't he seen it before now? The answer was obvious, he hadn't looked. The sound of an approaching vehicle caught his attention. It stopped outside, he heard footsteps, a thumping noise as the coal chute opened, and then a rumbling. Within seconds a blood-stained sack landed at his feet, Alan almost threw up. He backed away to the farthest point he could, gasping for breath. After what seemed like hours, he approached the sack, knelt and untied the length of cord that secured it and pulled it open. Trussed up inside, a large gash to the side of his head was Col Evans. Alan didn't register the departure of the vehicle, nor the fact that his phone had started ringing again, as he stared in disbelief. This was real, this was happening. He turned away shaking his head, wishing he was home in front of the TV.

Alan was breathing rapidly. He wiped his mouth on the back of his sleeve, then turned back to where Col lay helpless before him. He'd done this; he'd started the process that had led to another human being trussed up and deposited like so much meat. Didn't that make him as bad as Evans? His phone rang again, shattering the silence, Alan jumped, his hand shaking as he answered it.

'Bit late to be getting cold feet, Mr. Cooper.' Alan looked round at the camera; the red light blinked back at him. Whoever was watching him couldn't have seen his face the first time he'd rung. He checked the rest of the room, more cameras, more LEDs blinking away. He felt like a goldfish in a bowl, nowhere to hide.

'Now that you have established that we can see your every move,' went on the caller, 'let's get on with it, shall we?' Alan nodded dumbly, shock rendering him speechless. "Good, now if you open the desk drawer, you'll find a new set of instructions. By the way if you have any message for your ex-wife or the kid that helps in the shop just talk into the camera,' the caller laughed and hung up. It took a few minutes before what he'd said registered. Alan stood up facing one of the cameras.

'If you hurt them, if you...' his voice trailed off as he started to appreciate the futility of protesting. What did this maniac want? What did he have to do to protect Lloyd; even his ex-wife didn't deserve this? His imagination started to work overtime, as he stumbled to the battered old desk and opened the drawer. Another folder, fresh instructions, pretty much his original plan, his fantasy of how far he would go to exact his revenge on Col Evans.

'Everything you need to complete your task is in the next room, instructions on the process are listed on enclosed document,' and they were. Itemised instructions, down to the method of dispatch of his intended victim, which Alan had fantasised, would be a particularly noxious substance. In the beginning he had given the poison a fictitious name. His research had uncovered that something similar existed.

He'd found out how much he would need to administer to knock Evans out. He knew exactly how to revive him; he also knew the dosage that would end Col Evan's life. There was also a detailed section on how much blood could be extracted from his victim's body without killing him. Though exactly where Alan had come up with this form of torture he couldn't remember.

Technical matters, reminders, recording the whole process, it amounted to five A4 pages. So much more detailed than any plan that Alan had originated. Back then he had fantasised about his plan, visualising every nuance. He had been shocked to realise the enormity of his hatred and the relief the exercise had afforded. He was ashamed to admit that he'd experienced an almost sexual arousal when he thought about taking revenge on Evans. Then he would lose his nerve and decide to forget the whole thing, only to be buoyed up again by thoughts of revenge and encouragement from his mentor. He'd oscillated between a vast range of emotions. He slept badly, snapped at customers, and found himself unable to eat. Sometimes, quite suddenly his mind would clear, and he could visualise his preferred outcome in detail. He could imagine inflicting pain and humiliation on Col, hoping the experience would give him a level of peace by exorcising his demons. In the end he had to admit that nothing had changed in the real world. But despite his doubts, here he was, on the brink of acting out his plan. He knew the decisions were not entirely his own.

It was then that Alan realised that he was being bullied every bit as much as he had been at school. It was just that this time it was by someone he'd considered to be his friend.

26

The intercom buzzed as Alan sat at the counter, a cup of cold tea before him. He'd been staring at it for the last half hour, his sleep-deprived body protesting its fatigue. Deep down in his gut, Alan knew who it was, and he sighed in resignation as the two officers entered the shop. They went through their routine, asking his name, confirming that he was the one they sought, showing him warrant cards, DS Connett and DC Purdoe. Alan invited them to follow him upstairs to his flat and offered them a drink. He could put the kettle on, he assured them, no bother. They declined and sat down without being asked.

'I got one of your games for my lad,' said Purdoe, trying to set him at ease, 'good one that, football, he loved it.' Alan smiled nervously, trying to convey a relaxed manner.

'How long you been here Mr. Cooper?' asked Connett, he was older than his colleague and sounded a lot tougher.

'About, about six years now,' Alan cleared his throat mid-way through the sentence. He felt hot, giddy.

'Pay well does it, this Computer stuff?'

...*what a stupid question* Alan thought, if this is the best they can do?

'Are you familiar with a Colin Evans, Mr. Cooper?' There it was, out of the blue, it knocked Alan off balance. But what other reason would police officers have for calling on him, if not for this?

'Yes...yes, I went to the same school as him,' he answered, trying to sound as nonchalant as possible, 'why do you ask?'

'I believe Mr. Evans visited you here recently, what did he want Mr. Cooper?' asked Connett. Alan swallowed, remembering the day that Evans had come back into his life, and what he had had to do to get him out of it again.

'I really can't say officer, he seemed to want to talk over old times, then he left,' he admitted.

'... and you haven't seen him since?' the words bounced around in Alan's brain.

'No, no I haven't, why, has something happened to him?' he asked.

'Now why would you think that Mr. Cooper?' asked Purdoe, 'why would you think something had happened to him? Eh?'

'Alan,' Connett smiled, he looked smug, self-satisfied, as though he knew something that Alan didn't. 'Would it be possible for you to come with us to the station, there's a few things we'd like to discuss, and it would be better to do it there? You can get your lad to look after the shop, can't you?'

'Well, er, actually I have a class starting at ten o'clock, can't it wait?' he asked, knowing that it couldn't.

'Mr. Cooper, I think you ought to know that a body was found last night, and we have reason to believe that it was Mr. Evans. We found one of your business cards in his pocket, on the back was a time and date of the class you've just mentioned. Would you like to explain that Mr. Cooper?'

Alan knew that there was no point in refusing to go with them. In any case he wasn't sure he had the strength to carry on this charade any longer, despite his on-line mentor's warnings over the last few days. The threats had been graphic, details of what would happen should he give the police any information. Alan was sick to his stomach as he nodded his assent. Connett and Purdoe led the way back down the stairs and waited for Alan to tell Lloyd that he would be out for the rest of the afternoon. It was also enough time for him to slip a note into the lad's hand as he shook it. He smiled and patted him on the back.

'Thank you, Lloyd,' he said, 'I know you'll do the right thing,' as Lloyd took the note. Alan turned drawing himself up to his full height.

'Let's go then,' he said walking towards the two awaiting officers.

27

Porter was, eager to start the process. He found a message from Horton, no interview until I get there... wait until I arrive... several notes delivered over a period of hours early that morning. How the hell had he found out so quickly? Porter sighed; he had no option but to comply.

What the hell was Chetwynd doing giving him another crack at the case after everything that had happened? Must be something to do with them going through training at the same time. Porter shuddered at the myriad of images his thoughts had conjured up. Horton marched in an hour later, briefcase bulging, huffing and puffing.

'Let's get on with this shall we?' he blustered. All unnecessary showmanship in Porter's view, making himself look busy, when everyone knew him for what he was, incompetent. Porter was in no hurry now, having kicked his heels for the last hour. He wanted to make a point, to get Horton back in some way.

'Hadn't we better wait for Ms. Shaw?' he asked innocently, knowing that Horton would be annoyed at the reminder. 'After all, we did agree that she should observe the interviews from now on.'

His remark hit the spot, and Horton shot him a look of pure hatred. He cleared his throat as he busied himself with a sheaf of papers and walked ahead to the interview room muttering to himself.

'Preparation, that's the key, someone has to be on top of this shit!'

Porter shook his head. *You're certainly the top of this dung heap*, he thought, *to hell with it, let him bluster* he decided. In the meantime, he made his way back to the reception area to keep a look out for Ellie Shaw, praying she wouldn't be too late. That would give Horton yet another excuse to moan.

Horton had been furious when Ellie had been assigned to a more active role by Chetwynd. Bloody woman, why did she have to get involved, he had everything under control? *Doesn't mean I have to be civil to her*, he thought. Porter, on the other hand, applauded Ellie's actions, for setting the cat amongst the pigeons. He admired the work she had done with his team on previous occasions. He didn't give a damn about Horton, for the first time in weeks he believed they had a chance at solving the cases. He intended to offer her all the help and support he could.

28

Porter held a watch up in front of Alan Cooper's face. He turned his head to the side, refusing to look at it. Porter placed it on the table. Alan's heart thundered in his chest; he knew it immediately. His father had bought it for him shortly before he died. It was a fake Rolex, and they both knew it. The old man joked that with Alan's talent it wouldn't be long before he could afford the real thing. To his shame Alan hadn't even missed it.

'Do you recognise this watch, Mr. Cooper?' asked Porter, staring intently at Cooper.

'No... No, I don't think so... I'm... I'm not sure...' Alan answered, leaning as far back in his chair as he could. He was trying to put some distance between himself and the watch that he felt was reproaching him.

'Could you look at it a little more closely,' continued Porter. Alan glanced at the watch, shaking his head once more.

'For the tape, DI Porter is holding up the evidence bag for Mr. Cooper to gain a better view.' He reached out again, bringing the bag closer to Alan's face, so close that he could see the congealed blood. Alan recoiled as though he had been confronted by a venomous snake, shutting his eyes tightly.

'I may... I may have one like...' he stopped, swallowing hard, he repeated, 'I told you... I... I don't know... please, take it away.'

'Do you have an aversion to watches?' Porter asked innocently. Ellie, listening from the next room felt that question was inspired. He was wrong footing Cooper; he was good at this.

'N...No,' Alan stammered, 'look, I don't know anything about this watch, do you hear me?' He went on, his voice rising.

Without waiting for him to recover, Porter reached for a file and withdrew a set of pictures, lining them up neatly on the desk. He placed the last one face down. Then he pointed to them in turn. Alan stared resolutely at his folded arms, trying hard not to look at them.

'Please look at the pictures, Mr. Cooper, Mr. Cooper, I asked you to look at the pictures...' Alan sighed, there really was no choice.

'Number one shows the front view of the watch in question. As you can see there are traces of blood on the face and dried blood in between the links of the strap. Number two shows more blood on the back.' Porter waited, watching for Alan's reaction to the photographs. He cleared his throat and continued.

'You have just stated for the record that you don't recognise this watch, is that correct Mr. Cooper?' Alan's solicitor leaned towards his client and murmured into his ear.

'No comment,' he answered.

Here we go thought Porter, *I wondered how long we'd take to get to this stage.* He reached out for the final photograph, turning it over slowly.

'If that is the case, Mr. Cooper, how do you explain the presence of Colin Evan's blood on the watch, along with your DNA, and this....' he slid the final photo towards Alan, leaning back as the bemused man gazed at it. The picture showed the watch again, but this time the back had been removed. Alan could see the inscription inside it.

'Would you mind reading the dedication out loud, Mr. Cooper?' asked Porter. Alan's brain swirled in fear and confusion as he stared blindly at the words, he shook his head, *he couldn't, he just couldn't.*

'For the benefit of the tape,' said Porter holding up the photograph, 'the inscription reads, 'To Alan, revenge is sweet, followed by a date.' What exactly does that mean Mr. Cooper, 'revenge is sweet'?'

'No comment.' Alan's head was bowed, the fight having left him.

'... and the date, Mr. Cooper, the date is the day that Mr. Evans was killed, how do you explain that?'

'I can't,' began Alan, he lapsed back into 'No comment' as his solicitor cleared his throat.

'No comment, no comment, no comment' on and on it went. Ellie sat next to Mason in the next office, observing through the video link. She made notes regarding the suspect's body language and resolved to analyse it once the actual interview was over...provided Horton allowed her to take a copy of it. To hell with it, she decided, I'll kick up a fuss if necessary. It was about time that Horton took her seriously, although she couldn't see that happening any time soon. She was surprised that he'd allowed Porter to carry on the interview without interrupting him... so far. She noticed Cooper's increasing panic level. It was painful to watch. He kept up the litany of 'No comment' answers for several minutes, sometimes hesitating, almost as though he was on the brink of talking. Then he would rein himself in, holding himself tightly against Porter's interrogation.

Ellie had spent some time studying Cooper's profile the previous evening, it read like a favourable write up on a dating website. He was thirty-six, an expert in IT, with a First-Class Honours Degree, and an MSc in Computer Science. He had some minor, though quite lucrative contracts with medium to large firms nationwide. A small but neat shop just off the High Street in which he taught a variety of classes from 'Computing for the Terrified', usually for the elderly, to writing code, popular with the younger generation. He employed a part-time assistant, Lloyds Matthews, and had worked with the police in the past on data recovery.

Acrimonious divorce, no kids, small flat above the shop which he sometimes rented out, his own house, nice car, etc. etc., lots of plus points. Ellie studied him intently as the interview progressed. Not overly good-looking, but presentable, a little shy. His ruddy complexion made it seem as though he was constantly blushing.

Mason had slipped into the observation room to watch the interview a few minutes in, and now sat virtually motionless. Every now and then she wrote down a few words. Ellie had to try hard not to let her movements break her own concentration. Overall, Cooper wasn't the type she could imagine committing murder, let alone inflicting the kind of horror contained in the postmortem report. Graham had shuddered as he handed over a copy the night before, always solicitous where she was concerned.

Cooper's solicitor was Mr. Richardson, a dour looking man who said very little and looked like a character from a Dickens novel. He sat straight-backed next to his client. He was immaculately dressed, and took copious notes using a traditional fountain pen. Occasionally he would mutter a few words into Alan Cooper's ear and was asked several times to speak out for the tape. Porter had used a discreet earpiece through which Ellie could ask any questions she thought relevant. So far she hadn't used it, the DI was doing just fine, asking all the things that Ellie would want to know, and some questions she hadn't thought of. As far as she was concerned, everything was going well, everything except for the rushing noise she could hear, the one she recognised only too well, the one that usually heralded the onset of a migraine, or worse.

'Tell me about your relationship with the victim, Mr. Cooper' Porter asked, at which point Alan faltered, shifting his weight on the chair. He was obviously uncomfortable.

'I, er, I,' he stammered, 'It was….'

'Well, Mr. Cooper, what was it?' interrupted Horton, who had so far been silent. Porter had expected this to happen much earlier. Horton wasn't one to allow an interview to be conducted without interrupting. Now here he was, jumping into the process, threatening to shatter the tenuous link that had been building up.

Porter sighed; Ellie could tell he was furious. His body tensed up, and for a moment she thought he might hit his boss. The noise in her head was growing louder. She tried to shake it off, pressing her fingers into the dip below each ear, massaging round and round to relieve the tension. She tried focusing on the group in the next room, willing herself to calm down.

'Ask him to tell you about the time that he and Evans were at school together,' she whispered into the microphone, making Porter jump. He had forgotten she was there; he did as she asked.

'Yes, we…no comment.' Alan Cooper had turned pale. It was obvious to both Ellie and Porter that the question had hit a raw nerve.

'Did you and Mr. Evans have a friendly relationship?' Porter continued, taking up Ellie's initiative. Alan shook his head, his breathing rate increased; he gripped the edge of the table. Ellie could tell that the fight or flight instinct was kicking in. Alan stood up, banging his fist on the desk.

'I can't, I can't tell you...don't you see I can't tell you!' he yelled, just as suddenly he flopped back onto the chair, all the fight leaving him. He sat shaking his head, 'I'm sorry... so... so sorry, I should never...I didn't mean for it to go that far... I... I didn't have a choice...you have to understand... I...'

'Calm down Mr. Cooper, please!' Porter pleaded.

'He wants to say something, he wants to tell you, but he's terrified.' Ellie said, watching Cooper closely. The noise in her head had given way to a throbbing pain, searing through her skull as she almost fell forward. She gripped the table, her knuckles turning white as she channeled all her energy into staying conscious. Simultaneously, Richardson acted as though he had received an electric shock. He stood suddenly, shuffled his papers and announced that he considered this had gone on long enough now, that his client was entitled to a break. Porter and Horton started to protest, they had been in the interview room for barely an hour, the suspect had during that time been uncooperative...

Ellie was now in agony as she fought to stay upright but watched as the debacle commenced. They had hit on something with the question about Alan's childhood, and she was determined to find out more before the whole interview shuddered to a halt or she passed out.

'Ask him what was it that Col Evans did to him when they were boys?' she persisted. Porter asked the question, having to almost shout to be heard.

'Wha...what did you say?' stammered Cooper. Porter repeated himself as a hush descended on the room, like the pause when overloud music is suddenly switched off leaving the ears ringing.

'I asked you what Col Evans did to you to when you were boys,' Porter persisted, watching as Cooper dissolved into tears. He cradled his head in his hands and broke down as those present watched in morbid fascination.

'I can't do this,' he sobbed, 'I can't do it.'

Porter's instinct was to reach towards him, a reflex gesture which suggested that he too was affected by the plight of the devastated man in front of him. He thought better of it and bit his lip, thrown by the depth of Cooper's distress. Richardson cleared his throat and shuffled his papers, clearly intending to bring the interview to a halt. In the time it took for him to announce his intention, Cooper lunged across the desk grabbed the fountain pen and jabbed it several times into his own neck.

'You can't make me talk, there's no point. I'm dead anyway I'll never make it to court. He'll get me, I know he will, you don't know, you don't know!!!' he yelled. Blood sprayed out as his frantic words echoed around the room, over the desk, the photographs and the files as the three men tried to dodge the worst of it. Porter made a grab for Alan's hand trying to stop him.

Mason gawped at the scene, transfixed by Cooper's actions. It was only then that she saw Ellie lying on the floor.

29

The Doctor was brief. *Yes; his patient had inflicted wounds sufficient to be deemed as a 'serious injury'. No, they were not in themselves life-threatening. No, he was under sedation and couldn't be interviewed at this present time. Yes, they would be informed when it was acceptable to do so.*

'Mr. Cooper's behaviour will mean that he'll have to be assessed by the Mental Health Team to decide whether or not to commit him to a Psychiatric Unit,' he announced to a frustrated Porter. If this was the case, Cooper might not be ready for further questions for months, worst case scenario was that he may never be tried.

Porter had grabbed some clothes from lost property and looked incongruous standing in an old pair of jeans, a hoodie, a 'Bob Marley' tee shirt and a pair of trainers that were a size too big. They were clean at least, kept in reserve for overnight 'guests' who might disgrace themselves. At forty-five Porter considered himself too old to be dressed like some second-rate drug pusher.

He'd followed the ambulance to the hospital where he'd waited most of the night for news, dozing fitfully in an uncomfortable armchair. He left when he heard the breakfast trolley trundling towards him. He needed rest, or maybe breakfast, he couldn't decide which.

...No wonder my marriage broke up... he thought as he drove back towards his house. The morning mist huddled against the fields evaporating slowly, reluctant to break away as the sun started to warm up the landscape holding the promise of another beautiful autumn day.

Porter rarely dwelt on thoughts about his personal life, they served no purpose. He and Susanne had made their choices a long time ago. You couldn't do what he did and expect a beautiful vibrant woman to wait at home every night, not knowing if you would come home at all, let alone when. It got worse after their son was born.

Arthur was a difficult child; Susanne had been at her wits end, especially after they received the diagnosis that he was severely autistic. That was when she decided to work from home, isolating her even more. Arthur was three when she finally announced that she was leaving to live with her parents in Yorkshire. Porter rarely saw her or their son from that point. Now she was married to some hedge fund manager named Keith and had two daughters. Arthur, now nineteen, lived in a supported unit a few miles from his mother. He'd shown a remarkable talent for art and was drawing intricate and beautiful pictures which Susanne marketed and sold for high sums.

Porter received reports on his son's progress every year, photos of his work, and a bill for his share of the costs. It had been a financial struggle which kept him working long hours, but his resolve not to shirk his responsibilities had done him credit. Now his son's artistic success had outstripped his father's finances, and the cost of care was more than covered by Arthur's earnings. Porter's greatest sadness was that on the rare occasions that he managed to visit his son, Arthur barely recognised him.

'Enough of this,' he decided reaching the crossroads; turn left and he would be home within a few minutes, turn right and the station would be a few miles on… *no contest, he decided*… turn up at the station looking like this and they'd probably lock him up for vagrancy. He needed a shower and a change of clothes, that much was obvious. Within an hour he walked back towards his car, and headed to the station, his second home.

Coffee and a bacon sandwich set him straight. He could write up his witness statement and get that over and done with. He'd already left a message with Ellie Shaw's secretary asking if she was well enough to come to the station, if so, could they could meet up later. Then he dealt with several messages, including one from Horton, and booked his car in for a service.

Yesterday had been quite eventful, and one thing that stuck out in his mind was the look on Ellie's face, as medical and forensic staff filled the interview rooms. Porter couldn't recall seeing someone look so pale unless they were dead. She recovered quickly though, excusing her collapse on her extreme aversion to the sight of blood. But no matter how hard he'd tried. he couldn't get her to make eye contact. A few hours later, following a visit from Graham's team to collect forensic evidence, she insisted that she was well enough to drive home.

One thing was clear; he had to speak to Alan Cooper again, preferably before the Mental Health Team got their hands on him. Porter was convinced that Cooper could be the break they had been looking for. Mason had uncovered the history behind him and Evans. If Ellie Shaw was to be believed, the theme of revenge running through the whole case was about to be proved.

30

Several messages and a pile of letters greeted Ellie's return to her office. She was early and had hoped there would be no one there but wasn't surprised to find the office open. The aroma of freshly brewed coffee permeated the air, and she found Miss Pritchard sorting out and archiving old files. Several of the telephone messages, several were from Ellie's mother, which she would try to deal with at the earliest opportunity. Julia Morrison didn't like being ignored.

One was from Porter, to the point, no flim flam, could they meet at the station around 10am, he wanted to go over the details of yesterday's events before their meeting? Ellie found his request energising, they could present a united front. However, she had no idea what he meant when he referred to *'their meeting'*. The second message answered that question. Horton's secretary had called to say that Ellie was expected in his office at 2pm. She knew Horton wasn't happy about what had happened yesterday, on his watch.

She still wasn't sure it'd been necessary for Forensics to take Horton, Richardson and Porter's clothes away; watching them protest as Graham supervised the bagging and tagging. If the situation hadn't been so traumatic, she would've laughed at the smug looks on the team's faces as they stood garbed in coveralls. Despite their objections, Graham had stood firm.

'We can't make exceptions in procedure,' he said, trying hard not to look too self-satisfied. He was conscious of the seriousness of the past few hours, but the pleasure of being able to tell Horton that his chain-store suit would remain in the custody of the lab was priceless, he told her later.

Ellie shook her head. Not something to joke about, she reprimanded herself, especially given what had happened to her during that time. She couldn't get her head around it. She cringed at the unintended pun. Was it her imagination or had she and Alan Cooper connected in the instant he had reached for Richardson's pen? They'd made eye contact as he started stabbing at his neck, Ellie had felt his distress, and the pain he was going through, tension building inside her was an echo of his distress. But that was impossible, she was the other side of the two-way mirror, he couldn't have known she was there. She'd managed to convince Mason that the reason she passed out was an aversion to the sight of blood, although it sounded like a feeble excuse. Ellie knew it was something else.

Horton had snorted in derision at her explanation. Porter had an overwhelming urge to punch him. Cooper's actions had shocked her almost as much as the images she had seen just before she passed out. Where the hell had they come from? She hadn't even allowed herself to process them yet. They were too horrific to conjure up, yet there they were knocking at the door of her conscious mind demanding to be addressed. There seemed to Ellie only one person she could talk to, Odelia Mathers.

A tap on the door, John poked his head around it and cleared his throat, making Ellie jump.

'John! I, I didn't know you were back,' she stammered, 'when...'

'Horton called me last night, said there was a bit of drama yesterday. I was wondering why you didn't see fit to call me Ellie, besides which....'

Ellie very rarely experienced pure anger, but this was one of those times. 'How dare he,' she hissed, 'how dare he drag you back into this case now that...' she faltered, remembering who she was talking to. It wasn't John's fault that Horton had reverted to type.

'Ellie...Ellie please,' he walked towards her, his hands held in front of him in a gesture that was designed to placate her. 'Please, sit down and let me finish,' she sat, her strength deserting her.

'I had two calls last night, one from Horton, and the other from Chetwynd. She had nothing but praise for you, but she believes a fresh pair of eyes, a more experienced, more mature...'

'Ok, ok, I get the picture,' Ellie was still shaking, 'so you step in now, is that it, take over?'

'Now I didn't say that. I suggested that we could review the recordings together. Maybe we'll get something that was overlooked, that's all.' He was trying to reassure her, and she knew it, but something deep down whispered that the team's faith in her abilities were not as strongly established as she'd believed them to be. John called to Miss Pritchard to make some fresh coffee and sat down on one of Ellie's awful modern chairs. He squirmed as he attempted to make himself comfortable. Ellie watched him miserably, *serves you right*, she thought.

'Look, Ellie,' he leaned back sighing, 'this is getting serious, it can't be allowed to go on, good God, the body count is growing almost daily. Let's work together and perhaps we can solve this before anyone else is killed.'

Ellie sniffed, the last thing she wanted was to get the reputation for sulking, but she felt that this was her case. She didn't want John to take it back after she had come so far. But how far had she come, how much nearer was she to identifying the killer, let alone helping the team to catch him?

She watched him over the rim of her mug. The coffee hit the spot, restoring Ellie's reasoning faculties. Having John on board was no shame, she hoped the guys at the station would see it that way, although she knew that Horton would crow at having his 'expert' back. It was as though John had read her thoughts.

'Ellie, this is still your case, I'm just here to help, I promise, in fact, if you don't want me to come, I won't.'

He's serious, she thought, admitting that she could never live with herself if someone else died just because she'd missed some small detail that John might have picked up in a second. She could see the logic in what John was suggesting.

'No, no, you're right of course, we need a fresh perspective John. I'm sorry, I... who else is joining us?'

'Sorry, I should have said, DI Porter, no need to bother Horton unless we have to. Now... are you coming to the station, do you want a lift?' he asked. Ellie detected a hesitation in his voice, almost as though he was expecting for her to decline.

'No, I mean, yes, of course I'm coming,' she replied, wondering how on earth she was going to get back to her office if she accepted a lift with John, he anticipated her question.

'Taxi,' he suggested, 'you can get a taxi back, unless some kindly copper can give you a lift? Car park, ten minutes' he declared, jumping up and retreating from her office. Ellie heard the door to John's office close and grabbed her bag and jacket, she hurried to the Ladies', she didn't want to look a complete mess. This was all very rushed; she didn't like being rushed. She headed to the car park, stopping briefly to ask Miss Pritchard to re-arrange her one appointment of the day. The elderly secretary tutted, giving her a disapproving look. Ellie wondered whether John would have had the same reaction.

They rode to the station in virtual silence. Ellie would have liked to have kept it that way, but she needed to discuss Ruth's behaviour with John, and this seemed like a perfect opportunity.

She cleared her throat, unsure of how to bring up the subject.

'John, about Ruth...' she started.

'You needn't worry about her not taking her medication,' he interrupted, 'there's no need actually. Steve Mainwaring called me a few weeks ago, asked how she was. It was an interesting conversation,' he shifted slightly; he was obviously uncomfortable about something.

'It may be a breach in confidentiality, but he told me something that I've suspected for some time. Ruth isn't Bi-polar, he told her as much when she went to see him. He only told me because I expressed concern about how evasive she was being about her treatment,' he shook his head. 'For the life of me I'll never figure your sister out.'

Ellie felt like she'd been punched. What the hell was Ruth playing at? All the worry she'd put them through, the lack of co-operation, and there it was, Ruth inventing a condition to excuse her narcissistic behaviour. Her reaction morphed into anger, both at Ruth and then towards John.

'How long have you known about this, John?' she asked, so quietly that he barely heard her.

'Oh, about two weeks, I already told you that,' he answered as though she should be grateful that he'd mentioned it at all, 'why do you ask?'

She took a deep breath before answering. She kept her face turned to the window, her anger brewing as she fought to calm her thoughts before she answered.

'It would've been nice if you had told me straight away, that's all.'

Ellie battled to bring her attention back to Alan Cooper's interview and the images that demanded to be addressed.

I'll get through this meeting, she promised herself, *and then find out when I can talk to Odelia.*

31

The Interview Room was still cordoned off. There was nothing more to be done in there, but no-one had thought to take down the tape, they were waiting for Horton's say-so. No-one wanted to upset him any more than necessary. Porter was waiting for them in reception, he led them to a room on the third floor, well away from Horton's office.

'How are you feeling Ellie?' he asked as they settled down at one of the tables he had placed in front of the screen. His question took Ellie by surprise, and not just because Porter never used her first name when they were at the station. He noticed her confusion, 'after yesterday...how are you feeling?'

'Oh...better thanks,' she mumbled. She could feel herself blushing and busied herself retrieving her notebook and a pen. John cleared his throat, impatient to get on. He said little, not wanting to discuss the interview until they had had chance to watch it through. All three scribbled away as the recording progressed. Ellie found it hard to concentrate, the tension was almost palpable. She looked at the two men who appeared just as distracted.

'Maybe it would be better for us to watch this on our own initially, would that be possible DI Porter?' she suggested.

'How so?' asked John curtly, pausing the recording.

'No, I agree,' said Porter standing and stretching, although they had only been seated a short while. His vigil at the hospital was beginning to take its toll. 'I think we're expecting each other to come up with some eureka moment, and I can assure you that in my case, that's never going to happen!' he joked, winking in Ellie's direction. 'It won't take long to hook this up in the next two rooms; this floor is virtually deserted anyway.'

The third floor had been modernised two years ago, just before the last round of financial cutbacks had been introduced, but only a few officers had been through the process of updating their IT skills. It remained largely unused much to the frustration of the Celia Chetwynd, who had pushed hard for the funding of new technology. Soon they were sitting in separate rooms watching the recording. Ellie augmented the notes she'd already taken, noticing tiny nuances in Cooper's body language. He was obviously nervous throughout, almost wincing when pressed for answers. She noticed how desperate he appeared just prior to stabbing himself.

Ellie found herself tensing up as his distress increased, but then spotted something else, something she hadn't seen at the time of the actual interview. As Cooper stood up Ellie saw a light surrounding him, not very bright, but there, nevertheless. She pressed the remote to pause the recording, but as she did, the light seemed to travel across the screen, within seconds it had gone. The more she thought about it the more she was sure that the moment it had disappeared had coincided with the images that had invaded her mind. She rewound and pressed play, the light was no longer visible. She tried again, but it was no good, the light had gone.

'That's it,' she decided, 'I'm going mad!' She played the rest of the interview, but there were no other unusual occurrences, and as the recording finished an eerie silence pervaded the room. She was still staring at the screen when Porter knocked at the door.

'We're going to compare notes now,' he said, holding the door open in a way that brooked no argument. He saw her confusion; it reminded him of her past behaviour. He wondered what had happened to shake her newly found confidence. She was going to have to toughen up if she was ever going to replace John Prothero. For now, he tried what he hoped was an encouraging smile, and tried to soften the stance he'd taken.

Ellie swallowed hard, what had just happened? She hadn't slept well the previous night, so maybe she was overtired. Or had she really seen something on the screen?

Between them they managed to build up a much more rounded picture of what had happened. They'd all picked up on the comment that Cooper had made regarding a third party.

'Maybe we're looking at a vigilante group, or someone influencing people to commit these murders. You may have been right all along,' Porter suggested looking long and hard at Ellie and remembering the scorn with which Horton had greeted her suggestions. Ellie blushed again; John was also studying her, his mouth pursed into his signature gesture.

'I think you're on to something,' he conceded, 'Cooper may have confirmed your theory. From what he went on to say later in the interview, it certainly seems that way.'

'In which case, we need to start looking for the ring-leader, a 'Mr. Big', which is going to take some doing.' said Porter, 'He...they, could be working a much larger area than just this one. We need to see Cooper again as soon as possible, find out as much as we can before he gets scared off.'

'That much is obvious, if you don't mind me saying,' John observed, 'and we have no time to go over the obvious, I suggest we bring DCI Horton...'

The office door crashed open. A red-faced Horton overexerted from climbing the stairs stood in the doorway. Ellie suppressed a laugh, he looked as though he was about to explode from the effort. She wondered how on earth he got through his medical checks.

'What the hell is going on here?' he demanded, his face as red as the polo shirt he had been forced to wear due to his one good set of clothes being deemed as evidence. He'd teamed the shirt, which had obviously seen better days, with a pair of green slacks. Not a good look Ellie decided.

'Actually, we were preparing for your meeting this afternoon. If you'd bothered to ask, we would have clarified that point.' John said, adopting his most soothing tone which he still managed to infuse with a dose of acidity. It was a tactic he used with the more skittish patients he had to deal with. The DCI wilted slightly and backed into the far corner, trying to distance himself from the man who was obviously in charge.

Horton admired Prothero, but resented the ease with which he, Porter and the Shaw woman worked together. They seemed to be developing a close bond. He felt excluded, almost to the point of being ignored. His greatest fear was that if he couldn't take back the lead on this case, his position as SIO would be threatened. How many more chances would Chetwynd give him once she concluded that he wasn't up to the job? He'd already decided that should he be replaced by one of his team, he'd either apply for transfer, or resign.

Just a few hours earlier, Horton had once more been standing in Celia Chetwynd's office, where he'd been shocked to find the Mathers woman. To his total humiliation, he had been hauled over the coals in front of a civilian. Lack of results, failure to follow police procedure, and worst of all, '*Devicegate*' as he'd heard it called.

'Good,' Horton said at last, looking around at the others who watched him expectantly. 'Good to see that you to came in early, I was going to suggest something along those lines myself. Nice to see that you've taken the initiative, now that you're here, I think we should....'

'Hold on,' John interrupted Horton before he could continue, 'can't you see we're in the middle of something?'

Ellie glanced briefly at Porter, who was watching his senior officer deflate like a helium balloon left over from a long-finished party. She thought for a moment that she detected a hint of a smile, which disappeared when he realised that she was watching him.

'No, no of course not,' stammered Horton, 'I just...'

'Keep quiet and you can stay,' John snapped. Ellie watched in stunned fascination as Horton crossed meekly to a chair on the opposite side of the table and sat down, watching the three of them. John gathered together his notes and they continued their meeting, paying him little attention. Porter recapped Ellie's theory involving a 'Mr. Big' a controlling figure. He handed over to her, encouraging her to expound her theories.

'It appears that Alan Cooper was... is... terrified to implicate whoever else is involved,' she observed. She detected a low 'humph' from Horton but refused to look at him. John was nodding, which encouraged her to continue.

'What if this person, the one that could be pulling the strings, what if they are backing people like Alan Cooper into a corner? They could be threatening them, I don't know, maybe blackmailing them even, to commit the murders.' she suggested.

'Huh!' Horton was about to rise from his chair, John shot him a threatening stare.

'Let her go on,' he hissed.

'Well... I... this would explain why there are such diverse MOs. It could be because there are multiple perpetrators, connected in some way, but operating independently of each other... a sort of club... a murder club.'

'Right, that's it!' Horton exclaimed, jumping up. 'You think that someone has started, what, a social club for Psychos? Is that it Ms. Shaw...and you expect us to take that seriously?' He looked around at the two men for support. Ellie stared at her notes.

'What makes you think that this is a possibility Ellie?' asked Porter, his voice low, full of empathy.

'I... I don't know,' she stammered, 'it's a feeling I get, that... that the murders were orchestrated. I can feel it, sense it somehow.'

'You don't mean to say you think there's a possibility that she's right?' Horton demanded, shaking his head in disbelief. 'Have you all lost the plot?'

'I think at this stage it would be foolish to dismiss any possibility,' declared John, turning to Horton, daring him to contradict. He disliked this man; he disliked anyone that jumped to conclusions without considering all the possibilities. Ellie and Porter watched in amazement as Horton shrank once again under John's withering gaze.

'There's a lot of merit in your theories Ellie, it would be wise to go over the evidence again with them in mind. However, don't forget the possibility that these could still be unconnected murders. We can't dismiss the possibility that there may be multiple murderers out there, working independently. Of course, this will mean a lot of work for all of us. The links that you've already established do exist, but we need physical evidence, forensic evidence that will establish them without any possibility of doubt. We must examine this... or these cases with fresh eyes, which means starting again from scratch...' he stopped talking, distracted by a noise from the corridor.

The door opened; it was Connett. He looked for Horton, who had risen again and was about to admonish him for disturbing the meeting. Connett cut him short.

'Sir, sir we've just heard from the hospital, its Cooper. Sir, he's...' Connett stood gasping for breath, another victim of the stairs.

Ellie stood up suddenly, sending her chair crashing to the floor,

'He's dead,' she said softly, 'Alan Cooper's dead.'

32

Ellie sat in the furthest corner of the Black Horse Tavern. Porter had suggested that they escape before they got drawn into the chaos that was breaking out at the Station. He'd seen a look on her face, which had frankly scared him. He was also afraid that she would pass out again, and that this time she wouldn't have the excuse that she couldn't stand the sight of blood.

Ellie had so many conflicting thoughts spinning through her mind that she was finding it hard to focus on standing up, let alone getting involved with any more drama. Why had Cooper died from what were deemed as non-life-threatening injuries? How had this happened? Had he become another victim? Horton's knee-jerk reaction was to gather as many of the team that he could assemble.

Porter knew that it would take him several hours before he worked out the next step, and in any case if he missed them that much, he could always call them. As he left the station, he spotted Ellie sitting in reception, staring into space with a look of complete bewilderment. She needed a taxi she told him when he asked her if she was ok. She needed to get back to her office.

'Drink?' he asked before thinking through the implications of being seen leaving the station with an attractive woman, to hell with it what did he care? In any case no one in their right minds could think...

He got back from the bar with a pint of Boddingtons and a lime and soda for Ellie.

'Sorry, this is all they had,' he said, fetching two packets of plain crisps from his pocket. 'They stopped serving lunch half an hour ago.' Ellie smiled and thanked him, taking a sip of the drink. The ice clinked and beads of condensation ran down the glass. How she wished this was a nice Prosecco or even a Chardonnay... she sighed, would this longing ever go away? Porter noticed how uncomfortable she was as he swallowed a good third of his pint. God, he needed that.

'So, that was a turn up for the books, wasn't it?' he said, '...hope your husband can come up with something.'

'Do you?' asked Ellie turning on him. She pierced him with a stare that reminded him of John Prothero. 'Do you really? Because if he does...come up with something, you know what that'll mean? Another victim to add to the list, and it's already long enough as far as I'm concerned.'

Porter halted, his beer halfway to his lips, he wasn't used to such forceful outbursts from her. 'Sorry,' he said, '... that was insensitive, just wanted... I didn't mean...'

Ellie took a deep breath. 'It's ok, I... I know it's not your fault, I'm feeling a little out of my depth,' she confessed.

'Tell me,' he said, replacing his glass on the table and settling back into one of the wing-backed chairs that were a feature of the bar. He stared at Ellie, waiting for her to speak, she looked like a deer caught in the headlights of a car. He felt a strange twist in his chest, a feeling that he was unused to. By the time she had finished talking he had a clearer picture. He knew that she was terribly unsure of herself but finding out that she feared losing her place on the team... that he hadn't guessed. One minute she was at the centre of the case, the next John had been called in. She was frustrated at Horton's lack of confidence in her. Angry at herself for what she saw as her inability to express her opinions on the case... even of her abilities themselves. She had some theories, yes, but was afraid to express them in case she got the kind of reception that she had received that morning, both from Horton and even John Prothero.

'OK,' he said. She had run out of steam and sat looking dejected, almost shrinking into the large chair which seemed to swallow her fragile frame. 'Go over your theories again. Tell me what you think, and why you think it, sell them to me.'

She shuffled uneasily, she closed her eyes and took another deep breath, she let it go suddenly, moving around again... *like a cornered animal*, he thought.

'Ok, but please try and keep an open mind, I've been told that most of this stuff is a product of an over-active imagination.' She paused, still unsure of sharing something this contentious with someone she barely knew... 'I get these, feelings,' she murmured, causing him to strain to hear her, '... intuitions, my mother used to call them 'glimpses'. They're not based on concrete facts, just...feelings, like when you and Horton interviewed Cooper. I could feel his fear. He wasn't afraid of you, or that he'd been caught and arrested. He wanted to talk, he just couldn't, he was forcing himself to keep quiet, from telling you what had happened. It wasn't that I was caught up in the anticipation or anything, I was going through what he was feeling, the panic, the terror. He was afraid of someone, I'm sure of it.'

Porter had shifted in his chair, crossing his legs, his elbows on the arms, fingers steepled, watching her. It was obvious that telling him was a relief. She was unburdening herself and he knew better than to interrupt her.

'What I sensed in Alan Cooper,' she said, 'was that he was desperate to tell us the whole story. I don't think that he would have murdered Evans if he'd had a choice. I think he just wanted to teach him a lesson. But then something happened, he was coerced, threatened into taking it further. I've studied his background, he's not the type, doesn't fit the profile. We both know the factors that lead someone to commit murder, and heaven knows anyone could tell that Cooper had a long-standing issue with Evans. But it's not like he actively sought him out to exact his revenge is it? If his experiences when he was a child had caused so much damage why wait until now? I tried to discover a trigger, a driver, but it looks like Col Evans turned up one day out of the blue, and it sent Cooper into crisis mode. But can we really believe that he calmly organised a very elaborate murder scene, assembled all the equipment, committed murder then cleaned up, all on his own? It's just too much to accept, both his decision to commit the act, and the preparation for it,' she paused, took a sip of her drink, then continued. 'Horton and John, they didn't seem to ...' she sighed and shuffled in her seat, Porter stayed silent.

'In most of the current cases there are echoes of revenge, but the initial events happened years ago. What were the triggers that caused the suspects to act now, after all this time? What if... what if they became involved with a third party? Yes, I know I've suggested this before, but hear me out.' She'd seen Porter shift in his chair and was afraid to lose the thread of her theory again. 'What if this third party is someone who derives pleasure not from committing murder himself, but in driving others to? The satisfaction achieved would be the power he could exert over the individual he's controlling, making him the ultimate control freak.'

Porter's eyes narrowed as he took in every word, *she could be on to something here*, he thought, the links were joining up, a pattern, however slender, was emerging, and what she'd just outlined made sense. If he had learned nothing else in his career, it was that every case, however similar it seemed to another, was unique.

'Well if it means anything, I think you could be on to something,' he conceded, she looked up sharply, searching his face for any sign of insincerity. She saw none.

'Thank you,' she whispered, 'you don't know what it means to have someone believe me, there aren't many who take me seriously.'

'Oh, you'd be surprised,' he smiled, 'now let's try and crack this shall we?' Ellie felt a surge of confidence that Porter, with all his experience and an impressive track record had listened to her, it felt good. As for the images she had seen prior to passing out the previous day, and during her viewing of the recording that morning, those she kept to herself.

33

John stood looking out of the window; Horton's office was a tip, and it grated on his sense of how a workplace should be ordered, especially that of a senior police officer. He waited for Horton with mounting impatience. Just as he'd decided to leave, the portly DCI bustled in, a sheaf of paper in one hand, brief case in the other, and took his place behind the chaotic desk. He had kept John waiting for almost twenty minutes, an aberration in John's mind.

He had neither the time nor the patience to go over the latest information yet again. Making him wait was pathetic payback for the way in which he had spoken to Horton earlier. Even so Horton had subsequently pleaded with John to stay and 'clarify' one or two things. John knew what that meant, that Horton still didn't have a clue. Really, he had no respect for this man whatsoever, now if he were more like DI Porter, John mused as Horton shuffled his papers importantly.

Horton cleared his throat, '... you are staying for the meeting this afternoon, aren't you?' he asked, almost begging.

'No,' John replied secretly enjoying Horton's disappointment. 'I believe we covered the essentials this morning, and as I think I mentioned I have appointments this afternoon. I really have no more information on this case, or perhaps you think I am deliberately withholding something vital?'

Horton shook his head; he didn't want to alienate his only ally. He grunted, he would cancel the meeting if John wasn't going to be there, it would be pointless.

'Besides which you have a lot to consider, thanks to Ellie Shaw, don't you?' John picked up his briefcase sneaking a look at Horton. He was enjoying the other man's discomfort.

'About that...' began Horton, shaking his head and leaning back into his swivel chair. John cut him off before he could continue.

'You need to know, DCI Horton that I have every confidence in Ms. Shaw, and that that confidence is shared by Chief Superintendent Chetwynd. I think she made some extremely interesting observations, and that you and your team should be concentrating on them. In fact, after her performance a few weeks ago, I was confident that you had accepted the fact that I would be handing over to her on a permanent basis, a move also supported by your boss. Now, I must be going.' With that he turned and left Horton's office.

John was sure that Ellie and Porter had got everything in hand, and he had other things he needed to get on with. There were other calls on his time, hell that was the point of handing over to Ellie in the first place wasn't it, so that he would have more time to concentrate on his other work? His recent elevation to a post in a Government department was something that he had worked long and hard to achieve, he had no intention of giving it up now that he had reached his goal. The last ten years had seen many changes in his life. Practitioner, Professor, Consultant, it had been a roller coaster ride. Not just in his career but also in his personal life.

John had always considered himself a bit of a loner. Yes, he'd had relationships, but nothing long-term. Eventually he'd decided that women were too much like hard work to make the effort worthwhile, until he met Ruth. She was so different from women he had known in the past. A bit too different sometimes he had to admit, free-spirited, wild, and spontaneous. If he was honest, she was his complete opposite. He liked predictability in his life, Ruth was anything but.

After all these years, he still hadn't managed to figure her out. He doubted he ever would. She could be the most fascinating creature one moment, frustrating and annoying the next. He smiled at the thought of her, and of his son, his pride and joy; Max. A sudden bump bought him back to the present, he slammed on the brakes. The car skidded to a halt and stalled as he sat clutching the wheel, a flat tyre. John cursed as he opened the boot, this was all he needed. Calling the breakdown service was not an option; the reception here was so poor. He set about changing the tyre. It took him the best part of an hour, during which time he started to think about Graham and Ellie.

Graham had been his star student back in the day. John had had no qualms about recommending him for the post in the Forensics Department. It was partly due to his help that Graham had made such rapid progress in his career. When John's endorsement had subsequently resulted in

Graham obtaining a post at the University, it had sealed their friendship. John was delighted when Graham asked him to be best man at his wedding, which was where he'd met and fallen for Ruth.

Getting to know Ellie, on the other hand hadn't been plain sailing. She was a difficult person to read, almost obsessively private. She didn't open up to many people. John had perhaps got to know her better than most, and understood some of what made her tick, but even his expertise was challenged. During her first few months on the island, John had been instrumental in helping her come to terms with the Josie Blewitt case. It had been slow progress, but eventually she had gained enough confidence to get back to work, and even joined him in his practice in a part-time role.

He assigned her small steps at first, some counselling, Cognitive Behavioural Therapy, Hypnosis for minor phobias, not too demanding. As she settled in, he spotted how gifted she was. Later he suggested that she attend some of his lectures on criminal profiling. She shone, displaying instincts he had only seen a few times before in students. Soon she was assisting him at the local station, much to the frustration of Horton.

He knew she still lacked self-belief. She doubted every skill she possessed, and she did have some remarkable skills. She was bright, intelligent, knowledgeable, with an almost uncanny, no, unworldly ability to absorb and assimilate information. She would ask John's opinion on most cases she'd worked on, and he admired her grasp of them, joking several times about her supernatural abilities. Yet still she was unsure of herself, not trusting her judgement, he wondered if she ever would.

John wiped his hands with some antiseptic tissues that he always kept in his boot box and was on his way. The afternoon had almost gone, the evening was drawing in. Lights had appeared in farmhouses and cottages along the way. Most of the year was over, it seemed only weeks ago that they were seeing in the New Year. Yet here was autumn, creeping into the valley, leaves turning, winds turning chilly so that fires had to be lit earlier in the day. He really should try to spend more time with Ruth and Max. He hadn't finished work until late last Christmas Eve. Max was growing up, eight years old now. Soon he would lose the wonder of the season altogether. *Huh, not like me this, sentimental. Going to have to watch myself…* he thought.

The turning off the main road was sharp, the car handled well, and soon John was heading up the country lane and onward towards the house. For some reason, he could never bring himself to call it home. Ruth loved the house, but he… there was only one house he could call home, the one he grew up in, the one he shared with his parents and Grandmother, the one he had seen slip from his father's fingers as the old man had sunk into the abyss of alcoholism and bankruptcy… Russell Grove. It had taken a long time for him to acquire it, taking hard work and shrewd investments, but his patience had paid off when earlier this year he had managed to broker a deal with Ellis Franklin, one of the recent murder victims. John knew of course that Franklin wasn't the spotlessly clean individual that his cronies claimed he was… there was the matter of several thousand pounds that Franklin had asked him for to cover his 'expenses', for example. How was John to know that the money had been paid to a gang of thugs who would go on to intimidate the current owner, forcing her to sell?

The prospect of renovating his beloved former home had overridden his scruples in the end. Besides which, he'd had the foresight to conduct all his business with Franklin through a Limited Company that Ruth had set up during one of her 'speculative' periods. She'd spent some time and a considerable amount of money investing in the property market in a serious way but left him to sort out the mess she'd caused once she lost interest. She'd made some interesting purchases while the project had held her attention, though. She'd been rather adept at spotting 'little gems', but as soon as the novelty wore off, she would always move on to something else.

John had been forced to place the business in the hands of a Management service. When Franklin died it seemed wise not to muddy the waters by mentioning anything during the investigation. Besides, what had it got to do with a man wanting to regain his family inheritance, he asked himself? In the end he had discussed the matter with Horton, in a hypothetical way of course, and mentioning no names. He felt as though he'd covered his back, assuring himself that Horton wouldn't allow the matter to go any further, he was right. Now he looked forward to Christmas Day, when he could tell Ruth what he'd done, and see the look on her face as he showed her the keys to his new acquisition.

The track narrowed to the left, giving the first view of the house. The lights were on, Ruth would be there, preparing dinner for her and Max. Almost before the engine died, she was out of the door, auburn hair flying behind her, her loose bohemian-style clothes flowing. She threw herself into his arms taking his breath away. She clung to him as though she would never let go.

'Hey, watch it!' he said. It was always like this with Ruth, she was like an over excited puppy. He held her close; he still couldn't believe that this vibrant, beautiful woman was his wife.

'I didn't know you were coming back!' she shrieked delightedly. 'I didn't expect you!' she held him at arm's length and looked at him. He detected a look of hunger in her eyes, a look he knew well. He hadn't planned on staying, just long enough to pick up his things then leave for the mainland. He groaned, if he wasn't careful there would be another scene, and after the day he'd just had that was the last thing he wanted. Ruth saw the shadow cross his face. For a moment she faltered, then started to pull him towards the house,

'Come on,' she trilled, 'let's get inside, it's getting chilly,' her voice all light and tinkly. Sometimes he was enthralled by her, other times she annoyed him to death, this was the latter. In the last few hours his patience had been tested to the limit by Horton, now he was going to have to face the prospect of a tantrum from his wife when he told her he had to leave within the hour. John was not a person that liked to change his well-planned schedules. Having done so once today, he was not about to repeat the process, not even for his libidinous wife.

'Ruth,' he started, 'Ruth, I can't stay, I just came back for my things. I got caught up at the station, that's why I'm late,' he explained as she pulled him towards the house. He knew she wasn't listening; she had her own agenda and was deaf to his reasoning. Ever since she'd taken a unilateral decision that they should have another child, she'd taken every opportunity to get him into bed. She had charts based on some strange advice taken from the blasted Internet. Something about how women sometimes got pregnant straight away after coming off the pill. Ruth could see no reason for delaying.

More self-diagnosing, he thought distractedly.

As they reached the hallway, she steered him towards the stairs, but he held back.

'Ruth, you're not listening, I have to go, I have a meeting with Professor Parsons this evening, I'll be lucky to make it, without... you know.'

Ruth wound herself around him, in that way that he usually found irresistible. She stroked his hair, tickled his neck, slid her hand down his arm and onto his chest. She kissed him warmly; bit his ear, moves she used when they had all the time in the world for each other. John pulled away abruptly. He didn't mean to be cruel, but he was pushed for time, and she just wouldn't listen. Ruth staggered backwards, a look of surprise on her lovely face. He felt guilty as he saw her eyes fill with tears. She wrapped her arms around her slim body. She looked dejected, injured; an awful resignation pervaded her face.

'You... you don't have to be so, so cruel,' she stammered, 'a simple 'no' would have done.'

'I've been trying to tell you 'no', you just won't listen will you?' he sighed, 'Ruth, I've had a bad day, I need to leave within the next, he looked at his watch, 'twenty minutes, or I'll miss the meeting I've been trying to bring about for the last six months, and you want us to stop everything for a quick screw so you can get pregnant again. I'm sorry, but it's not going to happen, not tonight. Please, please try and understand, I don't have the time right now. Anyway, I'm really not in the mood.'

The tears fell then, he was sure she could cry to order. She had, after all studied drama for several years. She'd once boasted proudly of the time her tutor had asked her to cry on cue in an end of year production. Ruth had asked how many tears were needed and had produced the required number every time.

A war broke out within him. He hated seeing her like this, bereft that her hastily formed plan had come to nothing. Yet he was incensed that she could emotionally blackmail him the way she did. He'd allowed this situation to exist, and the sooner he set some clearer guidelines, the better.

'Well, if that's how you feel, maybe I should just leave you to get ready and leave…again,' she pouted. She needed to end this encounter in command position. She turned and walked away into the kitchen; her head held high. John was reminded of a film in which he had seen Vivian Leigh use the same tragic movements and sighed at his wife's theatricality.

As he made for the bedroom, he heard the front door opening and the sound of Max's voice as he was dropped off by his best friend's mother. There followed a stampede of feet as his son flew up the stairs to see him. John sighed again, more delays. He would have to spend at least a few minutes with Max. He comforted himself that at least he had had the foresight to pack his clothes along with the other essentials for his trip. Max bowled into the bedroom and threw himself into John's arms.

'Dad, Dad,' he bellowed, 'we did…we did about the Titanic today, the ship. It sank and we did all about it, why did it sink Dad, lots of people died, you didn't know that did you Dad?' Max took John's breath away with his excitement, 'and Mrs. Willets, she said, she said that lots of people froze in the water. What's it like Dad, freezing in the water? Can I have an iPad, Marcus has got one. Can I have one, please Dad, please?' The words tumbled out as John tried to disentangle himself from his son. Max was almost as good as Ruth for winding himself around someone's body. He sat Max down on the bed and looked at the boy whose face was glowing with health. He had never seen him look so well...his son was shooting up, eight years old already. Max panted, waiting expectantly for an answer to all his questions, looking adoringly at his father. John was momentarily torn, he didn't want to deflate Max's childish enthusiasm, but this evening's meeting was too important to cancel. As he began to speak, Ruth came into the room.

'Mom, Dad says I can have an iPad, can I... can I Mom?' he begged, Ruth agreed at once, much to John's annoyance.

'I said no such thing Max, and you know it!' he began.

'You did, you did!' cried his son, running to his mother and holding her around her waist.

'Don't be mean to him as well,' Ruth hissed, 'take your bad mood out on me not on him!' she held Max to her and rubbed his head, swaying in a comforting motion. She made *'there, there'* noises, which sent John into a meltdown. He took a deep breath trying to calm down.

'Ruth, I don't know how this started...actually I do know how it started, but I won't allow you to go on indulging Max the way you do. I didn't say he could have an iPad, in fact I didn't say a word, he made assumptions. I was going to suggest we discuss it as a possible Christmas present, but as usual you jumped the gun and gave in to him. Really, he's going to end up as spoilt as you are,' he tried to bite back the words, but they came flooding out. He was fed up with Max getting his own way, Ruth was always saying 'yes'. She gave in to the boy's every demand, it was about time he drew the line. Two pairs of steel blue eyes, identical in their shape, colour and ability to convey the most devastating hurt pierced him with their intensity. For a moment John was taken aback, was that a hint of hatred within them? He rose to his full height took a deep breath, reining in his anger.

'I'm going now,' he said, measuring every word. 'I'll be back in a few days; we'll talk about this then.' Both Ruth and Max knew what he was referring to, different in each case. They also knew by the tone of his voice, there would be no more discussion on the subject until he was good and ready. John picked up his case and left the bedroom. There was silence as he walked down the stairs and grabbed his jacket from the cloakroom. He closed the front door quietly, still fighting to calm down. He glanced up at the bedroom window as he placed his luggage in the boot. A strange feeling came over him as he got into the car and started the engine. He shook it off, he needed to prepare for his meeting; there was no time for any more distractions.

Driving down the lane he could see that the two of them had come out of the house and were standing on the porch. This was another of Ruth's little ploys to make him feel guilty. They were so alike, she and Max, united in their dejection.

It was the last time he would see either of them alive.

34

Lloyd Matthews sat in reception, his long legs jutting out in front of him. He'd gone over what he was going to say many times in the last few days, but no matter how he phrased it Alan Cooper came out looking bad. He sighed, nothing for it, he'd decided the previous evening. He had to tell them what he knew; he couldn't keep quiet any longer. The fire had been the last straw, standing on the pavement across the road looking at the burnt-out shell of the place he had regarded as his second home... Alan's shop. His gut told him it was deliberate. All that work, all that effort that they'd put into building up the business, everything that his mentor had taught him... all gone, even Alan himself. Lloyd missed him; it was like an ache somewhere in his chest.

Lloyd cleared his throat, emotion threatening to overcome his resolve to do what he could to redress events of the last few weeks. He didn't like police stations; he didn't like them at all. Not because he'd done anything wrong, it was just that he had encountered far too many police officers had jumped to unfair conclusions about him and his friends. He avoided them like the plague. He remembered his first car, a beaten-up Clio. Red it was, though when he bought it there were massive areas of rust around the sills and the wheel arches. He rubbed them down, filled holes, smoothed the bodywork, sprayed and polished his baby with a love he had never known for an inanimate object before. He was so proud of it he felt he would burst. During the first three months of driving his precious baby to and from Alan Cooper's shop, he had been stopped no less than eighteen times by a couple of keen young officers. They seemed determined to 'get him' for some imagined infringement of the Highway Code, if possible, for all of them. They failed...and his driver's licence remained clean as a whistle.

This developed into a battle of wits between him and 'them' to see if they could catch him out. They lay in wait for him, so that sometimes, out of pure devilment, he would take the longer route, smiling to himself when he pictured their disappointment. Sometimes he would see them later in the morning hanging around outside the shop. He'd chuckle, feeling as though he had got one over on them again. No, he had only known one decent copper in his life, and they had lost touch some years ago, shame though.

He checked his watch...11.45, his appointment was for 11.30. Five more minutes, he decided, and he would walk, sod the lot of them. A noise made him look round as Porter opened the reinforced door. At least it wasn't one of his former persecutors.

'Mr. Matthews?' asked the man, opening the door wider, 'can you come through please?'

Porter looked him up and down as Lloyd gathered himself together and rose to his full height. He wasn't in the habit of jumping to conclusions, but he could imagine this young man inflicting some serious harm if the need presented itself.

'Whas' your name please?' asked Lloyd, needing to establish a degree of control. He stood stock still, determined not to move until he had an answer. Porter smiled, he already liked the lad, recognising his need to be on equal footing.

'Porter, my name's DI Porter, thank you for coming, shall we go through?' he indicated the doorway. Lloyd stared at the open door, momentarily weighing up whether he should enter the innards of the beast known as *'the station'.*

'Hmmh!' he grunted, adopting an exaggerated swagger as he approached Porter. They made their way in silence, Porter stopping only to check that the room was prepared. Lloyd half smiled, sounds like they going to operate, he thought. A tall gawky woman came out from the side office and confirmed that everything was ready.

'Miss Mason!' Lloyd was taken aback, as the years fell away, his swagger vanished, and he dropped his affected way of talking. He beamed at DS Mason as though she was a long-lost relative.

'Lloyd?' she spluttered, 'what on earth…how are you?'

Porter watched, taken aback by the warmth of their exchange. They couldn't have been further apart on any scale. He cleared his throat as if to remind them that he was waiting.

'S… sorry Sir,' stammered Mason, stepping back, 'I… we… Lloyd was in my Sunday school class, he helped out with Scouts too,' she explained with a look of pride that Porter recognised as almost maternal.

'Yeah, an' Miss Mason, she put me onto computers,' Lloyd gushed, 'she really helped me… she did.'

Porter looked from one to the other, there was a real connection between them, one that took him seconds to exploit.

'I was about to suggest that DS Mason sit in with us, as a matter of fact,' he lied, seizing on the opportunity to make the lad feel at ease. Mason beamed, as Porter led the way to the interview room, he'd never seen this side of her. She and Lloyd chatted for a few minutes before he managed to call them to order. Their reunion would have to wait.

'Okay, so what was it that you wanted to talk about Lloyd?' he asked gently once they were settled, not wanting to lose the ground he had gained.

'Well, ok, so you know that Alan, right, you know his shop got burnt down, right, well I got to thinkin', there had to be a reason din't there?' Lloyd was straight into what he'd come to say. He'd thought this out, and he wanted to get it right, not for the coppers, but for Alan, for Alan's memory.

'It's like, well, I don' think it was no coincidence like. I think the fire was started for a reason,' he went on, then sat back as though he'd finished. Porter sighed, if this was all he had come to say, what a waste of time.

'We've looked into this Lloyd,' Mason said, 'we came to the same conclusion. There was a reason the shop was burnt out, we have to place it all in context now, and find out the motive.' Lloyd was responding to her, so Porter stayed quiet.

'Well, Miss Mason, err, sorry, I mean...' he faltered not remembering her police title. She smiled and placed her hand on his arm.

'Don't worry about titles Lloyd, I'm Miss Mason and always will be,' she said, patting his arm in encouragement. Lloyd smiled back at her and relaxed a little, gathering his thoughts. He took a deep breath and started again.

'You said that you need to place it all in contex' well, I think I know why they done it,' he paused, looking at Porter then back at Mason. 'I think they wanted to get rid of evidence. Alan, he was on them computers an awful lot jus' before, jus' before he done that bloke in. I mean more than usual, like. He was on them all the time I was there, and I was there almost all the time. An' when I used to walk into the room, the room where the computers were, he would shut down and like, be like I used to be at school when I was playin' on some game and the teacher walked in, you know?' he was babbling, almost incoherent as he reached the end of his tirade.

Porter sat down at the table; the lad had obviously given the situation a lot of thought. He could feel the familiar pull in his stomach that almost always told him that they were getting somewhere.

'Go on Lloyd,' urged Mason, 'I think you may be onto something here.' Porter smiled to himself, even if Lloyd gave them a load of hogwash, she would praise him, such was the bond between them.

'Well the afternoon that Alan was taken into, into, well when your lot came an' fetched him, I was in the back of the shop, with my mate. I heard what was goin' on, and then, then 'e come into the room like, and 'e gimme this note...' he faltered, realising the enormity of what he was about to say. Porter sat as still as he could, he was itching to know where this was going, but knew when to keep quiet. Mason patted Lloyd's arm again, as though she was calming a skittish horse. Lloyd looked at her and seemed to draw strength from her smile.

'You got to understand, Alan, 'e was good to me, 'e gave me a job, 'e trusted me. 'e said to me, in the note, 'e said 'Take my laptop, an' look after it, and if anything happens to me, you'll know when the time is right. Show it to someone, it'll tell them everything they need to know,' an' 'e was good to me, so that's what I'm doin' now like. I owe 'im, Miss Mason, I owe 'im.'

Lloyd slumped back in his chair; he was all but breaking down. He shook his head as he reached down and picked up his bag, opened it and extracted Alan Cooper's laptop.

35

Horton fumed. It was difficult to take the credit for something when everyone knew that you weren't there when it happened. He paced the living room floor, his favourite programme, flickering in the background. His attention barely registered the well-known characters that he revered and sought to model his career on. An old detective series, a box set that his sister had bought him the Christmas before last. He'd watched it over and over, trying to discover how his hero managed to work out 'who dunnit', episode after episode. He didn't seem to appreciate that this was a fictional force, the methods used almost archaic, or that he hero-worshipped a man bought to life when the director shouted 'action' and who effectively died moments later when he called 'cut'.

Horton was looking for answers, not only to the cases over which he now presided, but to questions about himself. He knew that the officers in his team looked at him with a little more scorn and treated him with a little less respect every day. They knew he couldn't cut it, even before he acknowledged it. What they thought of him hurt more than he would allow himself to admit.

…*Porter*, he thought, his temper building as he made each sweep of the well-worn, shabby carpet. *He was the problem, he made it look so easy. Swanning in with Cooper's laptop, showing off to the team, parading THAT lad, patting him on the back, smiling at Mason as she stood looking gormless as ever…* he sat down suddenly, making his cat, Percy, mewl in surprise.

'Sorry Perce,' he mumbled, the anger leaving him as quickly as it had appeared. He picked the cat up and stroked him. This creature was the only one he had any feelings left for.

'Come on, let's get some dinner, shall we?' the cat purred, snuggling his head into the crook of Horton's arm. Emotion overtook him, and he hugged the cat so tightly that it started to struggle, then hiss. With a sudden twist, it jumped from Horton's arms shaking its body free of the unwanted contact. Horton watched as the cat strolled, tail held high, into the kitchen without looking round. Within seconds it had squeezed through the cat flap into the night.

Horton shook his head, he really did cut a sad figure didn't he, if the highlight of the evening was that the cat was pissed off at him. Oh, and the next episode of a dated detective series. Things couldn't get much worse. He sighed as he examined the contents of the fridge, it was virtually empty, some cheese, a bit of leftover pasta, two slices of ham...ah well, he'd have to make do with that, couldn't be bothered to go to the corner shop. He chopped the ham and placed it on the pasta, grated the cheese on top and deposited the result in the microwave. He retraced his steps and prepared the front room, curtains shut, TV at just the right angle, footstool positioned for maximum comfort.

The knock on the back door was just a light tap. Horton walked towards it, almost tripping over Percy who had decided not to miss his supper after all. He'd re-entered the kitchen and jumped up onto the counter. Horton moved the faded curtain that covered the pane of glass in the back door, he could see nothing, the security light wasn't working. He dropped the curtain and he went back to the counter. The knock came again, this time more forcefully. Horton picked up the old cricket bat he kept by the larder door, calling out, his stomach turning slightly.

He knew that the neighbours on one side were away but wasn't sure about the others. His phone was in the front room, he backed away keeping the door in his eye line. With the kitchen light on he knew that whoever it was would be able to see everything.

There was silence, he let out a breath that he didn't know he was holding... maybe it was kids. He lowered the bat, he would get his phone, call the station, and get a car to do a circuit of his street. He'd tell them there had been a disturbance. The phone was on the coffee table, he reached out and started to dial. There was a sound of glass breaking, the thud of approaching footsteps. Horton turned, dropping the phone in surprise, making towards the front door. Before he could open it, he was in a headlock. He fell, reaching for support before feeling the sting in his neck. Within seconds he lost consciousness, his last thought was what Percy would do for his supper.

36

Almost total darkness, the only relief a faint glimmer under the door, a gap through which a howling draught blew. Horton was colder than he had been in a very long time. As his vision adjusted, he could just about make out his surroundings. He lay on a filthy mattress, his hands tied, he could just about see the orange cord. He moved his legs and heard what sounded like a chain. His ankles were shackled in manacles, which were fastened to an iron ring in the wall a short distance away. It took him a while to clear his head of the buzzing noise. He felt sick and thirsty, his head pounding, like the legacy of a bottle of whiskey. A door slammed, the sound echoing in the silence.

'Hello,' he called, 'hello, please…' he stopped… if he attracted attention, he might make his kidnapper angry; who knew what would happen then? On the other hand, whoever had brought him here would hardly forget about him, even if he kept quiet. As his head started to clear, anger welled up. To be in this situation… how dare anyone subject him to this? He would be the laughing stock of the station. Horton tried to pull his hands apart, then brought them up towards his mouth. He could try and loosen the cord with his teeth, but the end of it was tied around the manacles, restricting his movements. He tried shouting again…no response. He heard a car starting, whoever had bought him here was leaving. His stomach lurched once more. He had read of kidnapping cases when the victim had been left to die, starving to death, the memory did nothing to assuage his fear.

It seemed like hours before he could distinguish anything else in the room. During that time he imagined all kinds of scenarios, none of them ended well, he was scaring himself half to death in the process. He dithered with cold, his stomach growling despite his predicament. As the room grew lighter Horton could make out pieces of old machinery at the far end of his prison. They were rusty with age, partially covered with sacking. Piles of long-discarded tools lay scattered on the floor. He examined his restraints, there was no way he could free himself.

Two bottles of water and a pack of sandwiches lay just within his reach. His first instinct was that he should resist the urge to eat them. But he'd eaten nothing since lunch the previous day, and his growling stomach was becoming more insistent. At least he was being offered sustenance wasn't he, he tried to console himself. Maybe it was an indication of their intentions? It wasn't as though anyone would bother feeding him if they meant to kill him, was it? He was already salivating at the thought of the food lying nearby, who knew if it would be taken away, leaving him to starve?

Horton lay down and rolled onto his side. He reached over and picked up one of the bottles. He struggled to sit up, the exertion had made him out of breath, and he felt dizzy. It took a few minutes before he placed the bottle between his knees. It had a flip top with a thin piece of plastic sealing it. His hands were shaking, but eventually he managed to open it and raise it to his mouth, the cord restricting his movements. As he angled the bottle to drink it fell from his grasp and he could feel the water seeping into his trousers. He tried to grab it, hoping to save what he could, but it had rolled away. Horton was overwhelmed by his emotions as he slumped back onto the mattress. He couldn't tell if it was as a result of his current failure or a culmination of the last few weeks. Either way great sobs of frustration escaped as he fought to gain control.

The second bottle still stood by the mattress. Horton took a deep breath, *I can do this,* he told himself. He repeated the process, but this time managed to hold on to it. He took long gulps of water, then cursed himself for drinking too much. *I should have rationed it*, he thought.

He placed the bottle safely at the furthest point he could reach, then picked up the sandwiches, tearing the plastic cover open with his teeth. He almost dropped the packet on the floor, as he sniffed at the contents. Cheese and pickle, he hated cheese and pickle. Better than nothing though. He took one of the sandwiches and started eating, forcing the first few mouthfuls past the knot of fear that had formed in his throat. It was only then that it occurred to him that the food might be drugged, or even poisoned. He stopped chewing, but for some reason didn't spit it out. Either his captor was going to kill him, or he was going to allow him to live, he reasoned. If he was going to be killed there was nothing Horton could do about it. Whether he got shot, strangled or was poisoned, if he was going to die, he was going to die and that was it. Horton shrugged resignedly, at least he wouldn't die hungry, he started to laugh, and once he started, he couldn't stop. He tried holding his breath as hysteria gave way to panic, crying with frustration mingled with fear greater than he had ever known. The severity of his position had finally hit him. He'd read many reports during the past weeks, along with pictures of victims and suspects alike. Bodies tortured, limbs mangled, the memory was choking him as much as the food. He started to heave, then threw up on the floor, covering the other sandwich and the bottle of water in vomit.

He had to calm down, there was a slim chance that he could be released after all this was over. But would he, or was he kidding himself?

37

Earlier, Porter paced up and down the corridor. He'd been waiting for hours for news on the laptop. The officers allocated to deal with it, although way ahead of most at the station, were having problems. The station didn't have a dedicated tech department, something to do with restricted budgets. It seemed ironic that Alan Cooper himself had been their go-to expert in retrieving data. Lloyd remained at the station impressing those present with his knowledge. He introduced the team to various short-cuts that he'd learned from his mentor.

'I really need to go an' get my books,' he pleaded at one point far into their session. 'There's somethin' I'm missing.' Mason, who had been included in the group, patted his arm.

'I think you've done enough for one day Lloyd. Could you come back tomorrow maybe?' Lloyd agreed immediately, he'd do anything he could to help he told her as she stood and left the room to speak to Porter.

'We're into the device, but every one of these files is password protected. Lloyd has some ideas of how to get in, but it's taking time. We've been working as fast as we can, but the lad needs to rest... it's been a long day.' She spoke in a way that brooked no argument. Porter felt he had no option. It was a case of waiting. He needed any information that was on the laptop, but his patience was wearing thin. He made his way to the canteen, something to eat. He was greeted by Dorothy, closing the hatch.

'Sorry love,' she said, 'you can get a coffee from the machine if you like.' Porter wrinkled his nose. He hated vending machine drinks of any description and decided on a soft drink instead. He sat, orange fizz in hand, and mulled over the events of the day. Mason had been a revelation, who knew that she had a life outside the station. The rapport she had with Lloyd was amazing. If she hadn't calmed the lad down, they wouldn't be as far on as this. She'd managed to dispel his fears and given him enough confidence to sit with police officers and teach them a thing or two.

What with that and Horton's display of histrionics that morning, storming out of the station when he found out about Lloyd's revelation…it had been quite a day all round. Porter tried to phone Horton to let him know what was going on, but there was no reply. Horton must be on one of his famous sulks. It wasn't like him to miss an opportunity to take over any new moves in a case. His sudden absence was out of character.

Anyway, the atmosphere felt more relaxed without Horton there. He was a drain on everyone's energy, questioning everything they did, despite Chetwynd's intervention. Porter had always had him down as slow on the uptake, but no one could afford to go that slowly. Horton was holding back the investigation, and there was the risk that the body count could increase as a result. Porter felt uneasy about his lack of contact though. He checked his watch, 9.16, was it too late to phone Horton again? He decided it was.

'Be careful what you wish for, I suppose,' he murmured as he stood up and stretched his aching limbs. It'd been a long day, and he hated waiting around. 'Home,' he decided, 'I need some sleep.'

He reached reception at the same time as Lloyd. The youngster braced himself against the chill of the evening air as he opened the outer door. Porter called a greeting.

'All right Mr. Porter?' he answered, nodding to Porter in a far friendlier way than his initial contact.

'I'm well, thank you Lloyd, thank you for all your hard work today and for staying so late. Do you need a lift anywhere?' He didn't know if the boy had a car and didn't like the idea of driving off and leaving him to his own devices.

'You goin' anywhere near Jasmine Road?' Lloyd asked. Porter wasn't, but knew that Horton lived a few streets away, and his gut feeling was to check out his boss's house, exactly why he didn't know.

'Come on, I'll give you a lift,' he offered, and Lloyd fell into step, shortening his loping gait to match that of the shorter man.

If my Nan could see me now, he thought, *walkin' to a police officer's car without bein' suspected of doing anythin' wrong, and me spendin' all that time helpin' the police and runnin' rings around them*...thought Lloyd chuckling to himself. In his eyes it didn't get much better. They were silent on the ride, Porter felt it would be overkill to praise Lloyd any further, in case he felt that he was being patronised. Mason would've known what to say, but the lad was a virtual stranger, no matter how helpful he had been. It started to rain, and the steady sweep of the window screen wipers beat a hypnotic tattoo within the warmth of the car. Porter realised that Lloyd had fallen asleep. He manoeuvred his way through a set of road works and drove through the town. A diversion sign had cordoned off a side road, and Porter had to make a 'U' turn to take the alternative route; it would take him past Horton's house. Lloyd was snoring softly, totally relaxed. Porter decided to nip in and see if his gaffer was all right, hopefully before the lad woke up.

All the lights were off at Horton's house. Porter knew how frugal his boss was; he never paid for a drink at the pub and never bought the cakes at a celebration. In fact, the others in the team would joke about the pet moths in his wallet. Porter also knew that his boss was a bit of a night owl, watching TV until the early hours. This was comparatively early for him to have gone to bed. Porter felt the familiar prickle of suspicion starting in his gut and spreading throughout his body. It took seconds to assess the situation. The open front door, not obvious from the pavement, the umbrella-stand lying flat on the floor, the hall rug in a heap, all screamed recent struggle. Porter called out, no answer. A ginger cat, as big as a terrier rounded the corner of the living room door, running towards him in eager anticipation. Porter retraced his steps, contaminating the scene would not be a good idea. He reached the car in seconds and called the station. Lloyd woke to find blue lights all around him, he thought for a moment that they were intended for him, but soon relaxed and watched the proceedings from his grandstand seat.

38

Graham woke early, the central heating hadn't kicked in and he was shivering slightly as he turned over. Ellie hadn't come to bed and he sighed as he patted her pillow. He rose quickly pulling on a pair of sweatpants and a tee shirt. They'd both been so busy lately that there hadn't been time to talk things through, and although they were civil, Ellie remained distant, cold almost.

Making his way to the bathroom, he wondered idly if they would ever get back to normal, but what was normal? They hadn't had 'normal' since this case started. Ellie was getting in deeper and deeper and he worried about her, whilst at the same time being inordinately proud of her. He told her as much during a brief conversation over breakfast the previous morning, an oasis in their busy schedules.

'I feel the same about what you do,' she said. 'You take the wreckage of a human body and piece it back together. You present your conclusions, most of which are spot on; I don't know how you do it.' His work awed her, fascinated her, and if she were a little less squeamish might have drawn her down a similar path. But, for all her dealings with afflicted personalities, she remained averse to the sight of blood, and nothing she had tried had helped her to overcome it.

Graham washed his hands and caught his reflection in the mirror, he looked tired, and with good cause. The excess of adrenaline that they had lived with over the last few months had left them wrung out in the aftermath. For himself he wasn't so worried, he was used to working under those conditions. When he had a call in the middle of the night to go to a crime scene, his conditioning sent him from zero to full pelt in less time than it took to dress and get in the car. For Ellie, well, he believed that was a different matter. She wasn't used to the immediacy of it all.

He wondered if she was stronger than she appeared sometimes, if she didn't resent his concern about her overdoing it. He knew that he had to curb his concern if she was to have any chance of gaining confidence. She didn't need his constant questions about how she was doing. His main worry, though, was the fact that he'd been unable to find an opportunity to talk about the night she had observed his internet 'chat'. He needed to explain, to convince her that it really wasn't anything at all, that she had no need to worry. But the opportunity hadn't come up, and although they were managing to keep things civil, he could tell that something still wasn't right.

The kitchen was cold when he entered. Ellie lay on the couch with her feet on the floor, her head on a cushion. She was still holding her pen, sheets of paper scattered around. Graham touched her arm and she jumped. She was freezing.

'Sorry,' he said, moving around the couch, 'I didn't mean to startle you.'

Ellie rubbed her eyes, her breathing ragged. She reached for her sweater, shivering as he sat by her side. In one swift movement she was up, weaving unsteadily towards the island unit. She seemed to switch to auto-pilot. Coffee in the machine, mugs, milk, and sugar, hardly aware of what she did. Graham knew she was trying to avoid him, again. He also knew that the hug he'd planned wouldn't be welcome. She was watching him, just the odd glance now and then, but none the less watching him. Then he knew. She'd had the dream again, the one he dreaded her having, the one that would upset her for at least a few days. He didn't have to ask...he could sense it.

The dreams started at the same time she found out about his affair, just after Josie, when Ellie was...when he made the mistake that haunted him. He'd tried to tell her that it was all in the past. That sleeping with one of his students was something he'd regret for the rest of his life. He knew he didn't deserve her forgiveness, he hoped he could gain her understanding. She seemed to accept that they could put the whole thing behind them. Yet now and again, when she was under stress, she would have the nightmare again, Graham knew that there was nothing he could do. No amount of cajoling would bring Ellie out of her mood until she was ready. There was no point in asking what was wrong, he already knew. He just had to give her time. At least that's what usually happened, this time he wasn't so sure. He picked up some of the papers and started to read them. Ellie's looping writing scrawled over the pages. She re-joined him on the couch; he noticed that she sat at the opposite end.

'Just thoughts,' she answered to his unspoken questions, indicating the papers still in his hand. 'I must get them into order though; I'm meeting John at the office this afternoon; we're having a catch-up.' She leaned forward and took the papers from him, shuffling them together.

'Ellie,' he started, his voice low, concerned, 'don't push yourself too hard sweetheart.'

'Too hard Graham, too hard?' She rounded on him. 'People are dying Graham, people are dying,' she started to cry. He reached over to comfort her, but she stood up, grabbed her papers, and stumbled out of the kitchen towards the stairs. Graham sat back sighing, he felt exhausted. To follow her would precipitate another argument, she was best left alone. For what seemed like the millionth time he wished he could turn back the clock, and this time make different choices.

He needed to leave soon, the thought of the day's busy schedule bringing him back to the present. Ellie wasn't the only one who was in demand.

39

Their meeting was arranged for 2.30pm. Ellie had some time to sort out her paperwork. She shook her head as she tried to sort through the scrappy pieces of paper. The notes she'd made wouldn't impress anyone, especially John Prothero. She knew he would be driven to despair. She hated it when he read her notes, which he always insisted on doing. On their first case together, he had squinted and sighed, turning the papers this way and that. His opinion of her untidy presentation had been obvious.

'Do you usually use an ink-infused spider to write your notes Ellie? I do hope you arranged a suitable funeral for the poor thing?' he tutted, shaking his head at her scrawl. Ellie had laughed at the time but couldn't shake off the feeling of hurt at the criticism in his voice. Since then she'd made sure that her notes were at least legible.

Graham had woken her at 6.30, it was now 8.15. He'd left twenty minutes ago without trying to talk to her. Still, she told herself determinedly, he knew better than to attempt to appease her when she...was she so stubborn, that she couldn't even bring herself to call out to him as he left? They really did have to talk. But for now, she needed to sort out the mess that was her presentation before she met with John.

Ellie thought about their work together as she showered and dressed. She'd been delighted when he recommended her as his successor... delighted, though a little scared. In the time she'd known John she'd grown to admire his expertise. She'd learned a lot from the way he worked. When he was offered his current position and suggested her as his replacement, it had taken Ellie's breath away. She had never realised that he held her in such high esteem. Unfortunately, that euphoria didn't last long, and she crashed back down into reality as time after time Horton second-guessed her judgement. John had given her lecture after lecture on making sure that she put her point across forcefully, assuring her that eventually she would be accepted. But how could she when the problem lay with the boss of the very team she was supposed to be working with? Horton ran to John for his opinion at every opportunity. John seemed to make things worse. He would drop in whenever he was called on, and the whole circle would go around and round again. It had to be broken but telling John to 'butt out' of her job so that she could get on with it...well that wasn't a conversation she could imagine having any time soon.

She was drying her hair when the thought struck her. In consulting with John today, wasn't she also perpetuating the circle? Shouldn't she just tell him that she didn't need his help, that she had confidence in her own abilities and could work things through without running to him every five minutes? Wasn't she as bad as Horton? The thought shook her. While she continued to rely on John to back her up, she would never be able to function independently. At the same time tolerating Horton's attitude towards her would never establish the respect of the rest of the team. She acknowledged that she needed help with the current case, it was too big for her to handle alone. Ellie stared at her reflection, brush poised mid-air. To admit that she felt out of her depth would undermine her fragile position. To walk away from John's offer of help might mean she would miss something, which could mean that there could be more victims. But to carry on like this would mean that she might never be ready to work on her own. Conflicted though she felt, there was an unshakable feeling that told her she could do this. She could flourish in her chosen field. Now might not be the time to take that stand, but that was what she had to do eventually. It was a conversation that she had had with herself many times over the last few months. Today there was a lot more clarity, and she began to wonder if the meeting set for this afternoon was necessary at all.

Right now, she had a few hours to sort out the paperwork. They were beginning to take on some semblance of order as she typed them up. John would expect no less. Until she was able to launch her campaign to take charge in her new role, she still wanted to make an efficient presentation. When at last she was satisfied with the results, she packed them into her briefcase.

Her phone pinged, a text from Graham.

'Having coffee, nice group! Sorry about this morning. Love you,
xxx'

Ellie read the text a second time and started typing a
reply. She stopped. What was he sorry about? She knew he
was aware of her nightmare, was he sorry for that, she
wondered? Now was not the time to go rehashing old
hurts, and yet she couldn't seem to shake them off.

'Never known you to be phased by a class, love you too x' she
typed.

Ellie hated the phrase, *'Love you too,'* or *'Love you as well!'*
she saw it as an obligation when someone said, *'I love you',*
first. It almost always left the recipient in a position of
having to say it back. She always felt that not saying it
might raise a doubt as to whether the love was returned.
She shook her head, as if she didn't have enough to worry
about. Did she have to crowd out her mind with trivia?
She changed into her 'uniform', black blazer, cream blouse
and black trousers, punctuated with a bright patterned
scarf. John always observed the ritual of formal dress when
working. Just time for a coffee and something to eat, her
phone pinged again. She picked it up, expecting Graham
to continue their conversation, it was John.

'Change of plan, meet at mine, you know where key is. 1pm. DS
Mason joining us, explain later. John'

Ellie checked her watch, 12.25. How like John to expect
everyone to change their plans at the last minute. She typed
a brief *'OK'*, gathered her things and headed out to the car.

The journey to John's home wouldn't take long. She
could make herself a quick coffee there before he arrived.
That guy certainly knew how to make people jump; she'd
give him that. John was as precise about times as he was
about everything else, she thought, her admiration tinged
with a little jealousy at the reputation he'd built up. She

wondered if she would ever gain that level of respect from her peers. DS Mason was a bit of a curve ball though. Ellie wondered why she needed to be in on this meeting, and how on earth had John persuaded her to join them? She shrugged, who knew how John got most things done. He only had to click his fingers and the whole station responded. Perhaps this was just another sign that she was jealous. Ellie threw her things into the car and started down the drive.

The radio was playing her favourite piece of music '*Scheherazade*', as always it gave her goose bumps. She drove down the main road, and through the stunning countryside, slowing down as she reached the side-track which led to her sister's home. A van was parked by the side of the turning. Ellie had to swing out wide to get around it, there was no one in the driver's seat. Ellie wondered if it had been stolen or abandoned...not her problem. She had the impending meeting on her mind, and drove along the newly resurfaced track, the smooth ride was a complete contrast to the pot-holed approach to her own home. The last bend had always caught her out though, and she slowed to a crawl as she manoeuvred it...what she saw took her by surprise.

Ruth's car was parked at the side of the house. Ellie knew that she and Max were due to fly to the States that morning. A flare of annoyance caught her, if she and John were going to have a serious meeting, they didn't need constant interruptions from Ruth. She had the habit of flitting in and out to make sure they had enough coffee, or could she make them both something to eat, just to keep their strength up? Ellie immediately chastised herself. Perhaps Ruth was unwell, or something could have happened to Max. Without even speaking to her sister, she'd jumped to conclusions, something she wouldn't tolerate in others. A sense of guilt flowed like water into a bath. She'd experienced the emotion so often it was like an old friend. She had to stop taking herself so seriously. She really must make that appointment to see Odelia Mathers as soon as possible. Ellie parked the car and made her way to the front door, she hesitated, unsure of what to do. An overwhelming feeling of urgency surged through her, she needed to see Ruth, something was wrong.

'To hell with it,' she thought, as she knocked loudly, waiting for what felt like an eternity. She heard footsteps in the hallway, the door opened a crack and Ruth, her eyes red from crying, peeped out. As soon as she saw Ellie, she flung it open, and threw herself into her sister's arms.

40

Ruth appeared to be in full Drama-Queen mode. *She's had enough practice,* thought Ellie, and it took her several attempts to get her sister to talk coherently. Eventually she gave up and sat Ruth down with a box of tissues, while she made her way to the kitchen, intent on making coffee. She waited patiently as she listened to gut-churning bouts of nose blowing, then waited for the hiccups to subside before asking yet again what the hell was going on. John would be here soon, and Ruth being in this state didn't bode well for their meeting. Ruth seemed inconsolable, but Ellie knew that looks could be deceiving. She was used to the histrionics that often-accompanied Ruth's crisis points... the day she'd accidentally left her homework at school, the day she'd been overlooked as Head Girl, the day she was told that she had failed her first exams at College. They were all *'end of the world'* situations to Ruth.

Ellie managed to establish that Max was upstairs on his X-box, seemingly oblivious to his mother's distress, that was one thing off her mind. Ruth shredded yet another tissue, and its remnants fell like snow as she suddenly leaped up and strode to the window.

'Ellie,' she began, her voice shaking, her breath ragged, 'Ellie...I've...I've f-found something out...you need to know...you need to know Ellie,' she turned around, shaking with distress. Ellie watched her; it began to dawn on her that this was no act; her sister was really fighting to control herself.

I should ring John, she thought reaching for her phone to postpone the meeting, *warn him...what the hell?* Someone was banging on the front door with so much force that it rattled the windows. No one needed to bang that hard to attract attention. Ruth walked towards the hallway, disappearing through the door before Ellie could think to call her back. Something wasn't right...something was screaming inside Ellie's head to stop her. Ellie could hear Ruth's heels echoing on the hall tiles. The knocking continued as Max called from the landing.

Some force propelled Ellie upwards as she heard a man shouting, demanding to see someone...Marie...Maria...a bang...screaming...Max called out...another bang, followed by two more. She was halfway to the door when she regretted her impulse to get out into the hall. By then it was too late. Momentum carried her along as she twisted, trying to dodge back into the lounge, but instead she stepped into the path of the next bullet. Her head snapped around, and she saw a figure standing in the doorway. Despite the shadow cast by the surrounding trees, the figure seemed to be outlined in a bright light, a similar light to the one she had seen around Alan Cooper. Ellie's head ached, *the pressure, too much pressure* she thought, *I can't hold on to it all.* Images flooded through her brain, memories that didn't belong to her. She fell, her vision clouded, her consciousness evaporating like a dream just after waking. She kept her eyes on the figure, trying to imprint every detail on her memory.

It would be important, she thought...later...later when she and Ruth told the police what had happened. She felt a sharp pain in her side followed by...nothing.

41

John was late, he disliked being late, but it couldn't be helped, he told himself as he drove towards the house. He'd called in at the station to collect DS Mason when the news broke that Alan Cooper's death had nothing to do with his wounds. It was caused by a massive dose of morphine administered through his IV line. The perpetrator hadn't bothered to disguise their actions, discarding the syringe in a nearby rubbish bin; there were no fingerprints. With this new development, and the fact that Horton was missing, John felt compelled to offer his help...again. He couldn't leave Ellie with total responsibility.

They'd travelled in silence. John had given up trying to talk to DS Mason. How that woman had advanced to the position she was in was anybody's guess, she was practically mono syllabic. Still, she was right up to date with the current case and had a photographic memory to boot. It was always good to have a counterpoint for discussions, and of course a witness to what had been said, or done. Mason shuffled some papers, overwhelmed that she had been asked to sit in on this meeting. She was uncomfortable at the prospect of being away from the station. She sighed repeatedly, terrified that she might be asked for her opinion on the case. She wished Porter had been asked, anyone else but her.

John almost forgot she was there as he thought about the meeting. Ellie was proving to be a gifted profiler. He'd known from the start that she had the correct instincts. His faith in her was beginning to pay off. If only he could smooth her path with the others, his investment in her could start to pay off. Her clashes with Horton had escalated to the point of becoming embarrassing. Horton felt that John had 'dropped them in it' by taking on his new post, but he had been angling for a chance like this for so long that nothing would stop him accepting it. He'd have so much clout at last, a chance to make real changes. Besides, it felt like his reward for the hard work and dedication, in what was often a thankless job.

How many cases had he taken over, mid-investigation? He would have to catch up, acquaint himself with all the facts, come up with a profile, and hand it back to officers who at best were sceptical about newcomers. How many times had he endured their complaints when they realised that they had to go back to basics and cover 'old ground'? Then he'd have to defend his findings, suggest that this was a different perspective, when really you had all but nailed it and were waiting for them to catch up. Even when they found out you were right; they would never give you any credit.

Give Ellie her due though, this was a difficult case. The fact that she'd made as much progress as she had didn't surprise him at all. Perhaps he should have stayed behind and helped from the beginning? He needed to sort this sorry bunch of... John realised that he was gripping the steering wheel too tightly, and tried to relax, taking a few deep breaths. Maybe he could infuse enough confidence into Ellie this afternoon for her to take charge and do what he knew she had a gift for. He didn't mind helping her; he just couldn't keep responding to Horton's demands as well as bottle-feeding his protégé at the same time. He had his own work to focus on.

He felt calmer now, and the beauty of the autumn afternoon struck him momentarily as he approached the side road leading to his home. He saw the van at the mouth of the turning, he slammed on the brakes as the driver pulled out suddenly, directly into his path.

'What the f...!!' the engine stalled. Mason screamed and dropped a file, scattering the papers on the floor. The van sped off, leaving John watching as it disappeared into the distance. John took several deep breaths, restarted the car and turned onto the drive. Ruth's car, what the hell was she doing here? Ellie's was parked next to it...the front door open. A dreadful, sickening feeling grew slowly in the pit of his stomach. Ruth had been due to fly out early this morning, something was wrong. She wasn't meant...and if she was here, where was Max?

'Stay here,' he ordered, Mason nodded. John switched off the ignition, his heart racing. He tried to slow down his movements, to think of answers. He closed the door, walked to the house and disappeared inside. Within minutes he staggered out, falling to his knees on the porch.

Mason jumped out of the car and ran to his side. 'What...?'

John wailed, holding his head. 'Call...call someone...the station...' he screamed. Mason grabbed her phone and started dialing. She walked to the door, looked inside, cancelled the call and re-dialed 999. John managed to stand and follow her. Mason grabbed him and forced him around.

'Mr. Prothero…John, John, you need to come with me,' she said using all her strength to guide him away from the scene.

In those few moments John came to know the effectiveness of the officer he had so recently dismissed as incompetent.

42

He sat on the step at the back of the ambulance which was parked less than a hundred yards from the front door, a blanket around his shoulders. Someone had restrained him from entering the crime scene, for that was what his house had become. That someone was DS Mason. With strength of mind and a command of the situation that no one, least of all Mason knew she possessed, she forced him to stay outside until the police arrived. She'd executed a textbook handling of the situation and was now briefing DI Porter. John could see what was going on, he knew the drill. Images flashed across his mind, on the floor two bodies, adults. On the landing a smaller figure. He could only assume that Ruth and Max were home when Ellie arrived. It seemed like hours until Porter walked towards him. The look on the detective's face said it all… John howled like a wounded animal, shaking his head in disbelief.

'No, no, no, it can't be it's not them. They're not supposed to be here…they weren't…' he cried as Porter took hold of his shoulders. 'They weren't supposed to be here…they were due…to…this isn't how it's…'

'John, John, please, please, look at me John,' Porter pleaded, 'John, we can't be sure, we'll need to identify the two bodies. We mustn't jump to any conclusions yet.'

John grabbed onto his words

'T-two bodies?' he stammered. 'Who, who for Christ's sake?' He grabbed hold of Porter's jacket, pulling himself up to a standing position. The earth swayed beneath his feet.

'John, John, I'm sorry, it seems as though a woman and a young boy have been shot. There is a third casualty, but we can't confirm...we need confirmation before we...'

'Me... I'll tell you who they are,' John screamed. 'Let me see them, I'll confirm...' he shrugged himself free of Porter's grip. Mason stepped in front of him. Porter shook his head, pressing John back down on to the steps of the ambulance.

'John, you know that we don't do things like that, there's procedure to observe. You of all people should know that,' he said. John knew. He also knew that nothing he could do or say would wheedle his way around that procedure, not with Porter. Now if it had been Horton maybe he would have stood a chance of ending this nightmare.

The fight suddenly left him...he fell to the ground. The enormity of what he suspected had happened, and the uncertainty of its outcome finally overcame him as he lost consciousness.

43

John discharged himself from the hospital, despite being advised to stay in overnight. He sat in the hotel room, his house a closed crime scene. He could imagine it, the police tape, the Forensic team bagging and tagging evidence, stains in the hallway. He wouldn't allow himself to think about the casualties, he needed to distance himself from those thoughts. Emotions threatened to spill over each time the vision of desecrated flesh and oceans of blood entered his mind. He wouldn't give in to it, he couldn't give in to it. The phone rang as he rose to fetch some water, his throat burning with bile that threatened to choke him. He'd retched for almost an hour once he had locked the door to his room, and his stomach ached. He answered on the fifth ring, his hand shaking.

'It's Porter, I'm in reception,' the detective sounded like he was speaking through a child's string and plastic cup walkie-talkie. 'John, are you there?'

'I'll come down,' John answered and replaced the receiver. He splashed his face with cold water and grabbed his keys and phone. DS Mason stood by Porter's side, wringing her hands. She seemed to have shrunk back into herself, no longer the super-efficient detective she'd revealed that afternoon. Without preamble Porter said what he had come to say. Nevertheless, he seemed reluctant to say it.

'John, I know you want to get involved in this case,' he looked away and sighed, then bought back his full attention to the haunted figure standing dejectedly before him. 'You know that you can't because of your relationship with…' he stumbled, reluctant to cause further distress.

'…the two murder victims Detective Inspector, my wife… my son… who I've just identified, who died less than what?' John looked at his watch, 'five hours ago?' He spat out the words, pacing across the reception area, turning and re-tracing his steps.

'I'll see Horton in the morning,' he hissed, though Porter had the distinct impression he was talking to himself. He emphasised his words with a pointed finger, jabbing at the air as though he were taking direct revenge on whoever had done this to him. 'He'll fix it, he'll let me...'

'John...' Porter interrupted, 'John, DCI Horton is still missing, don't you remember?' John stopped suddenly, deflated. Mason cleared her throat.

'Mr. Prothero,' she said softly, 'you can't be included in the investigation team, it would be against procedure. You've suffered enough already don't you think? Let us deal with this, we have some leads. The van we saw leaving the lay-by has been found, leave this to us, sir, let us sort this out for you.' Her voice was hypnotic, and even Porter was soothed by her gentle tones.

John stared at her, as though her presence hadn't registered until that moment.

'That's *Professor* Prothero, if you don't mind,' he snapped. Didn't she understand what he was going through? He cast a contemptuous look over both officers before his expression softened slightly, fighting to regain control of his emotions.

'If that's all?' he snapped abruptly, turning towards the stairs. Porter cleared his throat, reluctant to delay him.

'Just one more thing, John. I haven't been able to track down Graham Shaw, do you know his whereabouts?' The look on John's face was one that neither Porter nor Mason would forget.

44

The lecture room was far too warm, the students lulled into a state of languid relaxation. Graham's lecture was entitled 'The Life Cycle of the Blow Fly', and he'd done his best to make the topic interesting. He'd almost finished, but the dim lighting and Graham's soporific tones which sounded boring even to him, were doing little to hold his students' attention. He was fighting a losing battle and he knew it. Having someone fall through the door was a welcome relief, to the students at least. They giggled at the sight of the man with shocking white hair flailing on the ground like a beached whale. He was followed by the tall thin woman who almost landed on top of him. Graham couldn't help being annoyed. He'd reached the point where he recited a little rhyme, something that would enable the students to remember particularly dull facts. He'd been anticipating the customary ripple of indulgent laughter, mixed with a few groans, but the moment was gone. He'd lost out to this buffoon's ignominious entrance. Graham adjusted his glasses...*who the hell?* He sighed he always knew when to call a halt to lectures that weren't going well. He'd lost them, and he knew it. Exactly when he would be able to repeat the lecture was in the lap of the gods. He wasn't obliged to run it but felt it necessary for those who had failed the module the previous semester. It was a stroke of luck that he'd managed to get them together at the same time.

'Ok, ok, let's calm down', Graham said, as two girls nearest the intruder realised that he may have hurt himself. They'd made their way to his side to offer their help. Graham raised the lights, he made his way over to the man, who was muttering apologies, getting to his feet as quickly as he could. He dusted himself down, recovering quickly. Graham was surprised when he recognised Porter, the woman's name he couldn't remember. Porter shrugged off her attempts to help him up, his annoyance and attempt to cover his embarrassment. Someone had brought a chair over and offered it to him. He refused it and stood at the side of the auditorium trying to look nonchalant. Something in his expression sent a spasm of dread through Graham, and his gut lurched. He was conscious of the rising volume of speculative conversation, and of the need to disperse his students quickly.

'Right, let's leave it there for the time being,' he announced returning to the podium. 'You have your module guides. I'd like you to read Timmins and Cousins' '*Determination of Timelines...*', chapters three to five, which should give you the information you need to make a start on this essay... pay particular attention to the marking grid Forrester,' he said focusing on a scruffy looking student who had previously demonstrated problems relating to the required criteria. Several in his group laughed, Forrester grinned... he liked Graham, they all did. There followed a general hubbub as the students prepared to leave, exalting in the shortened lecture. Speculation was running rife as to the reason. Graham noticed the stragglers, the ones whose curiosity levels exceeded those of their classmates. They wanted to know what was going on. In an odd way he was pleased that they had hung around, being inquisitive was a prerequisite on this course. You didn't get anywhere in Forensics without being nosy to the point of obsession.

'Thanks guys,' he called, tidying his notes and shutting down the presentation at the same time. He indicated the door and gradually the remaining students wandered through, leaving him and the two officers alone. He was playing for time, dreading whatever it was that Porter had come to tell him, sensing that this was personal. He snatched his brief case and strode towards them.

Porter sighed softly and began to speak.

45

Porter started with preliminary questions. His overriding concern was to get Graham to Ellie in case she didn't make it, although he was determined not to let on. So far, he had no idea if Ellie had sustained a life-threatening injury or something less serious. Until he knew he settled for the former. He'd long since decided that, no matter who he was dealing with, he would follow his own tried and tested procedure. That meant not revealing anything until he'd gathered enough information himself. This, he knew, would yield maximum results before emotion took over and his subject was consumed with either anger or grief... with Graham Shaw it just seemed heartless.

'This is difficult... I have to ask...' he began. Mason stood wringing her hands, misery etched on every crevice of her prematurely aged face. Porter cleared his throat again...did Graham know his wife's timetable for the day? Was she usually at her office on a Tuesday? Did he know why she would be at her sister's house? On and on he went, until Graham had had enough, he wanted to know what was going on, the reason for their visit. He demanded an explanation...Porter sighed. Mason bounced from one foot to the other, still wringing her hands, annoying both.

'Mason, go see if you can locate some drinks, please,' Porter suggested, eager to get rid of her. He could see the affect she was having on Graham. Her departure reminded Graham of a greyhound exiting a trap. Somehow, he couldn't remember her return.

The DI's words bounced around in his brain. Shot, Ellie had been shot... air-lifted to hospital, Porter wasn't sure which one. No beating about the bush now, Porter told it like it was, and how it was hit Graham like a brickbat. His staggered, grasping for support, his legs losing their strength, his body sagged as Porter helped him to a chair, then sat with him, waiting in his practiced way. His creed, had Graham known, *don't tell them any more than the essentials, listen for questions that follow.* Some people gave themselves away no matter how good they were at trying to hide facts. Not that Porter suspected Graham, but stranger things had happened in his long career.

The questions came, tentative at first, then faster like a tsunami... how, where, when? Graham tried to make sense of Porter's answers as they swirled around in his head. Ellie shot, a second woman dead, a young boy gunned down. John had identified them as Ruth and Max. Porter pulled no punches; he couldn't afford to. Could Graham think of anyone with a motive for the attack? When had he last seen his wife? They'd tried to contact him after the attack. Where was he, why hadn't he answered his phone?

No, he'd told Porter, he couldn't think of anyone who would do such a thing. He'd left home at around 8 a.m. yesterday morning and texted Ellie during a break. He'd meant to text her again after his lecture, but he couldn't find his phone. He'd been busy all day, then used the landline in his office to call her. He got her voicemail, left her a message, and crashed out on the sofa bed for the night. He hadn't spoken to anyone on his way to the lecture room, not until...

'So, you had no contact with your wife after you left the house yesterday morning?' asked Porter. Graham shook his head.

'Only the text I sent her... she replied, but no... look why are you... do you think I had something to do with this? How...' he spluttered.

Porter started to answer as his phone buzzed. Connett, telling him where Ellie had been taken. He relayed the information and Graham stood and grabbed his bag eager to get going. Porter placed a hand on his shoulder to steady him.

'I'll drive you,' Porter said, steering him out of the lecture room, Graham didn't refuse.

They travelled in virtual silence. Graham battled to make sense of it all. Porter glanced at him as they left the city behind. He was hoping for a look at the dynamic between the two of them, if she was still alive that was. They'd dropped Mason off at the nearest taxi office with orders to contact them with any developments.

Porter had the highest regard for Graham Shaw, they'd worked together several times, and had a similar clinical detachment, except for one case, almost eighteen months ago. A young woman murdered in a most brutal attack, and the only case that William Porter could honestly say had given him sleepless nights. It was the same for Graham, they discovered whilst discussing his report at the lab. He shook his head sharply, trying to dislodge the memory.

Graham sat staring out of the car window with unseeing eyes, his hands folded in his lap. After an hour Porter apologised, he needed to stop for fuel. They pulled in at the next services, ten minutes later they were travelling again. Porter knew better than to intrude on grief, but he couldn't rule out the possibility that Graham might have been involved in the incident, however unlikely. His habit of allowing the other party to initiate conversation was inviolate, but he began to wonder if for once, he should break his golden rule. The air in the car was growing stale, Porter wound down his window.

'She's my life!' Graham said suddenly, 'please hurry!'

'I am' said Porter, nevertheless speeding up. His years in patrol cars afforded him expert reflexes, and the journey passed rapidly.

He didn't get to see them together after all, the Professor and Ellie, she was still in surgery. He waited with Graham for an hour or so, then left, glad he'd taken the time to ferry him to an unenviable destination. There would be time later, first things first. He had a crime scene to visit, yet another incident board to set up. He only hoped that whoever was carrying out the forensics was half as good as the man he'd just left.

46

Graham stood slowly, stretching his aching limbs. The well-worn recliner that the ward sister had managed to procure was rapidly becoming less appealing. Two days had passed since he'd set up residence at the hospital. He'd spent most of his time holding Ellie's hand, occasionally drifting into a light doze, and trying to pry information out of the battery of doctors that darted in and out.

W*hat was the collective noun*; he wondered idly, *'an avoidance' perhaps?* That's what they seemed to excel at, avoiding his questions. He had to admit that it was no less than his stance when faced with anxious grieving relatives. Anyone placed in such a situation would at the very least prevaricate until sure of the facts. Somehow that was no comfort now that he was on the receiving end. They would breeze into the ICU, all white coats and clipboards, then within minutes be gone having muttered conspiratorially to each other, platitudes floating in their wake. Graham was sure that even if he had pinned them down to the floor, he would gain no more information. There was none, it was a waiting game now.

Ellie had yet to regain consciousness, but at least she was out of immediate danger. A bank of machines bleeped, monitoring her vital signs, nurses floating in and out to record them. He knew most of them by name now. He needed the loo. Hell, he needed more than that, he admitted. A shower and a change of clothes might help. Nothing to eat though, he couldn't face food, not yet. The corridor was empty as he passed the nurse's station, nodding to the only member of staff there.

'Breakfast trolley will be round soon Mr. Shaw,' she informed him. He muttered his acknowledgement and made his way to the visitor's toilet. The staff here had been wonderful, he thought as he washed his hands. He had access to a small area where he could make snacks, tea, coffee... all so that next of kin didn't have to leave in case... he stopped, a great surge of emotion threatening to overwhelm him. He made his way back along the corridor, wanting to get back to Ellie as soon as he could.

In his absence someone had tidied up, straightened the bedclothes, and replenished the water jug. He read the latest obs., no change. Graham took up his vigil once more, stroking Ellie's hand, talking to her, watching her face for any signs that she was regaining consciousness, thinking back to the lecture room and Porter's ignominious entrance. He tried to recall every word that had passed between them, it was no good. He hadn't heard half of what Porter had said, all he'd thought about was how quickly he could get to Ellie.

47

Ellie had imagined the scene over and over, Graham pulling up in front of the farmhouse, the door opening, going home. Later, when her in-laws had left, she lay exhausted on the bed. Was it only two weeks since...? She'd been shot in her right shoulder, a clean wound with minimal bone damage, but it ached with such intensity, even with the strongest painkillers possible. She found it difficult to concentrate on anything. Two cracked ribs, consistent with being kicked with some force, and considerable internal bleeding. The pain presented a dilemma every day, either relatively comfortable waking hours, or an unbroken night's sleep. Not, it seemed both. The side effects from the medication left her muzzy headed, and she was constantly thirsty. Apart from that, she told herself, she could cope.

The memories of what had happened at Ruth and John's cottage caused her the most pain, though. Images flashed unbidden into her mind. Even when she was able to sleep, her nights were punctuated with hideous dreams. Ruth lying on the hall floor, her body covered with blood. Max, one arm draped through the spindles on the landing. A blurred figure pointing the gun at her, shouting for someone. She couldn't remember the name... then silence followed by a dark figure moving towards her, a sharp pain in her side. At this point she would scream out in her sleep, hyperventilating, grabbing onto Graham, sobbing in his arms until her remaining strength was spent.

The next few days settled into a pattern. Graham's connection to the victims precluded him from working on the case, but he still rose early, as was his habit and attended to the minutiae of the day. He made coffee, which Ellie drank in bed as he made breakfast for them both. Afterwards he insisted she rest again, and she would try to read, which she couldn't concentrate on, resorting to staring out of the window. Graham was trying his best, and she appreciated his efforts, but treating her like this wasn't doing anything for her patience level. They hadn't spoken about the incident much, he understood her reluctance. Graham's parents visited, dropping off shopping and making small talk, but what Ellie really wanted was to be left alone to think. She developed a tactic which involved feigning interest in whichever was the least annoying TV programme. Once Graham felt she was content to manage without him for a while, he would tuck a rug around her legs and head upstairs to his office... *just to catch up with stuff,* he told her. Ellie wondered... she had never brought up the subject of who he had been talking to that night; somehow the opportunity had never arisen. It all seemed so unimportant now.

When he seemed determined to stay by her side, Ellie would surf through the channels, changing stations with lightning speed. She knew that Graham hated it when she did that, and that it wouldn't be long before he kissed her on the top of her head and tell her that he was heading upstairs. She would nod, and he would leave her, seemingly absorbed in her programme.

On Ellie's second day back, she became immersed in a chat show; the subject was 'Coercive Control'. Most of the programme's participants had fallen into a downward spiralling pattern of being manipulated by their partners. One woman, loud, not particularly articulate, told the avid audience about 'being jerked around like a string-puppet.'

Ellie felt uncomfortable, but in this instance, it wasn't because of her shoulder. Over the last few days she'd been thinking about the cases she'd been working on. She was sure that the murders that formed the core of the investigation had been orchestrated. Her theories formed the basis of the discussion she was due to have with John Prothero. Now a vivid image of someone pulling the strings, making the perpetrators do exactly what he or she wanted them to do had begun to form in her mind. It was so obvious really, playing God, directing the performance, like a writer, or a director on a film set, or...*a Puppet Master.*

48

No matter how hard she tried, Ellie couldn't persuade Graham to take her into town. He was adamant.

'You aren't well enough,' he insisted, 'just wait until after you see the doctor next week. Who knows, she may even suggest some physio.' He spoke to her in that semi-patronising way that people adopt when they are trying to placate a child. He moved around the kitchen making coffee, fixing breakfast, all the trivial tasks that Ellie couldn't manage for now.

'Graham, all I want to do is spend some time somewhere other than here. I'm going stir crazy,' she pleaded, knowing that she was fighting a losing battle. They'd had this conversation repeatedly in the last few days. Ellie could see Graham's point of view. He wanted her to be safe, and as things were, it looked as though things were far from that. Horton had been missing for over two weeks now. Graham wasn't about to put Ellie in harm's way again.

Ellie had a chronic bout of cabin fever. She read, wrote, walked around the farm and fed the chickens. But, although she insisted that she was well, she had to admit that even these trivial tasks exhausted her. By the end of the morning her shoulder ached with an intensity that she could hardly bear, and although she took refuge in her painkillers only as a last resort, she was glad of them and the nap she could take after lunch.

Graham on the other hand, aware that he couldn't take part in the postmortem on his sister-in-law or nephew, had left the house only to deliver a couple of lectures and a few tutorials given to his students. Their final year was coming up, dissertations needed to be discussed, and he wanted as much as possible to provide them with continuity. Their curiosity at having an actual murder happen on their own doorstep had led to more than usual traffic through his office. He was strict about who he saw, otherwise he knew that he would be at the University more than at home, where he felt ham fisted and clumsy dealing with his shattered wife. She wouldn't be alone though, he told her, he had arranged for his parents to come over and keep her company. Ellie sighed; a few hours alone with a chance to think seemed like bliss. Graham's own frustration was evident, especially when Emlyn Davies, the head of his department contacted him from the Lab.

'I don't want you to worry Graham,' he said, trying to sound reassuring. 'Everything's sorted out here, someone's been brought in to cover your duties. You take as long as you need, things like this can't be rushed. Must go now. Speak to you soon, bye, oh love to your wife,' he rang off, leaving Graham less than reassured. For one thing he didn't like the idea of a stranger poking about in his office. He called Cathy Beresford, his assistant to ask her all the questions that Davies hadn't given him the chance to voice.

No, his replacement hadn't arrived yet, Graham flinched. *No, she didn't know who it was...he didn't have to worry, a new office had been allocated, with new equipment no less.* There followed a five-minute tirade on how long she had been asking Emlyn for a new filing cabinet for *their* office, but oh no. Graham brought her back to the point.

'Try to discourage whoever it is from messing with my things, will you... and keep me posted when you can?' He pleaded, with the sinking feeling that he had been side-lined.

'Graham concentrate on Ellie, I'll keep things ticking, and no matter who comes in, they'll have to go through me to get into our office,' she promised. Graham told Ellie of his doubts; she could identify with his frustration. She desperately wanted to get back to work, to meet up with Odelia Mathers and ask her about her connection with Ruth. Something was urging her to tell Odelia what had happened at the Alan Cooper interview and later at John's cottage. She wanted to find the bastard who killed Ruth and Max, to confirm her suspicions that the cases were linked, to discover why John and Ruth's home had been targeted. But more than anything, she wanted to discuss Porter's progress on the case. She'd considered inviting him to the farm but doubted that Graham would agree.

Graham watched as Ellie walked to the window, wincing in pain. She tried to assure him that the gnawing ache had decreased somewhat in the last few days, but he knew she was only putting on a brave face. The fact was that the swelling was still evident, and her ribs ached like hell. She'd wrenched her knee during the attack, the ligaments were still healing. Strapping helped her to walk but didn't do much to ease her pain. The view, which she had loved since moving in, left her cold. She felt like a prisoner, wanting only some respite, both from the pain and from her home.

Graham was desperate to help, he had almost every practical aspect covered, but felt that it wasn't enough. Ellie almost flinched as his arms encircled her, he nuzzled her neck, she leaned against him, carefully folding her arms over his. They stood in silence for a few moments, she felt the warmth of him, and it comforted her.

'I know you're bored,' he murmured, 'but you need to get well before you dive back into the sewer. All I want is for you to be safe, and you can't be safe when you can hardly walk.'

Ellie could see the sense in that. She had to be patient, she had to heal, she had to get strong so that she could focus on catching whoever had torn their lives apart. Graham guided her back to the sofa, planted a kiss on top of her head, and went back to fixing breakfast. She sighed, a few weeks ago she would've been delighted to know that she was the focus of his attention. Now that she was, she found it somehow irritating.

Graham carried a loaded tray towards the coffee table, bacon sandwiches with a side of sautéed mushrooms, her favourite. Coffee in her 'Don't mess with me' mug, toast, butter, marmalade, it was all there. She smiled at her husband, who hovered, almost bowing as he presented the offering. Delicious, all of it, the best meal since…and her thoughts boomeranged back to Ruth's cottage…banging on the door…shouting…screams…the shots ringing out. She dragged herself away from the thought, concentrating on the meal, attempting to distract herself from the overwhelming grief that lurked a hair's breadth away. Tears threatened to spill over, Graham saw the transition and looked away, wondering how to break her state. Over the last few days he had held her many times as she sobbed into his chest, leaving her exhausted. This time he would try distraction.

'You'd better eat up,' he said as breezily as he could. 'You're going to need your strength this morning.' Ellie paused, *this was different*, she thought, *he's spent the last few days telling me to rest, what's he up to?*

'I was going to keep this until another day,' Graham went on having captured her attention, 'but as we have some time now…' he crossed to the utility room, and returned a few minutes later with a battered box. Ellie immediately recognised it as one she'd had shipped over when she moved to the UK, her heart sank. The last thing she needed now was to go through old photos and letters and whatever else was in there. Hell, she couldn't even remember half of what she'd kept. Graham detected her uncertainty, determined that she wouldn't wriggle out of the activity he had planned.

'Look hon, I know this might not set the world on fire, but at least it's something to do. We've been promising to sort out our clutter for years, now might be a good time, and look,' he made another trip and returned with an equally large box marked with his name. It had 'Uni Stuff' written on the side. Ellie sighed; she had to admit it was clever of him, to offer to sort her stuff first, when they both knew that his box contained nothing but his old notebooks. She knew when she was beaten. Besides, it would give her an excuse to move away from the food, which was beginning to make her feel nauseous.

'OK, wise-guy,' she conceded, 'let me go powder my nose, then we'll get down to it.' Graham laughed, standing between the two boxes, pointing first at one then the other, nodding and gesturing, *this one, that one*? There was no contest really, and an hour later they sat pouring over old photos, birthday cards and drawings. Ellie had intended to catalogue them 'when she had the time'. Graham's hope that the exercise would distract her was fulfilled as she reminisced over almost every scrap of paper.

'Do you remember when Mom's house was flooded a few years ago?' she asked him, placing yet another birthday card on the 'keep' pile. They were half way down the box yet not one item had been set aside for disposal. He nodded. It had been traumatic for Julia, and Ellie had gone back to the US to help her sort out the mess. Most of Ellie and Ruth's childhood keepsakes had perished, a further source of distress for them both. It'd been a particularly difficult time, and now considering what had happened to Ruth... he hoped that this memory wouldn't set Ellie back, and held his breath as she struggled to cope with her rising emotions.

'It would be nice to copy some of this stuff and create a book of some kind, the things that belonged to Ruth, I'm sure Mom would like that...' she stopped suddenly.

'Oh God, Graham, what do we do about the funerals? We haven't even talked about...'

Shit, he hadn't thought about that. They hadn't talked about what was going to happen when Ruth and Max's bodies were finally released. The postmortem had been completed a few days ago, held up by the backlog of cases in the Morgue, but it wouldn't be long before they were ready to be released. Ellie stared out of the window; tears coursed down her face. Graham reached her in one movement, touching her shoulder, ever aware of his need to be careful.

'Ellie... Ellie, come here,' he murmured, pulling her gently to him. 'We'll sort that out, don't worry about it for the moment. We'll have to meet with John and see what he wants to do.' Ellie stiffened in his arms, she hadn't thought of John, now the mention of him brought her back to the present.

'Yes, yes of course. We'll have to get together, talk to him about it, after all...' she pulled herself together. She would help John to arrange everything, determined to give them a fitting send off. Graham noticed the change in her energy. He knew she was fighting to take control of the emotions which up until a few minutes ago had played her like a violin. Sorting the box of memories out had been the right thing to do, he was sure of it.

Ellie pulled herself together as she reached over to pick up a scrapbook, smiling once more at the memories it evoked. Both her name and Ruth's were emblazoned on the front. Snippets of verse, pictures of princesses, drawings of stars, moons and horses jostled for attention. Inside a pasted-on letter written by Ruth...*sorry I stole your doll, I only wanted her to keep mine company, please don't tell Mom – Ruthie xxx*

It was a drawing of two dolls together in a crayoned pram with multi coloured blankets which Ellie remembered their Mother had crocheted out of spare wool. There followed recipes, poems, more drawings, some made her cry, others laugh out loud. She hadn't remembered Ruth being quite so prolific in her creativity, but then she was always so absorbed in reading her books to take any notice. This was a delight, Graham couldn't have suggested a better diversion, and she was grateful for it. True, some things brought her to the edge of tears, but that, she guessed was part of the healing process. She turned the next page. A sheet of paper fell to the floor, and she winced as she bent to retrieve it. It was tattered around the edges, almost like the treasure maps they used to make, tearing small pieces off to age the finished look. She unfolded it, the image searing into her brain.

The picture showed a figure, coloured red, slumped against a wall, attached to its hands and feet were lengths of cord, these in turn gathered to what could only be described as a puppeteers' control bar, held in a crudely drawn hand. Surrounding the figure were sketches of knives, guns and ropes. An area around the feet was a sea of red. Ellie gasped in shock, causing Graham to look up from a poem he'd been reading.

'Ellie, Ellie, what's wrong? What ...' he moved over to her side, as she turned the piece of paper towards him. He looked at the drawing, shaking his head, 'I, I don't understand...' he said.

'Look,' Ellie murmured, 'look at what's written at the bottom, Graham.'

WON'T STOP, CAN'T HELP IT, BEING CONTROLLED, BE CAREFUL HON....XXX

'What the hell!' Graham said. He read the words again, searching the drawing for more clues, shaking his head as he turned his attention back to his Ellie. She was scrutinising his face.

'That's Ruth's handwriting, Graham, and she didn't write that when she was a child, look at the date.... in the corner.' She pointed, her hand shaking as Graham re-examined the page.

'That's the day Ruth and Max were killed,' whispered Ellie, Graham nodded, placing the drawing on the table... now what?

49

Morning classes were in full swing. It was unseasonably warm, the room stuffy. Open windows caused problems as they allowed access to angry dying wasps drunk on fermented fruit. Several estimates for air conditioning had proved to be way outside Odelia's budget. An ancient fan had been set on maximum to alleviate the atmosphere and dispel the overwhelming smell of essential oils.

One day it'll give up, she thought, *and then what will we do?*

It didn't really bother her all that much, but lately she'd had several comments from her students. Something had to be done sooner rather than later. Odelia had focused on a new air conditioning system for so long now, she believed that it would have manifested. But there was still no sign of the significant sum it would cost. Perhaps that was it, perhaps she just needed to trust that it would come and relax. It's what she'd have told her Law of Attraction students to do, in any case she hadn't managed to pin the local authority down as to whether she could buy the place yet. Until it was hers, she was reluctant to invest that kind of money. Odelia wanted to transfer her practice here. Her business plan had impressed the bank manager, but something was stopping her progress.

'If you keep noticing that what you want hasn't arrived yet, you are focusing on it not arriving. According to the Law of Attraction, we get what we focus on, so it will continue not to arrive,' she answered when Shelly Pierce pointed out that the Lamborghini that she'd ordered in the last class hadn't materialised. Odelia smiled, packing up her Aromatherapy kit, it was all very well teaching this stuff, but sometimes it was a different matter when it came to practicing it. Still, all in all, her knowledge had stood her in good stead. She was happy in her belief system and the confidence that it bought her all she asked for, it was just sometimes it seemed to be frustratingly slow.

'Don't forget your towels next week please,' she reminded the group of people now packing their things as they prepared to leave, '…and your fans, don't forget your fans,' quipped Roland, a good-natured chap who attended almost every class she ran. 'Never know when old faithful is going to die on us!' he nodded to the fan which had now started to make a clicking noise.

'Better watch out Roland,' said Odelia, 'you may be more powerful than you think!' The group had made their way out of the building, hoping for some fresher, cooler air. Odelia and Roland walked towards what they had nicknamed the 'staff room'. It was a small kitchen come storage area with three chairs, a battered bookcase and a Formica table. Everywhere in the centre was spotless, just a little shabby. Roland had become a good friend, as well as being a devoted and loyal student. He was divorced, in his late 40's, and had recently moved back to live with his mother and a small terrier named Alfie. Odelia loved him for the slight oddball that he was. He made drinks as she packed away the morning's equipment.

'Sandwich sweetheart?' he asked placing her mug on the table, and retrieving a lunch box from his hold all, 'Fromage et…er… tomato,' she giggled, as she always did when he attempted to say something in French giving up halfway through. He reminded her of a character in a popular comedy show with his attempts to appear sophisticated. She suspected that he did it deliberately to make her smile.

The box contained much more than sandwiches. Fruit, a couple of Fondant fancies, which he knew she had a taste for, and a slab of fruitcake, made by his mother. Odelia rolled her eyes, although she eagerly anticipated a delicious lunch, his offerings were doing nothing for her waistline.

'Now don't you give me that look, young lady,' he tutted, 'you're practically skin and bone.'

She laughed, knowing that he would brook no argument, and tucked in. Their conversation strayed to the terrible things that had gone on in the cottage over yonder, and had she got any ideas about who could have done such a thing? Odelia didn't want to talk to him about it, not now, or ever. Since Ruth and Max had been killed, she'd had the worst nightmares she had ever had.

…*shock*, she thought, *it's just shock, it'll clear, and maybe then I'll be able to make some sense of it all.* She sighed, eyeing the last piece of fruit, smiling politely at Roland as he continued to probe. She didn't want to be rude, but she couldn't talk about this to him, and didn't think he would understand why. How could she, how could she tell anyone about what she'd seen? She closed her eyes, hoping that he would take the hint that the subject was off limits, but she could hear his voice droning on and on.

'Make it stop!' she pleaded inside her head…the phone rang. She dragged herself back from the semi-trance she was just about to enter and went into the small entrance hall to answer it.

It was Graham Shaw.

50

Odelia wasn't familiar with this part of the island. Graham had arranged to pick her up at 3.45, just after her last class. He felt uncomfortable at the thought of leaving Ellie alone, but she had reassured him that she'd be fine. He made her promise not to anything but sit and relax until they returned. For the life of him Graham couldn't understand why his wife would want to talk to Odelia, and he'd been quite offhand when he called to arrange for her to come over. He hadn't wanted to call her at all, but Ellie had insisted.

Graham found it almost impossible to tear his eyes from her face. Odelia was used to the reaction of people on first meeting her, after that it wasn't usually so uncomfortable. They travelled to the farm in virtual silence, as Odelia noted the depth of Graham's hostility. It was only when they arrived at the farmhouse itself that she managed to break the ice by enthusing over the view from the kitchen. Graham made sure that Ellie was comfortable, did she need anything, should he leave or stay?

'Stay,' Ellie whispered, holding on to his hand, 'please stay.'

Ellie had lost weight. The strain of the last few weeks etched in her pale face. Odelia crossed the room and stood in front of her, her hands outstretched. Ellie had slept during the last few hours. She'd dreamt about a time when she and Ruth had been playing in the stream at the bottom of their Grandfather's garden. It had been a special day for them both, and the memory of it was sweet. Now the sight of Odelia, her arms open, her expression one of caring concern, caused Ellie to break down again. Odelia sat next to her, placing her hand on Ellie's arm. Ellie leaned into her, sobbing as though her heart would break, before she finally pulled away and wiped her eyes, shuddering with emotion.

Graham felt like an intruder as he sat perched on the arm of the sofa. Ellie, having spent the worst of her anguish, showed Odelia the drawing. She studied it before reading the words out loud.

'WON'T STOP, CAN'T HELP IT, BEING CONTROLLED, BE CAREFUL HON....XXX'

Ellie and Graham watched as Odelia closed her eyes, allowing the piece of paper to flutter to the floor. She stood and walked to the French doors.

'I need a few minutes,' she said opening the door and stepping through onto the porch. She walked down the steps to the gravel path that wound through the lawn and up the slight incline. It ended at a stone bench which marked the beginning of a wooded area. Ellie and Graham watched as she sat down facing the house. The fading light was alleviated by the solar torches dotted here and there along the outline of the path. The fairy lights that they'd threaded into the trees for a party they'd held at the height of summer, punctuated the dusk. Almost an hour passed; Odelia sat motionless. Ellie could hardly see her when Graham remarked that she must be getting cold and went to fetch a shawl from the hallway. He walked towards the door to follow in Odelia's steps.

'No,' said Ellie, raising herself up with some effort, 'let me go, please Graham, I need to.' He handed her the shawl and watched as she limped her way slowly up to where Odelia sat. She eased herself down, and they sat in silence for a while, by which time Ellie started to shiver. Odelia rose abruptly from her seat as Ellie reached out for her.

'Don't touch me!' she snapped, she took a breath, her face softened, 'let's go inside, there's something I want to try, if you'll agree.' She walked back to the house; Ellie following a few paces behind. The light from the kitchen shone like a beacon, and the warmth enveloped them as they re-entered the building. Graham was watching them, he didn't look happy.

'Are you completely out of your mind?' he demanded. Ellie stared at him, she realised that he was talking to Odelia, 'she's sick for God's sake, she could catch a chill.' He grabbed a blanket and wrapped it around Ellie's shoulders.

'Be quiet Graham!' Odelia hissed, the tone of her voice silencing him. They both stared at her. She forced a smile, trying to dispel any tension.

'Please sit down,' she said soothingly. Graham did as he was told and joined Ellie. 'I want to try something…with your permission,' she said. They both nodded although neither knew why. They were finding it hard to resist her instructions.

'I'll need some paper and pens... these will do,' she picked up some scrap paper that Ellie kept on the kitchen counter, along with two pencils and placed them on the coffee table.

'Close your eyes breathe deeply and try to relax. I'm going to be very quiet for a few moments. You'll each feel a hand on your shoulder, don't worry,' she smiled, 'it'll be me.' They nodded again, not doubting her for a moment.

'When I take my hands away, I want you to open your eyes and draw or write whatever you see, if you see anything at all,' she could tell they were confused, so she explained again. Ellie looked at Graham, she was willing to try whatever Odelia suggested but was worried that he would dismiss the idea as ridiculous. His reassuring smile told her that he would give it a try. Odelia moved round to the back of the sofa.

'Okay,' she said, 'I want you both to relax, breathe deeply, and when it feels natural, close your eyes as they become heavier and heavier.'

She started to hum, some non-descript tune that neither of them recognised. Ellie felt her body relaxing. She glanced at Graham whose eyes were already shut. He seemed to be totally devoid of tension. They were sitting directly in front of the French windows, and the deepening darkness provided a perfect mirror. The last thing Ellie saw as her eyes closed was Odelia, surrounded by a silver-white light. Her hands were hovering, one over each of their shoulders. Ellie gasped as time appeared to freeze. Moments passed, but to her it seemed like hours. As they came back to full consciousness, they both opened their mouths to speak.

'Sshhh!!' instructed Odelia, who was now sitting on one of the stools at the breakfast bar, 'write down what you've seen.'

Graham's hand was shaking as he wrote. Ellie swallowed hard, trying to stem her tears. They handed their papers to Odelia, she placed them on the table. They had both written one word...

'Ruth'

'She's here!' Odelia said.

51

The red-brick building at the corner of Menchin Road and Post Office Lane was little more than derelict. Once a throbbing hub of business, it had served time as a Post Office, a B & B, various offices and, most recently, poorly designed flats. A dispute over ownership meant it had been boarded up for years, gradually falling into disrepair through neglect and a lack of a traceable inheritor. As such it was fair game for squatters.

Two of the five floors were empty, ransacked by those 'passing through'. The rest of the building was divided almost equally between two disparate groups. The first relied heavily on a variety of substances, the other well-intentioned self-proclaimed 'children of the universe'. The former lived on fast food and illegal highs. They claimed benefits they weren't entitled to, and shoplifted to fuel their habits, some burglary, blackmail, begging and extortion, the list was extensive.

The latter group despised that way of life, espousing honesty, treating their fellow man with respect. They were wandering workers, seasonal glass collectors, buskers, musicians, farm labourers. Most of the work they found was well below their abilities and intellectual qualifications. Some were ex-university students, drop-outs who took every opportunity to preach their disillusionment with life, disenchanted with their former dreams and ambitions. There were several hangers-on from especially poor backgrounds, following the pack in the hope of finding a place to belong. Most had been born with silver spoons, which they despised, denigrating their families with distain. Most seemed to have naive goals, find a piece of land, live off grid, get back to nature.

The locals had tarred them all with the same brush, labelling the building 'Hippy Heaven'. They gave the place a wide berth, as though walking too close would result in contracting a fatal disease, calling them 'layabouts', or the 'great unwashed'. Many an upright law-abiding citizen had been accosted by the ever-changing occupants for a fag or some change.

The building's facade was crumbling, pollution and neglect competing for ownership. Grubby, with broken windows, security boards wrenched from the gaps, it wore a cloak of defeat. Lead had long since disappeared from the roof, the copper piping missing from the third and fifth floors. The electric was still there, which was viewed as something of a miracle, the authorities had tried many times, they couldn't locate the source. It came from an empty shop two doors down, overlooked by the suppliers and long forgotten by the owners.

Charles Whittaker, who belonged to neither faction, had moved there after his wife left him taking their son with her. It was the only place he could find to shelter. Three months went by before he found out that the man he believed was the landlord was in fact the head of the 'druggies' as Charles came to call them. His name was Dirk, Charles laughed at that – *more like Dick*, he thought.

Every week Dirk would hammer on the basement door demanding the 'rent', and Charles, to avoid trouble would dutifully pay up. Eventually the sniggering of Dirk's gang made him wonder what was so funny. Rory the hippy told him, though not until he had wasted a considerable amount of his dwindling cash supply. When he found out, Charles was incensed. He was the only one handing over money to live in this shithole, money he could ill-afford, to a punk who spent it on drugs or pissed it up the wall the same night with his sniggering sycophants.

Charles planned the show-down with precision. He bought extra locks to tighten up his security, then launched his attack in the alleyway between the old post office and the equally neglected building next door. A metal pipe, held at the throat, with strength that Dirk could only dream about exerting, a hissed threat, his words chosen carefully for maximum effect. Charles knew how it went; he had been there many times before with more powerful opponents than this idiot. Dirk was a bully, and like all bullies he backed down when challenged. Charles' life seemed better from then on, more money, no rent to pay or hassle from Dirk and his cronies. They'd been shocked at the ferocity of the attack and left him alone. A few months later Dirk was found dead behind the Co-op, he'd overdosed in the car park. Charles hadn't missed him.

The 'Karma Kids', as he dubbed the others, were friendly, they even brought him various offerings from their skip diving forays. He dined on Gruyere, Onion and Leek Quiche from Waitrose, Cinnamon Bagels from

Tesco's and sometimes feather light strawberry tarts from that little French bakery down by the park. Occasionally he'd join them on the second floor, for what was a surprisingly sociable evening. He got to know Rory, Squidge and Mamsie, though most of the others by sight rather than name.

Charles had little to occupy his days, although he kept up a habit of working out, which helped him to maintain his fitness levels. It also afforded him a sense of purpose. He found an old bike in the alleyway, and spent some of his savings fixing it up. He started taking regular outings around the island. For other trips he relied on public transport which was surprisingly reliable in the area. Not that he had many places to go, just the Job Centre, his Probation Officer, or trips to see his psychiatrist. This was a condition of his probation. Failure to keep appointments would mean he would have to go back inside, and he had no intention of returning to prison, not for any reason. In any case, he liked his doctor, found he could talk to him, and tell him all about his crazy life, without being judged.

He started to look forward to his sessions, even though there had been that incident last month...he still wasn't sure what he'd said to cause the row. Now he saw another doctor...less keen on that one, but still.

Charles' life had become tolerable, and he settled down to relative normality. His days were routine for the most part, although he made sure that the other tenants were wrong footed as often as he could. He relished the knowledge that no-one was sure of his movements. Timers switched appliances on and off to throw them off the scent, he would laugh with an overblown sense of his ingenuity.

Then came the offer, the one he couldn't turn down, although he was curious as to how his new 'friend' had found him. An email picked up when he was using the computer at the library. Did he want to earn some easy money? Did he? He was down to his last few quid and applying for jobs was proving futile. At first, he was sure the offer was a joke, then he decided what the hell, he had to live didn't he? What did the authorities expect; that he would walk into an executive position with his track record? Seasonal work was all very well, but with zero hours' contracts and minimum wage. Hell, he'd earned a week's wages in a couple of hours before...but no he wouldn't go back to that. He'd promised Maria. But she wasn't there anymore was she, she wouldn't know? He didn't even know what this... he scrolled back to the beginning of the email... *Puppenspieler74* was offering.

He found the pre-paid phone at the designated spot; it was a game-changer. It was ready to use, someone had charged it up, and even put credit on. It rang at the pre-arranged time, Charles had what could only be described as a very in-depth telephone interview, an agreement was reached. The main questions centered on whether he had any scruples about what he would be required to do. Given that part of his reward would be information about his wife and son, he assured his new employer that he had none.

His first outing, which he was told to regard as a 'practical' interview, was to arrange for the disposal of his old boss, Rob Tranter. It was an exercise which Charles enjoyed more than he would allow himself to admit. He relished the sense of satisfaction he derived from having Tranter beg for his life before realising that he wasn't getting out of the encounter alive. He performed beyond expectations, he was told later, almost faultlessly, and would be rewarded accordingly. Charles' self-worth rose dramatically, and he awaited further contact with eager anticipation. He wasn't doing anything he hadn't done many times in the past; it was just that this time he didn't get to meet his boss face to face. The greater part of his time was his to enjoy, as others apparently cleared up the resultant mess.

Lately though, the demands placed upon him were increasing, he'd begun to get a little wary of the number of 'outings' he was being asked to carry out. He felt no guilt, that part of his psyche seemed to have had a by-pass, but although he was happy with the money side of things, the information about his wife seemed to have dried up. He needed more.

There had also been a number of 'episodes' that he hadn't experienced since before being prescribed his current medication. The symptoms didn't worry him much at first, but they were getting worse. He didn't want to go back to existing in a half-life of awareness if his doctor suggested different pills. He decided to ride it out for the time being and raise it at his next appointment.

It came as no surprise when Charles wasn't seen at the squat for several days. The lights came on and the radio played, the TV blared, the same pattern every day. Maybe if he had lived on another floor someone would've realised that something was wrong. Living in the basement with its separate entrance, meant that the rest of the occupants hardly ever saw him.

It was Rory that found him.

The Karma Kids' skip diving had yielded rich pickings that night; several bags of discarded food, almost fresh bread and a plethora of fruit and vegetables. Even after being shared out, it was still too much to eat. Rory selected a pepper and courgette mixture lying on a bed of seasoned cous cous… *not even out of date*, he thought shaking his head and tutting. He sorted out a slice of carrot cake to go with the main course, knowing it was Charles' favourite. He placed the meal into a recycled paper carrier bag and headed to the basement.

Rory liked Charles, partly because of the relative peace that had reigned after his show-down with Dirk. They often spent evenings sharing a bottle of something which Charles would procure, and Rory looked forward to. They would chat as they put the world to rights... or rather Rory would expound on his idealistic beliefs. Charles would listen understanding barely half of the conversation, but hypnotised by the younger man's fervency. The meetings took on a comfortable regularity which neither of them had expected.

Lately though Charles had become unpredictable, long absences, or ignoring the knock at his door, although Rory suspected he was in. Charles would listen for footsteps as his visitor, respecting the others' privacy, retreated upstairs, leaving his gift outside in the dingy corridor. Rory had recently discovered that Charles had family conflict going on. What with that and being treated for mental health related problems; Rory didn't want to intrude on his new friend's troubles. He was sorely tempted to say something when he'd discovered the number of pills Charles was taking, but he kept quiet in order not to appear judgemental.

The basement corridor was dark, the fading light outside fought for entrance against a filthy window. Rory felt his way along the walls, making a mental note to report the broken light bulbs to the building manager. He laughed at his own private joke. It had been a long time since he'd lived anywhere that had a maintenance man. He didn't mind, he preferred this life, but sometimes it would be nice to get things fixed he thought.

Shit! He stumbled, forgetting the ancient bike parked just to the side of Charles' door. He fell heavily, his knee connecting with the centre of the bike's wheel. The bag burst open, its contents skidding on the grubby oilcloth. Rory swore, pain searing through his leg making him dizzy. He sat still until the worst of it passed, then tried to stand, grabbing onto the offending machine to pull himself up. He could just about make out the food container and reached out to retrieve it, the cake he couldn't see. A light appeared behind the small stained-glass panel in Charles' door, Rory called out.

'Charles, Charles are you in there?' There had been no evidence of Charles' return that evening. In fact, Rory couldn't remember the last time he'd seen him. He hobbled to the door, knocking just in case, he called out again. The radio was on, not loud, just enough to give the impression that someone was at home. As Rory turned to leave, he could have sworn he heard the noise of a glass breaking. He stopped and turned back, battering on the door.

'Charles,' he shouted, 'Charles, are you ok?'

No reply. Rory bent down to look through the letterbox, which was a source of amusement to them both. The reclaimed door had been dumped on a skip at the end of the road and had replaced the plywood that had all but rotted away. The joke was lost on Charles until Rory explained the incongruity of its presence.

Rory raised the chipped enamel flap, positioning himself to peer through. That's when it hit him. It was a smell he would never forget.

52

Porter was at the station when the call came in. Then again, when wasn't he there these days? The search for clues to Horton's whereabouts had grown cold. No-one had come forward with any fresh evidence. Hope for the DCI was dwindling. Porter thought about the number of times he had despaired at Horton's ineptitude. There'd been times in the past that he'd wished... Ok, he considered Horton to be incompetent but for him to go missing like this? Even more frustrating was that there'd been no contact from whoever had taken Horton. Unless of course it wasn't a kidnapping at all, Horton might have become another murder victim. He studied the white boards... one for each of the murders. They seemed to multiply every other day. He knew that the answers had to be there, so why couldn't he see them? In the whole of his career Porter had never experienced so many unresolved cases at one time.

When you think about it came a voice from the other end of the room; *you've solved most of them already.*

'What?' demanded Porter, 'what do you mean?' Mason looked round, startled out of her silent contemplation of yet another file.

'B-beg pardon, Sir?' she murmured, staring across at him, her eyes as big as saucers. 'W-what did you say?'

'Never mind what I said, what did you mean, *'you've solved most of them already'*,' he demanded. Mason's reaction was starting to spook him, she was as confused as he was, he could tell.

'But...I didn't say anything, Sir,' she protested. Porter looked around the room. Lack of sleep was obviously starting to affect him. Mason looked at the boards, then back at Porter.

'Thing is, Sir,' she started tentatively, 'when you think about it, we have sort of tied up quite a bit, in one way,' she went on. Porter shook his head, was he going mad or had she beaten him to it? Mason took a deep breath, pointing at the boards, counting under her breath.

'We've got one, two, three, four, five, six, er...seven on here, nine if you count Mrs. Prothero and her son.' She waved towards the most recent board, bringing his attention back to the main cluster.

'Okay, number one is Ellis Franklin. We suspect that Noel Cooper killed him, so...'

Porter anticipated where Mason was going with her reasoning, 'Yes Mason, I know where you're heading, but we need proof. Just now we have none, no physical evidence, no witnesses, nothing... all just supposition isn't it?' Mason sighed; he was right; it was all hypothetical. They had nothing to prove their theories, at least not yet. They stood surveying the mass of circumstantial information crammed on the boards. Porter smiled, remembering how Ellie Shaw had done the same a few weeks before.

'There has to be a thread,' she told anyone within ear shot, 'something that joins the cases together.' Not long after they had discovered a tenuous connection, thanks mainly to Mason. Porter ran through it again, it never hurt to go back over facts. Sometimes they had the strangest habit of rearranging themselves which in turn could lead to new avenues of enquiry.

He skimmed through the notes. Alan Cooper bullied by Evans had given them both a link and a motive - revenge. Tony Berwick, who was known to the police for a series of minor assaults on young men, had been matched to a missing person's report on David Morgan establishing a connection between them. There seemed to be no end of connections, Mr. and Mrs. Parker and Franklin, Franklin and Nick Parker, but no proof in any of the cases. Morgan could have killed Berwick, no proof. He was sure that Alan Cooper had killed Evans, but then again no... Porter's head began to whirl again.

The phone rang, a body had been found in a squat, Porter didn't hang around. He beckoned Mason who snatched up her bag and jacket, and they raced to the scene.

53

The rats had been drawn en mass once they caught the scent. They'd treated Charles like a running buffet, his face was now a gaping hole. Identification, he was told by a Scene of Crimes officer, would only be possible from fingerprints, or teeth, if they could locate his dentist, DNA if he was on file anywhere. Robert Daventree, one of Professor Shaw's colleagues had been called in, despite his protestations that Graham was on call that night. He'd been told that the situation was 'complicated', and that he would understand when he got there. Porter didn't rate Daventree much, although he knew that his reputation was good, he didn't have Graham Shaw's finesse. But while he and Graham's stand-in dealt with the increasing workload, he would have to do.

Daventree appreciated why he'd been called out as soon as he got there. He was quick to grasp the significance of the 'shrine' as Porter called it. Pictures, newspaper clippings, drawings and maps were all pinned to the stained wall, forming part of a story, the theme of which was murder. A frayed light fitting swayed slightly as people upstairs moved around. It cast moving shadows that along with the overwhelming stench turned Porter's stomach. No one was immune, and no amounts of decongestant, however liberally applied helped. He was irritated by the signs that life was continuing amid the horror he was dealing with. Distorted laughter echoed from above, shouts between people speculating on the events beneath them.

'I want them out!' he shouted, 'all of them. This is a crime scene, for fuck's sake!'

The influx of curious people had been considerable as word had spread. Eager for gossip, people had gathered in the room above. Who knew if some of them were press? Floorboards creaked, the increasing weight causing them to sag perceptively, dust particles floated down on the crime scene. Porter had just cause to empty the building, and he knew how.

'Take them all to the station!' he shouted in the stair well, 'I want statements from the lot of them!'

Most of the druggie gang had already bolted. Those who had been too slow were the worst for wear. The Karma Kids seemed only too eager to help. Mason was sent to speak to them, re-joining Porter as he was talking to Daventree, interrupting their conversation.

'Sir,' she began, handing him her notes, 'you may want to see this.'

He read as far as the second page; she'd got a name...Charles Whittaker.

By the time they returned to the station a clearer picture was forming in Porter's mind. A shocked and sickened

Rory couldn't recall ever having seen the wall of clippings that Porter questioned him about.

'So, tell me about Whittaker,' Porter asked, 'anything would be helpful at this stage.'

Yes, Rory told him, he'd visited him in the flat, the last time being around four or five days ago. No, there was nothing unusual about the wall opposite the window. No, nothing pinned on the wall, just stained wallpaper.

'What about something like a curtain, a screen?' Porter asked him, fishing around.

'No, nothing,' repeated Rory, holding onto a bottle of water as though his life depended on it. He took regular swigs to try and quell the nausea that rose in ever increasing waves, afraid to close his eyes, afraid even to blink in case he saw Charles' face again. An idea struck him as he concentrated on the bottle.

'Look,' he fumbled around in the pocket of his oversized coat. He drew out a modern, expensive looking phone. Porter wondered how on earth he could afford it. Rory pressed a stream of buttons before passing the phone to Porter. A picture of him and Charles, taken barely a week ago making a toast to something, Rory couldn't remember exactly what. He'd asked one of the others to take the photo. It showed the wall in question behind them. It was bare except for an ancient torn poster for some rock band, confirming his statement. No clippings, no maps or notes...and yet the photos that Porter had recently pinned up on the board in the investigation room showed a plethora of pieces of paper which must have taken a considerable amount of time to assemble. Porter let Rory go, informing him that he would be required to make a formal statement later. They would need to keep the phone.

Rory didn't argue, he sped out of the station and staggered down a side street. There he retched until there was nothing in his stomach but bile.

Porter studied the photographs, even more convinced that the wall didn't look right. From what Rory had told him, Charles Whittaker didn't sound like the sort of person that would have the imagination to create it, it was too impressive. He examined the board that sported Rob Tranter's details, was this yet another revenge killing?

He grabbed his coat and made his way back to Menchin Road. A couple of the Forensic Team were still bagging and tagging as he hunkered down, hands clasped, looking at the wall. Something didn't feel right; he stared at it for some time. He stood up, pacing this way and that, scrunched up his eyes, nothing. It was like so many other walls created by sick fucks that he had dealt with in the past. Yet there was something not right about the placing of the neatly cut out snippets. The subject matter he recognised, of course, pictures taken from a distance, probably with a telephoto lens. Strange that they hadn't found a camera.

He would have known the two women anywhere, Ellie Shaw and her sister Ruth, the young boy was Max. Then there was John Prothero, and Graham. Mostly family stuff, a picnic on the lawn, some grainy quality to the pictures, but that wasn't unusual. The newspaper cuttings were all about John, some older reports of the cases in which he had played a major role. Others reported on his new position as Home Office Consultant. There were drawings, cartoons of mangled bodies, intricately detailed, coloured sketches of hideous forms of torture. The one that intrigued him the most was a portrait of a man hanging from a ceiling by his wrists, wounds evident around his ankles, blood pooling on the floor. They could have been copied from the scene of crime photographs of Col Evans. Had they been wrong about Alan Cooper? The thought unsettled him.

For all that the wall was overcrowded with information, Porter couldn't get over the feeling that it looked too neat, too contrived. Someone had tried hard to make it look like random chaos. It was a start, another link, a thread. Porter liked finding the end of a thread. It was when a knotted, stuck-fast ball of clues with no obvious leads was plonked into his lap that he was galvanised into action. It was just that this time, this time there was something different. He'd have to speak to John Prothero again, after all this was his field of expertise. But how could he approach the subject when the expert he needed to talk to was the very person who had lost the most already?

54

Graham didn't want to leave Ellie alone at the farm, but he was still on call in the event of an emergency. The first one came a few days later. Ellie promised him that she would rest, and so far, she'd kept her word. Odelia suggested that she should spend some time at the retreat that her mother ran on the south side of the island. Graham agreed that a change would do Ellie good, but he couldn't help worrying that she would outstrip what little strength she had managed to regain.

This morning, apart from a straightforward postmortem, Graham needed to clear up a mountain of outstanding paperwork. There were cases he had been in the middle of working on just before Ellie was...he needed to wrap them up. He made sure that Ellie had everything she needed, and she promised that she wouldn't overdo it as he left for the lab. It seemed strange to be driving there, even though he'd paid a few visits since Ellie had been shot. Graham didn't want to think about that day, not now, not ever if the truth be told, but he knew he couldn't avoid the subject forever.

He drove on along the main road, his mind pre-occupied with thoughts of Ellie, Ruth and Max. He swerved as an animal dashed out in front of the car jamming on the brakes, the car screeched to a halt. Graham sat frozen in his seat, his heart pounding, dizzy with shock. Suddenly a maelstrom of emotions, relief, sorrow, sadness, fear...feelings that he had managed to keep buried deep down inside for the last few weeks welled up. He gave way to it. Great waves swept through him as he sobbed until he felt empty and wretched. He leaned over the wheel, hugging the hardness of it to his chest, resting his head against his arms. He felt spent. He could remember feeling like this only once in the past, when he'd completed a cross-country run at school, his body pushed beyond its limit, exhausted. When he could finally breathe deeply, he felt oddly cleansed. A half empty bottle of water lay in the passenger foot well. Graham grabbed it, got out of the car and drank deeply before bending over and vomiting over the ferns. He searched in the boot and found a fresh bottle; he splashed a little over his face then drank again, this time slowly. Ironically, he felt much better than he had done when he left home a little over an hour ago. He'd been holding so much in. The careless animal, so nearly roadkill, had done him a huge favour. He got back in the car and drove on.

The lab was busy when he arrived. Graham needed to find out what was happening, if any progress had been made on the shootings. Cathy hadn't turned in; no-one had time to bring him up to date. He'd called Porter several times to see what he could find out, with few results. At this stage, he was told, details couldn't be discussed outside the investigation team, a fact that Graham already knew. It hurt to be on the outside of what was going on. Porter did however hint that there was little to connect the murder of his sister-in-law and nephew to the ones that Ellie had been working on. Graham wasn't sure. Anglesey was a small island, for so many murders to have taken place in such a short space of time was unbelievable. He felt there had to be a link, just like Ellie had suggested all those weeks ago.

This morning's postmortem was for a 'routine' sudden death, nothing untoward. A businessman sitting at the lunch table with two colleagues had suddenly choked and expired within minutes, despite desperate attempts to revive him. The body was prepped and ready, and soon Graham was immersed in his routine. He was surprised when he realised that he'd finished. The grossly overweight man had sclerosis of the liver. There was overwhelming hardening of the arteries, and an enlarged heart. Not surprising that he'd died, but what did shock Graham was that Brian Collins was only five years his senior.

So sad, he thought, shaking his head, *small changes in lifestyle could have prolonged his life.* What bothered Graham though was that he'd carried out the procedure on autopilot, something that he regularly warned both his assistants and students about. There was a high possibility that something could slip through the net if you didn't concentrate on the job in hand. He berated himself, and decided to check through his findings, this time giving all his attention to his subject. Once he was satisfied that there was nothing he'd overlooked, he washed his hands, leaving the closing procedure to the technician, Mark. The next few hours were taken up with the paperwork that went along with each procedure, dotting I's and crossing T's, bringing files up to date. It was routine stuff, but it needed to be done and the sooner he completed his work, the sooner he would be back with Ellie.

A sudden thought struck him. He was taking a lot longer to complete his notes than usual. He wondered if that was because he was out of the rhythm of things. It came as a shock when he realised that he was enjoying being back in the lab again, and that despite the nature of his work, it was a lot less stressful than tiptoeing around Ellie all day long. He had to admit that he wanted to stay there for as long as he could. The guilt he felt at this realization overwhelmed him momentarily. He loved Ellie, and wanted to help her though her ordeal, but maybe he wasn't giving her enough space? He thought about Odelia's suggestion. Maybe she was right; maybe they could do with some time apart? He hadn't slept well in ages. He filed some paperwork, shaking his head, what was the matter with him? His wife needed him; he should be there for her no matter what.

Voices in the hallway. He recognised one as Emlyn Davies, the other seemed familiar but he wasn't sure. The door opened and in they walked, first Emlyn followed by...Kara Billingham.

55

Graham had covered everything, Ellie thought gratefully as she turned gingerly onto her side. The sofa was comfortable, one side let down so that she could stretch out, he'd even fetched the duvet from the guest room. It was the duck down one, the one that he'd freaked out about when she told him how much it had cost. Ellie knew that she was filling her mind with trivia again. When she was thinking of something unimportant, she didn't have to think about...the realisation broke her fragile resolve. Other memories crowded in on her, not quite so happy. She'd been having the dream again, the one about him and....no, she wouldn't think about it, not now, not while she was alone and, it had to be said, lonely.

He had barely left her side since that awful day, just a few trips to the University or his office. Was it only a few weeks ago? His Mother or Father would turn up just before he left, so she was rarely alone. There was the time he went to fetch Odelia from the town, but he'd been back within an hour, somewhat of a record. She wished he would go out more often, he needed a break, as did she. She hadn't had time to think, it was almost as though he didn't want her to. But she needed quiet to recall parts of that day, it was important for her to remember. But Graham was always there, him or his parents, her 'babysitters'.

No, she thought, *that's not fair, it's because he cares. He wants to make sure I'm all right.* It did nothing to stem the feeling that he was overcompensating for something. He didn't know how to help her, especially when she lapsed into silence and sat staring out of the window. He'd try to get her to talk about anything to take her mind off what she really needed to do. The phone brought her back to the present. Where the hell was it? She fished it out from between the cushions. Porter... damn, she really didn't want to talk to him right now. He wanted her to go over her statement, and she wasn't ready. *But when will I be ready?* She swiped the phone to reply.

'Ms. Shaw,' Porter grunted, 'I'm sorry to bother you, I know this is a difficult time....' he hesitated. He wanted to be assured that she wasn't inconvenienced at all. She told him she was improving, and that yes, she was taking it easy. She almost added that she was doing a hell of a lot better than most people who have lost their sister and nephew to a mad gunman. The thought made her gasp, Porter heard it.

'Are you all right Ellie?' His tone caused her to swallow hard, biting back tears.

'Yes,' she whispered, 'I'm...I'm good,' she wasn't, and they both knew it.

'We can do this some other time,' he offered apologetically.

'No, please,' she sighed, 'what do you need me to do?'

They just happened to be on the island, he said trying to sound as though he hadn't planned it. DS Mason was with him. She could take notes, he suggested. Despite his concern for her welfare, she felt that he'd painted her into a corner. He was observing proprieties by using Mason as chaperone. He hoped that she would make an effective buffer if the situation became emotional. Porter knew his actions were mostly self-serving. He half-heartedly offered to postpone. Maybe they could arrange another time? Would she like Graham to be there? She reassured him that it would be fine, that she might feel more relaxed without Graham present.

'We'll be with you at 1p.m. then,' he confirmed. He still sounded unsure that he was doing the right thing.

The silence of the house closed in around her as Ellie waited. She could feel the tension building up. How had he known Graham wasn't there, she wondered as she straightened the covers and tried to relax? Was Porter watching her?

56

Graham knew Kara too well to believe that she had landed this assignment on the off-chance. She feigned delight at 'bumping into him,' even though he was sitting in his own clearly marked office. She must also have known that he was part of the team. Those factors alone cemented his suspicion that somehow, she'd managed to arrange everything, although just now he couldn't quite work out. Graham had heard of her success; the grapevine was adept in spreading such news. In a way, he was proud of what she'd achieved, but wary of his motivation in such pride. Now here she was standing in front of him. Even more disquieting was that she'd performed the postmortem on Ruth and Max without anyone informing him.

Later, sitting in the canteen, a mug of untouched coffee before him, he allowed this latest wrecking ball of a situation to settle into his consciousness. *I don't think I can cope with much more*...he thought. Was fate trying to finish him off, or was this the karma that Ellie often spoke of? Only moments ago, he had excused himself from the unnecessary introductions that Emlyn had been about to perform. Graham had fought the overwhelming urge to run. He managed to say that they had met, and that he was aware of how lucky the department was to have been sent such a talented practitioner to help them out. Kara stood watching him in silence, her glacial beauty exuding an aura of unworldliness. Graham could detect triumph beneath the polite exterior. He'd experienced her manipulative nature too many times to be fooled. His suspicions grew stronger, the tension he felt threatened to overwhelm him. He excused himself and fled to the comparative safety of the canteen.

How was it that he had been unaware of her assignment to the lab, let alone that she had performed the postmortem on Ruth and Max? Had he become so out of touch with what was going on at the lab? The answer of course was *yes*, and it made him angry. He'd always taken such pride in keeping his finger on the pulse of what was going on here, now he felt completely out of the loop.

His heart was racing; it was fear, that much was obvious. This was a potential disaster. Davies had recently offered him complete leave of absence and he wondered if he could take it, hesitating only because of the workload at the lab. But how could he remain as a functioning member of the team with Kara as one of his colleagues, even if on a temporary basis? Ellie's uncanny intuition would soon sense that something was wrong. His coffee was going cold as he considered his limited options. He ran his hands through his hair and rubbed his eyes, trying in vain to clear his head.

'Headache?' a voice at his side took him by surprise. He jumped up, knocking over his chair, his nerves stretched to their limit. Odelia stared at him in surprise. 'Are you all right?' she asked, shocked to see the change in him since her visit to the farm.

'Yes, yes, I'm, I'm fine…' he stuttered, in a way that told her that he was anything but. He picked up the chair and sat back down. Odelia placed her hand on his shoulder and kept it there for several seconds.

'I'll get some fresh coffee,' she whispered, and walked to the counter. Graham had calmed down as soon as she'd touched him. *What was it with her…* he wondered? He was as curious about her as Ellie was. His research had revealed little about her past. Graham had explored every source he knew to establish that she was genuine. He felt no guilt about his actions, justifying his actions by telling himself that his enquiries could save potential heartache and embarrassment. Nothing, no criminal activity, no recorded achievements, only a few write-ups on the retreat owned and run by her mother. This was the place that she wanted Ellie to visit, and if it would help, who was he to deny her that help?

Are you sure that's the real reason? Doesn't have anything to do with what just happened in your office does it? Graham turned around to see who'd spoken, Odelia was still at the counter, there was no one else there. He watched as Odelia turned and walked towards him, she smiled.

'I know you have doubts about Ellie coming to the retreat,' she said, almost as though she had read his mind, 'and I know that you're curious about me, will you let me try to put those doubts to rest?'

How could he refuse?

57

Porter was dreading seeing Ellie again. He was good with bodies and the aftermath of murder...those situations he could deal with. He was good with offenders, but victims? No, he wasn't good with victims, especially those who were suffering with survivor guilt. That was one of the reasons he'd asked Mason to accompany him. It was policy to have a chaperone when conducting an interview with a female, something that seemed unnecessary in days gone by. Mason would fill that role, and one of providing a buffer against his brusque way of interviewing. That and the fact that he couldn't, just couldn't deal with a weeping woman. He appreciated what Ellie Shaw had gone through, but there it was. Mason agreed at once, although she wondered if her inclusion was down to the fact that she seemed to be the only female officer available.

The lane to the farmhouse was rutted in places. Heavy rain a few nights ago had caused flooding in the area, widening cracks and washing away the smaller stones. It made for an uncomfortable ride. Mason clutched the hand strap, staring ahead, her face grim. She was silent as usual, and somehow this unnerved Porter.

'You ok, Mason?' he asked as they approached the final bend, she nodded, blushing at the same time.

'I was just thinking about the last time I was meant to meet with Ms. Shaw,' she confessed, her voice almost a whisper. Porter grimaced; realising that what had happened at John Prothero's home must have been a hell of a shock for Mason. He might have underestimated just how much.

'I'm sorry, I didn't think,' he started, embarrassed that he had assumed too much. Mason shook her head.

'It's ok, really, it's just that now and then...' she cleared her throat. 'Sir, I er...I was thinking, this morning...' she hesitated again, Porter waited. 'Do they know about Charles Whittaker?'

Porter almost stalled the car...*shit!* Had Graham found out? If he had, surely, he would have brought up the subject? On the other hand, if Ellie was still fragile...maybe he hadn't told her, maybe he didn't know, after all very few people did at this stage.

'I don't think it would be wise to bring up the subject at this stage, do you?' he asked, 'let's get her statement and leave it at that.'

Mason nodded; she saw the wisdom in both avoiding further distress for Ellie, and in not muddying the waters. They needed her statement, and this might be the best chance to take it...less formal than her coming to the station. All the same, she may well react badly when she did find out, which she would have to at some point.

Ellie welcomed them, offering to make drinks. She was annoyed when Mason took over. Having sat around for most of the day, she wanted something to do to stretch her legs, and perhaps break the tension that hung in the air. It was obvious that Porter had missed the memo when it came to empathy, even though he was genuinely moved by what Ellie had gone through. He hummed and hawed, shuffling in his seat as Mason busied herself.

'Err, thanks for seeing us,' he managed, wondering how on earth he was going to get through her statement if he couldn't get the ball rolling. Ellie's heart went out to him. She admired his interview techniques; she'd seen him handle the most obdurate of witnesses. This was different though. There was a growing respect between the two of them, and she always felt more confident when she was working with Porter, whereas Horton frightened her to death.

Somehow interviewing a colleague must be more difficult she thought *he doesn't know how to begin.*

'Shall we have some biscuits?' she said, getting up slowly and making her way around to the kitchen island. Mason shot her a glance that was both surprised and warm, a *'Well-done you',* reaction. Ellie winced as she reached for some chocolate digestives, which she knew Porter liked. She brought them back to the sofa, placing them on the coffee table. Porter smiled at her.

'Coincidence?' he asked, she shook her head.

'I got Graham to buy them,' she replied, 'we ought to rename them, 'Icebreakers!'" and it was, broken. Ellie tore into the packet; Porter helped himself to a couple and relaxed a little as he munched away before sighing.

'There is no easy way to do this is there?' he said, brushing the crumbs off his tie. Ellie shook her head.

'No, I guess there isn't,' she whispered. Mason sat on the footstool as Porter took out his notebook and a file.

It took them close to an hour to get through Ellie's statement. Porter had already written down everything he'd had heard her say on the few occasions that he'd been at the hospital. She confirmed most of it and added the details she could remember.

John had sent a text redirecting their meeting to his house because he had been delayed. She told him how surprised she was at finding Ruth and Max there, as they were supposed to be airborne at the time, and how upset her sister had been. Porter considered her comments before interrupting her.

'When was the last time you spoke to your sister?' he asked. 'Do you know what she was upset about?'

'The night before she was due to leave,' Ellie told him, 'she phoned me to say goodbye. We talked for maybe twenty minutes or so. She seemed fine, told me she'd been to see her doctor that day, and that we needed to talk more when she got back, that there was something that she needed to ask me about, that it was important, but that it could wait.'

Porter shifted in his chair. If this was going to end up in a discussion about personal medical details, he knew he was going to get uncomfortable. Mason detected the change in the atmosphere.

'Shall we go back to the events of the day, Ms. Shaw?' she asked, reminding them both of her presence. 'You were telling us about your arrival at the cottage.'

Ellie sighed; she really didn't want to go through this again, might as well get it over with as soon as she could. She recalled the events just after her arrival, how she'd spent time trying to calm her sister down.

Then someone was the banging on the door, Ruth left the room to answer it. The rest was still a blur, although she had recalled seeing her lying on the floor when she entered the hallway, shortly before…she paused. Porter stayed quiet, waiting for her to continue.

'… I was shot. From then on, it's mostly a blank, except that, I… I thought I saw something, just before I passed out. There was someone walking towards me from the other direction. I felt a sharp pain, in my ribs, and everything went black. That's all really, until I came around and Graham was sitting by the bed. I… I'm sorry, that's all I can remember.'

'That's fine,' Porter assured her, 'maybe something will come later, can you enlarge on a description?' he asked, hoping that she would be able to give him more of a clue.

She couldn't, the shooter was in the doorway with sunlight behind, and the impact of the bullet had spun her round so that she was facing the other way, she hadn't got a good look at all, she apologised over again.

'I'm not a very good witness, am I?' she asked, tears welling up. Mason took Ellie's hands in hers.

'You can't expect to be,' she whispered, 'trauma affects memory, it will come, just relax and allow yourself to remember.'

Both Porter and Ellie looked askance at the DS, who was patting Ellie's hand. She turned away, took a biscuit and dunked it in her tea.

It was almost three before they left. Mason refilled Ellie's water bottle and shuffled some magazines back into a neat pile. Porter gathered together his files and murmured a few platitudes along the lines of the whole team thinking about her and wishing her well. He was on his way to the door that the thought hit him.

'Did you say that you saw someone approach you from another direction, Ellie?' he asked.

Ellie thought about it for a few seconds closing her eyes to visualise the scene. Someone had walked around her, she could see their feet, dark shoes, she couldn't tell the colour for sure, but they were there in front of her face as she felt the cold of the tiles seeping into her cheek. Whoever it was had taken a step towards her and she had felt a piercing pain in her side as she passed out.

'I think we know how you came to sustain broken ribs now, don't you?' Porter observed as he saw Mason make a note of the new revelation.

'I think we do...' Ellie answered; he saw her confusion. She was trying to work something out, her eyes narrowed as realisation dawned. 'You know who did it, don't you?' she asked.

Porter sighed; he knew he'd have to tell her something. Keeping information from someone you knew you had to work with in the future was a risky business. But just how much he should tell her, that was the question.

58

Odelia thought about her conversation with Graham as she headed towards her office. After spending some time in the canteen where she outlined some of advantages she felt a visit to the Retreat could provide, they returned to his office. Graham had listened in a distracted way, but it wasn't his preoccupation that bothered her, it was the incident prior to her departure. She sensed that he was agitated; he kept looking towards the door.

Voices in the corridor, Graham jumped to his feet and suggested that she should come over to the farm the next evening to talk with Ellie. The office door opened; a tall blonde woman entered. She wore an unbuttoned lab coat, a pair of tailored trousers and a well-fitting blouse. There was a split-second delay before Odelia noticed her feigned look of surprise. It was obvious that the uninvited visitor had entered the office knowing that Graham was busy.

He introduced the woman as Kara Billingham, a pathologist who was on secondment his department and who'd performed the postmortem on Ruth and Max. Odelia watched his face suffuse with colour as he made the introductions. She also saw the almost imperceptible smirk of self-satisfaction on Kara's face as she stepped forward to shake Odelia's hand. Her grip was strong, Odelia almost winced, but she smiled back. There was something not right about Kara, something calculating, as though she was gloating about some victory.

The cat that got the cream, thought Odelia, she berated herself for jumping to conclusions. Then again, this was instinct, and when had she ever been wrong? Never, not in the long run. She gathered her things and moved towards the door, confirming the time for their meeting the next evening. She glanced back at Graham, still sitting at his desk. There was a look of desperation about him, as though he didn't want to be left alone with Kara. He was still babbling something about them having worked together in the past, and wasn't it a coincidence that she had been sent here?

'Professor Shaw,' Odelia pleaded, 'I wonder if you could help me with the door?' She juggled her handbag and her briefcase for effect, even though she could manage perfectly well. Graham sprang to his feet, and dashed towards her, confirming her previous suspicions. Holding the door open for her, he offered to walk with her to her car. She accepted, engaging in small talk until they had left the office.

'Best to avoid being alone with that one,' she whispered as he waited for her to unlock her car. He didn't answer, just nodded.

Did this woman know everything, he thought, *and if she did, would she spill the beans to Ellie?* She nodded as if he had spoken out loud, 'Best coming from you.'

As she pulled off the car park, she saw him unlock his own vehicle, *ahh*, she thought, *tactical retreat.* Odelia's sense of unease persisted as she thought about Kara's entrance into Graham's office. She had a certain look about her that was difficult to describe...then it came to her. *Predator*, she had the air of a predator about to strike.

59

Ellie was drained. She drifted into a deep sleep, glad that Graham wasn't due back for some hours. He'd promised to get a takeaway for them for supper. *He won't be happy when he finds out about Porter's visit*, she thought as she settled back on the sofa. Her mind was buzzing with the news about Charles Whittaker. *Ah well, too late now.* She would have had to give her statement sometime, better to get it over and done with. She was sure that Porter had stretched the truth about being on the island anyway, she was equally sure that he hadn't told her everything about Whittaker. Only that they had found his body, that he had some pictures which they were investigating, and that it looked as though it would take some time before they could piece everything together. Very vague, very up in the air, but she appreciated the brevity. She couldn't cope with much more for the time being.

But then again, why should that be a surprise? Everything's taking time, she thought with a sigh, realising how tired the encounter had left her. She tried to settle back, to dismiss the images that the last few hours had brought back, eventually she slipped into a fitful doze.

Ellie woke with a start; she'd seen the gunman in her dream, though not clearly, as she'd told Porter. Something was wrong though, something she couldn't put her finger on. She stared out of the window willing herself to remember, trying to relax and recall every detail. Then it came... it wasn't the sunlight that had prevented her seeing him...the sun wouldn't have been in that position at that time of day. Yet he was surrounded in light, just like Alan Cooper in the interview room. She'd seen the light move towards her in the same way, just as he fired at her. Ellie shook her head, trying to place her memories in order. She wasn't that sure of anything at all; maybe it was just her imagination. Her heart was racing as she searched once more for the phone, her hand shook as she keyed in Graham's number. The call diverted to his recorded message. Damn, she wanted to hear his voice.

'...leave a message, I'll get back asap,' she hesitated, unsure of what to say, she hung up still shaking. Drawing the duvet up to her chin, the last of her fragile bravado dissolved, she wept until her stomach ached, fighting for breath. It stopped almost as quickly as it had engulfed her as she heard banging on the front door. For a moment she imagined she was back in Ruth's house, she began to shake again. No one was due to call. She sat motionless, willing whoever it was to go away, determined to quell the terror inside. The silence was palpable, she realised that she was holding her breath.

More knocking, this time louder, more insistent, Ellie struggled to stand and made her way the hallway. She could see a figure through the frosted glass; Graham had warned her not to answer the door to anyone. She froze as the handle turned, hoping the caller would give up and leave. She knew the door was locked, but the knowledge did nothing to dispel her fear. Her pulse thundered in her ears; her legs started to lose strength.

'Ellie, Graham, please...' she recognised John's voice and gave a gasp of relief as she moved to open the door. John held onto the doorframe for support. Ellie reached out as he slumped towards her, his weight sending shockwaves through her injured shoulder. They stumbled into the kitchen; John fell onto the settee, where moments before Ellie had succumbed to her emotions. He began to wail, broken phrases, incoherent, slapping his forehead. Ellie stood still, her back against the island unit, knowing that in this state he could anything. She couldn't take much more... pain seared down her arm and into her chest. It was against her nature to remain outside of his reach, when what she wanted to do was to comfort him.

For nearly an hour she moved around cautiously, making what she hoped were soothing comments. John hardly seemed to know she was there. She watched him closely, prepared to move as quickly as she could if he tried to reach for her. She wasn't up to this. Eventually he appeared to be winding down, his energy spent. He sat for several minutes looking out of the window. Then, almost as though someone had switched off a light bulb, his eyes closed, and he fell into a fitful sleep. He slipped sideways, his body shifting into a foetal position. Ellie covered him with the duvet. She tiptoed into the hallway, not knowing what to do for the best. A car door slammed, the sound of footsteps on the gravel. Looking out of the window she saw Graham walking towards the house.

60

The decision was made, it wasn't a difficult one. Ellie would go to the retreat the next morning. They agreed that even without Porter and Mason's visit and John's sudden arrival, Ellie couldn't take much more. She needed a complete break; she was on the point of collapse. Graham blamed himself for assuming that she could cope. After his talk with Odelia he felt confident that a stay at the retreat was their best option. He also acknowledged that her absence would give him the breathing space he needed to address the elephant residing in the corner of his brain...Kara.

During the last few weeks, Graham had questioned whether Ellie should continue working in profiling at all. She disagreed, pointing out that they had no idea if what had happened at Ruth's home had any connection to her work. It could have been a robbery gone wrong, or any number of motives. Nevertheless, Graham had a growing belief that her work had somehow got them into this situation, the thought terrified him. The opposing voices in his head argued over and over.

It might not be her work, he reasoned, o*ther things, things over which they held a degree of responsibility, yes, but not her work, how could it?*

The devil's advocate in him whispered, *it brought her into contact with the kind of scum that would gun down women and young children, didn't it?* His convictions were backed up when Ellie finally broke the news about Charles Whittaker, a development he knew nothing about.

Graham considered the implications of what she'd said. He knew that psychiatric patients sometimes became obsessed with those trying to help them, but what had John done to deserve his treatment at the hands of such a low life? He tried to hold his anger in check. What was important was Ellie and her wellbeing, anything else was secondary. Driving home, he'd envisaged a quiet night, a chance to talk things over before telling her about Odelia's visit. But once there he'd had other things to occupy him. He managed to calm Ellie down, helped her upstairs, and stroked her head as she finally fell asleep. He'd returned to the kitchen and watched John as he slept fitfully, trying to guess what had caused him to break his self-imposed solitude so abruptly.

Graham had attempted to contact him several times during the last few days. He visited the hotel where he knew John was holed up but had missed him on each occasion. He wanted to talk to John, to let him know that he was there for him, but who knew with John? He was a law unto himself. Graham had persuaded his conscience that his brother-in-law probably had someone from the Family Liaison Department keeping an eye on him. With Ellie to worry about he felt he had enough on his plate. Now, looking at John as he twitched in his sleep, he felt guilty that he hadn't kept trying to get through to him.

John was dishevelled, unshaven, his hair greasy. Graham could tell from the pungent odour that he hadn't changed his clothes for some time. This wasn't like John; he was normally meticulous about his appearance. Graham shook his head, he had his reasons for being neglectful, he consoled himself, but how had John slipped through the net with the wealth of help that was available?

Graham retrieved the carrier bags that contained the takeaway, he'd dropped them in his dash to stop Ellie from falling. The food was cold, and anyway the last thing he felt like was eating, he pulled out the plastic dishes intending to throw them out.

'You could always reheat them,' came a voice from the settee. Graham turned to see John stretching. He turned and smiled shyly at Graham, 'I must look quite a sight,' he said.

Graham nodded, John must have been watching him reflected in the window, but he'd been too absorbed in his own thoughts to notice. He fetched two plates, spooned food onto them and re-heated them in the microwave. When they'd eaten, he sat back, glad that he'd forced the first mouthful down, each bite had been easier to swallow. John ate as though he hadn't eaten for days, and the food on offer was the finest cuisine, not a mediocre offering from a local Chinese.

'John...' Graham started, placing his fork down with exaggerated care.

'I know,' interrupted John, 'and I'm sorry, I didn't mean to frighten Ellie, I don't know what came over me, I just needed someone to talk to....' he gulped, overcome with emotion. 'Besides,' he added, 'I thought you'd be here with her.'

Graham winced, *I should have been*, he thought, clearing his throat. 'It can't be allowed to happen again,' he said calmly, 'she's not strong enough, and neither are you. You need help, John, no matter what you say, I know that's the last thing you want to hear, but there it is.'

They sat for several minutes, neither one spoke, each lost in their own thoughts. John stood abruptly, wiping his hands on his stained jacket.

'I'm going away for a while,' he said, gathering up his dishes, and carrying them to the kitchen. 'I'll let you know where I end up. In the meantime, could you let Porter and his team know? That way if something comes up, they can contact me.'

'John, I didn't mean for you to go away completely, let me help...' but John was adamant, and Graham knew that any further argument was futile. He left as suddenly as he'd arrived, despite Graham's protests as he followed him to his car. John turned as he reached it, causing Graham to step back in surprise.

'Let me know, won't you... just keep me informed?' he got into the car and was gone within seconds, leaving Graham staring long after the taillights had disappeared.

...*typical John*, he thought, *an expert at sorting out other people's problems, in total denial when it came to his own*. Apart from tonight Graham had never seen him so much as slightly ruffled when it came to his personal life. He comforted himself that John appeared to have reverted to something like his true nature.

...*I've got enough to worry about* he thought returning to the house. Within minutes he was dialing Odelia Mather's number, it was only later that he realised that he hadn't told John about Charles Whittaker.

61

Horton's body ached; it even hurt him to blink. He was having trouble keeping track of how long he'd been there. The thin mattress afforded little comfort. He tried to sleep but was conscious of the rats running around the perimeter of his prison. He flinched each time he heard them scuttling. He hated rats, more than aware of the damage they could wreak. He managed to drag out a torn sheet from under the mattress and had wound it round his head. It smelled putrid, but he hoped that it might give him a degree of protection.

The nights were the worst, not a flicker of light in the inky blackness. At least he had chance to study his prison during the day, although the prospect of an escape seemed impossible. A few times his hooded jailor had come to bring more water and sandwiches. There had been no verbal response, even though he had begged for his freedom, warning, cajoling, persuading, pleading, all to no avail.

The most dehumanising aspect of his ordeal though, were the toilet arrangements. He would be unchained, and half dragged over to the device they had provided for his needs. His trousers were hauled down around his ankles; strong hands would force him to sit down on what he recognised as a battered commode. His captor would wait in silence as he relieved himself. No toilet roll was provided, and he gagged at his own stench. Once he had finished, he was hauled back to the other end of the cell and his tether reattached. Then he was left alone once more. The fetid air reeked, causing Horton to retch on more than one occasion, the commode had been emptied only twice since his arrival.

Whoever was guarding him did what they had to do and left abruptly. He slept fitfully, it was damp and cold, and his lungs were feeling the effect of the moisture in the dank air. He coughed, his chest betraying the familiar signs of the recurring bronchitis he'd suffered from since childhood. For a couple of days, it rained continuously, hammering on the roof, wind howling through the walls. No one came to the barn, and Horton had to improvise new toilet arrangements.

On the third day his captor was back, fresh water, more sandwiches, only this time he placed the bottle into Horton's eager hands. He drank greedily, only to find himself feeling dizzy within seconds, his panic rising as he slowly lost consciousness. As he came to, he could hear distorted sounds echoing around his confused mind. He was blind-folded and could see only a thin strip of light if he looked down. He couldn't tell what was going on, only that there was someone else in the room with him. He lay as still as he could on the mattress. Something was being dragged around, banging, scraping, muffled voices... was that a drill whirring? Horton tried hard not to make a sound, to draw attention to himself would be a mistake. He heard the door creak, it banged shut leaving him in sudden silence. He lay still for what seemed like an eternity, terrified to call out. When he did there was no answer, but then no one had ever answered him. Hours passed and the room grew darker as he tried to clear his head, if only...a sound, the outer door being opened again. Using the last of his strength he pushed himself into a semi standing position. If they were going to kill him, he wasn't going to go lying down. Silence...had he made a mistake, dreamt that someone was out there? He saw lights flashing under the door, a voice called out.

'Armed police… is anyone there?' the door burst open; torches pierced the gloom. Horton fell once more to his knees. His first thought was that he would be the laughing stock of the station.

62

I t was a tip off, an anonymous call. The voice was disguised, the call only long enough to convey the message. The receiver had been left hanging, so the call was traced. Not that Porter had needed it; the caller's information was enough.

'Horton…Entwell's cowshed…not doing so well…' the caller hung up. They traced the phone, one of the remaining public ones, close to the farm itself. There were, of course no CCTV cameras in the area, no prints on the receiver. Porter knew that this operation was far too professional to have made those kinds of mistakes. Forensics pointed out some recently drilled holes high up inside the barn where they had found Horton. They couldn't confirm their purpose, most likely the whole thing had been filmed, another connection to earlier cases.

'Could be a back-board, something attached to it,' said one of the attending technicians, 'looks the sort of size you fix a camera to, in fact…' he took measurements, as he had of everything in the area. He was talking more to himself than to Porter, who knew that eventually there would be a full report. He was tired of following people around. He knew better than to question them while they were doing their thing.

Porter sighed deeply; then wished he hadn't as the combined stink from the drains and the commode caught in his throat, causing his stomach to lurch. How the hell had Horton survived these conditions for so long? Not that he'd had much choice in the matter. Still, he thought, it could have been worse. His boss could have been lying outside in a body bag. Taking one last look around the illuminated sight, he made for the open door through which his team had so recently burst.

The farm had been deserted for some time, yet another family business bankrupt. Porter could remember when this farm had been a thriving business. Thick mud squelched underfoot, *not ideal conditions for Forensics,* he thought as he spotted Graham Shaw standing in the back doorway talking to a technician. He made his way over.

No matter how hard he tried, Porter couldn't understand how Ellie's husband could carry on as though it was business as usual.

'Everything ok, Professor Shaw?' he asked nodding towards the barn, 'found anything?'

'Not so far, looks like someone's been in here regularly. We found copies of newspapers covering the time Horton's been missing, assorted rubbish, but nothing much otherwise. As a crime scene, it's a washout, won't get much in the way of footprints,' he turned as someone inside the house called to him, nodded to Porter as he disappeared inside the building. Porter decided he would leave them to it, he felt a bit like a spare part. Best go back to the station.

63

Ellie was exhausted. She'd spent the first two days at the Retreat either asleep or relaxing. Odelia realised that any activities that she'd planned, would have to wait. Her mother was of the same opinion. It was fortunate that Della Mathers and Ellie had hit it off from the offset. Ellie had been struck by the older woman's air of serenity; Della certainly lived up to the plaudits awarded to her and her work. They had only spoken a couple of times, but during those short interactions Ellie had been deeply affected by Della's calming presence. Ellie didn't have a clue why it was that just sitting and talking with Della quietened her anxiety, she only knew that once they parted company, she felt different. It was exciting and puzzling, Ellie's curiosity needed to be satisfied. She tried to question Odelia, but to no avail.

'We can talk later,' seemed to be the stock reply, 'rest now...build up your strength.' Ellie was beginning to feel as though she was being patronised, even though the advice seemed sincere. She knew that it made sense.

Odelia had spoken to her mother several times. It was obvious that Ellie had a great deal of healing to do. She'd progressed to short walks in the gardens, something she would have liked to have done at home but found impossible given the various distractions. She was sure that coming here was the right course of action but at the same time felt guilty that she'd cut herself off from Graham. As the days passed, though, she began to agree with what Odelia had said to her on the first day of her stay.

'You can't expect to be able to help anyone in the state you're in, Ellie,' they'd been sitting on a bench in the garden, the sound of the birds in the trees a backdrop to their conversation. 'Once you've rested and got yourself together, things will be better... look after yourself first.'

Ellie knew Odelia was right. She looked forward to Graham's calls every evening, but it was all she could do not to ask if he'd heard anything from Porter. It was three or four days after they arrived that Ellie had her first nightmare. It wasn't one that centered on Ruth and Max's death.

64

Odelia had grown up in the old house that was now the Retreat. It sat back from the edge of the cliffs by a good quarter of a mile. The rooms on the first floor gave stunning views out over the bay. The backdrop to the house, as well planned as any theatrical set, included well-tended hedges and shrubs. It lay in twenty odd acres of land. The long winding drive through an avenue of plane trees sheltered the main building from view until the very last bend revealed it in all its splendour.

The entrance hall was rather dark, but visitors who anticipated a sombre interior were pleasantly surprised once they were inside. The rest of the house was imbued with an incredible amount of light. The Great Hall, which served as a meeting place for group activities, boasted a pair of tall French windows which let out onto manicured lawns. The borders were planted with a variety of cottage flowers, giving the garden a relaxed feel. Here and there garden benches sat surrounded by seasonal blooms, and paths led off to areas designed for meditation and relaxation. Great statues of Buddha, St Francis of Assisi, Yin and Yang symbols and animals were placed so that the adventurer would come upon them as the path twisted and turned. Overall the illusion was that the main garden was huge.

A chilly sea breeze whipped the waves into a foaming frenzy. Odelia hunched her shoulders against the spray that was gradually soaking into her jacket. Not for anything would she miss her early morning walk, a habit she resumed every time she visited the retreat. The sand, a smooth stretch of almost unpolluted beach was patrolled every day by the guests. They took pride in retrieving and recycling any stray rubbish, leaving the area almost pristine. Odelia loved it here, even on a cold day like this. The watery sun gave off little heat, and Odelia knew that she would suffer if she stayed out much longer. Her overlong scarf provided some warmth, but she would have to turn back before long. Despite her thermal gloves her hands were becoming numb. She pulled off her gloves and examined her hands. Three of the fingers on her left hand were now a pale straw colour, her right hand wasn't much better. If she stayed out much longer, she'd be in agony once she returned to the warmth of the Retreat. She rubbed her hands together and blew on them to encourage the blood supply.

Hunger was just beginning to bite when Odelia spotted Ellie standing by the water's edge. Odelia knew that she'd been having trouble sleeping. She called out as she got closer, her voice almost swept away by the increasing strength of the wind. Even so Ellie heard her and turned, waving as she drew closer.

They didn't speak as Odelia put her arm around Ellie's shoulders and turned to head back. Much to her relief there was no resistance. They walked back in silence, entering the house by the side door, stepping into the warmth. Ellie stood in the small hallway looking lost, until Odelia steered her into one of several side rooms. She guided Ellie to one of the winged-back chairs. Ellie looked lost, her pale face revealing dark smudges under her eyes. Odelia took off her gloves, coat and scarf, and dumped them unceremoniously on a chair by the door. She rubbed her hands together once more to increase the circulation, hoping that she wouldn't get the agonising pins and needles which sometimes accompanied their recovery.

Ellie stared blindly into the flames as Odelia busied herself making coffee at the small drinks area. She offered a mug to Ellie, and they sat for a while, watching the fire. The crackling of the wood was the only sound other than the ticking of a mantle clock. As it struck the hour, Ellie sighed. Odelia waited, she'd resisted the impulse to start talking until Ellie was ready.

'Graham and I went to Budapest for our honeymoon,' Ellie said. 'It's a beautiful city, though sad in some ways, the war, what happened to the people, you know?' She talked as though Odelia wasn't there. 'On the last day, we visited the thermal baths. It was one of the strangest places I have ever been to. To be honest it spooked me.' Ellie laughed weakly as the memory of the hazy rooms, the lights ensconced in steam, came back as clearly as though it had been yesterday.

'We spent a long time there, it was January, and freezing outside. We didn't want to leave. Graham said his hands were shrivelling up, his fingers were all mushy,' she shook her head, 'so we got dressed and left.'

Ok thought Odelia, *nothing bad there,* she kept quiet as she watched Ellie's face cloud over.

'Something happened, around a year later,' Ellie seemed to fold in on herself as she told Odelia about Josie Blewitt, about the drinking, about Graham, the distance that had grown between them. Finally, about his betrayal with one of his students... Kara.

'He doesn't...' she went on, her voice strained with emotion, '...he doesn't know that I found out her name. It wasn't hard. He told me she'd left, transferred to another University. I did a bit of digging and came up with her name on a register of students. It didn't take long for me to find her on the Internet. She'd graduated with a First-Class Degree, something the papers in her hometown picked up on. There was a feature in one of the local papers. She looked just like I imagined she would.'

Ellie started to cry as she fought for control. She reached for a handful of tissues. '...and now, now I have this dream,' she sobbed as Odelia moved towards her. 'I'm there again, in the thermal baths, standing at the edge, watching...' she paused as a shudder ran through her body, 'watching them hold each other, kissing. Then... then she sinks into the water, and the thing is... the thing is, as she disappears, the water turns red, and she's gone. Graham turns to me...he's smiling, but he doesn't look...he doesn't look like himself...' Odelia put her hand onto Ellie's shoulder as she shredded the tissues to pieces. There was no comforting her, she stood and ran from the room.

Now that Odelia knew the identity of the woman in Graham's lab, she was even more concerned for Ellie's fragile state.

65

As Ellie entered her second week at the Retreat, her nightmares became less frequent. Her newfound practice of meditation and talking to Odelia and her mother helped. Ellie was grateful; a clearer mind enabled her to think. Now and then, as she drifted into a relaxed state, she thought she saw Ruth.

'I know she's trying to tell me something, I just know it...' she told Odelia during one of their discussions.

Odelia didn't seem to find it unusual and counselled her to be patient...that in time she would know what Ruth needed to tell her. It didn't sound odd to be told that, even though Ellie had never had much faith in the afterlife. Nevertheless, she had an unshakable feeling that she was never alone. It felt as though someone was constantly at her side, but when she turned around, there was no one there. She looked for an opportunity to speak to Della, she found her tidying up the borders at the front of the house.

'I love the garden,' Della said, slipping the secateurs into her basket, 'but there's always so much to do before winter.' She turned to Ellie and linked arms with her.

'Now, how can I help?' They walked towards the relative warmth of the green house, a great Victorian structure which stood at right angles to the main building. Ellie hesitated, now that she had Della's attention, she wasn't sure how to begin. Della paused occasionally to dead head a few more flowers, giving Ellie a chance to gather her thoughts. They were inside the greenhouse itself before she found her voice.

'I know I've been here some time now,' Ellie started, 'I... I know I've not had much chance to...' she stopped, exasperated at her inability to express her thoughts. Della took her time tidying away her tools. She took off her gloves and pulled out an ancient looking stool that sat under an equally decrepit table. She sat down, smiling at Ellie.

'I feel...I mean...I think I feel...oh shit!' Ellie shook her head in despair. She looked down at the quarry-tiled floor, noticing a line of ants making their way towards a gap down which they all disappeared.

'I feel like someone is with me, all the time… even when I know for sure that I'm alone. It's like sometimes when I'm just relaxing, I think I can see someone in the corner of my eye, but when I turn, there's no-one there.' She spoke quickly, the words tumbled out in one long rush. Della stood up and moved slowly across to her. She took her by the elbow and guided her back towards the recently vacated stool.

'Ellie, we haven't talked much since you arrived have, we?' she said, her voice almost a whisper. Ellie shook her head. Della moved to the table and leaned against it.

'You have a lot of healing to do before you're ready to start thinking about what's going on, the things you can do, your intuitions, your abilities. I don't want to start talking about those things now, because soon you'll leave and return to your husband, and that's just how it should be.' Ellie listened intently, although Della's voice was soft, it penetrated the still air. Every word resonated within her.

'for now I will say that I believe that you're not alone. I think that your sister is still with you in spirit and might eventually be able to tell you what she wanted you to know the day she died. I'm sure she'll find a way. The important thing is that you don't resist it, Ellie. Keep an open mind, because it's important that you find out.'

Ellie stared at Della. She had forgotten what Ruth had said that she had something to tell her. She only knew that her sister had been so upset she could hardly speak. It was only now that Ellie remembered how hard it had been to calm her down. Ruth had been on the point of speaking, but had stopped because of the banging on the front door. Just before...but how did Della know, when she herself had only just remembered?

Della smiled, *no*, she told Ellie, she didn't know what Ruth had wanted to tell her. Perhaps that was for her and her alone. But she was sure that if Ellie kept meditating and carrying out the practices that she was learning from Odelia that she'd soon find out. Ellie was torn, her faith in Della and Odelia's ability to help her healing process was not in question. But asking her to believe that her dead sister wanted to contact her to give her a message?

'How, how do I even start?' she asked. Della stood, beckoning Ellie to follow her. They made their way to the kitchen door, inside it was warm and smelt of fresh bread. Della crossed to the sink to wash her hands.

'If I recall, in the beginning, I used to ask for a clue, a sign, although that phrase has had something of a bad press in recent times.' Della laughed gently to herself remembering incidents in her past.

'What do you mean, 'in the beginning', the beginning of what? What's happening to me Della...tell me?' Ellie pleaded. Della moved around the central isle, considering her reply.

'Ellie, you must know by now that you have...abilities,' she said slowly, gently, choosing her words carefully to avoid spooking Ellie. Even now she was beginning to shake her head in denial.

'No, no, I'm just like everyone else,' Ellie said, starting to panic. She started to walk towards the door to the hallway turning her back on Della, she needed to leave, she didn't want to hear any more.

'Didn't you ever have a friend when you were little?' Della asked abruptly, 'someone that you talked to, played with, even insisted on setting a place at the table for,' she persisted. 'Someone that only you could see?'

Ellie stopped just short of the door. She felt a shiver of acknowledgement run through her body. It was a sign, she'd always felt, that what was being said resonated as the truth. Nevertheless, she shook her head in denial.

'Everyone has that,' Ellie insisted, taking a further step towards the door. 'All kids have an imaginary friend...Ruth had one,' she whispered. Della walked around her, took her hands and looked her straight in the eye.

'Not everyone Ellie,' she whispered, 'and almost without exception those that do lose the ability to communicate with them at around the age of five or six. Yours has grown up with you hasn't he Ellie? He still lurks there at the edge of your consciousness...you see him, don't you? When you're afraid or in a dilemma? Don't you talk to him, ask him for his advice, even though you've always claimed that you're just talking to yourself?'

Ellie gasped, that was exactly how it was. Her legs were giving way, her knees going weak. Della steered her backwards towards an armchair and helped her to sit down. She moved a footstool in order to sit closer.

'How... how do you know all this?' Ellie whispered, staring at Della, willing herself to calm down.

Della shook her head, smiling, 'Experience Ellie, just experience, keeping an open mind, and asking for guidance, it's that simple,' she replied. 'It's the living that complicate things.'

'You mean these imaginary friends, they're...they're dead?' Ellie demanded, shrinking further into the chair. What the hell was she doing here? Why had she agreed to come? Della patted Ellie's hand, realising that she was slipping towards denial.

'We'll talk about that at another time,' she said calmly, just for now think about your own experiences. I bet you remember things that you couldn't explain at the time, things that have always bothered you.' Ellie's breathing had quickened, her head was swirling, she felt dizzy, on the point of passing out.

'Take a deep breath, Ellie, and think back,' urged Della.

The memory came in a blinding flash, walking down the lane to the lake by her father's house, Ruth holding her hand. She'd seen him, Jacob, her 'friend' standing in the road, waving. She could see him so clearly; he'd called to her.

'Go back!' he shouted, 'go back Ellie, run back to the house,' and they had. Ellie trusted him, though she had no idea why. Ruth moaned, she wanted to go swimming, but Ellie insisted. Their father was surprised to see them walking back so soon, asking why they'd changed their plans. Ellie fobbed him off, claiming that she had a headache. He didn't believe her. The next day they found out that a lorry had dumped a load of chemicals not far from where they'd been heading. Some had seeped into the lake. Conservationists from around the district had moved in to try to stop an environmental disaster.

Their father hugged them. 'Thank God,' he said, over and over. 'Thank God you had that headache, sweetheart.' Ellie had looked over his shoulder; she could see Jacob standing in the doorway. He smiled, turned and left. She thought that was the last time she had seen him until...she gasped.

'Della, I saw him, I saw Jacob two days before, before...' she faltered, 'on my way into the station. He was standing on the corner, he waved. I didn't recognise him. I thought he was just some kid... I thought he was waving to someone else, but it was, it was him.'

Della was holding Ellie's hand, 'A warning, perhaps?' she suggested.

'If I'd known... if I'd paid attention.' Ellie whispered; her distress evident. Della took a deep breath, unsure if Ellie was ready for what she was about to say. She decided to take the risk.

'Ellie, please don't think that I'm being cold-hearted or unfeeling.' Della was trying to choose the right words; she spoke slowly and carefully.

'Some people believe that things are meant to happen, even something as horrific as the murders of your sister and her son. It's like arriving at the end of the path that we chose even before we're born. Nothing can or should be allowed to stand in that path and prevent our progress.' She stopped as Ellie gasped with shock, her face ashen, her mouth open, eyes bulging. How dare she, how dare she suggest that what had happened to Ruth and Max was pre-ordained. Della felt it was safe to go on talking.

'The day you meant to go swimming; Jacob warned you not to go. But if you were destined to end up in the lake, nothing would have stopped you. It would have been your path. As it was, he was there, looking out for you. It wasn't time for you to reach the end of your path.' She stopped, looking at Ellie to judge how her words might have been received. She could tell immediately that it wasn't good. Ellie snatched her hand away, shaking her head in denial.

'So that's it, you're telling me that I should just accept the fact that they're gone, be ok with it? They were murdered for God's sake; they didn't choose this 'path' or whatever it is that you're talking about. How dare you suggest...' she faltered. Della grabbed her hand again.

'Ellie, Ellie, please, calm down, you need to take a breath, please,' it was no good. Ellie was becoming hysterical. Della reached out and placed a hand on her head. Warmth seeped into Ellie's skull as she sank back into the chair and slept.

Della sighed, 'Nope,' she said to the room in general, 'too much, too soon.'

She could tell that the entities in the room agree.

66

When she woke Ellie was conscious of a deep sense of peace. The room was dark except for the flicker of the firelight. Everything was cast into shadow, and she heard rather than saw Della move.

'Feeling better?' Della asked as Ellie stretched, all tension having left her.

'Yes, I am, thank you. I'm sorry...' she started.

'No need, it's me that should be apologising,' Della said, 'sometimes I let myself get carried away.' Ellie could see her a little way away, sitting in a great leather chair.

'Della, how did you come to know all this? I know I asked you before, but who... who told you? There must have been someone, someone who let you in on...' she stopped, lost for the words.

'There was a point, a moment of crisis. One day maybe I'll tell you, but for now Ellie, trust me when I say that I was in a position not unlike your own. I needed help, not the kind that comes in a police car, or an ambulance, not even the kind where you sit down with someone with your qualifications. It was here,' she placed her hand over her heart, 'that needed sorting out. It seemed no matter how many avenues I explored; I couldn't find out how. Someone suggested that I should ask for help, for strength, for guidance, and it worked.'

'So, what are you saying, Della, that this is a religious thing?' Ellie asked. She detected a sharp intake of breath.

'No, no, not religious, and let's not get into that topic,' Della said quietly, her words measured and careful. 'I'm not sure what your views are, Ellie, but I would describe my experiences as spiritual, not religious.'

Ellie could tell that she had struck a chord. The trouble was she wasn't sure what kind of chord.

'So that's it, you just ask, and dead people help you?' she said. 'I've had always had visions of having to go through some complicated process like a Ouija board or holding hands around a crystal ball... and how do I know it's not all in my imagination?'

'Ellie it's not all about contacting the dead. There's no such thing as 'dead' in any case, just energy in other states of existence. Look,' she sighed, 'I don't feel that this is the right time and place to go any further. I think that you have enough to consider and trying too hard is worse than not trying at all. Just allow, Ellie, allow.'

'I don't understand,' Ellie persisted shaking her head. Most of what had passed between them had washed over her. Although she'd heard and remembered what Della had said, she understood very little.

'Take it step by step. Don't try to speed things up. For now, just practice asking and allowing. You'll get the hang of it Ellie, just like you got the hang of meditation,' Della was getting up, but Ellie was reluctant to let things lie. She wanted to know more, most of all she wanted proof. She placed her hand on Della's arm, causing her to sit back down.

'Show me how,' she pleaded, 'I need to know.'

Della smiled, 'You need to relax, ask for a sign, but then release the need to get one,' she replied, standing and crossing to the tea trolley in one swift movement.

'Tea,' she muttered in an effort to change the subject, 'we need some tea,' and busied herself with cups and saucers.

'Do you mind if I have coffee?' Ellie asked. She felt weary, if she had coffee now, she might just make it through to the evening. Then, perhaps she could hope for a good night's sleep, although she doubted it. Della's answers had left her more confused than ever. She watched Della preparing their drinks. No matter how bizarre her past seemed to her, they didn't shock her hostess in any way. Ellie had experienced a demonstration of Della's abilities, and had been left with the suspicion that she and Ruth had unfinished business.

Ellie sighed. It wouldn't hurt to give it a go, what did she have to lose. She settled back in her chair, placed both feet flat on the floor and closed her eyes, trying to remember everything that Odelia had taught her. Breathe deeply, evenly. Before long she felt a deep sense of calm.

Ok, she told herself, feeling slightly self-conscious, *so give me a sign*.

She heard Della place her coffee on the side table and opened her eyes. Della smiled, and the two women sipped their drinks in silence. The rhythm of the clock was hypnotic, as was the crackle of logs that Della added to the fire. The warmth of the room was easing Ellie's body into deeper relaxation when her phone rang.

'Graham, how are you, is everything all right?' Her questions seemed to come out in a rush as she tried to sound energetic. During his visits Graham had told her that she looked zonked out, and was she sure they weren't slipping her something to relax her? They talked for several minutes, before Ellie told him she intended to return in a few days.

'That's such good news, sweetheart.' Graham sounded near to tears, and she realised how difficult it must have been for him. He sniffed, trying to pull himself together.

'Yes, yes, it is isn't it?' Ellie managed. She hadn't realised how much she'd missed him. There was an awkward silence, neither of them knowing what to say.

'Is there any news yet, from the station I mean?' She heard him sigh.

'Only snippets love,' he admitted, 'you know I never knew what it felt like to be on the other end of what we do.' Ellie knew exactly what he meant.

'By the way,' he went on, 'who's Jacob?'

'W-Why do you ask?' she stammered, an image of her childhood 'friend' shimmering across her mind.

'I found a piece of paper on the floor in the kitchen. It said, 'Don't forget' and it was signed 'Jacob,' he went on, then thought he detected a gasp.

'Ellie, Ellie, are you all right?'

'Fine, I'm fine, I'll see you soon, love you.' She clicked the handset and stared at Della who had been watching her. She had her sign; she didn't believe in coincidences either.

67

Graham wasn't happy, and his unhappiness walked hand in hand with guilt. He hadn't felt this bad since his affair with Kara. Ellie was recovering, she seemed to be growing stronger every time he spoke with her, and for that he was glad. Although he hated to admit it, he'd been relieved when she left for the Retreat. The effort of sustaining empathy mixed with just the right amount of sympathy had worn him out, and there was the first layer of guilt. What could he say to her, how could he help her to cope with her grief? Despite his efforts, he had the impression that Ellie was shutting him out, and that hurt.

Then there was other reason for his relief, it gave him time to work out what to do about Kara. How could he resent Ellie not communicating with him, when he was keeping such a bombshell from her? He tried to justify his actions, telling himself that he was keeping silent to prevent Ellie any further distress. But he knew that there was a danger that the longer the Kara situation went on, the harder it would be to explain why he hadn't told her in the first place.

He wanted Ellie to get better. His motivation for supporting her trip to the Retreat was based on that, or was it? He asked himself that question a thousand times a day. To be honest it gave him a reprieve, and not only from having to try so hard to help Ellie. He was having to get used to the fact that Kara was becoming more entrenched in his little corner of the world. He'd been so sure that this part of his life was something that no one could take away from him, now it felt as though every day it was being eroded in front of his eyes. Only yesterday Emlyn Davies had informed him that Kara was being considered for a permanent post.

Graham was still busy with the on-going investigations. He'd arranged to take some leave when Ellie returned from the Retreat, but he dreaded that in doing so he would become even more isolated from what was happening at the lab. Besides, Ellie had hinted that she wanted to return to work as soon as she could. He would support her, of course, but if she did where would it leave him? He couldn't imagine anything less desirable than working alongside Kara, their paths crossing constantly. It would be stressful just being in the same building.

A few days ago, he had overheard her talking to one of the technicians, and realised that she was rapidly settling into her new role. Then he'd found out that Emlyn had asked her to re-examine some of the evidence in the on-going investigations. It felt like a slap in the face. Kara seemed to be in no hurry to move on.

The fact that she had been asked to carry out the postmortem on Charles Whittaker had left him with a feeling of having been overlooked. If he was being honest, he was beginning to feel a little jealous. With his meticulous work being checked over, and by Kara of all people, his resentment towards her was almost palpable. He tried to pull himself together, to analyse the situation rationally. He wouldn't have been allowed to take part in any of these cases, he was too personally involved. *But nevertheless,* he thought, *it's not right.*

The last phone call with Ellie had been brief, just long enough to arrange for him to pick her up in a few days. She'd told him that she missed him, and she couldn't wait to get back to the farm, but then she'd cut the conversation short when he told her about that stupid note. What the hell was that about? Despite his growing unease, he was happy she was coming back; seeing her growing strength each time he visited the Retreat had been one of few positive aspects of the last months.

He'd spent the morning tidying up an already immaculate house, resisting the urge to call the office. His resolve crumbled around lunchtime, and he reached for his phone, and started to tap in the office number. Maybe he could drive over, have a chat with Cathy…there was a knock at the door, he cancelled the call and made his way to answer it.

He had to admit, she looked stunning, the afternoon sun highlighting the streaks of blonde in her perfectly coiffed hair. She wore it loose framing her shoulders, around which was draped a wisp of a blouse. The narrow straps threatened to slip down as she turned to face him. It was obvious she wore no bra.

Graham knew from previous experience that her carefully calculated appearance was all for effect. For one thing the afternoon was chilly, bordering on freezing. He sighed as he remembered their previous encounters that had had nothing to do with work. He noted the skin-tight trousers the like of which he hadn't seen since Olivia Newton John had wiggled her way across a fun fair ride in Grease, and the low-heeled black pumps. She giggled, delighted at his reaction, slipping between him and the doorway before he had a chance to make a strategic retreat. When Graham caught up with her, she was standing in the kitchen, looking out of the French windows, seemingly enraptured with the view.

'You never told me your home was this beautiful,' she gushed, her arms wrapped around her waist, which had the effect of pulling the blouse even further down her shoulders. He couldn't help speculating how long it would continue to cover her modesty.

'Graham, it's perfect, you and…' she hesitated, he knew it was once again all for effect, 'Esme is it?' he didn't correct her, 'you must be so happy here.'

'What do you want, Kara,' he managed, his voice strangled in his throat, 'why are you here?'

She giggled again, walking slowly back to where he stood by the door, in case he needed to make a quick getaway.

'Oh, come on Graham, don't be like that,' she purred, 'I don't hold a grudge, why should you?' She was by his side now, warm, radiating energy; he could feel it in waves as she touched his shoulder. Her fingers almost burned his skin as she gently stroked the back of his neck. Her touch increased in pressure until she dug her nails into the hollow beneath his ear, and drew them back, marking his neck. He flinched, stepping sideways, hoping to place some distance between them. She closed the gap in two dainty steps.

'Anyone would think you're scared of me?' she whispered in his ear as her sinuous arms encircled his waist. He disentangled himself once more and walked to the open patio window. Stepping through he felt the urge to run but stilled his mind and controlled his rising anger.

'Kara, I want you to leave, if you don't, I'll…' he stopped realising that there was little he could do if he wanted to prevent the whole house of cards from crashing down. He shook his head, holding on to the fence that surrounded the patio. She laughed, a bitter-sweet tinkling sound that he remembered so well and hated with a passion.

'What will you do, Graham?' she asked, 'tell wifey, complain to the Head of Department? Hmm?' She laughed again, and in that moment, Graham understood for the first time in his long and distinguished career, what it was like to want to snatch the life from a fellow human being, to put an end to their time on earth, and not regret doing it. Kara laughed again.

'Don't worry my love, I'm going. Just wanted to deliver the news personally,' her voice had a deliberate singsong to it, it irritated his senses. His grip on the fence increased, he had never felt this angry, or this helpless in his life. It took him a few seconds before he realised that she had stopped talking. He looked around, and saw her, arms folded in front of her, smiling at his discomfort. She was waiting for him to speak first.

'Well?' he managed, turning to face her at last; he had to put an end to this charade.

'Oh Graham,' she pouted, 'you could be just the teensiest bit interested. She shook her head, sighing. 'Well if you're not going to ask, I'll be generous and tell you anyway. I'm staying on... yes, that's right. I've been interviewed and it's all arranged, I'm taking over from some old fogey who's just retired, you know, Doctor... oh why can't I remember his name?' she was obviously enjoying herself.

Graham stood stock still as she awaited his reaction. He was determined not to show his distress, she could wait forever, he wouldn't give her the satisfaction. After a few minutes she realised that he wasn't biting. Kara cleared her throat and stepped back into the kitchen. She picked up her bag and sat on the couch, taking time to arrange herself in a provocative pose.

'Such a poor host,' she pouted, 'not even going to offer me a drink?'

Graham hadn't moved, afraid that if he did, he'd do something he'd regret. Kara stroked the back of the couch, waiting for him to join her, her patience reminded him of his mother's cat waiting at the back door.

'You're no fun anymore Graham,' she whined, 'and you used to be such a hoot, remember that day when we...'

'Stop it Kara,' he hissed, 'stop it now, get out before...'

'Before what? We've been down this road before sweetheart, what can you do, think about it?' Kara stood, running her hands over her backside, smoothing imaginary creases out of seat of her trousers.

'I'll just pop to the powder room before I go, don't worry, I'll see myself out.'

Graham watched as she sashayed towards the hallway, he heard her footsteps as she climbed the stairs. She didn't know the house, of course, but he wished he had been quick enough to head her off and point out the downstairs facilities. Ah well, she'd be gone soon, and he'd have a chance to work out his next move. Moments passed, during which his mind flew this way and that, what the hell was he going to do? How could he explain all this to Ellie? Should he even tell her? One thing was for sure, he'd hold back until the last moment, nothing could spoil her homecoming.

'Bye sweetheart see you soon. Looking forward to working together,' Kara trilled, the front door slammed.

'Not if I can help it,' Graham muttered taking deep breaths as his anger gradually subsided. The sooner Kara was gone from his life, the better. He checked the time, pulled on his jacket and located his keys. He needed to get out of the house.

He was crossing the hall when he felt a nudge in his back that startled him, almost causing him to stumble. He looked around, had Kara slammed the door but stayed inside? There was no one in the hall, he heard a sound from one of the bedrooms and crossed to the stairs calling out into the silence.

'Who's there? Who's...Kara, it that you? Stop playing games...' he heard a door creak. She'd gone back upstairs; he was convinced of it. An icy feeling crept through his body as he made his way to the landing. Another sound, a sigh, a whisper... it came from the spare bedroom, the room that he had imagined decorating for... there it was again, and sobbing. What the hell was the woman playing at? He pushed open the door. A movement caught in his peripheral vision, as though someone had ducked into the en suite. Graham crossed the room, whatever Kara's game was, he was determined to put an end to it once and for all. The tiny room was empty. Graham stood staring at the vanity unit that housed the sink. To one side lay a small make up bag, one of Ellie's, the contents strewn across the tiled surface. He'd checked the room that morning and knew that he hadn't left these things out.

...you might want to do something about your neck... a voice whispered, close, too close. Graham jumped, spinning around at the same time, bumping into the shower unit.

'What the hell...?' he shouted into the empty room.

Several minutes passed before he could move. The chill in the air was palpable even though he had ensured the heating was on ready for Ellie's return. Graham grasped the edge of the sink, staring down into the bowl, swallowing repeatedly to quell the nausea that threatened to overwhelm him. He ran the cold water and splashed his face; fighting to regain control of his emotions. He replaced his glasses and looked at his reflection.

It was then that he understood the warning about his neck. Ugly red wheals had developed as a result of Kara's unwanted contact. He would have to use some of Ellie's make up to disguise them, make up that seemed to have been laid out for that purpose. What he didn't know was who, or what had alerted him to his injuries, and provided him with the means to disguise them.

68

As Graham dealt with Kara, John was leaving the cottage, undecided on his next move. He'd returned to the island without notice or fanfare, notifying the station a few days before to ensure he could return to the cottage. Even then he hadn't given them a specific date. The call had gone through to Porter.

'I'm going to need a few days to get my head around things,' he said, 'so don't tell anyone that I'm back. I don't want to be pestered, especially by the Press...you understand?' Porter understood.

'I only wished I could tell you some good news, he said, clearing his throat, 'you'll be needing to make arrangements, I suppose?'

'Arrangements? John repeated, he didn't...then he got what Porter was talking about. The funerals, he hadn't even thought...

One thing was for sure, he couldn't hang around here much longer. He grabbed his wallet and phone and headed to the car; his body ached from tiredness. He wasn't sure where to go, the office seemed like a good idea, although he could do with checking in at the station. He could see the front of the building in the mirror as he moved away; an image of Ruth and Max as they had looked just before... he slammed on the brakes, turning round in his seat to make sure that... *but that was wishful thinking,* he decided, shaking his head, trying to clear it.

He remembered the last time he'd seen her running towards him, her hair flying around her face. Max falling over as he ran up the stairs, throwing himself into John's outstretched arms, knocking him off balance in his eagerness to welcome him home. The argument they'd had might never have happened; John chose to erase the memory altogether.

He wiped away tears, forcing back emotions that threatened to engulf him. He had to find the strength to do what had to be done, to continue his life without them. Porter had offered to meet him at the house, but John refused. He told himself that he could only summon up the strength to do this if he was on his own. Now he wasn't so sure.

More than an hour passed as he sat locked in a world of memories. He knew what he had to do, make a move, it wasn't the one he had been planning. He started the car and headed down the drive. Within minutes he was on his way to Graham Shaw's place, angry with himself that he'd allowed the situation to beat him. He needed to talk to someone, just for a while at least, and Graham was the nearest he had to a friend.

As he approached the turning to the farm, he saw a bright red two-seater sports car coming down the lane from the direction towards the main road. John recognised the driver, what the hell was Kara Billingham doing here? He flashed his lights. There was no way that both cars could fit into the mouth of the lane. Kara raised a hand in acknowledgement and pulled onto the road. She seemed almost oblivious to him as she accelerated away. Within minutes John was knocking on Graham's door, he heard footsteps. The door was snatched open.

'Kara, I told you…' Graham snatched the door open; he froze when he saw it was John. His anger evaporated, and he stepped forward dragging the older man into an embrace before John had a chance to escape. John avoided close physical contact with anyone other than Ruth and Max, and now this. He managed to disentangle himself and step away. He could see Graham shaking, *just who's comforting who* he thought.

In the time that John had spent on the mainland, he had given little thought to how events had affected those left behind. The change he saw in Graham shocked him, and to a degree dissipated some of his own pain. Graham looked awful. He'd lost weight; his skin was the colour of parchment, his clothes creased. John was confused. On one hand he could appreciate that Graham was distressed about what had happened, not only to Ellie, but also to Ruth and Max. On the other he was angry, at least Ellie was still alive. He felt as though Graham was cashing in on his grief.

'What the hell's going on?' he demanded as he followed Graham into the hallway. This was not the return he had anticipated. Graham led him through to the kitchen where only moments ago Kara had stood mocking him. The cloying scent of her perfume still hung in the air, reminding him of her threatening presence. Graham pulled off his jacket and moved to the sink. He reached for the kettle, then banged it down on the surface, making John jump.

'Fuck this,' he growled, 'I need a drink...you?' John nodded and watched as Graham located and poured amber coloured oblivion into two tall glasses. John had never seen Graham like this...what exactly had gone on between him and Kara?

He didn't have to wait long to find out. In an uncharacteristic confession, Graham told him everything, then he refilled their glasses before going to the cellar to retrieve more alcohol.

As the afternoon wore on, John wondered idly how Ellie coped with so much temptation lying around so freely available. He would have asked Graham, but by then he'd fallen asleep on the couch, his empty glass in one hand. John moved his legs onto the cushions, covering him with a quilt, and headed into the lounge. Hell, now he would have to stay the night; he was in no condition to drive.

Sleep didn't come as easily as he thought it would. He lay awake for hours tossing and turning beneath improvised bedclothes. Eventually he returned to the kitchen, made coffee, and opened the patio doors, gasping at the change in temperature.

It was early morning as he gazed out at the scene he had never appreciated before. The ragged ribbons of night were parting, allowing a pale lavender sky the chance to peep through, clearing the way for the sunrise. The last of the stars hung low as John sipped his coffee.

How did he not know about Graham and Kara? He, who prided himself on his all-encompassing knowledge, how had this nugget slipped by? He glanced at his friend gently snoring gently on the sofa, all resentment at having his thunder stolen from him slipped away. Before he met Ruth, Graham was the nearest he had to family of his own. There had been a resonance between them since they'd met. Graham felt like the younger brother John had never had, their thought patterns overlapped, he'd been a joy to teach.

Enough, he decided, *I need to get on with my life*. He retraced his steps, covered Graham up with the blanket which had fallen to the floor. He left the farmhouse and drove home.

This time he had no fears about entering the cottage, it was time to move on.

69

Ellie was home, and Graham was determined that there would be nothing for her to worry about. He'd pre-warned his father not to make an issue of the 'home' harvest, a tradition that stretched back far into Jim Shaw's life, and which he looked forward to every year. His father promised nothing and felt vindicated when the first thing Ellie asked was how it had gone. She was surprised that they hadn't kept to their usual routine of gathering the fruit in their small orchard and turning the produce into jams and chutneys.

Graham had picked Ellie up from the Retreat, arriving late in the afternoon. Odelia excused herself, leaving the two of them to spend time over afternoon tea. Not that Graham ate much; he seemed distracted, eager to leave. Their departure was a drawn-out affair, with Odelia issuing warnings about not overdoing things. *It was good to be going home*, Ellie told herself as Graham headed down the sweeping drive, so why was she filled with a sense of foreboding?

Odelia waved as they left, she'd decided to stay on as she wanted to talk to her mother about Ellie's progress. Over the next few days they took long walks over the sands, where only days before Ellie had broken down and admitted the depth of her despair.

With Ellie's permission, the two women discussed her recovery. They each had their own specialist skills that could form the basis for the therapies that they believed would help. Ellie agreed to return, though whether it was with any degree of belief that she could be helped, or if she had just become so exhausted with the whole issue, was anyone's guess. Odelia hoped that it was the former. Having someone wanting to get better was essential, and they'd arranged for Ellie to return in a few weeks to begin her sessions.

The house beckoned them as they rounded the bend in the pathway leading to the kitchen door. The days were shorter now, the mornings frosty. Soon it would be time to turn the clocks back. Mrs. Pierce, who had worked for Della for many years, was buzzing around the kitchen making afternoon tea. The aroma of baking wafted towards them as they quickened their step towards the comforting warmth.

Once settled in Della's sitting room, a spread of sandwiches, scones and tea before them, their conversation resumed. Odelia stood before the log burner, hands outstretched to ease the stiffness from her fingers. She shook her head as she thought about the conversations that she and Ellie had had during the last few weeks.

'Ellie has a lot going on, hasn't she?' she observed, knowing that she was stating the obvious. Della nodded, pouring the tea and handing the cup to her daughter.

'She has,' she agreed, not wanting to intrude on Odelia's line of thought.

'We need to consider what to deal with first. I think it was right to allow her just to be for the time she was here. It certainly made a difference to her.' Once again, her mother nodded, sipping her drink as she watched the flames dancing behind the opaque glass of the log burner.

Odelia was both pleased that Ellie had agreed to work with them and frustrated that it would take some time to make measurable progress. Della's cup clinked as she set it down on the saucer.

'You must be patient, Odelia,' she murmured, as though she had read her daughter's thoughts. 'Ellie is a lot stronger than she knows, she has abilities that we can only dream about, not awake yet, but soon, all in good time,' she indicated the chair opposite.

'Now, sit down and enjoy this wonderful spread, we'll find a way, I sure of it.'

They sat for some time, each occupied with their own thoughts. The only sound was the ticking clock and the hissing of the wood as tiny pockets of resin were winkled out by the flames.

'Tell me about the cases you're involved with,' her mother said suddenly. Odelia stared at her. Where had that come from? For a good hour she related all that she knew about the murders. She spoke of Ellie's theories and described DCI Horton's disappearance. Of how he'd been ordered to take leave after his ordeal, and, of course about what had happened to Ruth and Max. She was staring into the fire when she sensed a change in the atmosphere.

Della's face was partially obscured by the wing back chair in which she sat, but Odelia could see her mother's hands gripping the arms of the chair, her knuckles were white. She moved to kneel by her feet, Della's shoulders were hunched. She looked as though she was in pain, and her eyes seemed to have disappeared into their sockets. Odelia grabbed her arms.

'Mom, Mom, what is it?' she tried to pull Della's body towards her own, but her mother sat rigid, resisting her. Odelia pulled her again, this time Della gave way and collapsed into her daughter's arms. Odelia held her tight, afraid to let her go. Della looked up, tears coursing down her face.

'We…I think…we…,' she faltered, 'we're all in great danger,' she whispered.

70

For some time Porter had noticed a shift in Mason's role within the team. He didn't need to be a detective to see that she was at her most comfortable when faced with paperwork rather than another human being. He hadn't realised just how much he had come to rely on her organisational abilities until after his latest meeting with Chetwynd.

The extent of Horton's incompetence had taken their breath away, they even suspected that his inaction could have led to the perpetrator remaining free, and ultimately to further deaths. A backlog of material had been discovered in Horton's office, unfiled interviews, evidence bags none of which had been entered into the general investigation, mistakes that had hampered the team from day one. No one had wanted to risk antagonising Horton, a fact that Chetwynd confirmed. She'd admitted to Porter that she'd been just as guilty as anyone on that score, but they were all going to have to take a share of responsibility. It was during their conversation that Porter began to suspect that Mason had been in direct contact with the Chief for more than one reason. If that was the case, he wanted confirmation.

Rather than ask outright, he decided to keep a close eye on her. Not that he didn't have enough to do, he thought as he walked back to the Incident room. It was just after 10 a.m. Most of the officers were out tracking down leads that the discovery of Horton's files had afforded them.

Connett was at his desk surfing the internet, awaiting Porter's return. Mason was busy pinning yet more information onto one of the many white boards that seemed to multiply every day. Neither of them had noticed his return.

Porter watched Mason as she worked, recalling his latest conversation with Chetwynd. In future, she'd told him, Mason would oversee receiving, copying and cataloguing any information. She would then send updates to both her and Porter. Mason had worked out a system which Chetwynd had sanctioned, and in view of her new status, she should be left to concentrate solely on those duties. This would mean that she wouldn't be dragged out of the station unless it was necessary, or she expressed a desire to return to her former duties. As neither of them could see that happening, it shouldn't be a problem.

Porter agreed; Mason's diligence was proving invaluable. Over the last few days every piece of evidence had been time-lined, the originals copied, and catalogued in chronological order. She had that side running in perfect order, so why was he uneasy about it all? He stepped forward as Mason turned, she smiled hesitantly, taking him by surprise. He had to admit she was in her element here, but the suspicion that she might be reporting directly to Chetwynd still dominated his thoughts.

Give her the benefit of the doubt, his gut seemed to say. *She's not the enemy you know.*

Porter shook his head; he needed more sleep. He headed for his office, thinking about his team, and his conversation earlier. After the incidents with Horton, Chetwynd had told him, morale had been at an all-time low, as if he didn't already know. If they factored in their painfully slow progress, she wasn't surprised that tempers were frayed. The longer their failure to make headway lasted, the less eager they were to follow what leads they did have. Her bosses were hounding her for progress, and the press were all but baying for blood.

The absence of John Prothero and Ellie Shaw had highlighted their value within the team. Chetwynd confessed that she had underestimated their contributions, only now appreciating the insights they provided. Horton had relied heavily on Prothero, eager for his input. His biggest failure lay in his unwillingness to share that information with the rest of the team to make himself look good.

'You do know that my team's attitudes changed dramatically with what happened to Ruth and Max Prothero, don't you?' Porter pleaded in their defence. He was angry at her attack on the officers who he knew were eager to bring about a result. They'd worked with little leadership for most of the case. Chetwynd smiled; she knew she had the right man for the job. Porter's defence of his colleagues backed up her opinion of him.

'DI Porter...Bill,' she started clearing her throat, 'you know, I've never understood why you didn't apply for the post of DCI when one became vacant a few years ago, after all you did pass your promotions exam. Any particular reason for your decision?' She tapped the desk with a pencil, staring at Porter as he shifted in his chair.

'I...it...err, wasn't the right time,' he mumbled, startled at the change of topic, 'stuff going on, you know how it is Ma'am?' Chetwynd smiled, she brought out an envelope from her desk and handed it to him.

'Read this, get back to me and let me know your answer. But remember, if we need to bring in a newcomer, there'll be yet more disruption. Quite frankly I for one wouldn't like to have to cope with that and the backlog of murders,' she smiled again, and stood indicating that their time was up.

'No pressure Bill,' she stressed watching his dawning realisation of what might be in the envelope.

Within the confines of his office, he focused on two aspects. Whether or not to accept promotion to DCI and with it responsibility for the entire shooting match, and who was feeding Celia Chetwynd information? He stood abruptly, crossing over to the window. He could see people going about their daily business, shopping, fetching their lunchtime snacks, hurrying to meet someone, maybe? He screwed his eyes when he saw Ellie and Graham emerge from a side street. The sight of them gave him an idea. Despite the efforts he'd made, the morale of the team was waning again, maybe he could inject some fresh energy into the enquiry. He grabbed his wallet and made his way downstairs. His hunch was that they were parked at the railway station and he headed in that direction. He was right; Graham was unlocking the car, Ellie waiting patiently, lost in thought. She jumped as he cleared his throat. Ellie thought he looked more cheerful than he had the last time she had seen him; it made her wonder what had changed. Graham had told her only last night how beleaguered he and his team were. Porter hummed and hawed for a few seconds. Ellie knew then that he hadn't just happened across them.

'I...err...I wonder if I could come out to the farm later, got something I'd like to ask you...a favour, sort of,' he managed.

Graham was wary, he was already shaking his head. Before he could say anything Ellie answered.

'Of course,' she said, 'around 3.30 be ok, I'll get some biscuits?' Porter swallowed hard, *after everything she's gone through*, he thought ...*I shouldn't be doing this*. She smiled and nodded, almost as though she could read his thoughts.

'Don't worry,' she murmured so that he only just caught her words, 'it'll be fine.' She got into the car.

Porter smiled back, until he looked up and saw Graham Shaw's face.

71

He planned what to say very carefully, going over intonations, choosing the right words, correcting tiny phrases. No pressure, no hassle, but in the end the suggestion that she could come and speak to the team came from Ellie herself. Porter breathed easier after that, even though he suspected that he had made an enemy of her husband for life. Graham started to protest, but Ellie shut him down in the nicest possible way, assuring him that she would be fine and that she wanted to do whatever she could to help.

Graham argued that it was still too early for Ellie to be doing anything but resting. Ellie on the other hand was in total control of the situation, Porter realised as he drove back to the station. She had changed, he acknowledged, almost to the point of being a totally different person. When she left for the Retreat, or whatever it was called, she had been on the verge of collapse. Now she appeared to have gained strength and had poise and control that weren't evident before. She'd reassured Graham, promising him that she wouldn't dream of overdoing it, and telling him that she would never forgive herself if someone else suffered due to her refusal to help. Despite his objections, she insisted that she'd be careful. In the end, they arranged for her to come into the station the next morning.

Porter sighed as he recalled Graham's reaction, which hadn't been positive. Naturally he was concerned about his wife; she had been through a traumatic experience. Ellie on the other hand, thought his idea was inspired, and was eager to take part. Eventually Graham had conceded, albeit unwillingly. Porter just hoped that he wasn't the kind to bear a grudge.

72

Porter had only been back a few hours when Chetwynd sent for him. He stood staring at his feet whilst the senior officer shuffled papers. How the hell had she found out about his trip?

'DCI Porter are you sure this is a good idea? You know that Ellie Shaw is closely linked with at least two of the murders that you and your team are investigating,' Porter sighed, *science of the bleeding obvious*, he thought irreverently, 'that's why she can't officially be a part of the investigation into those particular crimes, same applies to her husband...'

Porter sensed a 'but' coming. His eyes narrowed; he suspected that Chetwynd was about to throw him a lifeline. She handed him a single sheet of paper from a file on her desk.

'However, I've been doing a little digging of my own,' she said. 'There are precedents of personnel who may have conflicts of interest volunteering to contribute, as it were, not directly of course. But we, as the police, can't really stop them, can we? Then there's the fact that we don't really know if the murders of Mrs. Prothero and her son, and the injuries to Ms. Shaw are connected in any way to the other murders, the ones you suspect have been carried out by the so-called 'Puppet Master'. To be honest, and I've checked this out with higher powers, if Ellie Shaw is ready to return to work to investigate *those* murders, well, there is very little that we can do to stop her. She would of course have to have the all-clear from her Doctor, but as far as I'm concerned, she would be more than welcome.'

Porter could have punched the air, now they were getting somewhere, he could conduct the meeting he'd arranged with his Chetwynd's blessing. He checked his watch, he needed to get to his office and write a brief outline for Ellie. He hoped that this would galvanise the team back into action.

'You better get on with it,' Chetwynd smiled indulgently. Whatever Porter was planning to do, she trusted that it would be a hell of a lot better than Horton's efforts.

Hurrying back to his office, Porter realised that it was the first time that anyone had called him 'DCI'. Despite his quandary over accepting the post, it felt good.

73

It was some time before Porter realised that Chetwynd had slipped in to the incident room. It was a testament to the effectiveness of Ellie's speech that no-one else had noticed. The whole team was assembled, some standing, others perched on desks, a few seated. Some weren't even on the team itself, officers who'd begged to be allowed to join in during their spare time to try to help.

Ellie had spoken from the heart, with a strength that amazed everyone. She told of her own confusion as to the identity of the person they were seeking, of her dismay at the growing body count, her shock at the incident with Alan Cooper, and finally of her own experience. She was at pains to stress that she would remain one step removed from that actual investigation. She pledged her co-operation to assist wherever she could.

'In a way,' she observed almost to herself, 'we're almost there on the first three murders, having established motives if not hard evidence. The confirmation that someone, the 'Puppet Master' for want of a better name, may have orchestrated them has come to light thanks to Alan Cooper passing his laptop to his colleague. At some stage we may have to accept that evidence of third-party involvement in the other murders might never be uncovered. Of course, I'm not discounting anything, nor am I making assumptions.' A low buzz went around the room, most officers had felt this way, but few had expressed their opinions for fear of ridicule.

Finally, she spoke about Ruth and Max, some of her personal memories. How they would sit and watch the sun going down, Max playing in the meadows around the farm.

She reminded them about John and his loss. How he'd helped to solve innumerable cases in the past, and how, even though he hadn't been in contact for some time, she knew that he was as anxious as they were for results.

The effect was electrifying. Despite themselves the room rose as one and applauded her. She turned, affected by their response and walked slowly to Porter's side. It was then that he spotted the Chief, who nodded to him in approval. She allowed herself a slight smile before she slipped back through the door. Porter knew that Ellie had achieved the result he wanted. He was still trying to glue the team back into something cohesive, she had brought the element that was missing. He hoped that the fact that one of their own, and that was how they now regarded her, had suffered a huge loss would galvanise them back into action. Horton's abduction had been a shock, and his colleagues had made a determined effort to find him, but nothing could compare to the murder of a young woman and her son. He knew it was unfair, but there it was.

'Well done,' he offered as they sat down at his desk. 'You hit just the right note out there,' Ellie sighed.

'I just spoke from the heart,' she said, 'I hope it's enough.'

A knock at the door, Mason entered. She nodded to Ellie as she passed some papers to Porter. Ellie noticed how poised she seemed, not at all like the officer that had sat in silence at the farmhouse after making drinks for them all. Mason waited for Porter to skim read the first page, he nodded, 'Yeah, that's good,' he agreed, handing the file back. Mason headed towards the door, she hesitated as she turned to Ellie.

'I just wanted to say,' she murmured, 'well, we all wanted to…well done out there, it can't have been easy for you.' She nodded, turned and left, Porter looked at Ellie and smiled.

'Yes,' he smiled, 'well done.'

Ellie cleared her throat, 'let's get on with it shall we?' she said brusquely. Porter could see the sheen of tears as she turned her attention to the paperwork before her.

74

Ellie assured Graham that she was quite capable of looking after herself, she suggested that he return to work himself. He walked into utter chaos. He couldn't figure out why Davies hadn't notified him. It was frustrating to realise how out of the loop he was, but at the same time he was grateful that they'd given him and Ellie sometime after her return.

If only they'd known that she'd insisted on going back to the station so quickly, he thought. News started to filter through; Kara Billingham hadn't been to work for a couple of days. No-one had heard from her, and no-one had taken the time to find out where she was. Davies had called her mobile a few times, but the calls had gone straight to answer phone.

Graham was ploughing his way through a mountain of paperwork when he heard noises in the hallway. Muffled voices, a knock on his door, Porter entered, followed by Connett.

'Could we have a word, please Professor Shaw?' Porter began.

Graham waved them into his office, he could detect the official tone in Porter's voice. The energy surrounding Porter and his sidekick was tense, as he indicated that they should sit down. Porter hesitated, 'umming' and 'ahhing' a few times before clearing his throat.

'There's no easy way to say this,' he started. Graham looked alarmed and Porter held up his hand, forestalling his fears. 'Don't worry, this has nothing to do with your family Professor Shaw, it's just...' hesitation once more.

'This is rather delicate, given that...' Porter cleared his throat again. He shifted in his seat and sighed.

'What is your relationship with Kara Billingham?' asked Connett directly, pulling no punches. Porter's eyes never left Graham's face, as he struggled to respond. His heart sank, *how the hell...what did they know*? He tried to slow down his breathing, fighting to hide how much the question had rattled him, he failed.

'Why...why do you ask?' he faltered, Porter noted his response. He'd anticipated that Graham would deny a relationship, not make an enquiry as to why they needed to know. He smiled encouragingly, keeping his voice even, as he took back the lead from Connett.

'Professor Shaw...Graham,' he said gently. 'You must know by now; Ms. Billingham hasn't been to work for several days. Your department contacted us and in the light of all the...erm...*activity* in the last few months, we followed up on their concerns. Her landlady told us she hasn't been back to her digs, and we found this in her room.' Porter pulled out an evidence bag from a folder that Graham hadn't even noticed he was carrying. He placed it on the desk.

'Now, please answer the question, what is your relationship with Kara Billingham?'

Graham studied the photograph, now encased in plastic. It was a scene frozen in time, a memory that formed part of his nightmares. They were sitting at a table in a restaurant. Kara was snuggled up to him, he looked down at her. Her expression was one of obvious happiness, his was hard to read. They were younger of course, several years younger. Graham sighed, the years dissolved like a late spring frost on a sunny morning. There it was, karma, catching up with him after all this time.

Porter was speaking again, dragging Graham back to the present.

'Professor Shaw, please answer the question,' his voice insistent now. Graham took a deep breath and started talking, giving them a brief outline of what had happened. He told them how he'd become entangled in the trap into which, it seemed, Kara habitually led gullible men.

'So, you're saying you and Ms. Billingham had an affair whilst she was one of your students?' Porter confirmed, repeating what Graham had already told them, a tactic designed to clarify; to give the interviewee an opportunity to change or embellish their statement.

'Kara...Ms. Billingham had affairs with several people during her time in my student group. I knew nothing about them until sometime after our...liaison was over.' Porter could tell that Graham was choosing his words carefully. When people started to become selective about what they were saying, they were usually keeping things to themselves; at least that's what Porter had found in his long career. Either that or they were blatantly lying.

'Were any of these *'liaisons'* with other tutors at the University, Professor Shaw?' Connett asked, the inflection in his voice suggesting that he found the idea distasteful at the very least.

'I don't know what you...' Graham was beginning to feel very nervous about the tone of Connett's questions. 'Look, it's not as though she was underage or anything...she was only four years younger than...' he stopped as he wiped a hand across his forehead. He'd never considered that his affair would come back to haunt him in a professional capacity, if anyone found out...

'You'd get into serious trouble if the University found out, wouldn't you Professor Shaw?' Connett went on.

'When did you last see Ms. Billingham?' interrupted Porter, a question that Graham had been dreading. He looked down at his hands, they were clasped together tightly. He knew he looked guilty, how the hell...?

Porter stood, leaned down and placed his hands on the desk, his manner deadly serious. This was a different Porter to the one Graham had previously encountered.

'Professor Shaw, I'd like you to come with us to the station. We need to take a full statement from you,' he stood, smoothed out his tie and indicated the door.

'What's this about?' asked Graham, dreading the implications of Porter's request.

'Ms. Billingham's car was found abandoned this morning, so far there's no sign of her, we need to establish certain facts as soon as we can.'

He was all business now, no genial older colleague, no smiles and reassurances. Graham almost groaned as the two officers led him towards the waiting car.

75

It was a view, widely held by the people who knew him, that Gareth Wynn-Jones was a bit of a weirdo. Home was an eco-house perched a safe distance from a cliff edge. Most of the building had been ingeniously created from recycled materials, which Gareth would seek out using a rare concession to modernity, the Internet. When a building was scheduled for demolition, Gareth would be there.

His ancient Land Rover topped with a DIY luggage rack enabled him to transport useful materials back to his eyrie. Doors, floorboards, window frames, anything that could be recycled was lashed to the frame with ropes found on the beach. He would squirrel away his finds in his workshop, if not for immediate use, then for some future project. He'd even been known to visit the mainland from time to time, a prospect he always viewed with trepidation. He grew his own veggies, kept chickens, goats and the occasional pig, fed himself comfortably, and thrived in the outdoors life he'd carved out for himself.

Above all, though, Gareth was a realist. He had long since acknowledged that he could manage, but he wanted more, a few luxuries. Without compromising his principles, and thanks to his knowledge of the flora and fauna of the island gleaned from his parents, he managed that comfortably. He'd turned his skills into a rapidly expanding and highly popular foraging business. He sought out wild ingredients taking only as much as he needed to fulfil his own and his client's requirements. He charged the going rate, which sometimes astonished even him, and had managed to make his life much more comfortable.

Chefs at local restaurants placed their orders by a certain time each morning for delivery the next day. Sometimes he would have to decline a request, if it meant that the hunting grounds were on the opposite ends of island. He often suggested alternatives which worked out in the client's favour. He spent many hours discussing menus with them, explaining the availability of various herbs, vegetables and fruit, seaweed and seafood. The appeal, he knew, lay in the rarity value.

Keeping the location of his foraging grounds secret was of the utmost importance. Success was a double-edged sword, it afforded him a better lifestyle, but pricked at the edge of his conscience as he realised that he was bordering on becoming an entrepreneur, albeit an ethical one. It was an accusation that had been levelled at him by several of the locals at the pub that he delivered to on a regular basis. He had to admit that sometimes his activities didn't sit well with his eco-beliefs.

It was, therefore, a double blow when he approached one of his favourite sites and realised that the ground had been disturbed. His first thought was that he'd been observed on a previous visit, and that he had a rival poaching on his territory. His second was that holidaymakers had messed up yet another area. His third, upon clearing back a pile of leaves, was that he had better call the police.

76

Not much of a grave, thought Porter as he watched Forensics going about their routine, a routine which he had watched far too often in the past few weeks. Porter had taken a brief look at the body, long enough to recognise her, to see how badly she'd been beaten. He sighed and rather selfishly, he had to admit later, suspected that this might just tip the scales against him and end his career.

He tried to recall the number of victims they now had pinned up on the incident room board. He could just about remember their names, and that shocked him all over again. But he had nothing, no more leads to follow. If this was the same perpetrator, they were covering up their tracks expertly, almost as though…the thought struck him like a thunderbolt. The killer was an expert in covering up his tracks, someone who had the ability to clean up after themselves; someone forensically aware would leave nothing for him and his team to work with. What if the kingpin in this series of crimes had taken things into their own hands, and had had enough motive to murder someone himself? What if Graham Shaw wanted to get rid of Kara Billingham…or maybe…

If their theories about the murders were being based on revenge, this could be a pre-emptory strike. Kara Billingham had been murdered before she ruined… Porter shook his head, both to clear it and in disbelief. If his suspicions were right, more than one life would be ruined today. But it had to be done, he had to get Graham Shaw into the station again for questioning, even if it was to clear him of the brutal murder of his former lover, now on her way, beaten and bloodied to the overflowing morgue.

77

The cold air took his breath away. After an extremely uncomfortable session in the interview room, he realised the tenacity of DCI Porter. He'd also come to appreciate the techniques that the officer was expert in delivering. Now he was free to leave. They'd questioned him for hours. Not just about Kara, but about the other murders. He tried to answer, but all he could think of was Ellie's face, her hands gripping the back of the chair as she watched Porter caution him. Her skin changing from the healthy glow she had managed to regain during her stay at the Retreat, to a sickly greyish white. She shook her head as Porter's words had echoed around their kitchen. Graham watched her reaction, trying to reassure her. The look she gave him told him he'd failed.

'Graham Shaw, I am arresting you on suspicion of the murder of Kara Billingham, you do not have to...' the rest of his words were lost somewhere in the depths of Ellie's distressed howl as Porter placed the handcuffs on his wrists.

The ride to the station was reminiscent of the one to the hospital just after Ellie had been shot. Graham stared out of the car window, his body slumped, looking as though he was about to fall to one side. Then the questions started, the echoes of his inquisitors' voices ran around his brain, chasing each other as he tried to focus.

'How much do you know about the Internet? We have your laptop, your computer from work, we'll soon find out.' Their questions seemed to merge into a litany of accusations, all playing out on the backcloth of his mind.

'Where were you between 10 a.m. and noon on... Who were you with? What happened to your neck Professor Shaw?'

He repeated his answers, never faltering at any stage, until the last one. Porter held up a file, the results of the DNA test, taken on his last visit. His stomach, which up until that point had been clenched, seemed to give way, and he had to excuse himself to visit the loo. They knew, he knew they would find out, and now the results were back, he would have to tell them everything. It sounded bad, even to him. Kara's visit, how she had taunted him, her veiled threats to tell Ellie. It added up to near damning evidence, and what was worse, a motive.

Porter read out the results of the tests with meticulous care. The marks on Graham's neck, the DNA under Kara's fingernails, how did he explain them? Time of death was estimated at between 10 a.m. and noon, where was he at the time she was murdered? At home, he told them, sleeping off the hangover that her visit had caused. He'd cleaned up the mess from the previous evening before leaving to collect Ellie from the retreat.

'Can anyone verify this?' Porter asked. At first Graham couldn't think straight, he sat with his head in his hands, rocking back and forth, Ellie's painful howl echoing in his head.

'John...' he said suddenly, Porter looked up, a mixture of frustration that Graham might have an alibi, and relief that he had arguably the most reliable one of all. They locked him up in a dismal cell, it was just after midnight and he'd spent the next few hours curled up in a ball, a lightweight cellular blanket his only source of warmth. At 7a.m. someone bought him a mug of tea with too little milk and no sugar. But it was hot, and Graham warmed his hands as he grasped it to his chest.

At 10a.m. his door opened again; it was Porter. 'You're free to go,' he announced.

Just like that, thought Graham, as he threw off the blanket. The air bristled as he walked towards the custody desk. He was processed in a little over twenty minutes. He grabbed his jacket and belongings and left the station via the side door. John's car was parked opposite, and he called out and waved.

'Where are we going?' Graham asked as John drove away from the station. He didn't hear John's reply. He wasn't listening, he didn't care.

78

Floorboards creaked as warmth spread through the building. The last time Graham had been there was just after John had left the island. Both he and Ellie had been worried about security; his visit was meant to put their minds at ease. The old stone walls of the building, left empty for so long, had started to absorb the damp, and the place felt neglected. It was so different from when the place was lived in, Ruth had cultivated an air of warmth and homeliness.

Graham wasn't interested in the state of the house. His mind was on the confrontation that had just taken place between him and Ellie. It started when she unlocked the heavy bolt that barred his entry. He tried to justify her actions, choosing to believe that it was because of his absence rather than to ward off his return. Once he started to speak, Ellie had cut straight across him.

'I don't think it's a good idea for you to come back here right now, Graham,' she said, her controlled, clipped tones chilling him to the bone. She turned to John, 'would it be possible for him to stay with you for a while?' she asked.

This wasn't what John wanted. He had his own agenda without having to help Graham with his. He needed time to think, time to sort out what he was going to do now that Ruth...he sighed and was about to decline.

'In that case,' Ellie interrupted, 'you'll have to go to your parents' and stay there. You need to give me time Graham, time to think.'

Graham looked like a man on the receiving end of a body blow. Whatever fight he had left after his time at the station had gone. He held onto the back of the couch for support.

'Ellie,' he started, 'I didn't do it, I didn't kill….' he said shaking his head in denial.

'You don't get it do you Graham?' Ellie snapped, crossing to the window and looking out into the distance. 'Set aside for one moment the question of whether you did or didn't kill that woman,' she hissed in a voice that Graham had never heard before. 'This has to do with the fact that she's been working in your department for who knows how long. She came here to see you just before I came home, didn't she?'

Graham swallowed hard, to deny anything she'd said would be a mistake.

'How…how did you?' he stammered.

'Her lipstick was found upstairs in your office, and an earring I couldn't identify in… in our bed.'

So that was it, thought Graham. The urgency to go to the bathroom, the posturing on the sofa, the scratches on the neck, they had all been for effect. All in the hope that Ellie would suspect that there was something going on between them, to convince her that they had started up where they had left off all those years ago. He knew there was nothing he could say to convince her that it was a pack of lies, and he was too tired to try.

'I can't tell you what you need to hear right now,' he managed. 'I can only swear to you that there was nothing going on between Kara... I hoped you would believe me, but it's obvious that you don't...'

'Get out Graham. Get out of my sight,' she spat. He had, and now he was sitting in John's lounge chilled to the bone despite the warmth of the log fire. He noticed a glass of whiskey on the side table, heard the noise in the kitchen and downed the drink in one, staring at the dancing flames. John came through carrying a tray, bowls of soup and crusty bread, and some pre-packaged cakes, none of which interested Graham. They settled down, neither one in the mood for conversation, but Graham had to know something, hesitating even now to ask. John forestalled him, leaning over and pushing a bowl towards his side of the coffee table.

'You're probably wondering why I lied for you, Graham,' he said slowly. Graham shifted in his chair. 'It's quite simple really, I don't think you killed Kara, you're not the sort. That's why I told Porter that I stayed at your house, and that I didn't leave until noon.'

Graham stared at the fire. John believed him, that was something. But did he? *He said he didn't think that I killed her, not that he knew I hadn't.* He thought about John's words, there was a difference. Still if John believed him, maybe...in time...he could convince... he stood, emotion threatening to overcome him and crossed to the sideboard. The sparkling decanters seemed to dance in the firelight. Graham carried one back to his seat, refilling John's glass on the way. They sat drinking in silence.

It was the middle of the night when he woke up, not knowing where he was, he soon remembered. The fire had burned itself out, only wisps of smoke, and dully glowing charcoal evidence that it had ever existed. Graham shivered as he pulled a cover over his shoulders.

His world had shifted once again. He could appreciate that Ellie was angry with him for not telling her about Kara, but then she hadn't said she believed him when he'd protested his innocence. What was foremost in Ellie's mind, he wondered, infidelity, or murder? There had to be a way to get her to listen to him. There had to be an answer to the doubts and questions that filled his mind.

It was at that moment that he heard the voice, a whisper, the one he'd heard at the farmhouse the day of Kara's visit. It sounded like...Ruth.

Do you trust me, Graham?

He looked around, *I must have drunk more than I thought, either that or this was a joke?* He shook his head trying to clear it.

No joke, just a helping hand, if you want one. Now he was well and truly spooked...*trust me, Graham, it doesn't matter what you did or didn't do. I'll help you get out of this mess you've got yourself in, if you trust me. I know a lot of things Graham, but right now Ellie needs you...do you trust me Graham?'*

'I... I trust you Ruth.' Graham said out loud, sitting huddled in a quilt, in a rapidly cooling room. His wife doubted him, his marriage in the worst trouble it had been in since the first time he had betrayed her with Kara, what else did he have to lose except his sanity?

79

The phone rang, shattering her sleep. Ellie reached out, fumbling her way around the bedside table. Several thoughts flashed through her mind. Had Graham decided to try once more to contact her? In which case she was angry with him all over again. Had something happened to him? In which case she was...she didn't know what she was any more.

'Ellie Shaw...' she mumbled, attempting to drive sleep from her mind. Silence, '...hello, who is this?' she brought the handset from her ear and squinted at the display, *7191986*. She rubbed her eyes, trying to make sense of the numbers, they were vaguely familiar.

'Hello, who is this?' she repeated, ready to hang up. All she needed was some idiot playing tricks on her.

My birthday came the reply, Ellie dropped the phone. She sat up straight, trying to place as much distance between herself and the handset as she could manage... her birthday...Ruth's...July 19th, 1986.

I don't need the phone, but you know me Ellie, ever the drama queen. The voice was in the room, in Ellie's head. Clear, soft, with a tone she had never possessed in life...Ruth.

I'm so sorry you have to go through this, but it must play out this way. Trust me darling, I'll do all I can to keep you safe. You and Graham and your friends, I'll do all I can... the voice trailed away. The warm feeling that Ellie had felt enveloping her dissipated. She sat shivering in the dark, the only light was the sickly green glow of the display on the handset. Ellie stared at it. She must be dreaming, a nightmare maybe, but one that felt so real. If it was, she had to wake up. No, she was already awake. She grabbed her phone and pressed the call log. No record of a call. Her first thought was to ring Graham and tell him what had happened. Her second was not to, she was still too angry to ask him for help.

It was then that the bedroom door crashed open.

80

Gareth Wynn-Jones hauled on his waterproofs in preparation for a day's foraging. A few days ago, he had discovered a new crop of herbs under a hedgerow at the far end of a piece of common ground. He regarded the discovery as nothing short of a miracle.

Gareth made no excuses; he was sorry for the poor woman he'd discovered. No one deserved to be treated like that, but he had a living to make. Besides, he wanted to make a good impression on the young lady at the big house, the one with the hair like silver, and the calm peaceful ways.

They were at school together; Gareth had been fascinated by her ability to lure him into conversations that he wouldn't have dreamt of having with other students. Since then he had often wondered about her, but his solitary life meant that he didn't indulge in gossip. His home was close to the Retreat, causing him to speculate if this had been a sub-conscious effort to re-establish contact with her at some point. He'd been delivering to their kitchens for a few months, but it wasn't until a few weeks ago that he saw her, only from behind but he would have recognised that hair anywhere. He called her name, so quietly that even he could hardly hear it, but she heard, turned and waved. Since then he'd seen her a few times, nothing arranged, just 'bumping' into each other when he made his deliveries. They'd even had a drink together, something he hadn't done since his teenage years. He found himself able to talk to her like he used to at school, to her, to Odelia. It felt natural, easy, relaxed. She congratulated him on his business, on how popular he with the chefs on the island. He blossomed in her company. His life took on a new depth, and from then on, he took every chance he could to see her. He'd never asked her about her scars, and she'd never offered any information about them, neither seemed to feel it was necessary.

Gareth pulled on his boots fetching the battered windcheater from the back of the kitchen door. He took a quick look around as he headed outside, grabbing his bag as he left. The peace of the early morning enveloped him like a cloak.

Go to her, he heard. He froze, an icy finger travelling up his spine, *don't think, just go, trust me.*

Gareth left his gathering boxes on the doorstep, alongside his bag. He walked down the path and turned right towards the track that led to the beach. Why he did this, he couldn't explain. He headed across the long stretch of sand towards the steps cut into the side of the cliff. There was a path at the top leading through the woods to the village. From there he could take a shortcut to the Retreat. He had to start out now, before it was too late. It would take some time to reach his intended destination.

Why did he feel impelled to go? He didn't have a clue. All he knew was that he had to follow his instincts.

His instinct would change everything.

81

The scenery was breathtakingly beautiful, but it was wasted on Graham. His attention was on the road. His determination not to think of what might be happening to Ellie was the only thing that stopped his descent into panic. She'd sounded desperate when she called him; he'd struggled to understand her as he dragged himself out of a disturbed dream.

'Graham, you need to come, now!' her voice barely a whisper. He wondered if he'd heard her correctly in view of what had happened. 'Graham, did you hear me? You need to come down now, to the Retreat, please!'

...move Graham, screamed the voice. Images flashed though his mind; he cursed himself for overlooking the obvious. It was as though the answers to the questions they'd been asking themselves over the course of the

investigation had suddenly been downloaded into his brain. But more than that, he knew the identity of the Puppet Master.

The line went dead. He threw on his clothes and ran to the car.

Shit! He slammed the steering wheel with both hands. He'd intended to fill up with fuel the previous afternoon. He headed to the nearest petrol station, his hands shaking as he refueled, then realised that he had no money with him. How had his life spiraled so far out of control? He was anal about his methodical, almost obsessive ways. His routines were the backbone of his life, now they'd gone to hell in a handcart. Graham scribbled his details down, promising to return as soon as he could.

The car flew along the winding roads. He was driving too fast, but the adrenaline in his system enabled him to handle the machine with exceptional ease. His visits to see Ellie had embedded the route into his memory and he had no problem covering the miles in record time.

Suddenly, he was there. The huge azaleas loomed over the drive, the flowers had long since died back, but the leaves formed a theatrical backdrop to the manicured lawns. Around the last bend and there was the house itself. Huge, gothic, it never failed to impress with its forbidding facade. Now it took on a different guise, a beast, with his wife trapped in the belly. He was allowing his imagination to run amok, whatever was about to happen would require a calm mind, and he fought to control his emotions.

You know more about him than he thinks you do he tried to assure himself as he parked the car to the side of the house, *although not as much as I would like to know,* came the realisation. It took a few seconds to regain his composure.

...take your time, he heard, *he won't do anything until you arrive, it's not in his game plan.* The voice again, the one in his head, the one he had resisted so hard. He was sure now that it was Ruth. She was trying to reassure him, whilst almost knocking him over with shock. He knew she was right, that nothing would happen until he made his entrance. More than anything his adversary needed an audience, and he was the main ticketholder. He skirted around the house, taking in as much information as his overactive mind would allow.

Give me strength, he pleaded silently. A sense of calm, clarity of mind that he had not experienced in a long time enveloped him. It was a feeling that he knew of old, a detachment that he'd always been able to summon up at will. It had served him throughout his career. Lately he thought he'd lost the ability, now he greeted it like an old friend.

Graham reached the side door, only to find it locked. Hadn't Odelia told him that it was never locked?

...he locked it on purpose, this is far too important for you to use a side door, the words echoed in his head.

He walked around to the front of the house, all hope of making a secretive entrance gone. The great oak door groaned as he pushed it open. The hallway was dark after the brightness of the morning, and his eyes took a few second to adjust to the gloom. The smell of essential oils lingered in the air. Music started as he stepped over the threshold. It came from the main hall. The door stood slightly ajar, light seeping through into the gloom.

...and you thought I was the drama queen. Graham was getting used to the voice's presence. What if his instinct was wrong, what if this monster had already exacted whatever kind of retribution he believed he was entitled to, and there had already been a bloodbath?

...he hasn't, he wants to watch your reactions, trust me, this time the voice so clear he felt as though she was standing right next to him...*I am* she said. He couldn't help but look around as if he could see her.... nothing, nothing but a feeling. Graham breathed deeply, trying to calm his racing mind. He walked towards the door, gathering his strength for what lay ahead.

'Come in Graham. Please don't be shy; there are people here anxious to see you.' The command came from someone used to being obeyed instantly; someone who was used to having his demands met without question. Moments passed, they seemed like hours, Graham felt his insides lurch as he heard a scream.

'We said, 'Come in,' that was not a request!' This time insistent, an order.

... he'll take his time; his arrogance is your strength.

Graham swallowed hard. He pushed the door open. The curtains were closed, casting the room into semi-darkness. It took some time before his eyes adjusted.

'Please, take your time, we're in no hurry,' sarcasm dripped like acid. Graham squinted, trying to assess the room. He could see two figures seated at a table to his left. Immediately in front of him was a third figure kneeling on the floor. He noticed that the lights were being turned up by tiny increments, as though they were on a stage, and all those present were actors awaiting their cues. Several speakers were placed strategically to magnify the music and instructions.

...don't be intimidated, it's what he wants, you can do this Graham.

He could see Odelia, her face swollen, her tangled, matted hair hiding her face. She sat on a dining chair at the far side of the table, her upper body straining forward, arms behind her back, hands tied together. From where he stood Graham couldn't tell if she was conscious. At the other end sat Della leaning backwards, her body at an almost impossible angle. Blood covered her face; he could see her mouth parted slightly and suspected the worst.

...*keep calm,* the voice whispered.

Ellie knelt on the floor facing away from him, sitting back on her heels, her hands in front of her supporting her weight. In front of her was the curtained bay. Graham could hear her panting as she whimpered. Fear clutched his chest.

'Shut up!' screamed her captor, 'We told you what would happen if you said a word.'

Ellie's body convulsed as the electricity coursed its way through her body; she slumped back the moment it was switched off. Graham saw leads attached to her hands snaking back to the area behind the curtains. He stepped forward; he had no words, his mouth dry.

'Don't move!' the order reverberated around the room.

Graham looked around, the voice echoed around the room, but he knew it had come from behind the curtained area. For one irreverent moment he was reminded of the old man in the Wizard of Oz. Somehow the thought gave him strength.

...*let him know you know who he is.*

'How much longer are we going to play games, John?' Graham demanded. There was silence, then the sound of laughter.

'So, you know? Took you long enough didn't it, but then you've never been the sharpest tool in your postmortem kit. How did you work it out Graham? Did you guess all by yourself, or did wifey give you some clues, odd kind of pillow talk don't you think?' John stepped through the centre of the curtains and took a small bow.

...he could be a ringmaster about to introduce his audience to the main act, Graham thought as he watched in fascinated horror. John wore an immaculate black suit, white shirt, red tie, and highly polished black patent leather shoes. His cufflinks the gift that they had brought him for his wedding, the ones with the diamond chips, caught the light and winked as he raised his arm. He held a small device that reminded Graham of a television remote.

'You have no idea how many times I was tempted to tell you about our little game,' John said indicating the hall at large, 'but the opportunity never arose. It was never quite the right time. Still, now we can get you involved at last,' he crossed to the side of the window and pulled on one of the tasseled cords. The curtains parted, flooding the room with light, and once again John gave a small bow. Behind him in the bay window stood a large cabinet that Graham had never seen before. Cables led into what looked like a mixing desk sat next to it on a small table. They led back to the three women. Graham gasped as he imagined a myriad of possible outcomes.

'Impressive...huh?' John swept an arm towards the board, 'nothing we couldn't set up in a few hours, given that we were here last night. Our three participants proved a most interesting diversion, we had a lot of fun together, well, we had to test the equipment out, didn't we?' he laughed, indicating the three women.

...don't let him bait you, focus.

Graham's gut lurched once more, his imagination going into overtime. If John had subjected the others to his cruelty, God knew what he had done to Ellie? Graham looked down at her, she was shaking, her head down, whimpering.

'You bastard,' he murmured, 'you fucking bastard, if you've touched her….'

'What'cha gonna do Graham?' laughed John, his voice an obscene sing-song, 'bore us to death? From where we're standing it looks very much like, we're the ones in control!'

Graham looked around desperately, he saw a gun, perched on the top of the cabinet.

'Now, we're going to tell you exactly what we're going to do to your lady wife and her little friends.' John started a rhythmic pacing punctuated with a little skipping dance within the confines of the curtained area. Back and forth he paced, ticking off the points as he made them. Graham hardly heard him. He was reminded of a performance he'd seen at the local theatre, some play or other. Come to think of it they had been all been there, John, Ruth and Ellie. John had been highly amused at the time.

...*say something, take control.*

'You killed all those people, didn't you?' Graham asked, resisting the urge to dash forward for the gun, which he knew he'd never reach in time.

'No, no, no, no, far from it. We haven't killed anyone, well, not for quite some time.' John laughed, shaking his head at Graham's accusation. '...we may have helped a few people to die, but...no. Don't you know it's far more fun to get others to do the dirty work?'

'But why, what did they do to you?' Graham couldn't help himself, he needed to know.

'Oh, my dear, dear Graham, you don't get it do you? We don't care about the people who were killed, we hardly knew them. Mind you, there were some who had annoyed us for many years, but most of them we didn't know at all,' he chuckled. 'Come on Graham, haven't you ever felt like the world would be better off without the presence of certain individuals, Kara Billingham for example? Eh? Yes, we told you that we didn't believe that you could have...but you could have couldn't you, after all, she threatened your cosy little life, didn't she?'

...he's showing off, don't let him rattle you.

Graham felt the strength ebbing out of him...to murder someone was one thing, to murder a stranger, for no apparent reason, that was...monstrous. John was enjoying himself, holding court as though he were a king and Graham a courtier come to pay homage.

'What...what about Ruth and Max?' Graham heard himself ask, on an impulse that both scared and energised him...

...no, no, too soon!

John whipped around, no longer playing the genial twisted host, his face contorted.

'Let's tell you what happened, huh? Let's enlighten you as to whose fault their deaths really come down to, because we can tell you now Graham, it's not ours.'

Graham frowned; he had become acutely aware of John's phraseology.

'What's with the 'us' and 'ours' John?' he asked, 'is there someone else here?'

'Perceptive of you, Graham, very good, there is someone here with me, though not in any way that you would understand. He's always with me, always...I'm never alone you see,' he looked at the floor for several seconds, during which time Graham took a step forward.

'Ah, ah, ahhhhh!!!' said John, holding the device aloft, 'unless you want to see your darling wife squirm again, I wouldn't make any sudden moves. Now, where were we? But where are our manners? Please take a seat Graham, let me enlighten you, bring you up to speed.'

Graham could only watch as the charade unfolded. What the hell was he going to do now?

82

Porter had passed a troubled night. He had a quick shower, turning the water to cold to try and startle his body awake. He caught his breath as the icy blast hit him. He dressed, collected his briefcase and checked his phone... two missed calls from Graham Shaw.

The voice-mail message was brief, the situation, the address, the plea, the instructions, silent approach, the warning...and now a caravan of vehicles approached the Retreat. Porter drove one handed whilst talking into his radio, reminding them of the need for a silent approach. Anyone could become over-enthusiastic and trigger a situation they could no longer control. He recalled Graham's message...

DCI Porter, this is Graham Shaw, John Prothero is the Puppet Master, Ellie's at the Retreat...I don't know what condition she's in, he made her call me. Please...please can you come... silent approach...please hurry...

For all the situation was a grave one, Porter smiled, trust Graham Shaw to remind him to approach silently. He took a bend too fast, fighting to gain back control of the car, acutely aware that he would be no good to anyone if he crashed it.

83

Ellie hadn't moved for some time, Graham wondered if she was still conscious. He ached to reach out to her, to hold her and tell her everything would be all right. John had organised these theatricals to satisfy some sick need, to prolonging their suffering. Now and then Graham thought he saw Ellie's hand move slightly. Della and Odelia sat motionless on their chairs. He could see no visible signs of life from either.

...keep cool, don't let him get to you, trust me.

'We created a club, a society of sorts,' John was saying, 'entry to which was rather select, we won't bore you with the details. Let's just say the members of this club had interests which have always fascinated us. Our members were almost exclusively men, women tend to show too much mercy when it comes to the final act. They were all financially solvent, otherwise they would never be able to take the time out to fulfil their missions, but there were a few exceptions, David Morgan for one. Generally, people who could pass responsibility of the day to day running of their interests to minions and join in the fun, though some of the less well-off participants have given us the greatest amusement,' he was warming to his subject, Graham could tell.

...always was a fuckin' show off, observed the voice.

Graham almost chocked. John didn't notice as he crossed to the far window, strutting, hands behind his back as though he was giving a lecture or a sermon. He turned to admire the magnificent lawns beyond, rocking back and forth onto the balls of his feet. It was a habit with which Graham was all too familiar.

'Don't you want to know what the focus of this little group was...mmmm? Oh, come on Graham, don't look so sanctimonious, admit it you're dying to know.' John face creased into a parody of shock as he chuckled, 'dying to know, dying, oh that's a good one, we like that!'

Graham's mind was swimming, the voice in his head, the sight of his wife and the two other women to the forefront of his thoughts. He realised that John was watching him intently. This was a set piece; one which John had probably played over and over in his imagination. He wasn't going to allow anything to stop him from having this moment. Unless Graham could make a sudden, decisive and successful move to end it, the agonisingly slow dénouement was going to have to play out. For the moment John was in charge.

...that's it, calm and slow, that's the way he wants to play it, don't do anything to startle him, you know what he's like when someone tries to steal his thunder.

'We can tell you now, Graham, because soon you will all be dead. Now then let's get comfortable, shall we?' John crossed to a wing-backed chair and sat down, relaxed in his arrogance. He flicked an imaginary speck of dust from the immaculately creased trousers, and pointed to a strategically placed stool, motioning for Graham to sit on it. Graham felt compelled to obey.

'Do you remember some time ago, what was it now, seven, no, eight years ago?' he paused as though calculating how long it had been. 'Our findings based on research carried out by an American psychiatrist, we don't recall her name.' He waved a hand casually as if dismissing the work he was referring to, Graham was certain he had forgotten nothing.

Yes, thought Graham, he could remember the work, John had shown it to him, it was well presented, but the premise was slightly 'out there' for him, and had taken him by surprise.

'I can see that you know what I'm talking about, and flattered that you remember it, Graham, well done.' John said patronisingly. He went on to outline the subject of his own research.

It started the day he read a book on spirit possession, he said. It was a book which he initially dismissed as unlikely to say the least, but one in which he had become increasingly interested. As a psychiatrist himself, he felt it his duty to explore further, to either prove or disprove the main question. Was it possible that a departing soul, not ready to leave this world, could become attached to a living person, and thereafter impose their will on the 'host' thus affecting their behaviour?

If Graham remembered correctly, John had spent months preparing his paper. He'd become almost obsessed with the subject. It had affected him badly when his conclusions were dismissed, and in some cases even ridiculed by his peers. Things were beginning to fall into place. Graham looked back at John; he could see the delight on his eager face.

'That's it, that's it, take your time Graham, we have plenty of it after all,' he crowed.

'What did you do John?' Graham asked, almost afraid of the answer.

'You remember Howard Atkinson?' Graham did, in fact the very mention of his name sent shivers through him. Atkinson, a brutal serial killer who'd been committed to Broadmoor seventeen years ago after killing fourteen people, including three of his own family. Having been diagnosed as a Psychopath with delusional tendencies, and complex personality disorders, Atkinson knew he'd never be released. He'd kept the details of his crimes to himself, using them as a source of power. There'd been many occasions that he'd promised to reveal details of the final resting places of his victims, only to change his mind on a whim. John had found him fascinating.

'Permission to visit him was quite easy to obtain. A high regard with certain members of the Home office, and an impeccable reputation helped, of course. I was given unlimited access. The hope was that Atkinson would confide in me, but at that stage he never did. Part of the thrill of these meetings was that one could never be sure which of Atkinson's personalities would present itself. Ah yes, Atkinson was one of the most challenging cases in my long and distinguished career,' John shook his head. The memories of his time with Atkinson seemed to evoke an energy that made Graham feel sick.

Graham knew that Atkinson had asked John to visit him in the hospital wing before his death from pancreatic cancer. It was the day that Max was born. John had left Ruth's bedside within minutes of their son's birth to hurry to the mainland, arriving just in time to hear Atkinson breathe his last words. He'd never divulged what these were. Graham looked back at John, who was now almost bouncing up and down on his chair.

'Yes, that's right, you have it now Graham,' he screeched excitedly in a voice that wasn't his own, 'it's not just me sitting here. Atkinson knew, you see, we had talked about it many times,' Graham blanched, the thought too awful for him to contemplate.

'He wanted to live Graham, he wasn't ready to leave the world, so much more to be done you see. Most important of all, I wanted to know if the theories were right, could a soul who was unwilling to leave this life really transfer to another body?'

Graham shuddered again, events from the last few years were falling into place. The time John had shot his dog for no more reason than it was ill, they'd covered that one up by telling Max it had run away. John had assured Graham that it was an aberration and passed it off as stress. It took a few minutes before he realised that John had started talking again.

'We tried to recruit you; you know. Think of all the films we watched, all those gory ones with intense storylines, sometimes a little flimsy, admittedly, but nevertheless enough to make one lose one's dinner. We had fun didn't we, betting how bad the films would be, which one of us would find the bloodiest, who would hide their face first, who would walk out, or even pass out?' He chuckled at the memory.

'They affected you didn't they, more than once. We found it surprising that you, with your life's work delving into the innermost recesses of a person's body, could be in the least bit sickened by special effects on a television screen. It was easy to convince you that we were similarly affected, that we found them just as nauseating.' He studied the effect of his revelation on Graham.

The voice had gone quiet.

Graham remembered the times he and John spent drinking together. John had introduced what he called 'Scare Nights', starting with a few non-descript 'B' list disasters, rapidly escalating into more gruesome stuff. Graham suspected that more than one was a genuine 'Snuff movie'. John claimed he was conducting research into whether these films affected people who later went on to commit horrific murders. He wanted Graham's opinion, he said. But as they got progressively worse, with no noticeable discussion into the harm they could cause, their participation became a game to see who could locate the worst one; John always won. Eventually Graham started to dread them. John mocked him when the nightmares started. He had enough blood and gore in his job, he didn't want to watch it as entertainment. John had been solicitous at the time, and their 'Scare Nights' had fizzled out. Now that Graham thought about it, their companionable drinking episodes had begun to dwindle at the same time. It all made sense now.

'Yes, that's it, you're putting two and two together aren't you...clever boy!' John clapped his hands, standing to resume his pacing. He gave a little skip as he skirted his way around the bay window, then made his way back to the chair.

'You failed, by the way, by the time we had watched that last one, what was it called, the Driller, the Thriller, whatever, the one that made you vomit? Ha ha, and you told me it was a bad burrito, what a wimp! We knew then that you wouldn't make the final cut, so to speak.'

...insufferable, I don't know how I put up with you for so long! Graham jumped; the voice had been silent for so long he thought it had gone for good.

'Now, let's just make sure that the girls are ok!' he laughed pressing buttons on the device and flicking a few switches on the control panel.

Ellie jumped, twisting grotesquely. Graham screamed at John to stop, dashing forward, all caution gone. He grabbed hold of the gun and pointed it at his brother-in-law.

'Stop, now, I'll shoot. Stop, for God's sake stop!' he screamed his attention divided between his tortured wife and the maniac before him.

...no, no, not yet, not yet!

John smiled, he looked Graham in the eye as the trigger clicked, the gun was empty. Graham shook it as John laughed manically.

'You really believe we would leave a loaded gun anywhere near you? You, Graham with your cat-like reflexes? Don't forget we know how agile you are around the squash court?' he taunted. He switched off the current that had held Ellie in an arched position for the last few seconds that had seemed like hours. She collapsed back to the floor; Graham stepped towards her.

'No, no, noooo!!!' said John, his voice an obscene singsong, he waved the hand-held device and shook it towards Graham.

'Don't,' he pleaded. 'Please John, if we ever meant anything to you, don't hurt her anymore!' John paused, feigning consideration of his words.

'You...' he said, '...mean something to us? Now let's think...mmmm, no, got nothing Graham. Don't you get it, you meant nothing, you or your little wifey over there, nothing, nothing at all!'

'What about Ruth, Max, they meant something didn't they? This is Ruth's sister,' pleaded Graham hoping to stem the stream of bile that slaked off his tormentor like waves in the sea. John stopped dead in his tracks, lowering the device. His shoulders drooped; his eyes had narrowed dangerously. The fight seemed to have left him, dispelled by Graham's remark.

'Ruth...Max...' he whispered, more to himself than to anyone else, 'yes, they meant something. We loved Ruth, she was ours, she loved us. Max, he was our boy, my...my boy,' he paused, shaking his head slowly, 'and then, then they were gone, and it was her fault, her fault that they were killed, your darling wife. It wasn't supposed to be like that. They weren't supposed to be there, she called them back. Ruth told me that Ellie called her asking if she was sure about her trip; she put doubt into Ruth's mind, she got them to go to the house. It was only supposed to be her, but she made them come back, she killed them Graham, don't you see? You can see that can't you?' He was more forceful now, his voice rising to a crescendo. He was acting as though Graham knew what he was talking about.

'John, John please... let's talk,' pleaded Graham, 'I don't understand any of this, please explain John, you're the only one that can tell me what happened, I need you to explain,' he continued. He was afraid that Atkinson's spirit would take control again, he needed to expand this oasis of calm.

'Oh no, none of your games,' John shook his head, 'we know what you're up to my friend and it won't work. You're trying to delay the inevitable, trying to distract us so that you can talk us down. Ha, well done Graham, well done, but don't forget we perfected that technique. We use it on most of our patients after all, especially Whittaker. Yes, he was one of the easy ones. He didn't even notice when we swapped his medication for placebos. As for that little fracas at the office, we engineered that, it was a stroke of genius, don't you think, picking a fight and then threatening to have him re-arrested? It gave him reason to be dissatisfied, fabricated a motive. Feeding him false information about his wife and son, again, inspired. But then she bungled it, he was only supposed to find your darling wife at the cottage. But she...she phoned Ruth, got her to come back...my...my Ruth, Max.'

He stared past Graham, lost in his own thoughts. Graham stared back as John shook his head, looking round as though suddenly finding himself in a position he knew nothing about. He shook his head, focusing on Graham's, his face twisting into a contorted sneer.

'Simple case of transference, of course, that's what the Coroner will find,' he smiled. 'Oh, sorry Graham, I need to explain, you see transference is when...'

'I know what transference is!' Graham snapped racking his brain for a way to deal with whoever it was that now controlled John's body. John started to pace back and forth again, he seemed to be talking to himself as he looked around keeping a close watch on the people before him.

'Yes,' he said to himself, 'I agree, it has to be now. I've had enough of this; let's get it over and done with.'

'At least give me a motive John, you owe me that much. Tell me why all the murders?' Graham pleaded, stalling for time. He could see he was losing the battle.

'I owe you NOTHING!!' screamed John, whirling around, his face had darkened to a deep puce, 'nothing, do you hear me?'

...tell him you know you're going to die, but you need to know as a matter of professionalism.

What? Graham demanded silently.

...just do as I say, the voice soothed him, gave him strength. He repeated her words, and John seemed to calm down, lowering his hands to his sides.

'Interesting,' he said, 'that you should need to observe the niceties at this stage in the game. Very well, we'll tell you. Revenge and control, Graham, as your observant and very intelligent wife surmised, revenge and control. I observed Atkinson as he awaited death, and I was grateful for the opportunity to experience what had up until then been entirely based in theory, to prove that my peers were wrong. Besides, once I had tasted the freedom that came with having no moral compass, it was almost impossible to endure the periods when I was forced to adopt my former behaviour. Ruth and Max were my only regret, but

I had moments...' he stopped, memories stirring again, he took a few steps forward.

'But that's all over now Graham, thanks to your interfering wife and her last-minute phone calls,' he hissed, his face contorted in demonic determination, as he raised the control to shoulder level, grinning at Graham's horrified face.

At the same time a shocked Gareth Wynn-Jones pummeled on the window and Ellie's hand reached out like a striking snake and grasped John's ankle.

84

The police cavalcade had come to a halt at the end of the drive. All personnel had been briefed en route. They made their way through the trees and bushes to the edge of the lawn. From his vantage point Porter could see into the bay window, and the movement inside. He watched as John traversed the room, thanking any deity in general and none in particular, that his men hadn't been spotted yet. He froze as a figure walked around the corner of the house and approached the same window. The armed officers had taken up their positions. He had radio confirmation that they were ready to move on his word. Porter hesitated...what the hell was this guy doing here?

He wished he could make a better assessment, any attempt to approach could be detected due to the clear expanse of lawn in front of him. There was no hope of storming the building without causing a major incident. The option of firing tear gas was seductive. Porter stared through his binoculars; he had to make a move; he was running out of options. The man started banging on the window, shouting something that Porter couldn't hear. John dropped to the floor; it was over in a few seconds. John got up, and although Porter couldn't see his face very clearly, he detected a moment's hesitation before he turned and stepped out of sight.

'Go, go, go!!' he shouted, sensing his opportunity. A wall of officers moved as one towards the windows, screaming at the occupants of the room.

'Get down, get down, armed police, get down!' Shouts echoed as they stormed the room, dispelling the silence with their thunderous entrance. Graham, who had seen John drop then get back up, fell to his knees, his hands behind his head. The rest of the group couldn't move, and that was how Porter found them.

John was nowhere to be seen.

85

There was eerie calm as they checked out Graham, patting him down, forcing him onto the floor until they could be sure that he posed no threat. Others approached the women at the table. Ellie remained still on the floor in the middle of the room. Even she was patted down to check for weapons. Several officers left, searching for John. Porter could hear them on the floor above, throwing open doors, shouting to their colleagues that the space was clear before moving on to the next room. Outside Gareth had dropped down to the ground, his hands behind his head. An armed officer checked him out, then led him towards the ambulances.

Porter crossed to Graham, helping him to stand.

'Ellie,' he cried, 'please...let me...'

'Go!' Porter shouted, he realised that Graham was struggling to walk and placed an arm around his waist and half carried him over to where Ellie still knelt. Paramedics streamed through the doors, each armed with a medical case, some wheeling stretchers. Graham shrugged off Porter's help. He limped the last few steps on his own. Porter stretched out his hands to ward off the eager personnel, giving Graham a few moments before they took charge. They stopped as one, the only sound was that of the officers searching overhead.

Ellie hadn't moved since she had grabbed John's ankle and was bent into a hideous shape. He knelt beside her, gently touching her cheek, he scanned her face. He saw her eyelid flicker, she was alive! A surge of relief overwhelmed him as heard her whisper, and he leaned towards her.

'That hurt!' she murmured; Graham almost cried with relief.

86

Late November

The three women sat in the firelight, shadows dancing on the walls as they discussed their recent experience. The Retreat was temporarily closed to guests. Della and Odelia had returned there after a few days under observation, Ellie followed soon after. Each of them knew it would take some time to come to terms with, let alone recover from their ordeal.

Ellie had said little to anyone since that day, and not just about what she had seen in the seconds that she had held onto John Prothero's ankle. The information she did provide helped Porter to start making progress on the island murders. She knew details of John's secret hideaway at a seemingly abandoned house at Russell Grove, in which they discovered evidence of his activities. Ellie claimed she knew about the place from conversations she'd had with him in the past but had dismissed as unimportant. Considering what had happened at the Retreat, she said the details had taken on their true importance. Not that she sounded very convincing, even to herself. How could she tell anyone that she had somehow 'downloaded' all this information the second she touched John? She was convinced that no one would believe her, and unsure about how she could bring up the subject of Atkinson's crimes.

John's records confirmed her initial theories that there had been a Mr. Big, although how she hadn't suspected him baffled her. Porter was dubious. He knew that Ellie was holding back, and felt frustrated that she wasn't any more forthcoming, especially considering what had happened between her and Graham.

Ellie refused to discuss her reasons for not going back to the farmhouse. Porter didn't want to press the issue, but he couldn't believe that the only reason was her husband's failure to tell her about Kara Billingham's reappearance in his life. It irked him that this was yet another loose end.

'You're going to have to tell Porter at some stage Ellie, you know that,' Della said as she poured the tea. She was reading Ellie's thoughts... again. Ellie nodded.

'I will, but will he understand, or even believe me?' she sighed. 'I'll call him tomorrow,' she said sipping her drink and staring into the fire. *Oh my*, she thought, *that's going to be an interesting conversation.*

How to start, how to explain that in those few seconds she had seen images, not only from John's activities as the 'Puppet Master', but also from Howard Atkinson's life. She'd seen things that he'd had done, the acts of sheer depravity he'd indulged in. She had sketchy images of where the bodies were, how his victims had died. She'd lived their last moments. How on earth could she even begin to explain these things to Porter, when she couldn't understand them herself?

The most worrying thing though was that in all the memories that didn't belong to her, the horrific details that had been downloaded into her consciousness, there was not one that related to Kara Billingham, and if John hadn't killed her, then who had? Ellie's suspicions frightened her, and that was why she couldn't go back to the farmhouse.

Epilogue

Danny O'Neill sat watching the grey-tinged clouds scudding by. Rivulets of sea spray and rain chased each other down the panoramic window. He enjoyed travelling, taking the vagaries of the ferry crossing in his stride. He usually enjoyed a hearty meal on embarking, then a quick nap to prepare himself for the long drive across Ireland to his home. Today was the first time he'd ever experienced the nausea that had hit him as he drove onto the ferry, and he regretted mocking those of his employees who always seemed to throw up on the calmest of crossings.

He considered another visit to the loo, changing his mind as his stomach lurched once more. It would be a waste of time anyway. There was nothing left to bring up. Maybe it wasn't seasickness after all, he'd felt off colour for a few days, ever since the accident with that crazy maniac in the beat-up van.

Perhaps it was shock, he thought deciding to make the effort to go to the loo after all. It wasn't as though he'd been badly hurt or anything like that. Maybe it was whiplash that had given him a bad headache. Hell, if he was that badly injured, he wouldn't have been able to get out to check on the other guy. Weird thing was that all the other driver did was to hold onto his arms and stare at him in a scary spaced out kind of way. Danny had tried hard to pull away without seeming unsympathetic, but the guy had held on until the paramedics turned up and took over. Even then he was making a racket, shouting something about...

'Don't leave me, we have so much more to do!' as they put him on a stretcher and wheeled him away. What the hell had that been about?

Being kept overnight had been an inconvenience more than anything, but he'd managed to rearrange his travel plans. The dreams he'd had that night were disturbing though, bordering on nightmares. He'd woken up screaming at one point. The doctor had given him something to help him sleep and advised him to stay one more night, but he discharged himself and left just after midday.

The hospital car park was buzzing with police vehicles, and he had wondered who they were there for. Surely not for his accident, it was only an RTA after all, that would be overkill. It was only when he saw the headlines on the front of a local rag that he realised that, yes, they were there about his accident, well indirectly anyway. Something about him, what was his name? Prothero...that was it, being wanted for questioning into all those murders on the island. His head had hurt too much for him to concentrate on reading the details. He wanted to be out of there before he got delayed any more. He'd given the police his statement and they knew where to contact him.

The boat dipped and rolled as he made his way carefully to the men's restroom, and he wished his head didn't ache so much. The doctor had given him painkillers but had advised him against driving and he wanted to be home as soon as possible. The toilets were deserted as he washed his hands and face, hoping to clear the muggy feeling that sloshed around his brain. Danny pulled out a length of paper and dabbed his cheeks, he closed his eyes, shaking his head gently and breathing deeply. He held onto the sink as another wave of nausea hit him, his chin sank onto his chest. The tannoy pinged, bringing him back to the present. A warning about rough seas... as if he wasn't already aware. With an enormous effort, he dragged his head upright, struggling to open his eyes, he staggered backwards. His back hit the hand dryer as he tried to grasp for support. The face in the mirror wasn't his; he didn't recognise any of its features. It was over in a flash, but it floored him, sending his senses reeling. He crawled back towards the sink, dragging himself to a standing position, hardly daring to open his eyes.

Relief flooded his brain as he saw himself reflected. The nausea was passing, and he felt stronger as he cupped his hands and drank cool water in great gulps. He grabbed more paper towels to dry his face, taking deep breaths. This was much better; he might even manage a bite to eat.

Danny waited to be served, then carried his well-stocked tray to a table by the window. Yes, this was more like it, back to his old self. He drank some coffee and started on the shepherd's pie; the food was making him feel less spaced out. He relished each bite, feeling more cheerful as he ate. The wind had dropped; the sea was a lot calmer. He looked out of the window to see the sun breaking through. Things were looking up as he finished his meal, soon be back to normal.

Just one thing though, he thought between sips of coffee... *who the hell was Ellie Shaw and why was he so angry when he thought about her?*

...oo0oo...

Box of Lies

the 2nd book in the Ellie Shaw Series
by
J. Lewis-Thompson

A controversial, high-profile member of the Lords...
A popular Chef, author of several best-selling books...
The MD of a well-known High Street Chain…
All murdered, but how are they connected?
DS Mason can see a link, but can she make
her senior officers believe her?

Ellie Shaw's life is in pieces, she's finding it difficult to see a future in her chosen field of profiling. Let down by the most important people in her life, grieving for her sister and nephew, she considers her future carefully.

The residents of Anglesey are reeling from the shockwaves caused by the murders on the Island. The Investigation Team are eager to close up the case, but are shocked to find that it has been taken out of their hands, with a complete embargo on press coverage. With so many unanswered questions, this has left them in a state of limbo, and DCI Porter is not happy.

When DS Doris Mason comes to him with a new case, he's on the point of quitting the force altogether. When Ellie Shaw gets in touch, will he change his mind?

...oo0oo...

Acknowledgements...

...to everyone who has encouraged me to write. To Liz, Chris and Kate, to Emma, though she probably didn't realise it and to Georgia who is, well, Georgia.

...to Sarah U., your insistence that I didn't stop after the first chapter spurred me on.

...to Sue G., who edited and inspired.

...to Andrew S., who told me I could do it.

...to Michael S., who designed the cover, walked me through the formatting minefield, and listened to potential sub-plots *ad infinitum*. Oh, and fed me with inspiration and some of the most delicious meals I have ever eaten.

...and not least to Mrs. McGorty, who, a lifetime ago, expressed such surprise that I passed my GCE English, that she made me think...

...I'll show you!!!

J. Lewis-Thompson   April 2019

Printed in Great Britain
by Amazon

28079505R00188